WINTER FIRES AT MILL GRANGE

JENNY KANE

An Aria Book

ALSO BY JENNY KANE

First published in the United Kingdom in 2021 by Head of Zeus Ltd
This paperback edition published in 2021 by Head of Zeus Ltd
An Aria book

975312468

A CIP catalogue record for this book is available from the British Library.

ISBN (E): 9781801101974
ISBN (PB): 9781801101981

Head of Zeus
5–8 Hardwick Street
London EC1R 4RG
www.ariafiction.com

Print editions of this book are printed and bound by CPI Group (UK) Ltd,Croydon, CR0 4YY

Northmoor House— a place of endless inspiration.

'You are joking – aren't you?'

Harriet wasn't sure why she asked the question. Jason wasn't known for his sense of humour.

As their leading man slammed his mobile phone against the table, she glanced around the assembled members of The Outdoor Players. Only moments ago they'd been happily nursing their pints of beer or glasses of wine, chatting excitedly about the opening night of their winter show. Now the temperature in the room, despite the blazing log fire, plummeted to an almost arctic freeze.

Peeping at Rob through her curtain of hair, Harriet watched him suck at his bottom lip, hiding all but one of his brilliant white teeth.

'But the show is...'

'I know perfectly well when the show is, thank you, Rob!' Jason snapped. 'What do you expect me to do? Magic the flood away?'

Disappointment gripped Harriet. This was to have been her professional debut; an acting role beyond school or university productions. The first step towards her coveted Equity card. She had practised her lines three times a day for weeks. Now it looked as if she might not get to say them anytime soon – if at all.

Harriet was relieved when Matt, manager, director and producer of The Outdoor Players, knocked the base of his pint glass against the table, restoring order before panic took hold of the entire cast of *The Winter's Tale*.

'Let's start from the beginning. The phone call you just took, Jason – I assume it was from your parents? Can you give us the full story please?'

Every member of the cast stared at Jason.

'In a nutshell, the performance is off.'

ONE

WEDNESDAY DECEMBER 1ST

'So, you see, we need somewhere new to perform. I know it's a cheek to ask seeing as you don't know me, and I was going to call Tom because I *do* know him, but I didn't want to compromise him. I got the impression you're all good friends at Mill Grange, but as Tom is just an employee really, I thought maybe it should come straight from me, but...'

'Take a breath, Harriet.' Thea cut through the young woman's embarrassment. 'Let's start again. Are you asking me if I think Sam and Tina will let you use Mill Grange for some outdoor theatre?'

'Yes.'

'Right.' Thea grabbed a piece of scrap paper and picked up her pen. 'Now, tell me a little more about what you'd need, when you'd need it by, and how many people are involved.'

* * *

The scent of freshly baked cake wafted across the kitchen as the staff of Mill Grange drifted in from their various workstations and gathered around the large oak table that formed the heart of the house.

Thea, a mug of coffee warming her palms, watched as her best friend, Tina, poured a lemon juice and sugar concoction over the sponge she'd just extracted from the aged Aga.

'Seeing you bake a lemon cake always reminds me of the first staff meeting we had after my arrival at Mill Grange.'

Tina chuckled. 'That wasn't quite such a laid-back affair as our meetings these days, was it?'

Moving away from the sink, Mabel dried her hands, her powdered cheeks dotting with spots of pink as she sat next to Thea. 'I'm not sure if I ever said, but I really am sorry I was difficult in the beginning.'

Placing a consoling palm over the pensioner's hand, Thea shook her head. 'You were rightly wary of me. I swanned in from nowhere and started telling you how to restore the house you'd already been restoring for years. You were bound to have been put out.'

Throwing off his shoes, Sam took his regular seat nearest the open back door, ever ready to make a dash for the fresh air if his claustrophobia chose that moment to make its presence felt. 'That was nearly two years ago and frankly, Mabel, this place could not operate without you.'

'Thank you, Sam.' Mabel pushed her shoulders back, as she turned to Thea. 'You said you'd had a call from Harriet. That's Dylan's babysitter isn't it?'

'And future stepsister.' Fresh from working in the garden, Dylan's father, Tom, finished scrubbing the mud off his hands and picked up a mug of tea. 'Although, now she's at uni, she isn't looking after Dylan so much. I think he misses Harriet as much as he misses his mum, to be honest.'

Thea lowered her cup for a moment. 'How's Sue doing in Australia? Settled in?'

'I think so. Nathan likes being boss of the supermarket he's running and Sue is certainly embracing the local sunshine. I get the impression that their wedding plans are in full swing.' Tom found himself scowling as he thought about Sue, his ex and his son's mother.

Stirring some milk into her teacup, Mabel asked, 'What's Harriet studying, Tom?'

'Drama at Bristol.'

'Oh.'

Tina struggled not to chuckle as she recognised the effort Mabel was making not to comment on the fact that drama wasn't a "real" degree and changed the subject. 'How's Helen, Tom?'

'She's great, thanks.' A broad grin crossed the archaeologist's face. 'Up to her eyes in event organising for the Roman Baths.'

'Is she enjoying working from home?'

'Seems to be. The smallest bedroom is now her office.' Tom took a sip from his tea. 'And I can't complain. Since home is in Tiverton, near Dylan's school, that means I don't have to dash back to collect him at quarter past three every day.'

After putting the cake on the windowsill to cool, Tina joined her friends. 'As we're all here, shall we start?'

Sam nodded. 'The agenda isn't long, so let's hear what Harriet wanted first. Thea?'

Rolling her mug between her palms, Thea addressed the

group. 'I can't decide if it's potentially exciting or if it would be a nightmare.'

'What would?' Tina poised her pen over her pad, ready to take the meeting's minutes.

'As Tom said, Harriet is doing a drama degree. Her introductory term has just ended and she has landed her first professional acting job over the Christmas break. At least, she had.'

Tom blew into his tea. 'What's happened? Dylan was telling me how excited she was. Going to be the girl from Harry Potter he said – so I presumed Hermione.'

'Not quite. She does have the role of Hermione.' Thea laughed. 'But with an outdoor theatre company. They were due to perform Shakespeare's *The Winter's Tale* in the grounds of a farmhouse near Lacock, in Wiltshire, from 18th until 20th December.'

Tina opened her diary. 'That's in seventeen days.'

'Was, actually. Unless...' Thea looked at Sam '...they can find a new venue, the show is off.'

'And Harriet wants them to come here instead?' Sam exchanged glances with his wife, Tina, as he asked, 'What happened to the current venue?'

'There was a storm over a large part of Wiltshire last night. The farmhouse they were due to perform in has flooded. Apparently the thatch was old and this was the final straw, if you'll pardon the pun. The owners have had to cancel while they get some urgent renovation work done. The whole ground floor of the house needs ripping out and redoing.'

'That sounds awful!' Tina shuddered, glad that Mill Grange had a slate roof and was sat at the top of a hill.

'Dreadful though that sounds—' Mabel leant forward '—

the damage is all inside. If they are an outdoor group, why can't the show go on?'

'It's a health and safety issue.'

The old lady rolled her eyes. 'When isn't it?'

Tina scribbled a few notes on her pad. 'It's very short notice for them to change venue, especially to here. What are we, a hundred or so miles away from the original performance site? Presumably they'll have sold tickets that will need refunding?'

'That's what I meant by a potential nightmare. If we let The Outdoor Players use Mill Grange, then we'd have to find them an audience in double-quick time.'

Tom raked a hand through his hair. 'Harriet will be gutted if she doesn't get to do the play.'

'Let's be practical.' Sam got up and headed for the door. 'It's an outdoor performance, so let's see where it could be done. *If* we agreed.'

* * *

'It could be done here, on the main lawn, which has the advantage of being naturally sloped, so the performers could act at the bottom of the garden, with the audience looking out over them, as if they were in an indoor theatre.' Sam stretched a hand out over his vast garden. 'Or they could use the walled garden, which would give them a more secluded venue, I suspect with better acoustics, but less audience space.'

'And lots of chickens,' Thea added. 'Knowing Gertrude and co., they'd insist on joining in.'

Tina zipped her coat up higher. 'It's very cold. Did Harriet say anything about how they'd keep their audience from freezing to death, Thea?'

'I didn't think to ask, but as they are an outdoor group I'm assuming they have patio heaters and so on. We could advise people to bring blankets to wrap over their legs.' Thea saw Sam and Tina swap another look. 'You think this is a good idea don't you?'

Moving closer to his wife, Sam said, 'Obviously we haven't had a chance to discuss it yet, but in theory, yes.'

Tina agreed. 'The retreat did well, right up until the winter hit. So few bookings meant it was more cost-effective to close for December and January than keep going. Naturally, this means we aren't earning anything right now. This could be what we need to tide us over.'

'Assuming that The Outdoor Players are willing to pay for the use of the venue.' Sam looked sheepish. 'I'd like to say they could have it for gratis, but you know how much goes into organising an event.'

Thea agreed. 'Harriet didn't mention money. I think she was more calling out of desperation to see if you'd consider helping. But you have a point – the previous venue belonged to the family of a cast member, so they may not have been paying for it. The man to speak to is Matt Davis. He's the company's manager and also the one who produces and directs the plays.'

'Do you have his number?' Tina raised her pen over her clipboard.

'Sure.' Thea pulled a piece of paper out of her back pocket and passed it to her friend.

'We should pick Helen's brain for ideas. She's very fond of Harriet and event management is her thing.' Tom dug his hands into his pockets. 'If you did say yes, then there is a hell of a lot to consider. Do they bring the chairs for the audience, or are the audience expected to bring their own? Do we need to cater? Does the cast need accommodation?'

'Accommodation?' Tina's head shot up. 'That's it!'

'What is?'

'Presumably the actors would have had to stay in and around Lacock. I doubt the farmhouse would have been able to put everyone up, so they'd have been expecting to pay out for hotels or B&Bs. Why don't we do that?'

'Charge them to stay in the house and not worry about charging for the use of the acting space?' Sam approved. 'That would work, although, we aren't a hotel as such.'

'I wonder if Mabel would cook an evening meal. I'd happily do lunch and breakfast.' Tina took hold of her husband's hand. 'How many nights would it be for, Thea? How many performances?'

'The original plan was for four evening performances, so I assume at least five nights' accommodation would be required. Maybe a couple more.'

'What do you think, Sam?' Tina squeezed his gloved hand.

'I think we should go back inside, have some lemon cake, and ask Mabel if she'd be up for cooking up to three evening meals in principle. Then, when she says yes, which she will – we'll ring this Matt chap and offer him Mill Grange on the condition that they pay for accommodation and food, provide all their own equipment, and *only* come for a max of three performances and seven nights, assuming they need to arrive with time to rehearse. Sound good?'

Thea threw her arms around Shaun as he climbed out of his car. 'You don't happen to know *The Winter's Tale*, do you?'

Shaun's eyebrows rose. 'I'll be honest, that was not the first thing I thought you'd say to me after two months apart.'

'Would you rather I'd have led with the news that Mabel has made bacon sandwiches for lunch in honour of your return.'

'Too right. Although a kiss from my gorgeous girlfriend wouldn't go amiss first.'

'Before a bacon sandwich! I'm honoured.' Thea leant in for a kiss, only to have it curtailed by a question.

'The song by David Essex or the play by Shakespeare?'

'Sorry?'

'*Winter's Tale*.'

'Oh yes. The play.' Thea peered into the back of the car. 'That isn't all dirty washing, is it?'

Shaun chuckled. 'You sounded just like a wife then.'

'Oh.' Thea's cheeks coloured. 'Sorry, I just meant...'

'It's alright, I know. I was joking.' He pulled her closer.

'The weather was dreadful. I adore the North East coastline, but I don't think we had a single dry dig day for the entirety of the filming. At least it'll show *Landscape Treasures'* viewers that archaeology isn't just a fair-weather occupation.'

'Did you find it?'

'The Saxon farmstead?' Shaun grimaced. 'Ish. There's never much to find on Saxon sites. A few traces of hut post-holes. Usual stuff.' He opened the car's back doors. 'Why were you asking about a Shakespearean play?'

Thea heaved two overflowing carrier bags of grubby clothes out of the car. 'Dylan's stepsister, Harriet, has a role in it. Hermione.'

'Good for her.' Shaun hooked his rucksack onto his shoulder before grabbing a third bag of muddy clothes from the boot. 'It's a great play. I played Polixenes in an amateur production when I was at university.'

'No way!' Thea was amazed. 'I had no idea you'd trodden the boards.'

'It was a one-time event. I don't have what it takes to be in the limelight like that.'

'What are you talking about? You're a celebrity archaeologist! A television presenter! You're always in the public eye.'

Pushing the back door to the manor open with his foot, Shaun laughed. 'Believe me, it's very different. You know what it's like on *Landscape Treasures*. I only have to remember a few lines at a time, and if I mess up we can reshoot them. On stage, if you mess up, then everyone knows and no one ever lets you forget.'

Thea deposited the bags of washing in the hallway. 'That sounded like the voice of experience.'

'There was a tricky speech I had to do midway through the play. I left out *one* line. It wasn't major in the grand scheme of things. Didn't mess up the plot or anything, but the chap playing Leontes, David bloody Clark, would not let it go.'

Thea's eyebrows rose further. 'Not still bitter a million years down the line or anything?'

Shaun grinned. 'It put me off acting for life.'

'Shame. I bet you were good.'

'Probably about average, but thanks anyway.' Shaun inhaled as they walked towards the kitchen. 'Unless I'm very much mistaken, the sainted Mabel is already on sandwich duty.'

* * *

'I don't know how to thank you.' Matt gestured for Harriet to join him at his desk.

'Did Thea call you then?'

'Thea?' Matt's forehead crinkled. 'I spoke to a chap called Sam Philips. He said you'd asked him to call.'

'Sam. Yes.' Harriet nodded. 'He and his wife Tina own Mill Grange. Thea must have passed your number on. Thea is part of the management team.'

'Team managing what?'

'A retreat for recovering military personnel.'

'Isn't it a Victorian manor house?'

'It is.' Harriet shuffled her chair forward as she explained. 'Sam and Tina have transformed it into a recovery retreat for former service men and women who've had a bad time.'

Matt played a pen through his fingers. 'And you think it could be a potential venue for our show.'

'I realise it's a long way from Lacock, but...'

Matt held up a palm. 'No need to explain. As I said, we

owe you our thanks. I won't pretend such a last-minute – or distant – change of location won't be without problems, but better we go ahead than have to cancel. Especially as all the equipment is hired and we wouldn't get all our money back.'

'So, it *is* going to happen?' Hope started to unknot the tension in Harriet's shoulders.

'Providing the others agree.' Matt pushed a piece of paper covered in hastily scribbled notes across the table. 'Sam had a few conditions. What do you think?'

Harriet ran her eyes over the list, mumbling as she read, 'No charge for venue but there's a fee for accommodation and food.' She looked up, 'I'm guessing them not charging for the venue is a help, and we'd have all been paying for hotels and food so...'

'It depends how much the charge for accommodation is, but yes, no venue charge is certainly a help, especially as it is highly unlikely we'll be able to sell as many tickets. It's not in the most accessible location for an incoming audience.'

'When I first spoke to Thea she told me the locals are very supportive. And Tiverton is only fifteen miles away. It's a big town apparently, and then there's Bampton and...'

Matt looked at his companion more closely. 'You want this to work don't you, Harriet?'

'It would be – or have been – my first professional job.'

'Believe me, I understand how disappointed you'll be if it doesn't happen.' Matt tapped the top of his laptop. 'I've emailed the others asking them to attend a meeting in the rehearsal room at four.'

'Right.'

Matt indicated to the list in Harriet's hands. 'Sam suggested that we move the performance to January, but as we have other shows already scheduled, and you guys have a new university term to get back to, it has to be the 18th to the 20th December or not at all.'

Reading on, Harriet looked up at Matt. 'Only three shows, not four?'

'Sam didn't think we'd manage to fill more than three shows, and even then, he suspects more than two might be ambitious.' Matt sighed. 'As Mill Grange is in the middle of nowhere and time is short, I'm inclined to agree with him.'

* * *

Taking a swig of water from her bottle, Helen gulped down a couple of paracetamol she'd fished out from the recesses of her shoulder bag. Her head had been thudding for hours. Standing in the playground, waiting for Dylan to come out of his classroom, with what felt like a hundred screaming under fours running around her feet, she couldn't help but wish herself a million miles away.

Helen hoped her opinion concerning the lack of discipline from the parents around her, seemingly uncaring that their offspring were causing chaos, didn't show on her face.

Just because you're at least twenty years older than most of the mums here, no need to go all judgemental. Helen looked around her. The majority of parents seemed to be fresh out of school or college themselves. *I bet they all think I'm Dylan's gran!*

Trying to blank out the toddler strapped into the pushchair parked next to her, who was screaming to the full capacity of its lungs while being totally ignored by its associated adult, Helen focused on the activity within Dylan's classroom.

Come on!

The children had already trooped out to the cloakroom in batches to fetch their coats. The chairs had been stacked on the tables as per their daily routine, yet Mrs Harley was still talking to them and clearly, whatever it was she was saying, was causing excitement. *Wise woman, sending them into to a hyper state just as you release them into the community. That way we have to deal with the overexcitement fallout, rather than you having twenty-five mini dynamos on your hands all day.*

Helen immediately felt guilty. She loved Dylan as if he were her own. From the moment she'd got to know Tom, his six-year-old son had become one of the most important people in her life. She adored his enthusiasm for life and learning. Making up bedtime stories with him had become one of the highlights of her day since she and Tom had moved from Mill Grange to Tiverton. It hadn't been an easy decision to leave the manor, but they didn't want to take Dylan away from the school he'd only just settled into, at a time when his mum, Sue, had emigrated with her fiancé, leaving her son behind.

Helen looked back towards the classroom. Mrs Harley had a pile of letters in her hand and was striding towards the classroom door that led directly into the playground. A sure sign that she was about to release her charges.

Moments later, Dylan was sprinting to her side, brandishing a letter in his hand like he'd won the World Cup.

'Look, Helen. Can I tell Dad?' Dylan paused, a small furrow appearing on his forehead. 'He won't tell Bert will he? Cos I want to. Mabel and Bert will come won't they? Look!' He rustled the letter again. 'Mrs Harley says we can have four tickets. That's you, Dad, Mabel and Bert.'

Taking the letter from Dylan so she could discover what

he was talking about, Helen read at speed. 'This is fantastic. Of course you can tell your dad. Here.' Pressing a few buttons on her mobile, Helen passed it to Dylan.

Having been told many times that he was not allowed to walk around with a mobile in case he dropped it, Dylan stood like an immovable rock amid the swirling tide of children and parents, while he waited for Tom to pick up his call.

'Helen, can we go and tell Bert and Mabel later cos...' Dylan broke off as the line connected. 'Dad! It's me. Guess what?'

* * *

Harriet was sure Rob had been glancing at her whenever he thought she wasn't looking. *Or am I wishful thinking? He's probably just pleased we have a new venue, and as it was me who found it, he's looking my way. Don't read anything into something that isn't there.*

Matt was handing round printouts of Mill Grange's location. 'Obviously you can programme your phones or sat navs to get you to Upwich, but I have been warned that the mobile signal can be unreliable, so it seemed a good idea to have written directions to hand in case.'

'No Wi-Fi!' Jason curled his lip contemptuously. 'What the hell use is that?'

'It's only patchy sometimes.' Harriet felt defensive.

'And it's better than having nowhere to perform after all the hard work everyone has put in.' Matt gave Jason a hard stare. 'I trust your parents are alright and coping with the flood as best they can?'

'No, actually.' Jason tucked a stray hair behind his ear. 'I didn't think it would matter to the group, as I hadn't considered the possibility of the venue being replaced, but they've asked me to help them clear the house. Pull the carpets up and stuff.'

The way he spoke made it very clear that he considered such a task beneath him. Harriet found herself feeling sorry for his parents, until she realised that if Jason didn't come to Mill Grange, they'd have no leading man.

Matt had had the same thought. 'Are you telling us you are not going to be playing Polixenes?'

'Seems not.' Jason got up from where he'd been lounging on the edge of the stage, pulled his script from his holdall, and dropped it onto the floor. 'Can't say I'm that sorry if it comes at the cost of not being able to keep up with potential agents or missing out on future roles due to no Wi-Fi. Enjoy Exmoor, guys. I'll see you next time.'

Harriet risked a glance at Matt. His expression was thunderous. Jason was already at the door when he called after him. 'Are you seriously telling us that, after Harriet's bust a gut finding us a decent venue, we are down a lead role?'

'My family need me. What can I do?' Showing not one iota of remorse, Jason slammed the door behind him.

THREE
WEDNESDAY DECEMBER 1ST

'And to what do we owe this honour?' Bert held open the door to his and Mabel's cottage in the heart of Upwich. 'On a weekday too!'

Jumping up and down on the spot, Dylan was fit to burst with his news. 'I need to see Mabel too.'

'Of course you do. You know where to find her.' Bert stepped back as Dylan shot inside. 'Good to see you, Helen. Tom arrived five minutes ago. He's in with Mabel.'

Following the old man, Helen slipped off her shoes. 'I'm sorry to crash in on you so late in the afternoon, but there's no way I'd get Dylan off to sleep tonight if he doesn't talk to you both. Apparently this was "too big for a phone call".'

Bert chuckled. 'Well in that case, let's go in. The suspense is killing me!'

Mabel was in a stranglehold of a cuddle as Bert shuffled in with Helen. 'Do we have time to put the kettle on, Dylan?'

'Ah no! I want to tell you now.'

Easing himself into his favourite armchair, Bert caught Mabel's eye. His wife might rule every committee in the village with a rod of iron, but when it came to Dylan, she was putty in his hands.

'Go on then. Hot news your dad called it.'

Tom grinned at Bert. 'I'm very proud.'

The little boy frowned. 'You haven't told them, have you, Dad?'

'Absolutely not. I haven't even told Sam, Tina or Thea.' Tom put his arm around Helen as she sat down. 'You okay, love?'

'Long day – I'll tell you later.' She gave Dylan a thumbs up. 'Should we do a drum roll?'

'Yeah!' Dylan jumped off Mabel's lap and placed his palms next to Helen's on the top of the wooden coffee table.

'Ready?'

'Yes.' Dylan giggled as, in time with Helen, he drummed his palms against the side of the table, as if maintaining tension on a game show. 'One, two, three... and...' They stopped drumming and Dylan leapt to his feet. 'I'm going to be in the school nativity! I'm the innkeeper! I'm the one who gets to say, "No room at the inn!" And you can all come to see me be on stage and everything!'

Mabel clapped her hands. 'Oh, how wonderful!'

'Well done, young fella.' Bert patted his knee for Dylan to join him. 'Got a dressing gown and a tea towel at the ready?'

'Pardon?' Dylan looked at his dad. 'I help dry up sometimes, don't I.'

Tom laughed. 'You are very helpful. What Bert means is, will you need to provide your own costume?'

'A tea towel?'

'When we were little, the shepherds and the innkeeper used to have dressing gowns to wear, because they were a bit like the robes everyday people wore back then. We used tea towels on our heads, secured with a bit of cord, to look like the head coverings people wore.'

'Really?' Dylan looked up at Bert through his fringe, not sure if he was being teased.

'Really.' Bert cuddled him closer. 'Although thinking about it, I can't imagine why our teachers considered a tea towel a good replacement for a bit of plain material?'

'It was because everyone had tea towels, you daft man,' Mabel said affectionately, making Dylan laugh in the process. 'It was cheap and easy. Same went for dressing gowns. Everyone had one.'

Tom nodded. 'I remember the lad who played Joseph at one of my primary school nativities complaining because one of the shepherds had a nicer dressing gown than he did, and he was the star.'

'Did they swap dressing gowns, Dad?'

'Nope. My teacher told him off for complaining and made him the shepherd and the shepherd Joseph.'

'Really!' Dylan's eyes widened in surprise.

'Yep. Teachers were allowed to be tough back then.' Tom smiled as he saw Mabel and Bert share a look of tacit agreement that the world had gone soft.

'That won't happen to me will it?' Dylan turned to Helen. 'I've got dinosaurs on my dressing gown. That wouldn't be right for an innkeeper would it?'

'Don't you worry, I'm sure the school will find you an outfit to wear.'

'No, Mrs Harley said our mums and dads would have to make the costumes. They'll be another letter next week.' The joy went out of the six-year-old for a moment. 'Mum's a bit far away to help though.'

Keeping her inability as a seamstress quiet so she didn't disappoint Dylan, Helen said, 'We'll do our best.'

Sensing Helen's apprehension, Mabel said, 'I could do it. I'm not bad with a needle. But only if you're too busy – I wouldn't want to stop you doing it if you had an idea already.'

Helen sent a mental "thank you" across the living room. 'That would be ever so helpful. I'm not the greatest with a needle and work is rather full-on just now. Okay with you Dylan?'

'Yes!' He scrambled off Bert's lap. 'And you could help me learn my lines, Bert.'

'I'd be honoured, but don't you only have to say, "There's no room at the inn"?'

'No. Mrs Harley has had my part made bigger!'

'Has she now! Well in that case, bring me the script as soon as you have it!'

Mabel laughed. 'That's two theatrical productions to keep us busy this winter.'

'I can't wait to tell Harriet I'm going to be an actor too.' Dylan tilted his head towards his elderly friends. 'You will come won't you? It's on 16th December.' He turned to Bert. 'Shall we go and write it on your kitchen calendar?'

'What a good idea.' Bert heaved himself off the chair. 'Why don't you go ahead and find the biscuit tin while you're at it. This calls for a chocolate biscuit and cuppa celebration.'

As Dylan shot into the kitchen, Bert breathed out a ragged puff of air. 'Darn lungs. Slow me down these days.'

'You're alright though, aren't you, Bert?' Tom exchanged a worried look with Helen.

'Fit as a flea! I admit the pneumonia I had last spring knocked me a bit, but I'm just fine. Can't stand being so slow though!' He rubbed his palms together. 'Who's for tea and who's for coffee?'

* * *

'Helen!' Thea dropped a pile of retreat booking forms onto her desk as her friend poked her head around the door of the old scullery. 'What a lovely surprise. Tom said you were working from home today.'

'I was. And once we get home I will be again, but Dylan had news and he was desperate to tell Bert and Mabel.'

'News?'

'More than my life's worth to say. He'll want to tell you himself.' Helen pulled out the chair opposite Thea and sat down. 'He's tucking into biscuits at the cottage. I thought maybe we could have a coffee. Have you got time? It's ages since we had a catch-up.'

'Sure.' Thea's eyes narrowed. 'Are you alright? You look a bit, well...'

'Done in? Yep. That about covers it.'

Helen picked up her mobile. 'Why don't I text Tina to see if she wants to join us? Kitchen table or last orders at Sybil's?'

'Oooh, that is tempting.' Helen checked her watch. 'It's already half-four though. Is there time to visit the tea room?'

'There is *always* time to visit Sybil!' Thea laughed. 'She's open until half-six three evenings a week in the run-up to Christmas. Says it's worth having the coffee pot brewing while people come in to book their Christmas cake, pudding and pastry orders.'

'Then let's do it!' Helen was already on her feet. 'I could murder a scone or three. Hope she has some left.'

* * *

Sybil, her hands full of order papers, waved as they arrived. 'Hi, you two. Tina and a huge pot of coffee are in place. Be with you in a jiffy.'

Already sat at their favoured table at the back of the tea room, Tina leapt to her feet and gave Helen a hug.

'This is such a great idea.'

Helen smiled at her friends. 'It's just what I need. Thanks, both.'

'You okay?' Tina's concerned expression echoed Thea's earlier observation that Helen was not looking her usual unstoppable self.

'Tired.' Helen grabbed the coffee pot, inhaling the heavenly aroma as she poured some strong black liquid into her mug.

'So, what's wearing you out? The new job or the new life?' Thea took her turn with the coffee pot.

'Both.' Helen groaned. 'I don't mean that to sound as awful as it does. I love Tom so much, and Dylan too, but...'

Tina finished Helen's sentence as she pushed the Spode sugar bowl in her direction. 'With Sue in Australia, you have gone from being Tom's girlfriend, to his live-in partner, to Dylan's stepmum in just a few months. It's bound to be a big adjustment.'

'It's not just that.' Helen paused as Sybil arrived with a plate of steaming hot cheese scones and a pot of butter. 'Wow, I've missed you, Sybil!'

'Why thank you, Helen.' The tea room's owner gave a mock curtsey just as her phone rang. 'Sorry, I was hoping I could stay and chatter, but the second December arrives the entire village mobilises and wants to place their Christmas cake orders.'

'These smell amazing.' Helen picked up a scone as Sybil dashed off. 'Good job I've not got a big dinner planned for tonight.'

'I told Sam to get himself something. I won't be hungry for hours after a couple of these.' Tina began to fill two scones with hefty amounts of butter.

'It's a miracle you're so slim.' Helen laughed as she followed suit. 'Although I have to say you're looking fabulous. Married life suits you.'

Tina blushed. 'I can't believe how lucky I am.'

'Sam any closer to being able to go upstairs?' Helen licked some butter from her fingers.

'Not yet.' Tina chewed. 'He is okay with downstairs now – apart from where the corridor goes narrow and dark towards the laundry.'

Thea couldn't help laugh. 'Is that his claustrophobia or him trying to avoid having to use the washing machines?'

'I hadn't thought of that!' Tina grinned. 'It is good not to have to sit in the drawing room with the window open all the time now. It's so cold! Sam's convinced it's going to snow before Christmas.'

Helen laid down her knife. 'I suppose all those years living in a tent have made Sam attuned to the weather. Is Bert still helping him with therapy sessions?'

'Sometimes. Not so much since he had pneumonia.' Tina twirled her right pigtail through her fingers. 'To be honest, I think the fact that Bert used to suffer from claustrophobia helps Sam as much as the therapy does. He's a great example of someone who's worked out a way to live with it.'

'Bert was on good form when I saw him earlier, but

there's no doubt his brush with pneumonia has slowed him up a bit.'

Thea nodded. 'Mabel's constantly worried about him, but there's been no relapse. He'll have to be careful now the weather's getting colder.'

'I could take him some scones after we're done here. Warm his insides.' Helen refilled the coffee mug she'd already drained.

'Nice idea.' Tina sucked her buttery lips. 'New job okay, apart from being full-on?'

'It's great. It's *so* good not to be in overall charge of the Roman Baths anymore. I don't think I realised how stressful it was until I stopped doing it.'

'I bet.' Thea, who'd worked as Helen's second in command at the Roman Baths before she moved to Mill Grange, agreed. 'Mind you, being their chief event manager is hardly a walk in the park. How often do you have to go up to Bath?'

'Every other Monday. More often if an exhibition needs physically setting up. Sometimes I drive, but more often I go on the train. It's only just over an hour once I've driven up to Tiverton Parkway.' Helen smiled. 'Dylan is very good at not disturbing me when I'm in work mode. Well, most of the time anyway.'

'So you are managing to get things done?' Tina topped up her coffee. 'I'm not sure I could work from home.'

Thea and Helen both looked at her as if she was mad and waited for the penny to drop.

'Oh yeah.' Tina laughed. 'I'm so silly. I suppose Mill Grange is so big it doesn't feel like working from home by the time I've gone from the bedroom to the kitchen, and then back to my office in the attic!'

'It'll be all hands on deck with The Outdoor Players coming,' Helen said. 'Harriet is so relieved that the play can go ahead.'

'Blimey, news travels fast.' Thea wiped her hands on a serviette. 'Did Tom tell you?'

'Harriet beat him to it. She called to tell Dylan while we were on the way over here. It's lovely how close those too are despite the twelve-year age difference.' Helen's expression became troubled. 'You know, she wouldn't look out of place picking Dylan up from school. I swear she's the same age as most of the mums who wait in the playground.'

'She's eighteen!' Tina picked up her coffee cup.

'Nineteen, but yeah.' Helen shrugged. 'I feel like a granny when I go to collect Dylan.'

Suddenly, suspecting that she knew what was troubling her friend, Thea asked, 'Who do you talk to when you go to collect him?'

'Talk to?' Helen gave a humourless laugh. 'No one. Everyone already knows everyone. They're all friends from their own school days or from antenatal classes if the conversations I've overheard are anything to go by.' She shifted in her seat. 'I'm not eavesdropping, but most of them seem to shout at each other rather than just talk. It's difficult not to hear.'

'Ahh.' Tina caught Thea's eye. 'You a bit lonely over there, Helen?'

'Lonely? Tom's there every evening and Dylan of course. I just don't... It sounds silly when I say it out loud, but I don't fit. I don't understand the rules of being a parent in a social situation.'

'I'm not sure I would.' Tina's forehead wrinkled.

'But if you were the child's mother it would be different.

You'd already have met people at antenatal classes, play school, nursery and so on. It's like I've been parachuted into an alien world without a clue of the culture.' Helen sighed. 'Sorry, just having a whinge.'

'No need to be sorry.' Thea fiddled with her cup. 'I wish I could help, but I'll be honest, I haven't the foggiest what to suggest. I'll ask Shaun for ideas when I get back if you like, although why he'd have any thoughts on this matter I don't know.'

'Shaun's back?' Helen put her cup down with a thud. 'Why didn't you say? Don't you want to get back? You haven't seen him for weeks.'

'It's fine, honestly.' Thea dabbed up some crumbs with her fingertips. 'We're going to head to the pub for a drink later.'

'That wasn't said with enthusiasm.' Tina was now worried about both her friends. 'You guys are okay, aren't you?'

'Absolutely. It's just, well, after we were a bit ropey when you got married last spring, and then sorted ourselves out, I did wonder if maybe he'd...' Thea waved a hand to chase away her thoughts. 'Hardly matters. We're happy and that's what's important.'

Harriet's moment of dismay after Jason's bombshell had been short-lived. He'd no sooner sauntered from the room, leaving his fellow actors without their leading man, when Matt had got to his feet and scooped up Jason's abandoned script.

'Rob, I've understudied for the roles of Leontes and Polixenes in the past. Would you like to play Polixenes instead of Jason, or do you want to stick to being Leontes? You're more than capable of taking either role.'

'Thank you, but at this late stage, I'll stick with being Leontes.' Rob waved his script in front of him. 'I appreciate your confidence in me though.'

'Confidence that you've earned.' Matt acknowledged the student with a smile. 'Well then, if everyone's okay with me taking on the role of Polixenes rather than us wasting time we don't have finding a new lead, then I'll do it.'

Murmurs of relief echoed around the room as Matt turned to Rob. 'We'll do the scenes with you and Harriet first. Ready?'

'Ready.' Rob got to his feet as Harriet moved onto the stage.

'Okay then,' Matt referred to his stage notes. 'Let's go from where Rob, as Leontes, King of Sicilia, is asking you, Harriet, as his wife, to persuade me, as Polixenes, the King of Bohemia, to stay on the island. Act One, Scene Two.'

Harriet clutched her script for reassurance, but didn't open it. Willing the words to remain in her head as she took up her position directly before Rob, hoping that when she stared into his eyes as his adoring wife, he wouldn't see how much she fancied him.

* * *

The fire crackled in the hearth, sending out comforting wafts of wood smoke as Thea watched Shaun chatting to Moira, the landlady of the Stag and Hound.

The locals of Upwich had long since got used to having a television celebrity in their midst. Shaun Coulson, known to many of them as "the archaeology bloke" from *Landscape Treasures*, had been an accepted part of village life since he'd come to help restore Mill Grange in the months before Sam had bought the manor.

Thea could hear Shaun laughing at something Moira was saying as she poured him a pint of beer. He was pushing his fringe out of his eyes, raking a hand through hair that badly needed cutting, his tall frame towering over the bar.

She found herself reflecting on how important the pub had been to their relationship. They'd had their first real date in the back room, and it was thanks to Moira, with Sybil's help, that they had met in that same back room in the spring – a meeting that had gone a long way to prevent them from splitting up. And now, here they were, eight months later. *Together*. Thea knew she loved Shaun and that he loved her, but over the past few weeks she'd begun to wonder if they'd ever move on from where they were: a couple who lived together for part of the year, to a couple with their own home, or a couple with a family.

We certainly act like a married couple. Thea contemplated how many loads of washing she'd sorted for Shaun earlier.

'Your wine, madame.' Shaun placed a glass of Pinot before Thea with regal formality.

'Why thank you, kind sir.' Thea laughed. 'Fancying yourself a part in Harriet's play?'

Shaun sat next to Thea and looked into the fire. 'Not on your life.'

'That David bloke scarred you too deeply during your brush with Shakespeare, then?'

'Oh he did.' Shaun wrapped an arm around Thea's shoulder. 'I think I've missed a decent pint almost as much as I've missed Mill Grange.'

'And Mabel's bacon sandwiches.'

'Obviously.' Shaun put his glass down. 'Although, as I said earlier, neither the beer nor the sandwiches have quite the effect on me that you do.'

'I'm very pleased to hear it.'

'Ummm. I definitely would have to rate kissing you higher than Mabel's cooking.'

'And, if I'd kissed you after eating a bacon sandwich?'

'Orgasmic, obviously!'

Thea choked on a mouthful of wine. 'I have no answer to that!'

'Probably just as well. If Mabel found us making secret

bacon sandwiches to test the theory, she'd have something to say about it.'

'But not as much to say if she caught us sneaking off to bed in a post-sandwich haze of desire!'

'Oh hell, I want to do that now.' Shaun chuckled into his pint before changing the subject. 'Did you have a good time with Helen and Tina at Sybil's?'

'It was lovely. Sorry I dashed off so soon after you arrived, but we haven't seen Helen for ages. And although she's only ever a phone call or an email away, somehow the days disappear and we're not in contact that often.'

'Don't worry about it. It's not like we're only just together or anything.' He picked his pint back up. 'Helen okay?'

Thea digested the fact that Shaun didn't see them as a new couple anymore. 'She's finding some aspects of motherhood tricky, but otherwise she's okay.'

'I bet. I can't imagine taking on someone else's child like that. And let's face it, Dylan's a good kid. Some children would be a much tougher gig to take on.'

'I think that's the problem, the "taking him on" bit. She's joined the party without understanding the rules.'

Shaun unhooked his arm from Thea's shoulder. 'I've always thought the whole parenthood thing sounded fraught with landmines.'

Thea's stomach clenched; their moment of relaxed humour evaporating. 'I'm sure it's a roller coaster from start to finish. Worth it though.'

'Maybe.'

'Only maybe?' Thea bit her bottom lip, not wanting their first evening together in ages to dissolve into a row.

'Depends on the child doesn't it.'

'And the parents.'

'Quite.' Shaun examined the contents of his beer glass. 'Do you think Tina and Sam will have children?'

'They want to.' Thea set her eyes on the flames flickering in the grate. 'I can't imagine them leaving it too long. Tina's already thirty-three.'

'Same as you.'

'No, I'm a year older.'

'Oh, yes, right.' Shaun jumped up. 'Fancy some chips? I'm starving.'

'What? Right, okay. If you like.'

Thea kept her eyes on the fire as Shaun bounded towards the bar like a hyperactive puppy.

You always said you wanted children. Have you changed your mind?

A second later, Shaun was back.

'You're sat worrying about me not wanting kids aren't you?'

'I might be.'

'Well stop it.' He gestured to the bar. 'But if we are going to have a grown-up conversation about our future, I need fuel. Tomato sauce with your chips?'

* * *

'He was out like a light.' Tom sat on the sofa next to Helen and held out an arm so she could rest against his shoulder.

'I bet he was.' Helen closed her eyes. 'That's the trouble with Sue being in another time zone – if she wants to talk to Dylan we have to keep him up late if she wants to have a lie-in.'

Tom sighed. 'There's no way we'd have got him off to sleep if he hadn't told her his nativity news though.'

'I don't think I've ever seen him so excited.' Helen rolled around so her head was resting on Tom's lap. 'Thank goodness Mabel has offered to help with his costume. If it had been left to me, it really would have been a dressing gown and a tea towel.'

'I'd have bought him a new dressing gown especially. One without dinosaurs on it!'

Helen chuckled. 'Looks like it's going to be something of a creative winter all round.'

'What with two plays you mean?' Tom nodded. 'I told the others you'd be the one to ask for advice about organising it.'

The colour drained from Helen's face and she opened her eyes in alarm. 'You did what?'

As his girlfriend pulled away, Tom faltered. 'Well, with Harriet as one of the stars I thought...'

'That I'd somehow magic a few more hours in my day to organise the posters and tickets sales?'

'Hang on a minute. I didn't say you'd *do* anything, just that you'd be good for advice if it was needed. You're great at...'

'At event organising? Of course I am. It is my job, but then so are lots of other things! I have a heavy exhibition workload you know, and then there's the book I wrote about Mill Grange's fortlet, and...'

'The book? You've heard back from the publishers?'

Helen slumped back in her seat, her burst of anger deflating. 'This afternoon I got a huge list of the things they want doing before publication. And as the e-book version is out on 16th December.'

Tom's mouth dropped open before he interrupted, 'And they only just told you?'

'What?' Helen was confused by the question.

'That's a bit unfair.' Tom frowned. 'I know it can all happen quite quickly with digital imprints, but that's instant! How can you be expected...'

'Oh, I see. No...' Helen's face flushed. 'I've known the publication date for a while. I told you. Didn't I?'

'You didn't, love.' Tom ran a hand through his hair. 'I would have remembered something that important.'

'I thought I had. Sorry.' Silent for a moment, she added, 'At least the paperback edition won't be out until July, so we can breathe a bit on that.'

'That's what you meant by a creative winter all round.'

'Yes. I have a heap of promotional things to do to help sell the book, and although a lot of it is optional, I want to be professional about this. And it'll be good for Mill Grange, so...'

Tom held up his hands in surrender. 'I promise I only volunteered your advice. I wasn't expecting you to do anything. Anyway, Thea and Tina would have killed me if I'd added to your workload.'

'I'm sorry, I really thought I'd told you about the e-book launch when it came through last month. And I didn't mean to overreact about the play. I'm delighted for Harriet, but—' Helen scrubbed her hands over her face while a yawn overtook her '—did you hear the date of publication, Tom?'

Glad to change the subject away from their misunderstanding, Tom said, 'Yeah, on the 16th. Why didn't you tell me about the book's promotional requirements this afternoon?'

'It was a bit overshadowed by events. I didn't want to steal Dylan's thunder.'

'You would never do that. And...' Tom stopped talking as

the penny dropped. 'The 16th, that's the same day as the nativity.'

'Bingo!'

'Hell.'

'Quite. You should see how many articles and interviews they've lined up for me to do, and...' she paused as another massive yawn overtook her '...I'm so tired.'

'I know. The book and the new job and looking after Dylan. Can I do anything to help?'

'You do loads, and to be honest, it isn't the work as such, and the book wasn't hard to write once I worked out how to do it. No, it's, I don't know... the lack of human contact I suppose.'

'What about the mums at school?'

'It's like I'm from another planet.' Helen tucked her knees beneath her chin. 'I'm sure they're all lovely, but I have no common ground with them. Nothing to start a conversation with.'

Taking a spiral of Helen's red hair between his fingers, Tom pulled it gently outwards and let it go, taking pleasure in watching it spring back into a tight curl. 'I know what you mean. I'm never at home in the playground either. Everyone is so set in groups.'

'Exactly.' Helen yawned again. 'Come on, I'm exhausted. Bedtime.'

'How exhausted?' Tom took another lock of hair and teased it between his fingers.

FIVE
THURSDAY DECEMBER 2ND

Perfectly restored from the dilapidated state of shattered glass and broken lead fixings it had been in when Sam had first come to Mill Grange, the frost-coated Victorian greenhouse glittered in the early morning light.

'It looks as if someone has sprinkled magic over it.'

'You old romantic, you.' Sam winked at Tina as they walked past the vegetable beds and nearer to the glass structure at the back of the walled garden.

'True.' Tugging her woolly hat further down over her ears, Tina hoisted the bag of chicken feed she was carrying higher. 'I'm so grateful to your parents for getting it fixed as our wedding present. I love it.'

'It would make a good backdrop for the play.'

'It would,' Tina agreed. 'Depends on space though doesn't it.' She gestured to the chickens. 'Let's see what the hens think.'

'Good idea.' Sam lowered the watering can he was carrying over the fence that kept the Mill Grange chickens in place. Their coop, a palace among poultry abodes, formed the centrepiece of the walled garden, and was home to an expanding flock of hens, led by the unflappable Gertrude and her sidekicks, Betty and Mavis. They, unwitting sounding boards for all the problems to face Mill Grange's workforce, were only answerable to their constant hunger and the rooster, Tony Stark; so named as the way he strutted reminded everyone of Robert Downey Junior.

'What do you think then, girls?' Tina poured a line of chicken pellets into the narrow trough that ran along the centre of the pen. 'Fancy a bit of theatre in your lives?'

Sam chuckled in a way that reminded Tina of Bert. 'I can just see them all with little Elizabethan ruffs around their necks.'

'We'll have to be careful, or they'll be demanding parts.' Tina grinned as a hen hopped over her wellington boot and landed in the trough. 'Are there any chickens in *The Winter's Tale?*'

'Haven't a clue. I did *Macbeth* at school, and there ended my Shakespearean experience.'

'I always wished we'd done *Macbeth*. My school did *The Tempest*. We were taken to see it performed. I was expecting it to be in period, but it was done as if everyone was at a 1920s cricket match.'

'That sounds very different.'

'You can say that again.' Tina straightened up from where she'd been searching for eggs hidden in the hay of the henhouse. 'Here you go. Six today.'

'Thank you, girls.' Sam broke the ice on the three trays of water that acted as drinking bowls, and refilled them. 'That's good going in this cold.'

'I don't suppose we'll get many eggs now until the weather's better.'

Sam agreed. 'Might be an idea to warn Sybil that her café supply could be low for a while.'

'We could both go and tell her. Yesterday's tea room break made me realise how long it's been since you and I went together. We could sit in the garden.'

'You'd freeze!'

'And?'

Putting down the watering can, Sam gave Tina a quick kiss. 'You're a wonderful woman, Mrs Philips.'

'Good job you married me then isn't it.'

'True.' Sam's smile dropped. 'I am going to beat this claustrophobia, you know. We aren't going to have to sit outside every pub, restaurant and café for the rest of our lives.'

'I know.' Tina took his hand in hers. 'You have come so far since you came here. You sleep inside instead of in a tent in the garden; you eat in the kitchen and the dining room. You *are* winning and you *will* get there.'

'But I still haven't made it upstairs. Sometimes I think I'm getting nowhere.'

A cluck from Gertrude at their feet seemed to echo Tina's thoughts. 'You haven't spoken like this for a while, Sam. What's sparked the getting nowhere idea?'

'The house filling with strangers I suppose. Our usual guests get where I'm coming from. They've been there, one way or another. Military service is fantastic, but when it goes wrong, well...'

'It goes wrong big time.'

'Precisely. How can I explain to a group of actors that I can't go upstairs to change a light bulb, or fetch them extra blankets, or whatever?'

'Those situations are unlikely to occur, and if they do, we

will deal with them just like we always do. Harriet is aware of the situation; Tom filled her in.'

'He did?' Sam wasn't sure if he minded this or not.

'He asked me if it was a good idea. And before you ask, he only didn't ask you personally because you weren't there at the time.'

'Oh, right. Okay then. I suppose it's for the best.'

'She's unlikely to mention it unless she has to.'

Sam sighed. 'Sometimes I feel like the local freak. The man who bought a manor house, but has never set foot on its first or second floors.'

'Enough of that!' Tina picked up the bucket of hay-cradled eggs and the empty food sack. 'Let's get inside. I want to look up the plot for the play. You worry about them thinking you're odd for not going upstairs. I, on the other hand, don't want them thinking I'm ignorant because, if I'm honest, I'd never even heard of *The Winter's Tale* until Harriet called Thea.'

* * *

Thea took a pair of secateurs from their hook in the gardening shed and strode into the woods.

It hadn't mattered how many times she'd tried to get to sleep last night, her mind had refused to quieten enough for her body to relax. The conversation she'd had with Shaun in the pub – or rather, the fact of the lack of the promised conversation about their future, had replayed itself on a continuous loop through her head all night.

Their "grown-up" discussion had got no further than him asking if she wanted tomato sauce on his chips. A couple of the locals had spotted that Shaun was back from Northumbria and came over to their table to ask about his latest dig.

I should have moved the conversation back to having children as soon as they'd gone.

Thea took a narrow path leading to a holly bush, which would provide a plentiful supply of berry-bedecked branches that could be placed in large vases around the house in readiness for Christmas.

So why didn't you? Not sure she knew the answer to her own question, Thea got to work. Squeezing the cutters hard against a branch she could picture fitting perfectly in the porch to the house, Thea cursed under her breath. The branch she had chosen clearly did not want to be parted from the bush. 'It would have been nice if you'd stayed around to help me with this, Shaun.'

Knowing she was being unfair, since she hadn't even considered getting this seasonal task sorted until an hour ago, Thea wondered why Shaun had shot off to do his Christmas shopping so early. She didn't believe for a moment that he was worried about not finding a parking space when he'd driven off to Taunton at half past six in the morning.

* * *

'Come on, Dylan; eat up, mate.'

Tom posted his son's lunchbox into his backpack as Dylan munched his way through a bowl of cornflakes. 'We've got to leave in five minutes.'

'Okay.' Dylan crunched faster. 'I'm so excited about Mum coming I forgot to chew.'

Helen looked up from her breakfast and met Tom's eye. 'Sue is coming?'

Tom abandoned the rucksack and crouched at his son's side. 'Dylan, when did your mum say that?'

'On the Zoom last night. When you were... oh.'

'When I was what?' Tom fought to keep his voice level.

'When you went to get me a bedtime drink. I forgot to say.'

Lowering her toast to her plate, Helen asked, 'Can you tell us what your mum said, love?'

'That she and Nathan were coming to see Harriet in her play, and now they can see me in mine too! So exciting!' Dylan's forehead creased into worry lines when he saw the expression on his dad's face. 'It is exciting, isn't it?'

Getting in first, while Tom had time to compose himself, Helen said, 'Of course it is. It'll be lovely for you to see your mum. You must miss her, and I'm sure she misses you.'

'I do a bit.' Dylan played his spoon around his bowl, not catching Helen's eye.

Moving from her place opposite him, Helen sat next to Dylan and gave him a big smile. 'It's okay to miss her. I don't mind. I love you very much, but I'll never be your mum. Mums are very special people.'

Dropping his spoon with a milky splash Dylan said, 'You're a really good almost-mum though.'

'Thanks, Dylan.' Helen was surprised to find tears pricking at the corners of her eyes.

* * *

Helen hadn't been in her study for more than a minute before her mobile rang.

'Hi, love, did Dylan get in before the bell?'

'Just.' Tom tutted down the line. 'This is so like Sue. I bet she waited until I was out of earshot to tell Dylan she was coming over so it was a done deal.'

'You don't know that.' Helen suspected Tom was right, but didn't want to sound as if she was taking sides.

'I'm so sorry, love.'

'It's not your fault. It's natural that Sue would want to see Dylan in his first nativity. I'd want to if...' Helen faltered, before adding, 'But with only four tickets allowed, and Dylan having already promised Mabel and Bert tickets, I'll have to duck out of seeing him in action.'

'I hadn't thought of that.' Tom swore down the line. 'Surely Mrs Harley will understand. There's bound to be leeway for extended families, divorced parents and such.'

'I think four tickets *is* the leeway. Space for both parents and remarried parents. The days before fire regulations, when grandparents and siblings could be crammed into the school hall with the parents, are long gone.'

'But that's insane. It can't be right.'

'Trust me, one of my biggest bugbears is sorting out how many guests are allowed in an exhibition at any one time. It's fine. It's obviously me who shouldn't go.'

'No.'

'But, Tom, if I go, then either Mabel or Bert can't, and there is no way on this earth that is happening. Can you imagine how crushed they'd be?'

Tom's sigh echoed through the phone, as Helen fired her laptop into life. 'The fact is, there are only four tickets, so I will bow out. Sue won't be able to come every year. I'll see the next one.'

'He might not be in the next one.'

'We will cross that bridge when we come to it.'

Tom sighed again. 'I'd better go. I'm already late and the traffic wasn't looking too kind on the road out of town.'

'Have a good day at Mill Grange, and don't worry. I don't mind, honestly.'

Thirty seconds after hanging up, Helen burst into tears.

* * *

Thea pushed two mugs of tea across the table at Sam and Tina as Shaun came in with a handful of paper and a shopping bag.

'Here you go. Three jars of posh honey from the farmer's market in Taunton and plot notes for *The Winter's Tale*.'

Sam picked them up and flicked through the pages. 'It's not short then!'

'It's not the longest of his plays, but there's a fair bit to it. Comedy and tragedy go hand in hand with this one.'

Tina read the cast list in alarm. 'There are twenty plus roles here! We can't put up twenty people.'

'According to Harriet they aren't performing all the roles. Plus, some of the actors have two parts and they do the technical stuff themselves. There are just twelve of them and they're happy to share.'

Tina took a sip of tea. 'Can you give us a potted summary of the plot, Shaun? I'm not sure I've time to read that lot.'

'And why's it called *The Winter's Tale*?'

'No idea. I think it's just one of Shakespeare's typical enigmatic titles. There's a reference in Act Two when one of the characters says "a sad tale's best for winter".' Shaun tapped his fingers against the table as he thought how to summarise the play. 'It's basically about two friends, Leontes, King of Sicilia and Polixenes, the King of Bohemia. For the past nine months, Polixenes has been staying with Leontes, but Polixenes wants to go home to see his son. Leontes, however, desperately wants Polixenes to stay, but he can't change his friend's mind. So he asks his wife, Queen Hermione...'

'Who Harriet is playing.' Thea passed around a plate of biscuits.

'She is.' Shaun took a chocolate digestive and carried on, 'Anyway, Leontes asks Hermione to persuade Polixenes to stay – and she is successful.

'For some reason, rather than being chuffed, Leontes becomes convinced that his friend is staying because he's having an affair with Hermione – who is heavily pregnant by the way.'

'Harriet has to pretend to be pregnant?' Tina helped herself to a cookie. 'I guess the pillow, or whatever they use to make her belly bigger, will help keep her warm while she's performing.'

Thea dunked a biscuit in her coffee. 'Then what happens, Shaun?'

'Leontes orders Camillo, he's a Sicilian Lord, to poison Polixenes. Instead Camillo warns Polixenes and they both flee to Bohemia.'

'Always quick to overreact, these jealous men in Shakespearian plays.' Thea gave her boyfriend, who wasn't without a tendency to jealousy, a dig in the ribs.

Shaun stuck his tongue out. 'Anyway! Leontes gets his knickers in a twist and declares that Hermione has been unfaithful and that the child she carries is not his. He sends two trusted nobles to the Oracle at Delphos to ask if his suspicions are correct.'

'And they say he's wrong, and they all live happily ever after?' Sam asked.

'Eventually. Before then, Hermione has a baby girl, who is abandoned in the middle of nowhere. By the time word comes from the Oracle, saying that Leontes was wrong, the baby is miles away and Hermione has been put on trial.

'The Oracle sends word that Leontes will have no heir until his lost daughter is found. The word comes that Leontes' and Hermione's son, Mamillius, has died. The shock kills Hermione and...'

'Hang on!' Thea interrupted. 'That means they kill off poor Harriet!'

'Sort of.' Shaun laughed. 'After Hermione is dead, Leontes is filled with regret and vows to find his daughter.'

'And that's how it ends?' Tina pulled a face. 'Not very jolly before Christmas.'

'It doesn't end there.' Shaun picked up the last page of his notes. 'Heaps of time passes and Perdita, now sixteen, has been raised by shepherds. She becomes engaged to one of them. He is secretly an envoy from Sicilia who's looking for the lost girl.'

'Oh dear God.' Sam raised his eyebrows. 'Why is there always someone pretending to be someone they're not?'

'No idea.' Shaun laughed. 'Then, everyone gets back to where they ought to be, including Hermione, who comes to life again, via a statue of the deceased queen.'

Tina brushed some biscuit crumbs to the floor. 'That sounds complicated. I'm glad I'm not an actor who has to learn all those lines and cues.'

'I suppose they're used to it.' Thea checked the time. 'I'd better get on. I promised Harriet I'd do some posters and get a few notices out on social media.'

'I can take a few posters into the village if you like. I need to get the eggs to Sybil.' Tina got up off the bench. 'Do you have a list of the people coming and their dietary requirements yet? I'll get it to Mabel.'

'Harriet sent it first thing. I'll print it off.' Thea paused. 'Oh, and I got the holly cut ready to decorate the house. It's in the old store.'

'Thanks, that's great.' Sam raised his mug towards Shaun. 'How come you know this play so well anyway?'

'Didn't he tell you?' Thea flashed her eyes in her boyfriend's direction. 'Shaun played Polixenes at uni.'

'No way!' Tina and Sam spoke in unison.

'Yes way!' Shaun laughed. 'Less surprise in the voices would be nice though, guys.'

SIX

THURSDAY DECEMBER 2ND

Helen knew it was pointless, but she waited until all the children were out of the classroom and asked Mrs Harley if she had time for a chat anyway.

Quickly picking up that Helen wanted to speak to her in private, Dylan's teacher asked him if he'd help her by putting away all the paints left out on the art table. It took only a brief conversation, before a fully sympathetic Mrs Harley confirmed what Helen had already known. The four tickets per child rule was an immovable one. She was about to take her leave, when the teacher asked, 'How is Dylan coping without his mum being around?'

Helen directed her gaze towards the little boy as he happily organised the vividly coloured pots of poster paint into their overnight home. 'Very well to be honest.' She lowered her voice so Dylan couldn't hear her. 'He speaks to Sue most weekends. It's not as often as either of them would like, but the time difference is an issue. Dylan can't always stay awake to chat to her, and neither can Sue always be around. She has a new job, and I get the impression that life over there is fairly full-on.'

'And she is in a new relationship.' Mrs Harley nodded. 'Sometimes children can be... I was going to say forgotten, but that would be unfair. I just mean that, sometimes, especially with so much geography in between, everything beyond that relationship can be a little distanced.'

Helen found herself wondering if she and Tom were guilty of that too.

As if reading her mind, Mrs Harley smiled. 'I didn't mean you and Mr Harris. It is clear how important that young man is to you both. He talks about you a lot.'

'Does he?'

'He's so proud of you knowing so much about the past.' Mrs Harley pointed to a pile of exercise books awaiting her attention. 'We've been writing about what we'd like to be when we grow up. Dylan wants to be good at fossils like you. Apparently you gave him an ammonite that you dug up yourself?'

'Yes, a while ago. I found it at Lyme Regis.' Helen experienced an uncharacteristic urge to cry. 'That's lovely. He's very special to me.'

Mrs Harley slipped some exercise books into her bag. 'I'm sorry about the tickets. Truly I am, but if we changed the rules for one, then...'

'You'd have everyone wanting extras. It's okay, I understand, but I promised Tom I'd ask, just in case.'

Helen was almost at the door, with Dylan in tow, when the teacher asked, 'I don't suppose you fancy helping us out with the nativity, do you? We will be asking for volunteers to help out with rehearsals and behind the scenes.'

'Well I...'

'I know you work full-time, and it can be very tiring and, I won't lie, sometimes a superhuman amount of patience is required, but it would mean you'd get to see Dylan in action on the night, albeit from the side of the stage rather than out the front with Mr Harris.'

* * *

Harriet pulled the padded tunic over her head. It felt weird and looked weirder. Staring at her reflection in the dressing room mirror, she rested her arms on top of the fake baby bump.

'I know it'll look different once I've pulled Hermione's gown over the top, but...'

Laughing, Ali held up her own outfit. 'At least you'll have extra padding against the cold. If I don't wear thermals under this lot, I'm going to freeze to death.' Tugging on the thin, mustard yellow, tunic-style dress she'd be wearing as Hermione's trusted friend and maid, Paulina, Ali did a twirl. 'Let's see it then.'

'See what?'

'Your "I'm six months pregnant" walk.'

Harriet's eyebrows rose. 'Oh hell, yes! Pregnant women have a different walk don't they.'

'It's a heavy business.' Ali patted the fake belly. 'Here.' She threw Harriet's gown to her. 'Pop this over the top. Sexy though that grey pillow thing is, I can't help thinking you'll have a much better chance of winning Rob's heart if you look less like half a baked potato.'

Harriet went pink. 'What do you mean?'

'You know very well what I mean. You can't keep your

eyes off him. Can't say I blame you. He's a regular Jamaican Adonis!'

'Don't be silly.' Harriet hid her face by pulling the dark green silk dress over her head, glad when it caught on her ponytail, delaying Ali having to see her expression. 'He is playing my husband. I *have* to keep my eyes on him so I don't miss my cue to give a line.'

'Even in the pub?' Ali giggled. 'Now that's what I call dedication to the art.'

'Anyway, he's half-Jamaican.'

'Is that right?' Ali laughed, giving her friend a knowing look. 'Made sure you know all about him have you?'

'We're friends. I met his grandparents in the summer at the drama department's pre-degree show at Bristol.'

'And you've had the hots for Rob ever since.'

'If you mean I enjoy his company, then yes, I do. Just as I enjoy yours.' Harriet adjusted her bump, so that it hung in front of her and not off at the side. She'd only known Ali for a few weeks, but she'd liked her instantly. She was very direct and had a kind smile. She had also experienced much of what Harriet was about to face, having done the same degree at Bristol University some years earlier, before joining The Outdoor Players as one of their regular actors.

Moving forward, Ali helped Harriet tug her dress into the right place, so that it fell neatly over her bump. 'How's that? Comfortable?'

'Not even slightly.'

'In five years of acting for them, I can't remember ever being comfy in anything I've ever worn for The Outdoor Players. Cold yes, but comfortable – never.'

Pleased that Ali had dropped teasing her about Rob, Harriet tried not to wonder how she'd given herself away –

and if Rob had noticed. She risked another look in the mirror, reasoning that, although the bottle-green dress was an improvement on the greying under tunic, and the silk material light and soft in her hands, it was only just on the "ish" side of flattering. 'At least our dresses are long enough to hide our feet so we can wear our own boots, keeping our toes toasty.'

'This is true.' Ali adjusted her gown over her T-shirt and leggings. 'What do you think?'

'I think we look like two women who hate what they're wearing.'

'Good job we're alright at this acting lark then isn't it.' Ali checked her watch. 'Come on, dress rehearsal is in ten minutes. Let's go and show Rob you look gorgeous even in a gown made from an old dressing gown.'

Noticing the inlaid pattern on the fabric for the first time, and realising Ali was probably right about it having once been an evening robe, Harriet decided not to comment on what Rob might think about her appearance. It was hard enough concentrating on her lines, reactions, and where she had to stand when she kept having the urge to run her fingers through his tight black curls. And now, on top of all that, she had to work out how pregnant women walked.

* * *

Mabel pushed her clipboard over to Tina. It held an exhaustive list of all the food, drink and household supplies they'd need to order in before The Outdoor Players came to stay.

'I know there's a lot there. Some of it, the bathroom cleaning detergents and toilet rolls we needed anyway, but assuming they arrive two days before the first night so they can rehearse in situ, we are talking six nights, seven days.'

Tina's internal accountant was already adding up how much it would all cost. 'I think I'll have to suggest to Sam that we ask for a deposit on the rooms, so we can get all of this in.'

Not wanting to pry, Mabel asked, 'Are things that bad? I mean, if you need me and Bert to sub...'

'No. No thank you, Mabel.' Tina patted her friend's hand. 'We're okay thanks. But we'd hoped to be able to do this without dipping into February's food fund.'

'It will bring in money though won't it, having the actors here? It won't cost you anything ultimately?'

'We should come out with a small profit after heating, wages and food.' Tina tugged on her pigtails. 'Forgive me, Mabel. I must sound mercenary. It's just, between you and me, Sam and I hoped that, if possible, we'd save enough to have a short break in June or July. We thought we'd go camping somewhere away from Mill Grange. A sort of late honeymoon. Sam thinks he could manage one of those posh glamping tents.'

'That's a jolly good idea.' Mabel collected some apples from a box in the window, ready to make a batch of pies to freeze in preparation for their guests. 'It'll do you good to get away from here for a while.'

'You don't think we're greedy asking Harriet's friends to pay to come here?'

'Not at all. This is your business, not a hobby.' Mabel put down her apple peeler. 'Has that been bothering you?'

'A bit.' Tina pulled at her right pigtail. 'Daft aren't I?'

'Kind, not daft.' Mabel gestured to the larder. 'Fancy weighing me out some flour and butter before you go off to play with numbers?'

* * *

Harriet had forgotten how to walk properly.

She was fine until she got onto the stage and remembered what Ali had said about pregnant women walking differently. Now, it was all she could think about and, as Rob approached her in full King of Bohemia mode, all her lines flew out of her head.

Rather than pleading with Leontes to believe her when she claimed faithfulness to their marriage, a heartfelt speech she had known off by heart, Harriet found herself floundering, her face beetroot, as she parroted her lines from the prompt in the corner.

She imagined the unspoken reproach of her fellow actors radiating into her flesh as, finally daring to catch Rob's eye as he flawlessly delivered his reply to her speech, Harriet was relieved to see nothing but professional detachment.

'Are you alright, Harriet?' Matt didn't sound angry, but he did sound worried. 'You did this perfectly yesterday. Something on your mind?'

While thinking, *Yes, Ali knows I like Rob and now I've embarrassed myself in front of him – and I've forgotten how to walk,* Harriet said, 'Sorry, Matt – everyone – terrible night's sleep and well, it feels very odd wearing this thing.' She patted her extended belly. 'Sorry.'

'Right.' Not sounding convinced, Matt waved a hand. 'Shall we give it another go?'

'Yeah. Sorry.' Harriet's cheeks glowed as she shuffled awkwardly back to her position before Rob.

'Oh and, Harriet—' Matt gave her a gentle smile '—I assume Ali wound you up about getting the walk right now you're pregnant?'

'How did...?'

'You should have seen her when she played Hermione three years back. She walked as if she'd metamorphosed into a penguin. The cast never let her forget. Just relax and be you.'

The tension lifted from Harriet's shoulders. 'Okay. Thanks.'

Turning to Rob, she whispered, 'Really sorry.'

'Don't worry,' he whispered back. 'Oh, and you look great in that dress by the way.'

Harriet's blush returned as she responded, 'But it makes me look pregnant!'

'A beautifully natural stage of life.'

'Oh, well, ummm...'

Rob's face broke into a shy smile. 'I think Matt's waiting – we'd better get on.'

'Yes, yes of course.' Harriet swallowed. 'From the top?'

SEVEN

THURSDAY DECEMBER 2ND

'That is brilliant!' Tom was delighted. 'Mrs Harley is a genius. That solves everything.'

'Apart from the bit about me finding extra hours in the day, which I don't have, to look after children I don't know, in a place that makes me uncomfortable. Yep. Problem solved.' Helen stopped just short of shouting as she sat at the kitchen table. 'Oh, I gave her some posters for the play at Mill Grange. She's going to put them around the school.'

Tom bit his lip before replying. Helen helping with the nativity was the perfect solution to their problem, but one look at the dark rings around her eyes made him stop and think. 'You said yes to helping with the nativity without wanting to do it, didn't you?'

'Dylan was there and, well, all I could think about was how disappointed he'd be if Mabel and Bert weren't there. Not to mention Sue.'

Pulling out a chair, Tom sat next to Helen. 'What does helping actually involve? Not much surely? Don't you just have to be there for the show to get everyone into the right costume?'

Helen struggled not to let her laugh stray into the hysterical. 'It means after-school rehearsals twice next week and again the week after. It means helping dress twenty overexcited children. It means rearranging work so I can do that and...' Helen paused, licking her dry lips before adding, '... talking to the other parents who are helping.'

Guilt hit Tom as he realised how much the prospect of what she'd agreed to do terrified Helen.

'That's the biggest thing isn't it? The other parents.'

Helen crossed her arms over her chest, hugging herself tightly. 'They aren't *other* parents. They are *actual* parents. It should be Sue behind the scenes with Dylan. She's his mum and she knows the other parents.'

Tom tried to visualise Sue helping a gaggle of six- and seven-year-olds dress and keep them calm and quiet while their friends were on the stage rehearsing. It was an image that wouldn't square in his mind. 'Not the volunteering type, my ex.'

'Okay, so I can't picture Sue wiping other kids' snotty noses or stopping them from panicking if they get stage fright either. But then, I can't imagine doing those things myself.' Unfolding her arms, Helen picked up her phone and opened an email. 'Here, I had this today.'

Tom took the mobile; his lost smile coming back as he read. 'This is fantastic. Why aren't you bouncing off the walls?'

'I'm nervous. I've never done anything like this. Perhaps if I'd read that before I'd agreed to help at school.' Helen shrugged. 'But now it's just another massive step outside my comfort zone.'

'Your book is a step closer to being published.' He reread the email. '*Upwich: A Roman Fortlet*, will be part of the *Secret History* range. That's fabulous. I've seen that series in the library and bookshops.'

'Have you read the bit that comes under that? The list of things that *I* have to do *before* then?'

'Write three articles for historical magazines, pieces for historical website blogs...' Tom trailed off as he saw Helen pale as he read the tasks aloud. 'Let's go and sit on the sofa.'

'What will that do?'

'Make us more comfortable. Anyway, I can't cuddle you while we devise a plan of action on these hard chairs.'

'A plan of campaign that shows me how to volunteer at the nativity and launch a book at the same time, while doing my day job?' Helen blew out a ragged puff of anxiety. 'Although, I thought I might ask for a day's leave on nativity day so I'm not too tired to do my best for Dylan.'

'That's a great idea. Maybe you should book a few days off. Take a proper break.'

'I don't think that's an option just now. I've not long come back after eight months' sabbatical.' Helen hauled herself to her feet. 'Actually, Tom, I don't have time to chat properly now. I need to get at least another hour done or the next exhibition at the Roman Baths simply isn't going to happen. Sorry.'

'It's seven o'clock!'

'I lost an hour at school talking to Mrs Harley and if I'm going to be helping with the nativity on my book launch day, then I need to prepare as much as I can. I haven't even looked at the social media side of things yet.' After filling a glass of water to take with her, Helen headed for the kitchen door.

'But you've been working since seven this morning. You're knackered.'

Helen pulled a "this is how it is" face. 'I'll feel better once I've got a few things crossed off my to-do list. I'll see you in a bit.'

* * *

'I'm so sorry.' Ali passed Harriet a lager. 'I thought I was helping. I was pulled apart something chronic by the bloke who was directing when I played Hermione. Chris he was called. He gave me hell for my pregnant woman walk not being convincing.'

Ali pulled at the beer mat in her fingers, shredding it into neat strips. 'Matt always said Chris was a prima donna who revelled in getting under my skin. He did nothing for my confidence. I hadn't realised quite how true that was until I messed things up for you just then.'

'It's okay.' Harriet, who was used to Ali's mischievous sense of humour, and had assumed she'd been winding her up, was surprised by the concern on her friend's face. 'Don't worry about it.'

'Matt was just a cast member when I started with The Outdoor Players. I can't tell you how glad I was when he took over.'

'How long before you two became an item?' Harriet rescued the littered pieces of beer mat and heaped them into a small pile.

'We were friends first. For about two years, just over maybe.' Ali picked up her pint of lager. 'Then I cracked and asked him out. I'd fancied him for ages, but didn't think he saw me as anything other than a friend. He swears he was just about to ask me out when I beat him to it, but the jury is still out on that one.'

Harriet was surprised. 'Matt strikes me as so confident. I can't believe he didn't ask you first. You're so gorgeous.'

'Hardly, but thank you!' Ali did a fake bow.

'Now that was a very Shakespearian move.'

'I've had practice you know.'

Harriet felt awkward. 'Do you mind, you know, me playing Hermione instead of you?'

'Crumbs, no.' Ali pushed a tangle of chocolate-coloured hair from her face.

'You sure?' Harriet found herself putting her hands over her stomach, surprised to find the bump she'd been wearing nearly all day wasn't there anymore. 'I've only been here five minutes. You've had heaps of experience and, let's face it, you look the part far more than I do.'

'You mean I'm older.'

'Of course not. I mean, it's a Mediterranean story and you're Mediterranean. Plus, you know the play inside out.'

'You'd be surprised how much of it I'd forgotten.' Ali cradled her pint to her chest. 'I think I only got the role last time because I'm part Italian. Chris was all about the look. You're a better actor, Harriet – that's obvious.'

Harriet, her mouth opening and closing in surprise at the compliment, was spared having to answer.

'Are you fishing for compliments about your acting ability, Aliana?' Matt arrived at Ali's side and sat on the nearest empty chair.

'Might have been.' Grinning at her partner, Ali confessed, 'I was apologising for making Harriet self-conscious about her walk.'

'Ah.'

Ali took another mouthful of her drink. 'Mind you, if anyone can pull off walking like a penguin in an evening gown, it's Harriet.'

'You've only known each other a few weeks and already you two are like a couple of kids when you've had a few lagers.'

'True.' Ali put her drink down. 'Seriously though, Matt, how are we doing? The dress rehearsal, once I'd stopped helping, seemed solid. How are we set for the move to Exmoor? All the cast coming?'

Harriet found herself crossing her fingers as she waited for Matt's response.

'Everyone is up for it. Sam and Tina have been more than generous with what they are charging for food and accommodation.'

'You have told everyone Mill Grange isn't a hotel, haven't you? We'll have to make our own beds and tidy up after ourselves.'

'I've made it crystal clear, Harriet, don't worry. I've arranged for a couple of people carriers to take us down there. Sam said there's no way a coach would get near the house.' Matt picked up the tablet he'd laid on the table in front of him. 'Did you want me to copy you in on the emails?'

'No, I'm fine. I know it's silly, but I don't want to make it appear as if they are just doing us a favour – even though they are. This is Sam and Tina's livelihood after all.'

'Absolutely.' Matt nodded. 'And who knows, if the venue works and we manage to get a decent audience, it could be a place we can return to. Providing our performance doesn't scare them off!'

'As if it would.' Ali smiled encouragingly. 'What's it like there, Harriet?'

'Actually, I've never been. I have heard a lot about it from Dylan – my almost stepbrother. His dad, Tom, works there. I've seen lots of pictures. It looks heavenly. An unspoilt Victorian manor on Exmoor.'

Ali pointed to Matt's tablet. 'Do you have photos?'

'Thea sent loads. I kept meaning to show you, but...'

'I know. When you're in the "only three weeks until opening night" zone everything else goes out of the window.'

'Yep.' Matt started to flick through his emails. 'I'll find them for you. I'd like your opinions. There is some indecision as to which garden we'd be best to perform in.'

'Two gardens?'

'And a wood.' Harriet added, 'And an archaeological excavation.'

'Seriously?' Ali picked a menu off the table. 'I think I need sustenance if I have to do thinking this late in the evening. Pizza?'

'Good idea. Pepperoni please.' Harriet was about to fish some money out of her bag to give to Ali, when her phone burst into life. 'Oh, it's my dad.'

Harriet's forehead creased in concern as she moved to the quietest corner of the pub to take the call. 'Hi, Dad, you okay? Whatever time is it over there?'

* * *

'You okay, Harriet?' Ali placed a heavily cheesed pepperoni pizza, in the middle of the table for them to share. 'You look a bit pale.'

'I'm fine.' Harriet picked up a slice and took a large bite. Instantly, she regretted it, as the piping hot cheese hit her tongue. She blew inwardly, trying to cool the mouthful so she didn't have to spit it out.

'Careful, it's just out of the oven.' Ali picked up Harriet's lager and passed it to her. 'Quick, take a sip. The last thing you need is a burnt mouth with all the lines you've got.'

'Thanks.' Harriet took a gulp and wiped her mouth on a napkin. She looked round. 'No Matt?'

'He's gone home to practise his lines. He wasn't expecting to be acting in this one.'

Harriet raised the pizza slice back to her lips and blew on it hard. 'I can't believe Jason dropped us in it like that.'

'I can.' Ali changed the subject. 'Are you sure you're alright? You look a bit peaky.'

'Just hungry.'

'You were fine before you spoke to your dad.' Ali checked her watch. 'Won't it be about dawn over there or something?'

'Seven in the morning. Dad's always been an early riser. He was already at work.'

'Wow. Keen.' Ali saw a shadow pass over Harriet's face. 'Look, I know I'm a nosy busybody, but I'm a trustworthy nosy busybody, so, if you want to talk about it, feel free. If you don't, then you can tell me all about your crush on Rob instead.'

Harriet couldn't help but laugh. 'It's that obvious, huh?'

'Yep.'

'Also pointless. Rob is *way* out of my league.' Harriet wound some of the stringy cheese that hung off the pizza around her fingers. 'He's also the best actor of all of us. If anyone in the players is going to make it... and well...'

'Well what?'

'Well nothing. I have a degree to get on with and a career

to build. And so does Rob. Plus, I have some pride; if he liked me, he'd say so.'

'But he's so cripplingly shy.'

'So am I.' Harriet put down her food. 'When it comes to men anyway.'

Seeing that Harriet wasn't going to be sharing any gory details about her fantasies where Rob was concerned, Ali asked more gently, 'And your father's call?'

'Dad and Sue, that's his fiancée, are coming to see the play.'

Ali's huge green eyes sparkled with surprise. 'All the way from Oz? Wow, he must love you a lot.'

'Umm.'

'That was a loaded "umm".'

'Sue has a little boy, Dylan. I've told you about him.'

'The lad you babysat for when you lived in Devon?'

'That's him. He's lovely, and soon to be my stepbrother. Just six years old, but not one of those spoilt, annoying six-year-olds. He's lovely to be with.'

Ali picked three slices of pepperoni off her pizza, saying, 'I can feel a "but" coming on.'

'But—' Harriet gave a drawn-out sigh '—when Dad was offered the job in Sydney, he and Sue just went. They left me and Dylan behind. We weren't even asked if we'd like to go too. Their only children. Dylan has his dad, Tom, and his dad's girlfriend Helen, but who do I have?'

The food in Ali's mouth suddenly felt very large as she chewed. 'I'm so sorry. I had no idea. I knew he lived in Australia but...'

'Oh it's okay. I wouldn't have gone. I had my life here all sorted with uni, getting an acting career going and all that, but since Sue came along, I've become a very low priority for Dad. He's always believed in what he called "hard life lessons" – that everyone should be independent and sort out their own problems.'

'Stand on your own feet kind of thing?'

'Yeah.' Harriet sighed. 'I get that now, but it was a tough lesson at eight years old.'

'He must love you though, or why come back to see the play? It's a hell of an expensive trip for a two-hour play.'

'He has a meeting over here apparently. In Bristol, a couple of days before Dylan is in his school nativity. They're coming to see him as well.'

'Okay.' Ali frowned. 'That's convenient I suppose. Gives them a triple reason for a trip. And it's nearly Christmas. They'll want to see their offspring at Christmas won't they?'

Harriet gave a shallow grunt. 'They'll be home again by then. Apparently it's a whistle-stop visit paid for by the company. I need to get two play tickets for the 18th. They go back on the 19th. I've just been told how much they're looking forward to their first Christmas on the beach.'

'Oh.' Ali shifted awkwardly. 'You know you could come to Matt and me, but we're off to Italy to see my folks and...'

Harriet held up a hand. 'It's okay, I wasn't asking, but I appreciate the offer. I'll be fine.'

'I sense your father is a little *sconsiderato*.'

'Pardon?' Harriet lifted her glass of lager.

'It's Italian for thoughtless. Has so much more impact than in English, don't you think?'

Harriet smiled. 'It does and he is – although I'm sure he has no idea.'

Ali shoved the plate closer to her friend. 'Now, we can either talk about this some more, or you can tell me what it is that makes Rob the bee's knees as far as you're concerned. And for heaven's sake, help me eat this pizza before I munch it all.' She pointed to the bag containing Harriet's costume for the play. 'Honestly, woman, don't you know you're eating for two!'

EIGHT
TUESDAY DECEMBER 7TH

Helen pulled off her gloves. Her palms were clammy despite the coolness of the air, and although she was walking far slower than usual, her pulse was racing. The park that buffered the side of West Exe Primary School seemed bigger today; the straight, flat path mountainous and full of unseen bear traps.

This is ridiculous. Checking she wasn't running late, even though she knew she was early, Helen aimed for a bench and sat down. *You've stood before hundreds of people and spoken for hours on Roman Britain. You have led countless school trips around the Baths. You ran one of the biggest tourist attractions in England for years. All you have to do is go and help out a teacher for an hour. That's it.*

Wrapping her arms around her chest, Helen could see the group of parents growing outside of the school gates, waiting for the moment when they'd be allowed into the playground. Pulling her scarf and coat around her, Helen sat still until the sound of the bell, indicating the end of the school day, echoed across the crisp winter air.

This is for Dylan and Tom. You don't have to enjoy it.

Getting cross with herself for being so feeble, Helen walked a little faster than before, heading not for her usual spot by the classroom door, but to the reception office, where Mrs Harley had told her she'd be signed in and given a visitor's pass. Then, formalities over, she'd be escorted into the hall where, to quote Dylan's teacher, "the fun and games would begin".

* * *

Tom checked his watch. *Damn.*

He'd been so engrossed in sorting out the paperwork for the next season of work with the retreat guests due to start their archaeological training in February, that he'd missed his chance to send Helen a text wishing her luck.

Dylan had promised to look after her, and although Helen had claimed she was looking forward to the adventure, Tom knew she was scared stiff about helping out with the nativity.

Tom imagined his son and friends excitedly waiting, with ill-concealed impatience, for their opportunity to shine on the school hall's stage. His smile dipped as he remembered Helen's pale complexion that morning. He knew she'd hardly slept, for she'd woken him twice tossing and turning, before he'd discovered over breakfast that she'd given up trying to sleep at about four a.m. and gone to work on one of the articles to promote her book.

Knowing he wouldn't be able to concentrate on his work until he'd heard from Helen after the rehearsal, Tom headed to the kitchen in search of a hot drink.

'Hi.' Thea reached another mug down from the rack that

hung within reach as she poured herself some coffee and waved it in Tom's direction. 'Tea?'

'I think I'll go with coffee if there's any going.'

'You okay?' Thea dropped a teabag into the mug. 'Not like you to drink coffee – normally you go for tea.'

'Consider it an act of solidarity with Helen.'

'Sorry?'

'She's just gone into her first nativity rehearsal.'

'Ah.' Thea passed Tom his drink and picked up the biscuit tin. 'Then you should also eat chocolate. That would be what Helen would do if she was here.'

'That's true.' Tom gave a half-smile. 'Has Helen said much to you lately?'

'I had an email about the nativity and about how nervous she was about going into the school.' Unsure if Tom knew just how uneasy the playground pick-ups made his partner, Thea kept her reply vague. 'She never liked groups of strangers, even when she worked at Bath.'

'She dealt with them though, didn't she?' Tom dunked a chocolate digestive into his mug.

'And she did it well, but that was her job. This is rather different.'

Tom brushed some biscuit crumbs from the table to the floor. 'That's the bit I'm struggling with. It's for ten minutes a day. She doesn't have to do anything other than stand there and wait for Dylan to appear and then leave.'

Feeling awkward, Thea cradled her mug in her palms. 'Have you spoken to Helen about this?'

'A bit.'

'But you don't get it?'

'Do you?'

'To an extent.' Wishing Tina was there to help her out,

not sure if the conversation they'd had with Helen about how tough she found certain aspects of her new life had been confidential, Thea said, 'The impression I get, and it is just *my* impression, is that Helen's out of her comfort zone. When it's work, no matter how tricky the situation or the people she has to deal with, she knows her subject and has professional confidence.'

'But she's so good with Dylan. She's a natural parent. How can I get her to see that?'

Thea stirred her coffee. 'She loves him as if he was her own – but he isn't. Coming into Dylan's life late, Helen doesn't feel as if she fits in with the parents.'

Tom stared into his mug, wishing he'd asked for his coffee to be extra strong. 'What can I do about that?'

'I honestly don't know. Perhaps this nativity will help. After all, it's throwing her into the heart of the fire.'

'She'll have no choice but to talk to other parents you mean.'

'Yes.' Thea blew through the vapour rising from her black coffee. 'At the very least, she has a stepchild at that school. It's a uniting point to start from.'

'I hope you're right.'

'Whatever happens, you know that Helen won't let Dylan down. If she's struggling with the situation, no one will ever notice.'

Tom stared into his mug. 'She's good at hiding her feelings. At least, she usually is. Lately, I don't know... perhaps she's just taken on too much.' He looked up at Thea. 'Do you think Helen is alright?'

* * *

The noise had been deafening as twenty children ran around, high as kites, shrieking and jostling each other at top speed. Helen, her back to the hall's stark white wall, had had to physically fight the urge to run to the toilet block and be sick. The relief she'd experienced when Mrs Harley had produced a whistle from the recesses of her skirt pocket and blown it, sending her charges into instant motionlessness, had been overwhelming.

'Thank God for that.'

Helen felt an instant rush of affection for the teaching assistant who'd uttered her mutual muted relief at the cessation of noise.

'I know it's a good idea to let them have time to get rid of the excess excitement,' Miss Walters whispered, 'but sometimes I wonder if it's such moments that keep the manufacturers of headache cures in business.'

'I'm glad you said that. I thought it was just me.'

'Nope.' The teaching assistant kept her eyes on the assembled children. 'You're very kind to volunteer. As you can see, help is thin on the ground.'

Helen had assumed that the other parents hadn't arrived yet. 'Just me and you?'

'Yep, it's...' Miss Walters paused as her eyes fixed themselves on a girl at the back of the group who was trying to secretly unwrap a sweet; seconds later, the child was blushing and the sweet was being returned to her pocket '...understandable. Most parents want to see their kids from the front, so...'

'Makes sense.' Helen fiddled with the keys in her jeans pocket as her gaze fell on Dylan. *Yet another difference between me and the real parents.*

'Are you okay?'

Helen plastered her professional smile on her face. 'Bit out of my depth.'

'You'll be fine.' Miss Walters gestured towards Dylan. 'He's a great kid.'

'He is.' Helen hastily added, 'You know I'm not his mum, right? I'm just his dad's partner.'

'You made that sound like a nasty secret.' The teaching assistant's eyebrows rose. 'A third of the parents here are step-parents you know.'

'Really?'

'Sure.' Miss Walters pulled herself away from the wall as the children gathered obediently around Mrs Harley. 'I'm Carol by the way.'

'Helen.'

'Right then, Helen. Cometh the hour, cometh the assistants!'

* * *

Helen read the text with relief.

Hope you survived okay. Don't do dinner. I'll get take-away on the way home. Love you. Tom xx

'Your dad's picking up a takeaway.'

'Yeah!' Dylan ran in circles around Helen on the way home. 'Will we get takeaway after every rehearsal?'

'Sadly not. But tonight will be nice.'

'Can I play in the garden when we get home?'

'Do you have homework?'

'Mrs Harley said the rehearsal was homework. It was fun. Did you like it?'

'I did.' Surprised to find that she wasn't pretending, Helen added, 'You were very good at your lines.'

'I promised Bert I'd practise them with him.'

'I remember. He'll like that.' Helen could picture Dylan, being the innkeeper, while Bert pretended to be all the other characters. 'And now that we have an idea what the school want you to wear, Mabel can start sorting that out.'

Dylan skipped on ahead as they meandered through the park towards home. 'Miss Walters is funny.'

'Funny?'

'Yeah. She tells jokes. Really silly ones.'

'She must have been too busy to tell me any.' Helen could imagine Carol having an army of cracker-style puns at the ready to cheer any worried or upset pupil. 'I liked her.'

Dylan grinned. 'She's my reading teacher.'

'Is she?'

'Yeah. We go to the library and get books that are too hard for the others.'

'Is that so?' Helen chuckled. 'That's very good, Dylan. You don't show off about that to your friends though I hope.'

'Nah, that would make me a meanie.'

'Good boy.'

Stopping at the edge of the path that divided the park from the road home, Dylan waited for Helen to catch him up. 'Did you hear me telling everyone you know all about the nativity because you know about the Romans?'

'Well, I'm not sure that's quite...'

'My friends think you're cool.'

'Oh.' Helen blushed. 'Really?'

'Course.'

NINE
TUESDAY DECEMBER 7TH

'It wasn't so bad then?' Tom scrunched the fish and chip papers into a ball and passed them to Helen to put into the kitchen bin. 'Dylan clearly had a great time.'

'I have to hand it to Mrs Harley – she knows how to get the best from her charges.' Helen stacked their dirty plates next to the sink, ready to be washed. 'I was saved from conversations with other parents because it was only me helping out, thank goodness. But, as Carol Walters said – she's the teaching assistant who helps run the accelerated reading scheme – the *real* parents don't want to volunteer, because they'd rather be out the front in the audience when the time comes.'

Wincing internally at the reference to "real parents", Tom said, 'You're a brilliant parent to Dylan. You only have to look at the pair of you together to know he sees you as a mum.'

'That's nice, but...' Helen put down the cups she'd been carrying from the table to the sink '...I don't know. It's so hard to explain.'

She kissed Tom's cheek. 'Either way, it doesn't matter. With the exception of the deafening noise at the start, it turned out to be fun. The kids are so keen and, apart from one or two wrigglers who have to be virtually sat on before you can get them to pay attention, they're a good bunch. You were right. I had nothing to worry about. I'm silly really.' Avoiding looking at Tom, Helen moved away from the sink. 'Now, I'd better crack on.'

'You aren't working tonight are you?'

'If that book is going to be out on time, I don't see I have a choice, do you?'

* * *

Guilt.

Helen closed her eyes and counted to ten in the hope it would clear her mind.

Why do I spend so much of my time feeling guilty?

She exhaled slowly and opened her eyes. Her to-do list looked back at her, mocking her inability to have crossed anything off it after 3 p.m. that day.

'Mabel would tell me to put less on the list.' Helen knew she missed everyone at Mill Grange, even though she'd only worked there for eight months. Aside from the fact she'd met Tom at the manor, her colleagues there had quickly become friends. And although she had friends at the Roman Baths, they were more of the work-time-only variety, whereas Thea, Tina, Sam and Shaun were all-weather friends. She didn't know what she'd do without them.

I am without them.

Helen was alarmed to find tears forming in her eyes.

'Don't be so bloody ridiculous, woman!' She grabbed a

tissue and blew her nose hard. 'All you have to do is pick up the phone or dash off an email or go in with Tom to say hi.'

But when?

Her gaze returned to her list. What with her day job, the book, making sure Dylan got home from school safely, and chatting to him when he popped into her study because he wanted someone to talk to, or he needed help with his homework, or simply wanted a cuddle... and now the nativity. Then there was the housework and...

'No, that's not fair. Tom and I share that. That isn't an issue,' she muttered to herself as she took another tissue from the box and dabbed her eyes. 'I know that Tom is, right now, doing the clearing up in the kitchen and if I asked him to, he would do all the cooking and the cleaning and...'

A wave of tears overtook her as she muttered, 'There isn't even time to call Thea to chat for five minutes, and I can't tell Tom because he'll think I'm not coping, and then I'd feel a failure and...'

Helen's throat caught in a ragged snort. Angry at her self-pity, she took a third tissue and sat up straight. 'As if wallowing like this is going to help! You're wasting time you do not have, woman!'

Logging onto her computer, Helen opened her work inbox. Deciding that she was too tired to write a promotional blog, she hit her exhibition admin instead.

The first email awaiting her had "*Children of Roman Britain*" written in the subject line. Immediately, Helen's mind filled with pictures of Dylan's class. She could visualise them perfectly; each child clutching a piece of paper with the nativity script printed out, their individual lines highlighted in bright yellow.

The couple who'd been playing Mary and Joseph, the

stars of the show, were regarded with awe by the shyer members of the class and envy by a few who believed they'd do a better job in the roles. It had taken Helen back to her own childhood. An image of herself at six years old came back to her; she'd desperately wished she had the nerve to volunteer to be the angel or a shepherd, but knowing, even then, that her lot in life was to be a passing villager.

'I had a good time.' She exhaled, the pent-up tension of the day releasing itself after her tears. 'I made the children laugh. They liked me.'

The realisation came as a surprise. 'I suspect I have Dylan to thank for that.'

She opened the email to be confronted with a detailed proposal for an exhibition planned for the Baths the following summer. An event celebrating the history of children in Roman Bath.

Helen opened her diary to add in the dates and work out when she'd have to begin preparing for exhibits to be ordered and delivered. She was about to calculate an estimate of how much space would be required to house such a display, when her concentration was robbed by a new thought.

Do I mind not having children?

She withdrew her hands from the keyboard and sat very still.

Where did that come from?

She swallowed against her dry throat. *I came to terms with not having kids years ago.*

Another image imprinted itself on her mind. It was Dylan, not long after Sue had left for Australia. He was showing her the photo album his mum had put together for him before she'd gone. Dylan as a baby, Dylan as a toddler,

Dylan's first day at school, Dylan at the fair, exploring a castle, climbing a tree, getting muddy in the woods...

Tom had been in some of the pictures, Sue in a few, but mostly it was just Dylan.

No pictures of me.

'Of course there weren't, you idiot! You hadn't met any of them then.' She wiped her hands over her eyes. 'What is the matter with me? Why am I being so bloody emotional, so irrational? I'm turning into...' Helen groaned '...my mother.'

Oh no...

Grabbing her diary, Helen flicked clumsily through the pages. After going back three months she stopped looking.

That would explain everything. The quick emotions, the irrationality, the lack of concentration... and it *had* happened to her mother.

With shaking hands Helen logged off the computer and left her office. She needed to talk to Tom.

* * *

Helen could hear his voice through the partially open bedroom door. He was reading to Dylan from one of his favourite picture books. She had read the story so often that she no longer needed the book, and could just hold up the pictures and narrate it verbatim.

Tempted to go in, she stopped herself, not wanting to interrupt their father and son time. Instead she headed to the bathroom. One glance in the mirror, made Helen glad she hadn't joined them. Her face was streaked with dried tears and her eyes were puffy and bloodshot.

Running some hot water, she scrubbed at her face, attacking the wrinkles that felt as if they were appearing all over her complexion. Ignoring the voice at the back of her head that told her she was being paranoid, Helen shut the bathroom door. Tugging off her clothes, she hopped into the shower, cranking the temperature gauge up to as hot as she could stand it.

Grabbing the shower gel, Helen soaped and scoured herself until her skin shone and her shoulders were bruised from the pelt of the water.

'I. Am. Not. My. Mother.'

The words came out in angry bite-sized pieces as she raked her fingernails through her scalp, flattening her tight ringlets against her head.

Suddenly she stopped moving. Letting the water cascade over her head, neck and body, Helen placed her palms flat against the tiles and began to cry.

Her shoulders shook as her tears mingled with the shower water. Images of her mother when Helen had been a little girl – kind, fun and forever smiling – morphed into images of her mother on her daughter's twenty-first birthday. She'd become distant and clingy all at the same time, her emotions darting from one extreme to the other at any given minute. Then, next day she'd been fine. The following week she hadn't. Every day after that had been a lottery, presenting Helen with either "normal" mum, or a woman who acted as if she had no sense of space with minimal control over her body or vocabulary. A trip to the doctor had delivered the news that she was experiencing early menopause. He'd sympathised with Helen, explaining that her mother was going through "a very severe experience".

'I can't be like her. I can't!'

Despite the heat of the water bouncing off her body, Helen shivered. Goose pimples dotted her flesh as she slid down the side of the cubicle, curling herself into a ball, steam fogging up the glass door.

'I'll get worse. This is just the beginning, and it can take years to develop properly and...' She gave a massive sniff, choking as she inhaled steam and water alike. 'Tom won't want me anymore, and I'll lose Dylan and...' Resting her head on her knees, Helen surrendered herself to the outpouring of grief that abruptly overtook her.

TEN
TUESDAY DECEMBER 7TH

'Helen?' Tom knocked on the bathroom door. He could hear the shower running.

Secure in the knowledge that his son was already sound asleep, worn out by the excitement of playing the innkeeper for the first time, he stepped into the bathroom.

'Helen?' Tom blinked against the humid mist that hung in the air. Droplets ran down the mirror and dotted the window as he made out the shape on the cubicle floor. 'Oh my God!'

Pulling a towel off the rack, he threw open the shower door, switched off the water and knelt down. Ignoring the puddle he'd knelt in, he threw the towel around his girlfriend's shoulders and pulled her to his chest.

'Helen?' Frightened, Tom smoothed her sodden hair from her eyes. 'Please, Helen, talk to me.'

'Tom?' Helen, her eyes blurry from her tears and the humidity of the shower, tugged the towel around her shoulders as the cold air from the bathroom hit her.

Levering Helen to her feet, Tom began to dry her. 'Lean against me.'

'You'll get wet.'

'Too late for that.' He continued to battle down his panic. Allowing herself to be massaged dry by the towel, Helen rested against Tom as he moved her arms, one at a time, so he could wipe off the water. She was like a rag doll. Limp and floppy.

'Come on then.' Tom's voice was unnaturally jolly, but Helen didn't seem to notice. 'Bedroom time. Sit on the bed while I rig up the hairdryer.'

Swathed in her thick fluffy dressing gown, Helen gripped the robe over her chest.

'Shame.' Tom nodded in the direction of her cleavage.

'What is?'

'I was enjoying the gap.'

'Gap?'

'Before you closed the robe properly, there was a small gap. It was giving me a tantalising peep of your delicious chest.'

Helen gave a ragged sigh. 'Hardly delicious. Not now, and certainly not for much longer.'

'Are you kidding me?' Confused, Tom sat on the bed next to her, a hand automatically reaching out to play with a strand of her curly hair. 'You were gorgeous the day I met you and will be until the end of time.'

'Things change though don't they?' Bringing her knees up, Helen tucked them under her chin. 'Women especially. Our bodies change and there's nothing we can do to stop it.'

Resting a finger under her chin, Tom lifted Helen's face so she was looking at him. 'Can you tell me what's going on?' He spoke far more calmly than he felt. 'You haven't been yourself for a few weeks and I just found you in a foetal position in the bathroom.'

Helen licked her lips. 'I was on my way to tell you. To talk to you. But you were reading to Dylan and I needed a shower, so...'

As her voice trailed off, Tom coaxed, 'Please tell me. I'm frightened, Helen.'

'*You're* frightened?'

'Yes!' Tom raised his voice, before quickly lowering it again. 'The woman I love, the most capable and strongest person I know, just fell apart in the shower. Of course I'm frightened.'

Helen pushed a strand of wet hair from her eyes. 'I'm... I'm not sure where to start, but I think... No, I'm sure.'

'Sure? Sure of what?'

Taking a deep breath, Helen unfurled her legs. 'I'm sorry about the shower. I started to cry and I couldn't stop. It was as if every part of me was so tired I couldn't even stand. Then...' she wiped a wet ringlet from her forehead '...I remembered my mother. How she was when... And now it's happening to me too.' Helen gripped Tom's hands in hers. 'I'm so sorry. So, so sorry.'

With no idea what she was talking about, Tom held her close, inhaling the fresh scent of coconut shower gel. 'Tell me about your mother. You've never really spoken about her.'

'It was always just me and Mum. She was great and then...' Helen grabbed a tissue and gave her nose a hard blow, before sitting up straight, her tone abruptly practical. 'Early menopause. All of us go through it, but for her it was about as bad as it could get. It affected her memory first. She forgot words for things. A bit like mild Alzheimer's – but sporadic.

Then she got tired and emotional all the time. She was only forty.'

'I see.' Tom held her gaze as he realised what Helen was telling him. 'How long did her menopause last?'

'A decade.' Helen grimaced. 'It left her with a depression she never got out of. I'm sure, if she'd been happier, she'd have fought harder when the cancer came and... Well, she didn't. No, that's not fair – she couldn't. She had no energy left and so I lost her.'

Tom felt the weight of her palm in his, and was suddenly afraid to ever let go. 'You're afraid you're going through early menopause too? The tiredness and emotional roller coaster bit?'

'You noticed huh?' Helen tried to smile.

'Just a bit.' Tom's throat constricted as, shuffling up the bed, he held his arms open. 'I don't know if you need a hug, but I certainly do.'

Crawling into his arms, Helen whispered, 'I'm so sorry, Tom.'

'What're you sorry for? You haven't done anything wrong.'

'But I'm going to age quicker and get fat and be ratty and forgetful. You won't want to sleep with me anymore and I might frighten Dylan if I go all peculiar and...'

'Whoa there!' Tom held her close. 'We don't even know that's what's happening yet. You've had a massive life change lately – you could just be worn out. Exhaustion can be a real nightmare once it gets hold.'

'But I've always overworked and I've always been fine.'

Feeling bad for how much extra work he had hoisted upon Helen since they'd got together, Tom whispered, 'I'm sorry, love. I've added so much to your burden haven't I? It was me who encouraged you to write the book. And what with Dylan and working from home and...'

Helen placed a finger to his lips. 'None of this is your fault. Logically, I know it isn't my fault, although...'

'It's not your fault.' Tom kissed her forehead. 'If we're talking logic, the obvious thing to do is to make an appointment to see the doctor.'

Helen pulled a face. 'I suppose so.'

'You don't like doctors?'

'I'm never ill, so I can't say I have an opinion either way. I was just thinking of the hassle of registering with one locally.'

'But you have one in Bath, don't you? Where you are going to be working tomorrow.'

'Yes, but...'

Tom smiled as he interrupted. 'Make an appointment.'

Helen rested her head on his shoulder. 'I should have thought of that, but I didn't. You see what I mean, Tom? It's the obvious thing to do, but I didn't see it. That's how it was for Mum. She started to miss the ordinary. She was really clever, and then suddenly she wasn't. She went all – I don't know – frumpy in the mind and the body. She was vivacious one minute and then mentally hunched the next.'

'You're *still* very clever. And if you think for a single minute that you aren't sexy anymore then I clearly need to spend more time convincing you otherwise.' He twirled a wisp of hair around his fingers.

Helen laughed despite herself. 'Tom, I have soggy hair and am wearing a dressing gown that's older than Harriet.'

'Is that so?' Tom unhooked his arm from Helen and moved so he was sat in front of her. 'In that case I need to do two things, the second of which is ordering you a new dressing gown.'

'And the first?'

'I need to check that bit of flesh I saw earlier. Just to make sure it is as beautiful as I recall.' Tom looked solemn. 'In fact, I can predict a thorough exploration of all areas. In the interests of academic research, you understand...'

Helen checked her watch. It was 6 a.m. already. If she didn't leave for the fifteen-mile drive to Tiverton Parkway station soon, she'd miss the only direct train to Bath before midday.

'Got everything?' Tom pulled a T-shirt over his head as Helen slipped on her suit jacket.

'Think so.' Helen gave him a nervous smile. 'I may not be able to get an appointment just like that.'

'But you're going to try, aren't you?'

'You used your "Dylan, do your homework" voice then.'

'Sorry, love.' Tom gave her a quick hug. 'I'm worried about you.'

'I know. I'm worried about me too, but not as much as I was. Thank you.' She gave him a slow kiss. 'You made me feel amazing last night.'

'You are amazing.' Tom gestured to Helen's handbag. 'Do you have your diary in there?'

'Of course. Why?'

'Won't the doctor want to know when your last period was?'

'She's bound to.' Pulling the book from her bag, Helen leafed through the diary. 'That's what made me make the connection with early menopause. I was looking through it last night before my shower. I haven't had a period for eight weeks, and they've been erratic, to say the least, for the past two years. That's what it was like for Mum.'

Tom hesitated before speaking. 'Don't take this the wrong way, love, but have you really missed two periods, or have you simply forgotten to write them down? Sue was a devil for getting her dates wrong.'

'I suppose I could have forgotten. That's another symptom of menopause, being forgetful. Mum did that a lot – and she'd forget words. She'd say bath when she meant bridge or child when she meant cat; silly substitutes that she'd often not even notice.' Helen groaned. 'I told you that last night didn't I. About forgetting words.'

'It doesn't matter.'

Picking up her bag, Helen gave Tom a goodbye kiss. 'I'll call you as soon as I know what's what.'

Tom nodded. 'I'm sorry I can't come with you, but...'

'Dylan and work. Believe me, I know.'

* * *

The zip at the back of Harriet's dress slipped a fraction as she crossed the stage. Glad her back was not visible to the small audience of cast members, telling herself only the top of her neck was exposed, she delivered Hermione's line with the required disbelief.

'What is this? Sport?'

Harriet avoided looking at Rob, even though he was stood less than a metre away from her. *The zip only slipped a bit.*

Your dress is not going to fall down. Concentrate! Rob's giving his lines.

'...let her sport herself with that she's big with; for 'tis Polixenes has made thee swell thus.'

Resplendent in the regalia of Leontes, King of Sicilia, Rob swung round. Hoping the level of haughty hurt Matt had told her to apply was evident, Harriet felt the zip slip down a few more teeth. Lifting an arm, clutching at her shoulder, as if in offence, but really holding her dress up, she carried on, 'I'll say it is *not* and will *swear* that you should believe me, whatever you think to the contrary.'

Harriet gripped the green fabric in her fist as she focused her eyes on Rob.

Even if the dress does fall down, all Rob would see is the cumbersome pregnancy cushion. At least the zip has broken now, and not while my father was watching.

Harriet gave Hermione's lines on autopilot while her subconscious decided the time was right to relive the conversation she'd had with her father.

Why was I surprised?

Harriet knew there was no reason why she should be hurt that her father had made it sound as if finding time for her was a favour.

'Seeing as we're here anyway, and stopping by to watch Dylan's show, we thought we should watch yours too.'

Which basically means, if you weren't here "anyway", and if Dylan hadn't been in his first nativity play at the same time as my first professional acting job, you wouldn't have bothered visiting either of us.

Not hearing the lines she spoke as she countered her onstage husband's accusations, the pressure of her father's last words to her played through Harriet's mind.

'I hope you'll be word perfect by the time we get there. It's a long way to come for such a minor theatre company's performance.'

Harriet gave an internal groan. *What does he expect? My first role was hardly going to be with the Royal Shakespeare Company!*

Dragging herself back to the present, she began Hermione's speech in defence of her honour. Wrapped up in the delivery of her lines and the emotion of the moment, Harriet lifted her hands out towards Rob in supplication, letting go of her dress in the process. A second later she coloured a vivid crimson as she felt her dress slip downwards.

Rushing forward, Rob caught the silky fabric before it hit the stage, and hooked it back up over Harriet's shoulders.

Taking a brief bow to the applause of the cast, he looked as embarrassed as Harriet felt as he murmured, 'Here, let me check the zip.'

Determined not to look at Ali, who Harriet knew would be mentally applauding with glee at Rob being the one to rescue her, she muttered, 'God, how embarrassing!'

The brush of his slender hands on her neck did nothing to diminish the flush to Harriet's skin as Rob flicked her ponytail to one side so he could refasten her dress.

'The zip's bust.' He caught Harriet's gaze for a second, before hastily averting his eye line to the dress. 'Here.' Rob pulled a safety pin from his costume. 'My tunic needs mending too, but I can spare one of my safety pins to stop you falling apart.'

Harriet's flesh warmed beneath his touch as Rob deftly pinned her dress together.

'I umm, yes... thank you.'

Rob stepped back as Harriet turned to Matt. 'Sorry, I didn't realise.'

'No problem. What matters is that your lines were flawless.' Matt called to Ali offstage. 'Can you do a check of all the costumes later, love? We need to make sure no one is going to come apart mid performance.'

'I'll add it to the list.' Ali tapped the task into her phone. 'But I'm not the best seamstress.'

Feeling the need to atone for holding up the rehearsal, however unintentionally, Harriet said, 'I'm not bad with needle and thread. I could have a go.'

* * *

Ali nudged Harriet's elbow as they headed to the changing room after the rehearsal was over. 'Nice one.'

'What?' Harriet frowned.

'Volunteering to mend the costumes. You'll be able to spend time alone with Rob while he tries his outfit on. Shame it's his tunic and not his trousers that need mending.'

Harriet's body immediately reminded her of the sensation of Rob's fingertips on her neck. 'For heaven's sake Ali, I offered to help so you didn't have to do it.'

'Let's call it an added bonus then.' Ali chuckled. 'Thanks though. It does save me a lot of work.'

'I can't believe my dress fell down in front of everyone!' Harriet pulled the offending article over her head and rolled it into a ball.

'Revealing your "oh so sexy" grey baby bump.'

'If my father had been here, he'd have dismissed us as amateurs and walked out.'

Ali tilted her head to one side. 'His coming to watch the play has really got under your skin hasn't it.'

'A bit.' Harriet confessed, 'I'm probably overreacting.'

'Not something you're given to.' Ali untied the apron she wore as part of her costume and changed the subject. 'So, when are you going to ask Rob out for a drink to say thank you for saving your dignity in front of the cast?'

'Oh, I...'

'If you're about to say you can't do that, then log on, woman! It's the twenty-first century. You are allowed to ask a bloke out for a drink, especially to say thank you for something.'

'I know.' Harriet felt awkward. 'I don't have time. I'm off south tomorrow.'

'Is that tomorrow? That's come around fast. Thanks for being our advance guard.'

Harriet smiled. 'It makes sense for me to go on ahead. I can check out the best place for the stage and so on.' She pointed to the green dress. 'I'll take that and the other costumes that need fixing with me and mend them while I'm there.'

* * *

Tina pulled a tray of chocolate chip muffins out of the Aga as Sam arrived at the kitchen door. One inhalation of the fresh-baked-cake aroma and he disposed of his wellington boots at a faster speed than usual.

Tina grinned. 'As ever, your timing is perfect.'

Sam patted his stomach. 'It's a good job I walk so many miles around the grounds each day, or I'd be sporting a serious belly thanks to your cooking.'

'Complaining?' Tina gingerly transferred each hot muffin from the tin to a cooling rack.

'Nope.' Sam headed to the kettle. 'But if those aren't for us to eat now, I'm going to be terribly disappointed.'

'You can have *one*, and take one each to Thea, Shaun and Tom. The rest are going into the freezer for when our guests arrive next week.'

'Not Shaun.' Sam took some mugs off the dresser. 'He's had to dash off to check out a local venue for the next TV series.'

'Oh. Thea never said.'

'It was a bit last-minute. Be handy if he has a dig to do on the doorstep though.' Sam nodded back at the muffins. 'You not having one then?'

Tina collected five plates from the larder. 'Of course I am.'

'Coffee?'

'Please.' Tina gestured to a mountain of muffins cooling on the dresser. 'That's the third batch ready for freezing. Do you think that'll be enough?'

'Are they for the guests or for interval refreshments during the shows?'

'Interval?' Tina's right hand automatically came to her pigtail and twirled it through her fingers. 'I hadn't thought of that. Do you think we should provide refreshments?'

Sam took a mouthful of muffin. 'Would bring in a few more pennies wouldn't it. Help us pay for extra staff to cover us when we have our long overdue honeymoon.'

Adding "interval snacks and drinks" to her list, Tina kicked her shoes off under the table. 'I know we do this sort of thing all the time for the retreat, but this seems more daunting.'

'Only because it's new. The retreat workload was daunting before we got used to it.'

'True. Perhaps I'll ask Sybil to provide scones for the interval.' Tina pulled her coffee mug closer. 'There's something else we need to do that we forgot to put on the list.'

'What's that?'

'Christmas isn't far away and, apart from the holly Thea cut, there isn't a decoration to be seen.' Tina gestured around her. 'I'd put money on the actors expecting to see a Victorian manor house bedecked in decorations.'

Sam dabbed some crumbs from his plate. 'I keep forgetting Christmas is so close. Somehow it feels months away.'

'It's in less than three weeks.' Tina tapped a pen against her pad. 'It would be wonderful to decorate the house so Mill Grange looks festive.'

'You're right. I'll ask Shaun and Tom if they'll fetch us a Christmas tree and get the decorations down from the attic.' He fidgeted his mug of tea in his hands. 'I'd hoped I'd be able to get up to the attic by now. But...'

Tina reached a hand out to him across the table. 'Come on. Sam, we've been through this. You're doing well. You'll get there.'

'I know.' He sighed. 'It still frustrates the hell out of me though.'

'When are you seeing Bert next?' Tina pushed her feet back into her shoes and got up.

'This afternoon. Unless there's too much to do here, then I'll...'

'There will never be too much to do for you to miss your therapy chatter with Bert.' Tina gestured to the last muffin. 'Can you take that out to Tom?'

'Sure.'

'I hope he's okay? It's not like Tom not to appear with a hopeful look on his face as soon as I've finished baking.'

* * *

Helen closed the door of her office at the Roman Baths and leant against it. For the first time, she wished it had a lock. She'd been craving adult company ever since she'd been to Sybil's with Thea and Tina, but now all she wanted was to be alone.

Looking around her office, which had once belonged to Thea, Helen took in the space, hoping that its familiarity would bring her comfort. The cluttered desk, the open laptop, the pile of used cups ready to be washed up, the often opened tin of biscuits. The coffee machine that Thea had bought long ago, and had left behind when she left the Baths for Mill Grange; such was her haste to leave her past behind her.

Blowing out a gust of breath, Helen opened her eyes and headed for the coffee machine. She watched the black liquid stream into her mug with a hiss of heat and took a chocolate biscuit from the tin, crunching into it without registering what she was doing.

The presence of her mobile phone felt heavy in her jacket pocket. Laying it face up on the desk, Helen stared at it, not sure if she was willing it to ring and put her out of her misery, or if she never wanted to hear it ring again.

Knowing Tom would be waiting for her to call, Helen bit into another biscuit before picking up the phone and firing off a text.

Seen doctor. She was very helpful. Did some tests. Results in a few days. Helen. xx

Helen sank into her seat. *It wasn't a lie.* She told herself as she inhaled her drink's comforting aroma. 'I *did* have some tests and I *will* have some results in a few days. The doctor's educated opinion, however—' she reached for another biscuit '—I got immediately.'

Helen took a sustaining gulp of coffee. 'Mother, you have a hell of a lot to answer for.'

TWELVE

THURSDAY DECEMBER 9TH

With her rucksack hooked over her shoulder, and a holdall full of costumes that needed mending in her hand, Harriet walked up the sloping driveway. She'd been warned it was hard to spot the entranceway to the manor, but the taxi driver she'd met at Tiverton Parkway railway station had found Mill Grange without getting lost among the narrow country lanes.

Harriet's stomach churned with a combination of nerves and excitement as her boots crunched along the gravel, disturbing a confused-looking pheasant, which didn't seem to know which direction to fly off in. A few paces later she crested the hill and stopped dead.

Mill Grange sat before her in all its dignified splendour. Dylan had told her so much about the house; about the grey roof and the walls that went shiny in the sun, as well as his old attic room and the big garden. What he hadn't told her was that it was breathtakingly beautiful. The photos she'd seen had not done the place justice.

The grey roof was really a rich blue slate, dotted with lichen. The granite walls, far higher than she'd imagined, felt welcoming as Harriet walked towards a large set of double doors. She loved them on sight. Wooden, arched across the top, with a big round doorknocker off to one side, they looked as if they'd been designed by someone who wanted to make Mill Grange look like a doll's house.

'Wow.' Harriet breathed the word out as she walked forward, not quite sure which direction to go in. To the left, a gravelled path led around the side of the house, which, she presumed, would take her to the rolling garden that Dylan had told her about. To the right a mini car park, with a few cars parked up, led to what Harriet guessed was the back door. *Or should I head for the main door and knock?*

Her indecision was interrupted by the sound of a Land Rover coming up behind her.

Harriet waved shyly as she saw Tom park. They'd met a few times during the period before she'd left for university and Sue had been preparing to go to Australia, but with the tension of Dylan being left behind, it hadn't been the easiest of atmospheres to get to know someone. Harriet had mainly been around to look after Dylan, while his parents planned how to sort out long-distance shared custody.

'Harriet! Hi there.' Tom climbed out of the Land Rover. 'Great to see you. Dylan is very excited about seeing you being famous.'

Harriet laughed. 'I think his idea of famous and everyone else's might be quite different. How is he?'

'On good form thanks. Over-the-top excited about being in the school nativity.'

'Dad told me.' Harriet turned away at the mention of her father.

'You okay?' Tom smiled.

'Yes. Sorry.' Harriet gestured towards the house. 'Nervous. New people and all that. You know.'

'I do know.' Tom grinned. 'However, you are in luck, because these new people are about as good as it gets.'

'Thea, Tina and Sam certainly seemed lovely over the phone and email.'

'They are.' Tom pointed to the passenger door of the Land Rover. 'This chap isn't too bad either.'

'Thanks mate.' Shaun winked as he got out of the vehicle. 'Such an effusive introduction.' He stepped forward, his hand outstretched. 'You must be Harriet. Pleased to meet you.'

'You're Shaun Coulson!' Realising too late that she sounded like a fangirl, Harriet hastily added, 'Sorry. I hadn't realised you were the Shaun that Dylan talked about.'

'Afraid so. I'm Thea's partner. I'm also—' the archaeologist pointed to the trailer attached to the back of the Land Rover that the curve in the drive had previously hidden from Harriet '—chief helper and odd-job person at Mill Grange between filming jaunts.'

Pulling herself together, Harriet took a step forward. 'Now that is a big Christmas tree.'

'Fabulous isn't it.' Tom unstrapped some of the ropes holding the tree onto the trailer. 'It's going in the drawing room. Tina wants the house all Christmassy before your friends get here.'

'That's so kind.' Harriet felt some of her nerves dissolve. 'I bet this place looks incredible decked out for Christmas. Can I help?'

'I'm sure you can.' Tom wound a coil of rope around his arm, before dropping it into the trailer next to the tree. 'But for now, let's get you inside. I don't know about you, but I'm gagging for a cuppa.'

* * *

Helen washed her hands thoroughly and sat on the side of the bath. 'This is a waste of time.' She stared at the stopwatch that was counting down on her mobile phone. 'I ought to be checking my inbox and reading copyedits.'

Sixty, fifty-nine, fifty-eight...

The seconds passed so slowly.

Complaining directly to her phone, Helen wiped her clammy palms together. 'I've just spent fifteen pounds I did not need to spend.'

Forty-nine, forty-eight, forty-seven...

Helen's insides were doing backflips.

'It's impossible. I'm forty-one.'

She felt sick.

'I will simply have to start taking evening primrose oil in enormous quantities, do more exercise and accept that my brain isn't what it once was.'

Thirty-eight, thirty-seven, thirty-six...

'I am *not* my mother. Who knows, if she hadn't got ill during her menopause, then maybe she'd have come out the other side and been her old self again.'

Twenty-nine, twenty-eight, twenty-seven...

'Maybe I'll get a crossword book and do one every day. Help keep the mind sharp.'

Nineteen, eighteen, seventeen...

Leaping to her feet, Helen averted her eyes from the timer. Her forensic following of the falling numbers was going too fast now.

What do I do when it gets to zero?

* * *

'That was the most delicious sandwich I have ever eaten. Ever,' Harriet pronounced across the kitchen table.

'Told you they were good.' Shaun smiled.

Thea laughed. 'I swear Shaun would do literally *anything* for one of Mabel's bacon sandwiches.'

'Did I hear my name mentioned?'

Harriet looked up as an old woman bustled into the kitchen, a crisp white apron around her waist, her grey hair a tight halo of curls, a determined glint to her smiling eyes.

'Mabel, this is Harriet.' Tina tapped the space next to her, inviting Mabel to sit down. 'You have another fan for your sarnies.'

'Dylan's babysitter?'

'That's me.' Harriet took a seat. 'I hoped I'd get to meet you. Dylan talks about you and your husband a lot.'

'How lovely.' Mabel lit up. 'Bert and I are very fond of him.'

'The feeling is entirely mutual.' Tom smiled. 'He's looking forward to Bert helping him learn his lines. Although, to be honest, there aren't many to learn. He...'

'...excuse me.' The vibration of Tom's mobile against the table broke him off midstream. 'It's Helen.'

As Tom left the room to take the call, Harriet turned to Tina and Sam. 'Thank you for letting us come here. You really have saved the day.'

'Our pleasure.' Sam chewed his last mouthful of sandwich. 'You're doing us a favour too you know. Helping pay those winter fuel bills and so on.'

'Apart from a pile of mending, which I need to do before the others arrive on Tuesday, I'm here to help. Anything that needs doing, tell me, and I'll do my best to do it.'

Tina's eyes fell to her list. 'You may regret saying that!'

'Seriously, I'm happy to help.'

'In that case—' Thea got to her feet '—why don't I show you to your room and then I'll bring you up to date on ticket sales.'

'And then,' Sam added, 'you can take a look at where the show could take place.'

Mabel chuckled. 'If you thought you'd have nothing to do, lass, then you are in for a surprise.'

* * *

Tom found himself hesitating before picking up Helen's call. It was one thing theorising about Helen having peri-menopausal symptoms, but having it confirmed was something else entirely. While he knew he'd stick by her, Tom couldn't help wondering how he'd cope if the emotional blips Helen had been suffering worsened.

'Hi, love.' Tom winced; his voice sounded unnaturally jolly again. 'Any word from the doctor?'

'Not yet.' Helen crossed her fingers in a manner she'd adopted when she'd lied as a child. 'I just wondered how Harriet was. Did she arrive okay?'

'All good thanks. She's having lunch with the others.' Tom's brow furrowed. 'You sure you're alright?'

'Yeah. I'm sorting through my emails.' Harriet stared at the bathroom wall, wondering if he could hear the echo that told him she wasn't in her study. 'Don't forget I have the second rehearsal after school, so I'll probably have to work late again to make up the time.'

'Oh, I thought that was tomorrow. My mistake.'

'Tomorrow?' Helen got up and walked to her study so she

could check her diary. 'Oh yes. God, I could have sworn it was Friday today. Sorry.'

'No problem, I'm always getting my days muddled.'

'No you're not. But you're kind to pretend.' Helen kept her eyes on her desk. 'I'll chase up the doctor. Maybe they've just forgotten to call.'

'Good idea.' For the first time since they'd become a couple, Tom didn't know what else to say to Helen. The silence down the line stretched out until he caught sight of Tina through the kitchen window. 'Why don't I see if we can visit Bert and Mabel this weekend – and the others of course. I know Mabel is dying to get going with Dylan's costume.'

'I'd like that.' Helen shifted uneasily in her seat. 'I miss the Mill Grange folk.'

'We miss you being here. It's not the same without you.'

'Thanks, Tom.' Helen stared at the pregnancy test she'd not let go of since she'd got up the courage to look at the result. 'I'd better get on then. See you later.'

* * *

Helen had managed to answer three emails, and was just beginning to think that losing herself in work was the way forward, when her mobile burst back into life.

The number was withheld. Tempted to ignore it, a nagging voice at the back of Helen's mind told her it could be the doctor calling back. She'd made herself call the surgery as soon as she'd done the test. Now she wished she hadn't.

Pull yourself together!

'Hello, Helen Rogers speaking.'

'It's Doctor Sanders. Well, how are you feeling?'

Grateful that her doctor had got straight to the point,

Helen said, 'I have no idea. Relieved, terrified, excited and more anxious than I've been in the whole of my life.'

'A standard response. That's good.'

Hearing the good humour in the doctor's voice, Helen asked, 'What happens now?'

'We get you in for a general check-up.'

'I had one the other day.'

'You did, but now you've done a test, I need to get you to do one here to make it official. Then we can book blood tests and so on.'

'So, it might not be true then? I need to have a proper test?' She wasn't sure if this was good news or not. Her heart constricted in fear – *Oh my God, I want it to be true.*

'It's simply a rubber stamp. I'm sure your test is correct,' Doctor Sanders reassured her down the line. 'Congratulations, Helen, you're going to have a baby.'

'Was that Mum?'

Dylan came bounding into the living room. He was clutching a small rucksack that Helen had filled with a change of clothes for when he inevitably got covered in mud or chocolate, or both, while they were at Mill Grange.

'It was.' Tom held out his arms, enfolding Dylan in a cuddle. 'She said to say she loves you and that she's sorry there wasn't time for you guys to chat today.'

'Oh.' Dylan's smile faltered. 'I was going to tell her about Helen helping at school yesterday. She made everyone laugh.'

'Did she?' Tom's eyebrows rose. Helen hadn't said anything about the rehearsal apart from that it had gone quickly.

'Yeah. The girl playing Mary was off sick, so Helen was Mary. She was great.'

'That's good then.' Tom considered how fast Helen had eaten her dinner and dashed off to hide in her study until bedtime, claiming there was a lot to catch up on if she wanted to take the whole weekend off. 'I hope Mary is better soon.'

'Me too, Helen won't fit in the costume.' Dylan giggled. 'Although she tried! It was *so* funny, Dad.'

'I can imagine.' Tom ruffled his son's hair. 'Have you got everything you need?'

'Yep.' Dylan pointed to his school bag. 'I'm taking that so I can show Bert my play words.' He suddenly looked shy. 'Do you think Harriet will want to see them? They aren't *big* play words like hers.'

'Of course she will. Whatever made you think Harriet wouldn't want to see them?'

'When I Zoomed with Mum, Nathan said Harriet's was a proper play and mine was just a school thing.'

Biting back the temptation to share his opinion of his ex's future husband, Tom said, 'I'm sure he only meant that Harriet's play is longer. She will want to see your script. Promise.'

'Okay.' Dylan let go of his dad. 'I'll fetch Harold. He can come can't he?'

'Always room for a dinosaur in the car, you know that.'

As Dylan skipped off to fetch his cuddly toy, Helen came into the living room. 'How was Sue?'

'Demanding. She wants me to book her and Nathan a room at the Stag and Hound while they are in Upwich.'

'Poor Moira.'

'Quite. She's a landlady who doesn't deserve such difficult guests.' Tom sighed. 'I'd better do it though.'

Helen tilted her head to one side. 'She didn't speak to Dylan this morning?'

Lowering his voice, Tom said, 'She didn't even ask after him. Poor Dylan. I just lied to him. Made him think his mum was simply in a hurry. Do you think that's okay?'

'Lying so you don't hurt or confuse someone?' Helen's cheeks pinked. 'Oh yes. That's okay. That's lying to be kind.'

* * *

Harriet looked at the ringing mobile. Even before she answered it heat dotted her cheeks.

Stop it, you're not sixteen!

'Hi, Rob, how's it going in Bristol?'

'Great.'

Harriet tried not to think about how much she loved his voice. It was almost velvety; taking on a musical lilt when he was passionate about a subject.

'I've not started on the sewing, if that's what you're ringing about?'

'It's not that, although I did want to thank you for taking my tunic. I would have done it myself. In fact, I could have fixed your zip too. My grandmother taught me to sew when I was little.'

Surprised that Rob was offering up information about himself without being asked, Harriet felt a faint ray of hope. 'You're probably better at it than I am then. I'm a bit of a "patch it up and hope for the best" sort of seamstress. I just felt bad about disturbing the rehearsal with my dress issue. I wanted to make amends somehow.' From her position, swaddled in five layers of clothing, on a bench in the garden, Harriet watched the winter sun hover behind the trees of Mill Grange's woodland, trying to burn off the frost that coated the lawn before her and Exmoor beyond as she added, 'I didn't get the chance to thank you for saving my dignity.'

Harriet could hear Ali's voice nagging at the back of her head. *Ask him out for a drink to say thank you properly.*

'My pleasure.' Rob sounded serious. 'I wouldn't have wanted you to be embarrassed in front of everyone.'

'Oh, well. Thank you.' The memory of his fingers at her neck sent a hot flush through Harriet as Rob went on.

'I'm ringing on Matt's behalf. He's up to his eyes packing the stage props with the others. The thing is, we need to know roughly how big the stage area is going to be. Any chance of you measuring the space they've got in mind for us?'

'Sure.' Harriet looked across the garden. 'I'm sat looking at it now.'

'Now? But it's freezing out there.'

Harriet laughed. 'We'll be acting in these temperatures. I'd pack your thermals if I were you.'

She sensed Rob's smile as he said, 'This is why I was hoping to get a role in The Outdoor Players' summer production, rather than the winter one!'

Harriet was surprised. 'Really? I didn't know they'd done auditions for that yet.'

'They haven't, but Jason let slip that it's going to be *A Midsummer Night's Dream*. I've always wanted to be in that. I only went for this production in the hope I'd be seen as keen and be considered for reauditioning in the future.'

'You mean you assumed you wouldn't get a role this time, but would make enough of an impression to be asked back to retry?'

'You've got it.'

'But you're good. I mean, *really* good.' Harriet leant forward, as if this would show the man who couldn't see her how earnest she was.

'That is very kind of you, but I've lots to learn.'

'Haven't we all.' Harriet could hear him shuffling, and presumed he was sat somewhere, probably in the rehearsal room. She'd have put money on him sucking his bottom lip.

After a pause that was slightly too long, Rob added, 'You're good too. Look, umm... I just wondered...'

A crash in the background made Harriet jump. 'What was that? Are you okay?'

'Yeah.' Rob stood up, and Harriet could hear the Doc Marten boots he habitually wore clumping across the wooden floor. 'Matt and Ali just dropped the harbour of Bohemia.'

'Hope it's not damaged. What were you going to say?'

'What? Oh yeah, look, I'll have to go. I'll tell you when you call with the stage measurements. Bye.'

Harriet cradled the phone in her gloved hands. *Was he about to ask me out?* She shivered as the sun was blanketed by a thick grey cloud. *Or was he simply going to ask me to remind Mabel he doesn't eat meat?* Climbing to her feet to see if she could find someone to lend her a tape measure, Harriet sighed. *Or he may have been about to ask me not to sew up his tunic after all. Why did I say I couldn't sew when I can? Rob probably thinks I'll make a right bodge-up of it now.*

* * *

'That is one hell of a tree.' Thea brushed soil from her palms as she straightened her back. 'Next year, remind me to ask Sam to help us bring it indoors.'

Shaun gave the trunk a final push into the thick soil they'd piled around it, supporting it within the large bucket-like pot they'd secured it in, and stood back to admire the effect. 'I'll second that. I swear it wasn't this heavy when we collected it from the farm.'

Positioned next to the fireplace in the drawing room, the tree, almost seven foot tall, held its thickly pine-needled arms out with picture-perfect symmetry.

'It's going to look like something from one of those magazine articles when it's decorated – you know "how to have a perfect Christmas" sort of thing.'

Shaun slipped an arm around Thea's shoulders. 'Shame we don't have time to decorate it.'

'We couldn't even if we did.' Thea felt unexpectedly sad. 'It's not our tree or our home. We're just helping Tina and Sam out. It's theirs, not ours.'

Shaun frowned. 'We're here for Christmas though, aren't we?'

'You know we are.' Thea exhaled quietly. 'I meant that this is just somewhere we live and work, between filming in your case, whereas this is Tina and Sam's *home*. Sooner or later they'll have a family and they're not going to want us around twenty-four-seven.'

'Well, no, but we're good for now.' Shaun glanced at the clock on the mantelpiece. 'No point in worrying about tomorrow. Besides, you're due at Sybil's in forty minutes and I've got to nip out.'

'Nip out? Again?'

'Yeah.' Shaun bent down to collect a few fallen pine needles from the carpet. 'That site we're considering for *Landscape Treasures* – the local one. It might be a goer. As I'm handy, the production team have asked me to go and talk to the landowner about costings and fees and so on.'

'Couldn't they do that by phone or email?'

'Well yes, I suppose. But well, I'm here aren't I. Hadn't you better go?' Shaun gave her a quick peck on the cheek and put his hand to his ear as if listening for something. 'I swear I can hear scones calling you.'

* * *

Tom could hear Dylan and Sam laughing in the garden. Every now and then he'd see Sam pass the window followed by the very top of Dylan's bobble hat as they carried armfuls of foliage that Sam had cut back into a pile for a bonfire.

'They're good lads.' Bert sighed. 'I hate that I can't keep on top of the garden as much as I'd like to. Sam saves me a lot of work.'

Tom's eyes remained on the large picture window. 'Dylan's in his element. You're doing me a favour keeping him occupied and I dare say Sam is happy to help.'

Bert leant forward. 'You wanted to ask me something.'

'How did you know?'

'Living with Mabel for so long, I've picked up some of her intuition.' The old man smiled kindly. 'You're worried about Helen.'

'I don't know about intuition. That's either witchcraft or you've got our house bugged.'

'Or,' Bert confessed, 'it could be that Mabel told me she was sure something was bothering Helen last time she saw her.'

'And, as ever, Mabel is right.'

'Well—' the pensioner's eyes went back to the window '—I suspect we have about five minutes before your son runs in wanting us to light the bonfire, so, now's your moment.'

'You're in danger of becoming the village's agony uncle.'

'Helen?'

Tom pulled a face. 'Yes, right. It's probably nothing, but...'

Bert raised a hand. 'Any sentence that starts with "it's probably nothing" is usually something.'

'Point taken, I'll get to it. Helen hasn't been right for a while. I mean, she's not been smiling much, been forgetful, worrying about things that wouldn't normally rock her. That sort of thing.'

'Not smiling? I can't imagine her without a smile.' Bert's hand enclosed the top of the walking stick he'd taken to using over the past few months.

Tom lowered his voice. 'Helen thinks we're here so you and Dylan can read his lines, but I sent an SOS to the girls, and they obligingly invited Helen for a cuppa. She needs to see her friends.'

'Only natural.'

Tom agreed. 'She was so much happier after she saw them at the beginning of the month. I'm hoping she'll confide in them.'

'You think this is more than Helen missing her life at Mill Grange?'

'Between you and me, she's had tests to see if she's having an early menopause. Her mother did, and...'

'Ahh.' Bert looked solemn. 'Mabel had a rough go of it for a year or two with that.'

'Helen's seen a doctor and is awaiting test results, but I know she's not telling me what's going on in her head.'

'Probably because she loves you and doesn't want to worry you.'

'As reasons go, I like that one.' Tom ran a hand over his cropped hair. 'I'm hoping she'll talk to the girls.'

'You know—' Bert sped up as the sound of Dylan and Sam taking their boots off at the back door floated through the cottage '—it could be something far simpler. Working from home is tough you know. Keeping focused on your work when you are surrounded by household things that nag at you that they need doing now.'

'That's true.' Tom whispered, 'And the book is preoccupying her. It's out soon. There seems to be a lot of marketing-type work that we hadn't expected.'

'The book is out soon?' Bert was surprised. 'I had no idea.'

'She forgot to tell me too.'

'Ummm.' Bert tapped Tom's knee. 'That lass has a lot on her mind. And it's nearly Christmas, and the nativity, *and* Sue is coming over. Could be hormones, my boy, they are hellish things for our women, but it could just as easily be life doing its thing.'

'It's so obvious when you say that. I should have spoken to you earlier.'

'You sounded like Sam then.' Bert chuckled. 'Now then, I suspect we are about to light a bonfire.'

The tea room was packed and Helen was grateful to Thea for reserving a table. The first to arrive, Helen was glad to have a moment to collect her thoughts. *Do I tell them?*

Hooking a sugar cube from the bowl on the table, Helen sucked it between her tongue and roof of her mouth. *No. I have to tell Tom first.*

Remembering how she and Tom had first got to know each other here, sat awkwardly at a table for two, Helen smiled. Not knowing what to say to each other, they had hidden in work conversations, even though – she'd learnt later – he'd already been as attracted to her as she had been to him.

What if he leaves me? We're in our forties and he's already got enough hassle with Sue being a distant, and difficult, parent and...

Helen stopped her thoughts before they veered from irrational to unfair and took another sugar cube from the bowl, crunching it through her teeth.

I'll be forty-two before the baby comes. She reached for

another lump of sugar. *I'll be in my late fifties when I'm dealing with teenage angst.*

The idea made her nauseous.

Helen ran a tongue around her mouth, catching a few granules of sugar that had gone astray. She knew there was no need to wait. Even if her brain was slow on the uptake, her heart and her body had already accepted what her doctor had suspected the minute she'd sat in her surgery.

I'm having a baby.

Trickles of fear coursed through Helen. But not just fear. Excitement. And something else, something she couldn't quite define; a sense of rightness.

Rightness? Come on, Helen, don't go all dippy-chick.

Selecting a third sugar cube, Helen was about to pop it into her mouth when she remembered part of the long list of advice the doctor had given her. Something about pregnancy leading to poor gum hygiene, and how it was important for her to look after her teeth during the next few months.

She dropped the cube as if it were on fire. Hoping no one else had seen her ploughing through the sugar bowl, Helen was relieved to see that Sybil and her waitresses were too busy to notice her.

Picking up the menu, Helen was attempting to distract herself by reading through the list of foods on offer, when a shadow fell across the table, announcing the arrival of Thea.

'It's great to see you.' Thea gestured towards the kitchen. 'Tina's dropping some eggs in to Sybil.'

'The hens still laying?'

'On and off.' Thea smiled. 'You know how it is in the winter. Gertrude and co. need their energy to stay warm rather than lay eggs.'

Helen muttered, 'I miss those chickens. Is that silly?'

'Not at all.' Thea shook out a paper napkin ready to dab up the crumbs she'd inevitably make. 'I missed them when I was away filming with *Landscape Treasures*. They're so human – if you see what I mean.'

'I do.' Helen fiddled a teaspoon through her fingers.

'Are you okay, Helen?' Thea leant towards her friend. 'You said last time that you were tired, and that the new life in Tiverton was taking some getting used to. Is there something else?'

Unsure how to respond, knowing this was the perfect opening to take if she was to confide about her unexpected situation to her closest friend, Helen missed the moment as Tina and Sybil arrived in a flurry of activity.

'Twice in one month, Helen!' Sybil clapped her hands. 'Just like old times. Usual?'

Hoping the sense of loss that shot through her at the "old times" comment didn't show, Helen looked into Sybil's happy face. 'That would be lovely, thank you. Oh, and a glass of water as well if that's okay?'

'No problem at all.' Scribbling a note on her pad, Sybil looked at Thea and Tina. 'The same as Helen?'

'Why not?' Tina laughed. 'Be a shame to ruin the habit of a lifetime.'

* * *

Harriet sat with her back to the Aga and looked at her notes.

'Thank you so much for helping.' She smiled at Shaun. 'I was getting nowhere fast trying to measure the garden on my own.'

'My pleasure. The meeting I'd sorted has been postponed, so I'm all yours.'

Harriet put a line through some of her scribbles and wrote a little clearer. 'My handwriting is terrible.'

'So's mine. Thank goodness for computers.' Shaun sat down and waited for the kettle to boil. 'Coffee?'

'Thank you. I don't think I've had so many coffee breaks in my life.' Harriet bit her lips together. 'I didn't mean to sound ungrateful.'

'You didn't.' Shaun rubbed his hands together. 'We do drink heaps of coffee, although we rarely stop while we drink them. It's partly to keep us hydrated as the work can be so labour-intensive, and partly because it's freezing! I don't envy you having to perform the play outside.'

'I'll be wearing many layers under my costume and there'll be patio heaters dotted about.'

'It's an odd play to choose. I mean, I know it's called *The Winter's Tale*, but it's set in sunshine.'

Harriet nodded. 'You are not the first to mention this. Do you know the play?'

'Once upon a time I played Polixenes. My one and only appearance on stage.'

'Really?' Harriet sounded more surprised than she'd intended. 'That's great. You'll maybe have an idea of whether the space Sam is suggesting is big enough then.'

'You aren't sure?'

'I haven't a clue, but having seen the scenery that Matt is intending to bring, I'm a bit concerned that the main lawn will be too big. A smaller, more intimate setting may work better.'

'Well, in that case—' Shaun got to his feet and made the coffee '—grab a mug and follow me.'

* * *

'I forgot to say...' Thea paused in the middle of buttering a scone '...Shaun and I got the tree in. It's an absolute beauty.'

'Thank you! I know Sam and I could have done it, but we're so busy.' Tina sighed. 'I ought not to be here really. If we're going to be ready for the actors, then...'

'I'm sorry.' Helen stood up. 'I'm so selfish. I didn't think. Of course you don't have time for this today.'

Tina and Thea exchanged glances as Tina put out her hand and rested it over Helen's. 'What do you mean? Of course I have time. There's always time for friends. I was just having a little panic. Take no notice.'

Thea tapped the table. 'Come on, Helen, sit down and tell us what's up.'

'It's nothing.' Feeling stupid for overreacting, Helen slid back into her seat.

'It obviously isn't nothing.' Tina shook her head. 'You've put up with me fretting about Sam and his claustrophobia for months *and* Thea worrying about Shaun during their "are we together or not" episode in April. Now it's your turn.'

* * *

'It's perfect!'

Harriet knew at once that this was where the play would work best. 'When Sam showed me the space before I hadn't thought in terms of scenery size.'

'Let's see what the chickens think.' Shaun strode towards the coop in the centre of the space that ran out before them. 'I take it you've been formally introduced?'

'Not really. But to be fair, I haven't been here long. I've spent most of my time helping Thea to sort out ticket transfers and advertise locally.'

'Many sales?'

'Surprisingly, yes, considering it's such short notice.' A rush of nervous adrenalin shot through Harriet as she thought about the people who'd booked to watch the show. 'The first night is looking very healthy.'

Shaun chuckled. 'The folk of Upwich will be curious to see what's going on at Mill Grange this time. Sam is very good to the community, so when he does open the doors to the public, they all tend to flock in for a nose round.'

'Well, whatever the reason, Matt – he's our producer and director – is pleased.' Harriet took a sip of coffee. 'The final night's performance is looking a bit feeble ticket sale wise though. It may be that it doesn't happen.'

'Or perhaps, if sales are low, we could tuck in the performance area and make it feel more intimate. Give it a personal feel.'

Harriet regarded Shaun with renewed curiosity. 'You're good at this.'

'It's working in television. If you don't learn how to put a positive spin on everything fast, you don't survive.' He raked a hand through his hair. 'Now then, to more important matters. Let me introduce you to Gertrude and Tony Stark.'

* * *

'Early menopause? Like with your mum?' Thea was horrified on her friend's behalf. 'That does not sound fun.'

Tina tugged at her pigtails. 'I'm so sorry, Helen.'

'Thanks.'

'And you think this is happening to you, now?' Thea asked tentatively.

'I did.' Helen stared at the bowl of sugar cubes.

'Did?' Thea tilted her head to one side in enquiry. 'Past tense?'

'I went to the doctor. Had some tests, which were negative.'

Tina blew out a sigh. 'I bet you and Tom were relieved.'

Helen shifted awkwardly. 'I shouldn't have said anything. I umm... I haven't told Tom I've had the all clear yet.'

Thea caught Sybil's eye, and mouthed "more coffee?" before saying, 'Helen love, you have to tell him. I bet he's worried sick.'

'I know.' Helen took a sugar cube, crumbling it between her fingers. 'But it doesn't change anything. I mean, I'm still down in the dumps and emotional and stressed and not myself.'

Tina spoke gently. 'You mean that, awful though early menopause would be, it would be a reason for feeling off-kilter.'

'Exactly.' Helen kept her eyes averted from her friends. 'It's only a matter of time before Tom starts to think I'm unhappy with him and Dylan. I'm *really* not.'

'You have to tell him the doctor called.' Thea sat back as Sybil came into view with fresh coffee.

Waiting until thanks had been offered and the empty coffee pot had been swapped for a fresh one, Helen said, 'I know. But...'

Tina suddenly sat up. 'Why not come back here?'

'What?' Helen's forehead creased in confusion.

'Work at Mill Grange again.' Tina looked at Thea, who was already on her friend's wavelength and nodding furiously.

'That's so kind, but I haven't long started the new job at Bath and...'

Tina interrupted, 'Keep that job, but do it here. Mornings only maybe, to fit in with Dylan's school hours.'

'That way, you'd be within reach of people to talk to when the going gets tough,' Thea added.

Helen's mouth opened and closed, but no words came out.

'Is that goldfish impression you saying yes?' Tina toasted her friend with her coffee cup.

'I'd love to, but I don't know. It would mean both me and Tom driving independently to Mill Grange if I was coming home before him, which would be a bit of a waste of petrol, not to mention bad for the carbon footprint. And then there's...'

Thea interrupted, 'There are all sorts of problems, but it is possible. Even if you only worked here once a week, it would break up the time alone wouldn't it? I'm only guessing, but that is the main problem – isn't it?'

'It is.' A sense of lightness crossed Helen's shoulders. 'Thank you.'

'One condition though—' Tina dropped a sugar cube into her friend's fresh coffee '—you tell Tom you've had the all clear from the doctor.'

'Okay.'

Tina pointed to Helen's mobile. 'Now.'

'Now?'

'Right this second.'

FIFTEEN
SATURDAY DECEMBER 11TH

Tom sat on the bench opposite Sybil's Tea Rooms in Upwich village. Having left Dylan in Bert's capable hands, he'd gone to reserve Sue a room at the Stag and Hound. His phone had rung on the way back to his friend's cottage.

'Thank God for that,' he muttered as he looked across at the café. Tom was tempted to dash over and give her a hug, but something held him back.

Helen had sounded as relieved as he was that the doctor had called to tell her she was not suffering from the menopause. More importantly, by the tone of her voice, Tom could tell she was chuffed to bits that Tina had offered her the chance to work at Mill Grange whenever she felt like it. Yet, he sensed that she was still holding back about something.

Why did the doctor call on a Saturday?

Tom started to walk through the village. *It was probably a receptionist passing on the test results, rather than the doctor. City-based surgeries open on Saturday mornings.*

Slipping his phone into his pocket, Tom saw Bert's

cottage ahead of him. *Looks like you were right as usual, Bert. Helen's just struggling with life's adjustments.*

* * *

Harriet glared at the green thread she'd brought with her. Gritting her teeth, she tried to thread it through her needle for the third time.

'Hello, Harriet, you need some help there?'

'Oh, hi, Mabel.' Harriet felt caught out, unsure if she was supposed to be sat at the dining room table. 'My costume needs mending, but this needle is defying all my attempts to thread it.'

Looking at the silk dress waiting for its new zip to be sewn in, Mabel shook her head. 'Now then, that cotton is *almost* a match for the material, but not quite, and as the dress is silk, you'll need silk thread. Come on.'

As the old lady strode off purposefully, Harriet followed. Passing through the double doors that linked the dining room to the lounge, they moved on through another door, which took them into the drawing room.

'Here you go.' Mabel pointed to a deeply seated sofa by the bay window. 'Look behind there, in the very corner.'

Not sure what she was supposed to be looking for, Harriet wedged herself between the wall and the sofa's arm, wriggling forward until she was in the dead space between the seat and the window. 'Oh wow.'

'Beautiful isn't it. My mother had one, although I'm sure that is rather older than hers was.'

Harriet found herself confronting a Victorian roll-top sewing cabinet. She pushed back the top and gasped. It was like a miniature Aladdin's cave. A seamstress's treasure trove.

Tightly packed, the cabinet held neat rows of rolled skeins of cotton thread, silks, tapestry wool and packets of needles, pins, hooks and eyes and poppers.

'There'll be a silk to match your dress in there.' There was no doubt in Mabel's voice as Harriet continued to hunt through the cabinet's layers. 'If you dig down, you'll find a faded paper bag holding an assortment of zips. One of them is bound to be a better match than the modern one you've got there.'

'Are you sure it's alright to use some of this?' Harriet's hand hovered over the myriad of coloured threads. 'Won't Tina mind?'

'She won't.' Mabel grinned. 'But I can ask if you're worried.'

'Would you?' Harriet felt awkward. 'Everyone is being so kind here. I don't want to take advantage.'

'No wonder Dylan is such a good lad. Tom and Helen are such good influences, as is his babysitter.' Mabel nodded in approval. 'You have a dig around and find what you need for that costume of yours, and I'll call Tina to make sure she is happy for you to use anything from the cabinet.'

Mabel had gone to the kitchen to fetch her phone before Harriet could respond. Picking out a coil of bottle-green silk thread, she was about to slide out of the confined space to fetch the dress so she could match the colour, when her eye fell on a wooden container hidden at the bottom of the cabinet. Pulling it out carefully, Harriet opened the hinged lid. The rough box, obviously handmade by someone not practised in the art of carpentry, was stuffed to the brim with buttons.

Harriet had always loved buttons. Trailing her hands through the collection of plastic, metal, wooden, bone and even ivory buttons, toggles and clasps, she found herself picturing the garments they must have come from as Mabel reappeared.

'There's something special about buttons, don't you think?'

'I do.' The old lady sat on the sofa and smoothed the dress over her lap. 'Every fastening in that box has a story and a life that's gone before.' She tapped the seat next to her. 'Tina said yes, so why don't you dig out a zip to go with that thread and we'll see what can be done.' Mabel paused. 'If you don't mind me helping that is? I'll leave you to it if you'd rather. I know I tend to interfere a bit.'

Experiencing a rush of affection for the little woman on the sofa, Harriet said, 'I'd be very grateful for your help. I'll be fine with the buttons, but the zip may be beyond my skills. I only volunteered to do all the mending to compensate for slowing a rehearsal.'

'How did you do that, dear?'

'It's a bit embarrassing,' Harriet muttered. 'My dress sort of fell down.'

'*Sort of* fell down?'

'Rob saved it.'

'Is that so?' Mabel didn't miss the brief flash of light that crossed Harriet's eyes as she mentioned her co-star. 'Come on then, let's get your dress mended, and you can tell me all about your gallant hero.'

* * *

The fragrance of leek and potato soup hit Harriet's nostrils as she sat at the dining room table. Her stomach growled in hopeful anticipation of a delicious lunch to come as she examined the zip that Mabel had deftly sewn into Hermione's costume. The stitching was so neat; she knew there was no way she could have done such a good job.

Now, as she sewed on three shiny, military-style buttons she'd found in the box onto the tunic, Harriet wondered what she'd say to Rob when she called him.

The old lady had seen through her in seconds. Unlike Ali, however, she had not encouraged her to ask Rob out, but on listening to Harriet talking about the dress incident, the play in general and her hopes and dreams for a career on the stage, Mabel had looked her straight in the eye and said, 'Good people gravitate together. If he is the right good person, you'll find each other.'

With that, Mabel had gone to make a bulk batch of soup.

I can see why you like Mabel so much, Dylan.

Harriet smiled. She was looking forward to seeing her small friend later.

Her eyes strayed from Leontes's tunic to the notebook holding the stage measurements that Matt had requested. *Just call! They need the information you have. You don't have to make anything of it.*

'Rob said he had something to tell me.' She told the buttons. 'It's going to be something really boring isn't it.'

But it might not be.

* * *

Relieved to see Helen laughing as she and Tina discussed hopeless Christmas presents various exes had got them in the dim and distant past, Thea felt happy. It was just like old times, the three of them together, putting the world to rights.

'Why don't you stay over tonight, Helen?' Thea leant

back in her seat. 'You and Tom could use his old room, and Dylan could have your old room. Not a holiday exactly, but a change of scene would be nice and...' Realising what she was doing, Thea abruptly stopped talking.

Tina frowned. 'You okay, Thea?'

'I forgot myself. Sorry.'

'Sorry for what?' Tina looked at Helen, who shrugged.

'I offered your home out without even thinking. I mean—' Thea looked apologetically at Helen '—I'm not saying Tina wouldn't have offered it herself, just that Mill Grange is Tina and Sam's home. I just stay there and...'

'Okay, that's it!' Tina waved both hands in Sybil's direction as if an emergency had struck. 'I don't know what's got into you two these days, but we need wine.'

SIXTEEN

SATURDAY DECEMBER 11TH

'It's heavenly. There's even a greenhouse at the end of the walled garden, which would make a fabulous backdrop to the scenery. A bit of clever lighting and it could look like an Italian hothouse garden.'

Aware that she had been gushing, Harriet clamped her lips together and waited for Rob to respond.

'It does sound perfect.' Rob's voice rang with enthusiasm. 'And the size of audience space in the walled garden you've given is what Matt had in mind I think. I'll pass all this on to him.'

Wondering why Matt hadn't called himself, and hoping it was because Rob had wanted to talk to her, rather than because he was a nice man and was just helping out, Harriet changed the subject. 'The sewing is done and tomorrow I'm helping Tina and Thea do a big push on selling the last few tickets. The locals have embraced the idea of a play here in double quick time.'

'That's a relief,' Rob said. 'I was a bit worried, what with the house being so remote.'

Defensive on Mill Grange's behalf, Harriet said, 'Not that remote. There are loads of little villages and towns handy.'

'You've fallen in love with the place haven't you?'

Harriet could hear the amusement in his voice. 'Maybe a bit.'

'Well, I can't blame you for that. Looking at the website pictures, it does look stunning.'

'It's beautiful.'

'Then I'm bound to love it too. I am drawn to the beautiful.'

Before Harriet could comment, Rob added quickly, 'Must go. See you Tuesday,' and she found herself listening to a dead phone line.

* * *

Tina placed two small glasses of Pinot before herself and Thea. 'You sure you don't want one, Helen?'

'I'd love one, but the doctor said no alcohol until I've had more tests on Monday.' Helen crossed her fingers under the table.

'Let me get this straight.' Tina twirled a pigtail through her fingers. 'On the one hand you, Helen, are battling an emotional blip while life adjusts itself. Meanwhile you, Thea, are feeling bad about inviting Helen, Tom and Dylan to stay when you don't own the house, even though it is your home and you are perfectly at liberty to have guests to stay – especially Helen and family, who are part of the furniture at Mill Grange anyway.'

Thea muttered, 'That sounds about right.'

Helen dropped sugar into her coffee. 'I can blame overwork and hormones for my bouts of insecurity. What's brought this on with you, Thea?'

'Shaun, I guess.'

'Why, what's Shaun done?' Tina asked.

'Apart from rattle on about how excited he is about the play coming to Mill Grange, and popping off to visit potential *Landscape Treasures* sites or to Christmas-shop every five minutes – absolutely nothing.'

'Ah. I see.' Tina sat back in her seat. 'Let me guess, he hasn't a clue he should have done a certain something by now?'

'Not the foggiest.'

Sunday December 12th

After wrapping a scarf around her neck, Thea pulled on her coat, and rammed her bright red bobble hat down over her head. The frost that had crept across Exmoor in the night had turned the green lawn silver and the air so sharp that it sent pinpricks across her face the moment she opened the kitchen door.

Blowing out softly, Thea watched as the air frosted her breath. She loved the atmosphere at this time in the morning, especially in winter. It was so unstirred, so fresh; ready to carve the first signs of life onto the world that day. Digging her gloved hands into her pockets she stepped out of the shelter of the kitchen's doorway.

Thea had been craving a solo walk since waking at five o'clock. Lying next to a sleeping Shaun, her imagination had gone into overdrive and she'd been getting dangerously close to overthinking and creating problems where there were none. Knowing she'd be more rational if she had some exercise, as soon as six o'clock came around, Thea had snuck out of bed and hurried into as many clothes as possible, determined to share her thoughts about the conversation she'd had with the girls with the chickens, before going for a gentle hike.

Patting her pockets to make sure she'd remembered to pick up the pepper slices she'd selected for the hens' pre-breakfast treat, she took a single step outside the house – and then stopped.

A set of boot prints had already crunched across the grass that morning. Thea hesitated. *Who was it?*

She shook herself. It could only be Tom, Helen, Sam or Tina. Shaun was fast asleep, the prints were too big for Dylan's little feet, and she doubted very much if Harriet was in the habit of getting up before eight o'clock in the morning.

What if it's someone who isn't supposed to be here?

Thea's heart beat faster as she stepped back under cover. Her gaze landed on the wellington boot rack that Sam had built not long after buying Mill Grange. There was a pair missing.

* * *

The gate of the walled garden gave a frost-muffled squeak as it was pushed open. As Helen hadn't peered around, Thea assumed she was so engaged in conversation with Gertrude and her cohorts, that she hadn't heard it.

Thea hesitated. *Perhaps she'd rather be on her own?*

Flexing her toes within her boots, Thea decided to say hello. If Helen wanted to be alone, she'd throw the snack to the hens and keep going, if not, she'd invite Helen to walk with her.

Despite the early hour, as Thea crossed the garden she could see Mavis and Betty pecking at the chilly earth, while the rooster stalked around the edge of the coop as if he was a soldier on sentry duty. She could hear Helen talking, and realised her friend still hadn't noticed she had human company.

Not wanting to startle her, Thea coughed softly, sending an extra gust of icy air out before her.

'Oh!' Helen swung round. 'Hello.'

Thea hurried forward. Her friend's face was red, and there were lines of tears, now dried, which the cold had coated, leaving sharp streaks across her cheeks.

'Helen?' Thea wrapped an arm around her shoulders. 'Whatever's wrong?'

'Nothing.' Helen ran a hand across her chapped face. 'I couldn't sleep so I thought I'd seek chicken wisdom.'

'And the fact you've been crying and your face looks sore?'

Helen gave a half-hearted smile. 'Probably looks worse than it is.'

'We should go inside. Those tear lines could chap your cheeks if you don't warm up soon.'

Helen pulled her scarf higher over her face, so that just her eyes peeped out from between it and her hat. 'See, all better.'

Not convinced, and privately vowing to get Helen inside as soon as possible, even if she had to physically frogmarch her along, Thea asked, 'Has Gertrude worked her magic on you?'

'It's always worked before.'

'But has it worked this time, or are you pretending?'

'Sometimes I forget how well you know me.' Helen

sighed. 'But no, I'm not pretending. I do feel better for airing my thoughts with the poultry. Is that why you're here?'

'Yep. I thought I'd seek chicken solace and then take a walk in the woods.' Thea pulled a few strips of red pepper from her pocket and threw them into the chicken run.

'Blimey.' Helen was surprised as six more hens appeared, stampeding towards the unexpected treat. 'I'd forgotten how much they liked peppers.'

'Don't tell Mabel, but I pinched a fresh one, rather than taking one that was on the turn.'

'My lips are sealed.'

For a moment they watched the chickens devour their snack, before Helen said, 'What you were saying at Sybil's yesterday, about Shaun I mean – the girls here and I were thinking that you should ask him to marry you. You know, rather than wait for him to ask you.'

Thea's eyebrows shot up so far that they were hidden by her hat. 'I never mentioned marriage. Only that we're a bit stuck in a rut. Shaun's got all comfortable and acts like we'll be as we are forever.'

'Same thing.'

Thea grimaced. 'Sometimes, I forget how well you know me, too.'

'That makes us even then.' Helen clapped her hands together to spark some heat into her numb fingers. 'You went on to say about wanting to find a place for the two of you though, somewhere that is your own beyond Mill Grange.'

'I hope I didn't offend Tina. I mean, I know she said I hadn't, but I wondered afterwards...'

'Stop right there.' Helen held up her palm. 'Tina under-stood perfectly. You and Shaun have been together longer than Tina and Sam, yet they are married and have a home of their own.'

Thea tried to concentrate her thoughts as she watched the chickens fight over the final piece of pepper. 'It's the home more than marriage. It doesn't matter if we're married or not, but a place of our own...'

'A ring is lovely, but a mortgage is commitment, right?'

'Right.' Experiencing the same sense of awkwardness that had washed over her in the café, Thea said, 'It's not that Sam or Tina has ever made me feel like a lodger, far from it, but I'm ready for a home of my own again.'

'Do you miss the place you had in Bath?'

'The place itself, no, but having my own things – to be able to choose the colour of the walls. The little things I suppose.' Thea realised she hadn't thought about the home she'd had before she came to Mill Grange for a long time. 'It was the Christmas tree that made me think.'

'Because you didn't like to decorate it you mean? Because it wasn't yours?'

'Did I say that?'

'Several times.' Helen giggled. 'You'd had two glasses of wine by then.'

Groaning, Thea kept her eyes on the chickens. 'I can't remember the last time I had more than one glass of wine, total, in the evening, let alone during the day.'

'You also said that, with Shaun working away for half the year, you'd probably end up living alone a lot anyway.'

'I remember.' Thea winced. 'Tina told me not to be so silly and that I could live at Mill Grange as long as I liked.'

'And she meant it.'

'I know, but...' Thea paused, stamping her feet against the hard ground '...you're all moving on while Shaun and I are stuck at the dating, semi co-habiting stage. He's so cosy with the arrangement – and so am I in a way, but what happens when children come along?'

'Children?' Helen swallowed. 'How do you mean?'

'Babies. Here. Tina and Sam both want kids.'

Looking away, Helen muttered, 'Of course. Sorry, half asleep.'

Thea licked her lips and then regretted it, as the chilled air froze over them. 'I think we should go inside.'

'You wanted a walk.' Helen watched as Mavis wrestled a slice of pepper away from Betty.

'I did, but I think you need to talk to someone.'

'I'm fine.'

Thea tilted her head to one side. 'I'm going to light a fire in the lounge. There will be hot chocolate.'

Helen shuffled her feet. 'You know how to tempt a girl.'

'I'll even give you marshmallows.' Observing her friend's continued worried countenance, Thea whispered, 'Can I ask you a question?'

Raising her eyes to meet Thea's, Helen gave a defeated sigh, 'You've guessed haven't you?'

'You didn't drink the wine and, although I don't know much about the menopause, I'm pretty sure you don't need blood tests *after* you've been told you're not suffering from it.'

Helen crossed her arms over her chest. Her whisper was so quiet it almost dissolved into the breeze.

'What if Tom leaves me?'

SEVENTEEN
SUNDAY DECEMBER 12TH

The fire crackled comfortingly in the grate. The smell of wood smoke filled the air as the two friends sat on the carpet, their backs resting against the sofas, their feet toasting before the hearth.

Hot chocolate mugs in their hands, lost in their own thoughts, Thea and Helen watched the dance of the flames until the clock on the mantelpiece announced the arrival of half past six and broke the spell.

'I suspect we have about thirty minutes before Tina and Sam get up.'

Helen glanced towards the closed living room doors. 'I hope we haven't disturbed them. Sometimes I forget they sleep downstairs.'

'I'm sure it's okay – we're a fair way from their room.' Thea lowered her voice anyway. 'Do you want to talk about it?'

Helen held her mug under her chin. 'I do, but I haven't told Tom yet so...'

'Understood.'

'But, what if...'

Thea placed a hand on her friend's arm. 'He'll be thrilled.'

'What if he isn't?' Helen focused on the orange lick of the fire. 'His experiences with Sue when Dylan was a baby weren't exactly fun, but the idea of doing this alone...'

'Alone?' Thea gave a firm shake of her head. 'Whatever happens, you will not be alone.'

'Thanks, but as much as your support is fabulous, not to mention Tina and Sam's, it isn't quite the same.'

'No. I don't suppose it is.' Thea sipped her hot chocolate. 'Do you know when you're due?'

'The doctor guessed I was about eight weeks gone, so that would be July. But I haven't had the official test result yet.'

'Is that the test you are having tomorrow?'

'Yes. Although, the doctor said tomorrow is just a formality. I'd already done a home test and that was positive.'

A smile crossed Thea's face. 'You're going to be a mum! And a summer baby too! It's fantastic. You'll be brilliant.'

'Do you really think so?'

'Yes! You're incredible with Dylan. This little soul—' Thea dipped her head towards Helen's belly '—is going to be a very lucky baby indeed.'

Temporarily choked with emotion, Helen whispered, 'But I'm so old.'

'You're not!'

'I meant old for a first-time mum.' Helen sniffed. 'It makes everything so much riskier. I'll need extra tests and there's a higher chance of problems along the way.'

'Or there might be no problems at all.'

'I'll be fifty when my child is eight years old.'

Unable to deny that, Thea said, 'How about you take

Tom for a walk on the moor today? I'll Dylan-sit. Shaun can help me. You need to talk without distractions.'

'But isn't it all hands on deck with the play promotion today?'

'We'll manage without Tom.' Thea spoke as if the decision was made. 'This is important.'

Helen stared into the fire, resting her empty mug on her stomach. 'It's so strange you know. I never...' She cleared her throat and started again. 'I always wanted a family, but the right person never came along. Once I got to thirty-five I made peace with not having children, and then I came here.'

'And everything changed. As Bert would say, that's the miracle of Mill Grange for you.'

Helen gave Thea a dig in the ribs. 'Don't be soppy, you know what I mean. Although—' she played a curl of hair through her fingers '—you met Shaun here didn't you? And Tina met Sam and...'

'Now you're getting soppy!' Thea tucked her feet up under her before her toes overheated. 'Anyway, I met Shaun at a conference years before I came here. I thought he was a total idiot.'

'So you did. I remember that conference!' Helen laughed. 'So, thinking about it, this is your fault.'

'What do you mean?' Thea pointed at her friend's stomach. 'Unless biology changed while I wasn't looking, that is very much the work of one Mr Tom Harris.'

'No! I mean, if you hadn't come to Mill Grange, then I wouldn't be pregnant.'

Crossing her legs, Thea laughed. 'You mean it's my fault because if I'd stayed in Bath with you, I would not have met Shaun again, so I would not have found the fortlet in the garden, so would not have called you for your advice. You would, therefore, not have visited Mill Grange to see it, and so would not have fallen for Tom the moment you set eyes on him. That's what you mean?'

'Yep.' The firelight made Helen's myriad of freckles shine. 'See, all your fault.'

'Well, if it wasn't for my ex, John Sommers, and his stalking, I would never have come to Mill Grange, so really, that makes it all his fault.'

'Or it could be Minerva's fault?' Helen laughed.

'And how are you making this the Goddess of Wisdom's responsibility exactly?'

'You always used to ask her for advice.'

'Still do sometimes.' Thea remembered the statue of the Roman goddess that sat in her office at the Roman Baths. She'd been her sounding board and silent adviser for years before the manor's chickens had adopted the role.

'You asked her about Shaun and about whether you should move to Mill Grange. You told me you did.'

'So I did! That does it then, it's her fault.' Thea chuckled. 'A Roman goddess is to blame! The culprit is found!'

'I should get her out of storage and keep her in my office!' The sound of footsteps heading in their direction, wiped the smile off Helen's face. 'You won't tell anyone will you?'

'Of course not,' Thea said, 'but I can't promise Tina won't guess too.'

Helen nodded. Her mouth was suddenly dry; the merriment of the moment wiped away.

'Tell Tom today. You'll never relax until you do.' Thea collected up their empty mugs and clambered to her feet. 'I'm convinced he'll be pleased, but if by any chance he isn't, nothing changes the facts. You are going to be a mum, and that is a fantastic thing.'

'I'm going to be a mum.' The words came out in hushed awe. 'I think I need a cup of coffee.'

'That's more like it!' Thea scrambled to her feet. 'Just be grateful you want one.'

'What do you mean?'

'Lots of women can't stand the smell of coffee from the minute they become pregnant.'

'Oh my God!' Helen was horrified. 'And there I was worried about giving birth!'

* * *

Thea watched as Dylan selected an orange crayon and applied it to the paper with the same level of care she'd give to excavating a crumbling mosaic.

'What are you drawing?'

'A bonfire.' Dylan didn't look up as he took a red crayon from his pencil case. 'It's the one in Bert's garden.'

'It's very good.' Thea smiled. 'You obviously looked at that fire carefully. They have all sorts of colours in them don't they.'

'Mrs Harley says I'm good at drawing.'

'She's right.' Thea knew how much time Tom and Helen had spent with Dylan, talking to him about all the colours in the flames when watching the bonfires they often had at Mill Grange. *They are going to be great parents, because they already are.*

'I'm sorry Shaun isn't here to keep you company while I'm busy. I thought he might take you for a walk, but he's had to pop out.' Thea pointed to the other end of the kitchen table. 'Harriet and Tina will be here in a minute. Will you be okay colouring while we chat about the play?'

'Yep.' Dylan grabbed a brown crayon and drew in some logs at the base of the fire. 'I'll listen. I'm good at plays now. I could help.'

* * *

The wind whipped their hair and scarves around their faces as Tom and Helen reached the highest point of moorland at Haddon Hill. Eyes streaming, unable to talk as the wind would have taken their breath away, they grinned at each other as they admired the view. Three hundred and sixty degrees of stunning Exmoor beauty. From where they stood they could see woodland, scrubland, the huge expanse of water known as Wimbleball Lake, and beyond to farmers' fields and patchworks of hedged gardens surrounding the occasional dwelling.

After a few minutes of searching, Helen's gaze found what she'd been hunting for. Huddled together, almost the same colour as the moor around them, a group of Exmoor ponies stood, their heads bowed against the wind. The last time they'd walked up here, almost three months ago, one of the ponies had had a foal with her.

I suspect it's in the middle of the huddle, being protected by its mother and her friends. The thought made Helen draw breath. *If Tom freaks, at least I have my friends.*

She looked around at him now. Tom. Former squaddie, self-confessed disaster with women and archaeology tutor at the retreat. To see him working with former military personnel who, for a variety of reasons, had been invalided out of the services and had come to Mill Grange to learn practical skills for the civilian life ahead of them, you'd never guess he'd been a man without purpose for so long.

Then Mill Grange did its thing.

Aware she was teetering on the brink of falling into a Disney-style fairy tale entirely of her own making, Helen took a steadying breath. *It's time.*

Slipping a gloved hand in his, Helen headed towards a path that ran towards the shelter of the woods. Her mind raced as they walked downhill. *How am I going to start?*

The temperature felt considerably less encroaching as the path took them along a row of fir trees, which formed the border of the Christmas tree farm, where Tom and Shaun had fetched Mill Grange's tree.

'That's better.' Tom smiled. 'As much as I love the view up there, that breeze was getting a bit personal.'

Despite her nerves, Helen laughed. 'And you a former soldier! Life at Mill Grange has softened you up, mister!'

'Cheek!' He kissed her cold face. 'I'm so glad Thea offered to Dylan-sit. I've really missed having time alone with you.'

'Me too.' Helen spoke the words on automatic pilot, and although she knew she meant them, her heart sank. In a few months' time they'd have no time alone at all – not for years.

'I haven't liked to ask about the book lately.' Tom gave her a sideways glance as they walked. 'You've had so much on, asking about it felt like rubbing it in.'

'It's fine. I've almost written the blogs and only have two interviews left to complete.' A fresh wave of guilt swept through her. 'I ought to be doing them now. They need them tomorrow.'

Tom shook his head. 'You needed a break more than you needed to work. Tomorrow will sort itself out.'

'You're right.' Helen stopped and peered into the mass of

Christmas trees to her left. 'I always think it's a shame that the ones growing here are left undecorated.'

'There's hundreds of them.' Tom gestured to the rows of trees. 'That would be a lot of fairy lights.'

'We should get a tree for the house.'

'We could get one while we're here, if you wanted to?'

'I'd love that. Dylan could decorate it before bed.'

'You wouldn't feel it was just more for you to do? I don't want to add to your load or anything.' Tom said carefully, 'I know you aren't suffering from early menopause, thank goodness, but you're still tired.'

'It's just a Christmas tree. I love Christmas. This will be our first one as a proper...' Helen trailed off.

'Family? Why is it so hard to admit you're part of a family now?'

'It isn't, I...' Helen tensed as Tom's face creased in frustration. Crossing her arms over her chest, she took a deep breath. 'The thing is...'

'What? What's the thing, Helen?' Tom's brow furrowed further. 'I've been treading on eggshells for weeks. I want to know why. Please! Tell me.'

'Okay then.' Helen looked straight into his eyes. 'I'm pregnant.'

'Pregnant?'

Tom's eyes had gone so wide, Helen could see the flecks in his irises as she added, 'Yes. We're having a baby.'

Tom's expression went blank. Stepping back from Helen, he stared at her, his mouth opened – but no words came out.

'Tom?' Helen reached an arm out to the nearest tree trunk to steady herself. Her legs started to shake. 'Tom?'

Helen's legs felt weak. She thought she was going to be sick.

In her imagination she'd played out every scenario – every way in which Tom might react to her news; from joy to anger, to simply turning and walking away. She had not pictured him showing no reaction at all. It was as if every emotion had been wiped from his face.

'Tom?' Helen suddenly felt angry. She'd been so worried about his reaction, about him leaving her – and now she'd been brave enough to tell him, he didn't even have the courtesy to speak. Even if he wasn't pleased, she thought he loved her enough to ask if she was alright and how she felt about it.

I'll give him until the count of ten. Then I'm going home.

By the time she'd counted to five, and Tom still hadn't said anything, Helen had made up her mind. Tears leaked from the corner of her eyes as she silently turned and walked towards the car park.

Thea was wrong. Fishing a tissue from her pocket to wipe her eyes, Helen placed a protective hand on her stomach. 'Don't worry, Mummy loves you.'

Tears were streaming down her face by the time the sound of running feet came up behind her.

Tom placed a hand on her shoulder. 'Helen.'

'What?' Helen shrugged him off and kept walking.

'Did you really say that?' He almost had to jog to keep up with her now. 'That you are going to have a baby?'

'Yes. *Our* baby.' Helen stopped moving. 'I hoped you'd be happy, but I was still terrified of telling you. Terrified you'd be angry. That you'd leave me.'

'Angry? I'm not angry.'

Helen felt uncertain. Tom hadn't shouted, but nor had he said anything positive.

Pulling off his woollen hat, Tom dragged a hand through his close-cut hair. 'That's why you've been so emotional. Hormones, but not menopausal ones?'

'The very reverse of menopausal ones in fact.' Helen sighed. 'I want this baby, Tom, but if you don't then...' Her words faded; a vision of Dylan's face as she told him she was leaving choked her words.

'Don't?'

Helen put her hands on her hips as she stared into his eyes. 'Tom, are you in there? Are you okay?'

'Okay?'

Helen knew her frustration was in danger of merging into another round of frightened tears. 'Please will you stop parroting every word I say, and say *something* about the fact I'm carrying your child? *Anything!*'

Diving forward with unexpected speed, Tom pulled Helen close. 'Am I okay? The most amazing woman in the world is having my baby. God, I love you, Helen Rogers.'

'You aren't cross?' Helen breathed her words into his jacket. 'You just scared the hell out of me.'

'Sorry, love. I was...' He gave his head a shake as if trying to wake himself up from a dream. 'Why would I be cross?'

'Because we've only just got used to the house and sorted out a routine with work and Dylan and everything will change. My office will have to be changed into a nursery and —' Helen spoke faster and faster '—I'll have to give up work for a while and there's so much to do and we'll be such old parents, and Dylan might hate not being an only child anymore and we won't sleep much and there won't be much sex anymore, and I know nothing about being pregnant or having a baby or raising babies, or...'

'Whoa!' Tom held her out at arm's length for a moment so he could stare into her eyes. 'You're missing the point here. We are going to have a baby. *A baby!*'

'*I'm* missing the point?' Helen stared at him, still not sure if she could trust that Tom was pleased, or if he'd simply worked out the right words to say. 'You're the one who's been gormlessly staring into space.'

'Shock.' He pulled her close again. 'I can't believe it. Are you alright?'

'You *really* aren't angry? You're not just saying the things you think I want to hear?'

'Are you kidding me?' Tom kissed the top of her head and squeezed her tighter. 'Tell me *everything*. What did the doctor *really* say to you when you went to see her? When is our baby coming, and when do we get to go shopping for cots and teddy bears?'

* * *

'We've earned this!' Thea rested back against her chair. 'I'm so grateful to Sam for looking after Dylan.'

'He's in his element. He loves playing in the garden with Dylan. And once Shaun gets back they're planning a trek through the woods.' Tina smiled. 'Where is Shaun this time? More shopping?'

'Another trip to check out that excavation site apparently.' Thea looked sceptical, before shaking off the thought that Shaun might be making excuses not to be around her. She raised her glass of mulled wine up to Harriet and Tina, who did the same.

'To the success of *The Winter's Tale*.' Tina savoured the sensation of the spiced red liquid coating her throat. 'Oh that's nice. I need to ask Moira where she got this from. Be good for refreshments at the interval.'

Harriet smiled. 'You're so kind. I can't thank you enough for how much you guys are doing for us.'

'It's good for us too. I'll just pop and ask Moira about the mulled wine before I forget.'

As Tina got up, Thea leant towards Harriet. 'She means it you know. You're helping them too.'

'Really?'

'*Really.*' Thea leant forward as she explained. 'The retreat is in its early days, and although it is working and, in time, the archaeological site in the grounds is going to bring in tourists, the house eats money.'

'I can imagine. I struggle to pay the heating bill in my student house.'

'And you don't have staff to pay or guests to provide for.'

Harriet watched Tina talking to Moira at the bar. 'And I bet they don't charge as much as they ought to.'

'How did you guess?' Thea grinned.

'Tom told me they have kind hearts, and he was right.'

'Their thinking is, and I have to agree with them, that if

they charged enough to make a decent profit, then the people who would benefit most from their time at Mill Grange wouldn't be able to afford to come.'

'And that's what it's all about for them isn't it.' Harriet could see Moira scribbling down something on her order pad as Tina produced a bank card from her mobile phone case. 'Helping people first, money second.'

'It is.'

'They are lucky they can afford to do that.' Harriet sounded wistful.

'Very lucky, and they know it and don't take it for granted.' Thea asked, 'You okay?'

'Sorry, yes. I was just thinking about my dad.'

'Nathan? I've not had the pleasure yet.'

'But you've met Sue?' Harriet ran a finger around the rim of her heavy pottery mug.

'At Tina and Sam's wedding.'

'Dad is very like her, but more...' Harriet paused.

'Driven?' Thea volunteered.

'That is one way to put it,' Harriet agreed. 'I think I need another one of these. You want one?'

'Definitely.'

Harriet had just got to her feet, when Tina reappeared, complete with a tray of more drinks.

'I made an assumption!'

'I was just on my way to top us all up.' Harriet smiled. 'I'll get the next round. Thank you.'

Tina tapped the side of her mug. 'Moira is ordering in two dozen bottles for the interval refreshments. I'd rather buy it from her than the wholesaler. Support local, and all that.'

'You do a lot for this village don't you?' Harriet gripped

her mug. 'I hope my dad and Sue are kind when they stay here.'

Tina and Thea exchanged a glance before Tina said, 'The people of Upwich have been very good to us.'

Thea smiled. 'You'll meet a lot of them – or see a lot of them – when you're performing. Most of the tickets sold have gone local. Although, several folk are coming in from Tiverton and Bampton as well.'

'And Taunton,' Tina added. 'Not to mention a few hardy souls that are travelling from Wiltshire, after transferring their tickets from the original location.'

'They must be making a holiday of the show.' Thea took another mouthful of mulled wine. 'Even in winter Exmoor is a stunning place to visit.'

Harriet grunted. 'I'd put money on my dad complaining it's too cold within five minutes of arrival.'

'You okay, Harriet?' Thea rested her elbows on the small wooden table before them. 'I mean, you seemed quite excited about the play when we were working out how much food and drink we'll need and so on, but now...'

'I'm sorry. I am excited. It's my first professional performance after all. It's just that my father isn't the easiest man to please. I'll be nervous enough as it is, but with him in the audience...'

'Adds pressure?' Tina asked.

'Even if I gave an Oscar-winning performance it wouldn't be good enough.' Harriet felt her shoulder droop. 'Goodness knows what Rob will make of him.'

'Rob?' Thea asked. 'The guy playing Leontes?'

'Yeah.' Harriet knew she was blushing. *Why did I mention him and not Matt or Ali?*

'Mabel said you were mending Leontes' tunic. That'll be

for Rob then.' Tina twiddled a pigtail through her fingers. 'Nice is he?'

'I had to mend my dress too, and there was a cloak for Ali that needed a rip sewing up. She's playing Paulina, maid to my character, Hermione.'

Thea winked at Tina. 'I think that means Rob is nice.'

'You're as bad as Ali. She's always teasing me about Rob.'

'Sorry.' Tina wrinkled her nose. 'I hate being teased. I didn't mean to do that. It's just, you looked so low when you spoke about your dad, and then you said Rob's name and your face lit up.'

Thea decided to let Harriet off the hook. 'This Ali, she's a good friend then?'

'We haven't known each other that long, but we just sort of hit it off.'

'Sounds good.' Tina held her palms up to the nearby fire. 'Is she a student too?'

'Graduated.' Harriet thought of her friend. 'She is Matt's partner. He's the producer and manager of the company. Ali ought to be Hermione really, but she went for a smaller role for some reason.'

'Or maybe you did a better audition?' Thea tilted her head to one side.

'You're very kind. I suspect, however, it's because she's had a bit of a crisis of confidence with this play. Someone undermined her rather when she was last in *The Winter's Tale*.'

'That's cruel.'

'It happens.'

Suspecting that Harriet was worried that her father might do the same to her, Thea moved the conversation on. 'So you are Hermione, this Rob is Leontes. Who's playing Polixenes?'

'Matt. It was a chap called Jason, but it was his parents' house that got flooded, hence the change of location.'

'You wrinkled your nose as if you'd smelt something bad when you said *Jason*.' Tina stretched her feet nearer to the fire.

'It isn't a disaster that he's not in the company for this one. He's a bit full of himself.' Harriet hid her face in her mug. 'I know it's early days in my career, and I'm usually okay at dealing with people like that, but there's something about Jason that gives the impression he wouldn't be beyond stepping on anyone who gets in the way of his desire for stardom.'

'One of those.' Thea found herself thinking of her ex-boyfriend, John, for the second time in a few days.

'But Rob's not like that?' Tina's tone was mischievous.

'You said you weren't going to tease me?' Harriet couldn't help but laugh.

'Think of it as curiosity. I'd like to know who will be sleeping in my house.'

'He's just a nice guy, that's all.'

'And?' Thea asked.

'He's going to be big. I mean, he ought to be, he's a great actor. Natural talent rather than someone like me, who just desperately wants to act. It's a different thing.'

'I'm sure you have natural talent too,' Thea said.

'You're very kind, but when you watch the play, you'll see what I mean.'

Tina asked, 'What's Rob like otherwise?'

'He's tall and slim.' Harriet found herself unable to keep the smile from her face as she described her co-star. 'Beautiful dark skin. His dad's parents were Jamaican.'

'Nice.' Thea grinned. 'Does he have kind eyes? Kind eyes are very important.'

'Very. And a shy smile and a nice laugh.'

'Then that's all we need to know,' Thea declared.

'Absolutely, anything else after that is just window dressing.' Tina picked up the menu from the table. 'Sandwiches?'

'Yes.' Harriet knew she'd need to eat if she wasn't going to doze off. 'That mulled wine was stronger than I thought. I'll get them.'

'Thanks.' Tina scanned the list of sandwiches on offer. 'Tuna and mayo for me please.'

Thea smiled. 'Cheese and pickle. Oh, and maybe a round of black coffee. Extra strong.'

NINETEEN

SUNDAY DECEMBER 12TH

Sam watched Dylan. Sat on the sofa nearest the Christmas tree, the little boy was eating his lunch while flicking through the book on King Arthur he'd been given on the day Sue had left for Australia. Sam remembered how Helen had sat there with Dylan, distracting him with tales of Lancelot, Merlin and the Round Table until his sobs had died away and he'd fallen asleep in her arms.

It had been about a year since Dylan had sat with him, on that same sofa, as he'd waited to be interviewed for *Landscape Treasures*. The battle he'd had with himself not to flee from the captivity of the four walls had been terrifying.

Sam hid a groan of frustration as a cold sweat broke out on the back of his neck. The first signs that his demon was beginning to surface. Going to the window, he struggled against the urge to open it. Sam knew if Dylan wasn't there he'd have flung it open or, more likely, he'd have left the room and dashed outside.

You can't open it. The boy will get cold. And you can't leave because Dylan will ask why you're going.

Hoping his companion wouldn't notice that he was shaking, Sam thought through the mantra Bert had taught him to help when a wave of claustrophobia sparked a panic attack.

It happened. I couldn't save them, but I tried. Other people are alive because of me.

From behind him, Sam could hear the drum of Dylan's feet against the side of the sofa. They were kicking back and forth in time to the chews of his ham sandwich.

You can't do this now!

'You okay?' Suddenly, Dylan was at Sam's side. 'You've got your scared-of-stuff face on.'

You are in your own home. It is safe. Nothing is going to go wrong.

Dylan put his hand on his friend's leg. 'Shall I get Bert?'

'Sorry, mate.' Sam leant down and picked Dylan up. 'I'm fine.'

'Good.' Taking Sam's answer at face value, Dylan pointed to the tree. 'Why isn't it decorated?'

'Not had time.'

'We got time now?' Dylan's face lit up. 'I've decorated your tree before, remember?'

'And a great job you made of it. That was when you helped me with the television people.'

'You were scared.' Dylan whispered a confession: 'I was too. Don't tell Dad!'

'My lips are sealed.' Sam felt a surge of love for his young charge. 'I'm sure you could help, but I'm afraid the decorations are still in the attic.'

'We could get them.' Dylan spoke as if it was the easiest thing in the world.

Which is what it would be to anyone else but me.

'It would be a surprise for Tina. Unless she wanted to

decorate it herself. Although, she'd let me help, wouldn't she?'

'Of course she would.' Sam smiled at Dylan's worried expression at the thought of being left out of manhandling tinsel. 'Anyway, this is more a guest Christmas tree, for when Harriet's friends come. We'll have a little tree of our own in our room once everyone has gone.'

'Two trees!' Dylan's eyebrows rose so high Sam laughed. 'That's awesome.'

'Isn't it.'

'So, could I help you do this one then? It would be a nice surprise for Tina, wouldn't it?'

The sweat that had started to dry on Sam's neck became sticky again. New dots of perspiration joined the old ones; covering his chest as well as his neck and back. 'Tina probably would like it crossed off her to-do list, but the thing is...'

'Come on then!' Dylan jumped from Sam's arms. 'Let's help Tina! I know where they are.'

'But we were going to have a walk weren't we?' Sam found himself being tugged across the drawing room carpet and towards the main stairs before he realised what was happening. 'Dylan, I...'

Any second now the headache is going to arrive.

'It's okay – I fetched the decorations with Tina last time. I know where they are.'

Sam's lips had gone dry; in stark contrast to the rest of his body, which was swimming in sweat. The staircase was right in front of them. It was wide at the bottom, but he knew from the video calls he'd had with Tina, Thea and Shaun, when they'd shown him his home while he sat on a garden bench, that the corridors above got narrower the higher up the house you climbed.

As the yank of Dylan's hand urged him to go faster, Sam managed to blurt out, 'We should go slowly – the stairs are well polished. We don't want to slip.'

'We're okay!'

'But, Dylan, if you slipped and hurt yourself, you couldn't be the innkeeper anymore.'

Not sure what had made him say that, Sam was nevertheless relieved by the effect. Dylan instantly began to walk with almost exaggerated care.

The first three steps were taken. Sam took a handkerchief from his pocket and wiped his forehead.

You can do this. You can do this. The roof is NOT going to collapse. It is NOT going to...

'Harriet said she liked my innkeeper lines.' Dylan took another careful step upwards. 'I don't understand her lines though.'

That's another step. Tina will be so proud. You can do this.

Trying to focus on what Dylan was saying, Sam mumbled, 'Shakespeare can be a bit complicated.'

Dylan paused on step five and looked up at Sam. 'I wish you could come to my play.'

Not sure if stopping made it easier or harder, Sam squeezed Dylan's palm, as much for his own reassurance as the boy's. 'Me too. You'll tell us all about it afterwards though, won't you?'

'Promise.'

Sam took hold of the banister with his free hand. In that moment he wasn't sure he could move again. His legs were as heavy as lead, and his head pounded.

'You okay, Sam?'

'Headache.'

'Shall we sit here for a bit?' Dylan promptly sat on the

stair. 'I'm seeing Mabel later. She's going to measure me for my costume.'

'That's exciting.' Sam sat next to his friend. He looked at the grandfather clock in the hall below them. They'd travelled less than three metres out of his comfort zone.

'Sam?' Dylan's enquiring eyes stared at his friend. 'Bert said you had claw-stroaber. He said that's why you have windows open a lot.'

'Claustrophobia. Did he?'

'Yes. What is it? I'm not going to catch it am I? There aren't any windows in the school hall, and I don't want to miss being the innkeeper.'

* * *

'How do you think Dylan will take the news?'

Tom couldn't stop looking at Helen. Every few paces, her hand firmly in his, he'd pause in his stride and stare at her; shaking his head in happy disbelief.

'Tom? Are you with me?' Helen tapped his arm. 'I asked if you thought Dylan will be okay with having a brother or sister. He's been an only child for so long. I'd hate to make him feel second best.'

'He'll be in his element! Someone to build Lego models with.'

'Eventually.'

'Eventually.'

'I hope you're right.' Helen frowned. 'However hard it gets with sleepless nights and everything there is to do, we must keep doing things just with Dylan when we can.'

Tom draped an arm around Helen's shoulders. 'We will. Sometimes it won't work, but we both know we'll do our best.'

Helen walked faster. 'Come on, I'm getting cold.'

'Takeaway coffee from the van in the car park before we go home and tell everyone?'

'Definitely yes to the coffee, but let's not tell everyone yet.' Helen hoped Tom hadn't guessed that Thea knew already. 'Let's get the first trip to the doctor over with first. I mean, let's get it in writing as it were. I'm not twelve weeks gone yet. I don't want to tempt fate.'

'Fair enough,' Tom agreed. 'I was getting overexcited.'

'Which is a good thing.' Helen peered up at the crisp blue sky that was nudging its way through the sheet of cloud. 'I hope nothing goes wrong.'

* * *

Dylan rested his head on Sam's arm as he listened.

'So, you see, you can't catch claustrophobia. It is something that happens to someone.'

'After something bad.'

'Usually.'

Dylan was quiet for a while, before asking, 'Should I get the decorations on my own then?'

Sam was tempted to say yes, but knew he couldn't. If Dylan got hurt getting the boxes out of the cupboard in the attic room he'd never forgive himself. 'No, but I'm not sure I can go up there yet. I'm so sorry, Dylan. I wanted to.'

'That's okay.'

Sam hugged the boy close, the disappointment on the lad's face cut him in half. 'You really wanted to decorate the tree didn't you?'

'And surprise Tina.'

'Me too.' Sam got to his feet and glanced up the

remainder of the stairs. He exhaled slowly. 'Look, I'm not going to promise this will work, but, if you keep talking to me, Dylan, then maybe we can try. But...' Sam's hands shook '...if I can't do this, please don't be sad.'

* * *

'That's the second time I've had alcohol at lunchtime this week!' Thea massaged her temples. 'And I'm fast remembering why it isn't something I make a habit of.'

Tina laughed. 'Me too. Maybe it's the release from having no guests for the first time in ages. Less responsibility.'

Thea grinned. 'I rather like being irresponsible in the face of a lovely winter fire.'

'I'm obviously a bad influence.' Harriet grinned back.

'You are.' Tina laughed. 'But we've sorted out loads of admin, we have the refreshments sorted, our audience is looking healthy and Mabel and Sybil are on top of the catering. And we've had a proper relax. Perfect.'

Thea stirred a spoon through her coffee. 'All we need to do tomorrow is make up the bedrooms and check the bathrooms are equipped with loo roll and handwash.'

Harriet saw the fire flicker; guttering as someone opened and closed the pub's main door. 'Everyone's going to love it at Mill Grange. I can't wait to show Ali around.'

'And Rob?' Thea tilted her head to one side.

'Just when I thought you'd dropped the subject!'

Tina laughed again. 'We promise to be on our best behaviour when he's here, but it seems to me that you owe him a drink after the dress moment.'

'That's what Ali said.'

Thea raised her cup. 'I think I'm going to like Ali.'

* * *

Dylan was talking so much that he barely left a gap for any return of conversation. Sam was glad, because he didn't have enough air in his body to breathe and speak.

He was vaguely aware that Dylan had given him a blow-by-blow account of the order of performance for his school nativity and was now retelling the story his dad had read him last night.

I couldn't save them, but I tried. Other people are alive because of me.

Dylan had finished the story and was now saying something about Glastonbury and dragons. Sam was not entirely listening, but the sound of the lad's happy voice as he walked with him – sometimes slow, sometimes rushed – was keeping his legs moving one in front of the other. Then – magically he was on the top step.

You did it. Whatever happens now, you made it upstairs.

Sam tried to take in his surroundings. The corridor was wider than he'd imagined, and as he walked past a row of closed bedroom and bathroom doors to his left and right, he was drawn forward by the sense of natural light. He began to run, towing a surprised Dylan after him. 'I didn't know.'

'What didn't you know? About George and the dragon?'

Sam embraced the little boy. 'No, although that was very interesting. I didn't know the corridor up here had windows along it.'

Dylan's forehead wrinkled. 'But you can see it from outside?'

Sam opened his mouth and then closed it again. *Idiot, of course you can. You've known all along that you could see out from up here.*

His breathing was still fast; the thump in Sam's head eased a fraction.

'Are we stopping here?' Dylan asked as he pointed forward. 'The attic is just around the corner and up the stairs.'

'We're really close aren't we?'

'Really really close.'

'Okay.' Sam gripped his free hand into a fist, digging his fingernails so deep into his palms to deflect his mind from the narrow set of stairs he knew to lie ahead, that they'd be marked with half-moon impressions for days. 'Let's give it a try.'

TWENTY

SUNDAY DECEMBER 12TH

Dylan punched the air and did a little dance.

'You did it, you did it!'

Sam had no voice with which to reply. He'd dealt with the narrow stairs to the servants' quarters by galloping up them and hurtling straight into the attic bedroom, which doubled as Tina's office. Flinging open the window the second he'd arrived, Sam now leant as far out of it as he could, taking desperate gulps of cold air.

Calm in the face of his friend's discomfort, Dylan headed to the door that led into the Mill Grange's roof space. 'I'll get the boxes shall I?'

Sam knew he should say no. That he should get them because they might be heavy. He had no idea if the closed-off attic space was safe or not. But he couldn't speak.

The sound of Dylan opening the door was quickly followed by the noises of cardboard being dragged along and the young boy humming happily to himself as he worked. He might have heard the boy say, 'This one has Christmas decorations written on it!' but Sam wasn't sure.

His head was pure fog. All he could do was breathe.

A second later a noise broke through, and Sam heard Dylan panting as he tugged a second box from the cupboard, followed by the lighter grabbing and plopping sound of a carrier bag full of tinsel being dropped onto the floor.

Out of the window, Sam saw Shaun walk into view. What would his friend think of him for letting Dylan into the attic space on his own? Anything could have happened to him. *Tom would kill me.*

Mustering himself, keeping his eyes fixed on the garden, Sam called across the room. 'Dylan, can you come here?'

'Sure.'

Sam gulped some moisture into his throat. 'I'm sorry I couldn't help you.'

'It's okay. I've got it all.' He beamed. 'Shall we go decorate the tree now?'

Sinking to the floor, his legs too shaky to stand, Sam asked softly, 'Dylan, could you get Shaun, please? He has just come home.'

The little boy looked serious again. 'You having a claws-foaber minute?'

Sam nodded.

'I'll fetch Shaun then. You stay there.'

As if I can do anything else.

* * *

Harriet couldn't remember the last time she'd laughed so much. Even her friends at university, when they went out for cocktails and to nightclubs, didn't laugh like Thea and Tina when they'd overdosed on mulled wine, good coffee, and the heady freedom of time off from work.

'You know—' Harriet wiped a hand across her eyes '—you two are proof that overworking can send people to hysteria.'

'It's not like what we were saying was that funny.' Thea shook her head.

Tina giggled. 'It's our age. Everything seems funny sometimes.'

Harriet smiled. 'Especially the idea of Sam, Shaun and Tom all dressed up as giant vegetables and running around the garden. Although... how did we get onto that again?'

Tina picked up her coffee and took a sustaining sip. 'It was when Thea said that your Rob sounded a knockout. Then I said it reminded me of the TV show *It's a Knockout*, which you'd never heard of, being so young and everything...'

'Ow!' Thea nudged her friend playfully in the ribs. 'We only remember it because we saw repeats on one of those catch-up channels. We aren't old enough either!'

'Oh no, we're definitely young and sprightly.' Tina wrinkled her nose with a giggle.

As the euphoria of the moment's silliness died off, Harriet sighed. 'Anyway, he isn't *my* Rob.'

'You'd like him to be though, wouldn't you?' Thea spoke gently. 'Not easy is it, having feelings for someone and having no clue how they feel in return?'

'It's rubbish.'

Tina checked her watch. 'Look, why don't we have a bit of cake to soak up all the liquid? Then we'll see how Sam and Dylan are getting on.'

'Good idea.' Thea got to her feet. 'I'll go this time. I fancy some of Moira's chocolate orange cake.'

'Moira bakes too?' Harriet was amazed. 'Does everyone in this village do everything?'

'It can seem like that.' Tina grinned. 'But no, Sybil makes

the cake across the road in the tea rooms. That is somewhere you *have* to go before you go home.'

'Sounds good.' Harriet looked around the pub. The patrons had changed several times since they'd arrived, but there was a couple in the far corner of the pub that'd arrived not long after they had, and were still there. Every time Harriet glanced in their direction, they were holding hands across the table, paying no attention to anyone or anything but each other.

Tina noticed the direction of the student's gaze. 'You okay?'

'Yeah. I'll just nip to the loo.'

Tina gestured subtly to the couple in the corner as Thea arrived with the cake. 'I think Harriet is maybe a touch wistful.'

'Ummm.' Thea was thoughtful. 'If this Rob is a nice chap, but is as shy as Harriet says he is, then you and I may have to meddle.'

'You sound like Mabel.' Tina took her slice of cake and inhaled the delicious aroma of chocolate and orange.

'What can I say?' Thea said. 'I learnt from the best.'

* * *

'Don't you dare scare me like that again!'

Having sent Dylan to wash his hands after being in the attic, Shaun sat a pale Sam on the sofa in the drawing room.

'Sorry, mate.' Sam was close to tears. 'If you'd been here, I'd never have gone up. Where've you been anyway?'

'To sort Thea's Christmas present.'

'Not to a dig site?' The thump in Sam's head made him want to shut his eyes.

'Not this time, although she thinks I have.' Shaun reached out to shake Sam's hand. 'Oh, and there's another thing.'

'What?'

'Bloody well done!'

Confusion creased Sam's face as his friend pumped his arm up and down. 'What? But I... Dylan, he could have fallen through the ceiling!'

'No he couldn't. This house is as solid as they come.' Getting up, Shaun hauled one of the boxes of decorations nearer to the tree. 'Don't you get it? You have been *upstairs*. You went, not just to the first floor, but to the *top* of the house. That is huge.'

Sam stared at his hands as he held them out before him. They were shaking. 'I did, didn't I?'

'Bert is going to be made up! Not to mention Tina.'

The sound of Dylan running along the corridor made Sam look round. 'That boy is never going to understand just how much I owe him.'

Shaun whispered, 'He will, because when he's older, you'll tell him.'

* * *

Helen climbed out of the Land Rover and looked up at the granite walls and slate roof of Mill Grange. Although the sun wasn't high in the sky, as it had been the day she'd first seen the Victorian manor house, the winter light glinted off the granite, making it shine in places.

'A penny for your thoughts?' Tom asked as he saw her stare up at the house.

'I was just thinking about this place. Tina and Thea were

saying it was magical, that somehow being at Mill Grange sorts things out.'

'How much wine had they had at that point?'

Helen laughed. 'A fair bit, but in an odd way they're right. I mean—' she placed a hand on her stomach '—I would never have dreamed...'

'I know.' Tom kissed the top of her head. 'It is going to be so hard not telling everyone.'

'Only for a while. Once I'm safely past twelve weeks, then we'll let people know.' Helen took his hand. 'Come on. Let's see what Dylan's been up to.'

* * *

Sam watched from the sofa as Dylan, Shaun, Tom and Helen circled the tree in fairy lights, and tinsel. He'd intended to help, but he didn't yet trust his legs not to go out from under him as his brain wrestled with the fact he'd been upstairs.

You've done it once, which means you can do it again.

He took a drink from the glass of water Helen had fetched him as soon as she and Tom had heard what had happened. Sam smiled; he'd never forget the expression on Tom's face as he'd heard what Dylan had helped him do. Nor would he forget Dylan's continued attempts to say claustrophobia properly for the rest of the afternoon.

Shaun passed the boy a large gold star. 'Ready to pop this on, then?'

'Yeah!'

Scooping him up, Shaun lifted Dylan so he could place the final decoration at the top of the tree.

'It looks amazing.' As Dylan came to her side, Helen

switched the drawing room light off, so that only the fairy lights and fire lit the room.

The blue, white and gold bulbs shone, reflecting in the shiny baubles that adorned every inch of the huge tree.

A lump came to Sam's throat as he held a hand out to an oddly subdued Dylan.

'Are you alright?' The little boy pressed his face close to Sam's ear. 'Did I make you poorly?'

'Not at all. My claustrophobia did that. You made me braver. You did a good thing. Thank you.'

'Promise?'

'Promise.' Sam held him tight.

'Bert won't be cross with me then?'

Suddenly understanding, Sam held his little friend tighter. 'Because you helped me when he wasn't here?'

'Helping you is his thing.'

'Bert will be thrilled, Dylan. Would you like to be the one to tell him all about it when you go and fetch your costume from Mabel later?'

'Could I?' The boy's face lit up. 'Don't you want to?'

'If it wasn't for you, I'd never have been to the attics. You should tell him.'

The sound of footsteps and chatter in the corridor outside made Sam and Dylan clamber to their feet.

'Tina.' Sam breathed the word, before heading to the doorway to the drawing room, just as his wife and her friends came in.

'Wow!'

'Do you like it?' Sam heard his own voice as he spoke. It was hoarse, despite the water he'd been drinking.

'It's beautiful!'

Tina turned to thank her friends, but they were already

disappearing from the room with calls of 'It's time to put the kettle on.'

'What is it? What's happened?' She looked from Sam, to the tree, and back again. 'And who got the decorations out of the attic?'

TWENTY-ONE

MONDAY DECEMBER 13TH

'If I'd known you'd react to me managing to go upstairs like that, I'd have done it months ago.' Sam raised an arm so Tina could lay her head against his shoulder, as they snuggled beneath the bedcovers.

Tina smiled as she stroked his chest. 'I can't believe you did it. I'm chuffed to bits.'

'I wouldn't be that proud if I were you. I doubt I could do it again in a hurry.'

'You still *did it*.'

'Only because I didn't want to let Dylan down. I was a mess up there. I needed Shaun to help me down again.'

'Well, I'm proud of you, so there.' Tina rolled over so she was lying on top of Sam. 'And however you got up there yesterday, and however you got down, doesn't change the fact that you climbed up to the attic and got down again.'

'Ummm.' Sam nuzzled the side of her neck. 'I have to say, I'm enjoying my reward for seeing the view from the top of the house.'

'Stunning isn't it.'

'It is, but not as stunning as my current view.' Sam peered across to the alarm clock by their bed. 'Only five o'clock – we just have time...'

* * *

Helen let the shower pound against her shoulder muscles. It seemed a lifetime since she'd fallen apart in that very cubicle.

Butterflies danced in her stomach at the thought of the doctor's visit to come, but although she was nervous, now she had Tom's support she felt a lot better.

A yawn escaped as she switched off the water and swathed herself in a towel. It was going to be a long day. Doctor's in Bath, then back home to work – the social media posts for the book needed scheduling and she had a heap of emails and tasks piling up for the day job. Then there was the nativity; there was a rehearsal that evening, and – Helen gave a sigh – Sue and Nathan were due to arrive tomorrow.

That shouldn't bother me. Sue is Dylan's mum and she has never been unkind to me.

Helen wiped the towel over her arms. *She's never been particularly nice to me either, but then, why would she be?*

Tired before the day had even begun, Helen sat on top of the laundry basket and listened to the sounds of her family getting ready for work and school. She could hear Tom asking Dylan if he had his costume ready for the rehearsal. Helen's smile worked its way back across her face as she remembered Dylan, high as a kite from helping Sam get to the attic and decorating the tree, struggling to stay immobile while Mabel checked that the tunic she'd made him fitted.

Bert had almost been as bad. Bowled over with the news

of Sam's achievement, he'd not been able to stop himself from repeating the same words over and over: 'He did it. I knew he would. I *knew* it.'

After hearing the same sentences at least a dozen times, Mabel's patience had snapped, and she'd spoken through gritted teeth. 'Yes, dear, Sam did it. We are all happy for him. Do you suppose you could go and be proud in the kitchen while you make us some tea?'

'You alright in there?'

Tom's voice brought Helen back to the present. 'Just drying. Be with you in a minute.'

She passed the towel over her stomach and paused. *Stay safe in there, won't you.*

* * *

Mabel wasn't alone when Sam came into the kitchen after feeding the chickens their breakfast.

Bert jumped to his feet, his arm outstretched. 'You did it! I said you would.'

'Several times.' Mabel rolled her eyes as she gave her husband an affectionate smile.

Sam shook his head. 'My performance was nothing to make a fuss of.'

'Nonsense! Now then—' Bert brushed his hands together as if the matter was closed '—you've done it once, so you'll be able to do it again.'

Sam grinned. 'That's exactly what I hoped you'd say.'

'And you were spot on.' Bert tapped the clipboard that Mabel had placed on the kitchen table. 'But not today. Lots to do before these actor types arrive. So, how can I help?'

'You sure you don't mind pitching in?'

'Wouldn't be here if I minded.' Bert smiled. 'And as young Dylan told me Tom had asked for the day off to get his Christmas shopping done in Bath, I thought an extra pair of hands might come in – well – handy.'

* * *

'Hey, Harriet, just checking all good for tomorrow. Matt thinks everyone will be with you by ten. Is that too early do you think?'

A bleary-eyed Harriet felt her pulse zip up a notch as Rob's velvet voice came down the line. 'That should be fine. That's almost midday here. Everyone gets up awfully early.'

'I haven't woken you, have I?'

'No,' Harriet lied as she held her duvet to her chest against the chill of the room. Her eyes caught the time on her clock; it was already half past nine. 'I'm not up though.'

There was a brief pause on the line. Harriet had the briefest suspicion that Rob was picturing her in bed, but quickly dismissed it as wishful thinking on her part.

'I wondered – and please say if you don't think it's a good idea – I wouldn't be offended or anything.'

'Offended about what?' Harriet reached an arm to the chair that operated as a bedside table and hooked a jumper towards her.

Rob cleared his throat. 'I have my own car, so I thought I'd drive over separately, rather than come in the people carrier with the others.'

'And you're worried about parking space?' Harriet threaded an arm into a jumper sleeve, and swapped the phone into her other hand. 'I can't imagine that being a problem. The drive is pretty big. Most of the audience will walk up from the village, so there should be room for you.'

'Great. Yes.' Rob hesitated again.

'Wasn't that what you wanted to ask?'

'No, well. Yes. Actually, I wondered about coming to Exmoor today. Do you think Sam and Tina would mind?'

* * *

'Hi, um, sorry to interrupt.'

Tina turned from her work. 'You alright, Harriet? You look flustered.'

'I am flustered! Rob wants to come today. What do I say?'

Tina smiled. 'You say yes of course. The rooms will be ready by lunchtime.'

Thea looked up from where she'd been tackling an email. 'You'll have to take him to the pub for dinner though. Mabel won't have enough food.'

'Of course she'll have enough...' Tina stopped talking as she saw the expression on Thea's face, before starting again. 'Rob is very welcome to come, but perhaps you could tell him that we aren't quite ready to cater. Maybe he'd like to accompany you to the pub this evening?'

Harriet looked from Tina to Thea and back again, understanding what they were saying. 'You two are brilliant.'

As Harriet dashed off to return Rob's call, Thea's gaze returned to the list of booking enquiries for the retreat she'd been dealing with. 'Is it me, or is Harriet quite excited about Rob coming?'

'Whatever gave you that impression?' Tina smiled. 'I'll call Moira and reserve them a table.'

'Won't they think we are interfering?'

'Possibly.' Tina picked the phone up anyway. 'I'll tell Moira that if Rob or Harriet call, then she should cancel my booking.'

'Do you know Rob's surname then?'

'Rats, no, I don't.' Tina pulled a face. 'But it would be Harriet who booked wouldn't it, as she's here?'

'Probably.' Thea tapped open an email. 'Reserve it anyway. If we are going to meddle for the greater good then we might as well go the whole hog.'

* * *

The hospital waiting room smelt of antiseptic and apprehension. The chairs, grouped in twos or fours, sat in roughly regimented rows, each set punctuated by a small table holding piles of out-of-date magazines and empty paper cups.

Helen watched as Tom booked her in at the reception. She hadn't expected this. At least, not yet.

'All checked in.' Tom took her hand as Helen tried to force down another cup of water.

'You're using your "it'll be alright, Dylan" voice.'

'Sorry.' Tom shrugged. 'As much for my benefit as yours.' He peered around them. There was no one else there. 'Are we out of hours or something?'

Helen took another swig of cold water. 'Normal surgery time finished half an hour ago. Doctor Sanders has managed to slot us in as an extra.'

'Right.' Tom took Helen's cup from her and took a drink. 'But isn't it a bit early for a scan? Sue didn't get one until she was twelve weeks.'

Helen tried to steady the nerves that were shooting around her entire body. 'Sue wasn't over forty.'

Tom passed the cup back. 'Sorry, love.'

'Not your fault.' Helen tried to drink some more and winced. 'I know they need me to have a full bladder, but if I have any more water I swear I'm going to wet myself.'

'How much have you drunk?'

'Six cups.'

Tom peered up at the large round white clock on the wall opposite. 'I'm sure they won't keep us much longer.'

'Hope not.' Helen crossed her legs, then remembered that Doctor Sanders had told her not to do that, and uncrossed them again. 'At least I wore a skirt today. Can you imagine the faffing if I'd had my dungarees on?'

'I rather like your dungarees.' Tom smiled. 'You were wearing them the first time I saw you.'

'So I was.' Helen rested her head on his shoulder. 'Fancy you remembering that.'

'Not just a pretty face.'

Helen shuffled uncomfortably on her plastic seat, and whispered, 'It'll be okay, won't it?'

Trying not to let his own nerves show, Tom agreed, 'Absolutely.'

'But. What if...?'

Helen's concerns were curtailed by the arrival of a young man wearing nurse's scrubs.

'Helen Rogers?'

'Yes.' Helen got up too fast, and had to battle not to be sick. She could feel her insides gurgle, they were so waterlogged.

'I'm Arjun. I'm a student midwife. I have to ask if you are

alright with me being present during your scan.' He held his palms out. 'I promise I won't be offended if you say no.'

'I don't mind. Tom?'

'Not at all.' Tom shook Arjun's hand. 'You don't know how much longer we'll have to wait do you?'

'No time at all.' He waved a hand out before him. 'Walk this way.'

TWENTY-TWO

MONDAY DECEMBER 13TH

Harriet ran her eyes over her lines. Since she'd arrived at Mill Grange, she hadn't practised them as often as she'd intended to. Now, with Rob due late afternoon and Matt, Ali and the rest of the cast arriving the following day, Harriet felt time running out on her.

Would I be this nervous if my father wasn't coming?

Curled up on the sofa nearest the Christmas tree, she closed her eyes. Harriet pictured the walled garden in her mind and tried to imprint her memory of *The Winter's Tale*'s few bits of scenery over it. Starting from Act One, she then ran the play through her mind, scene by scene, act by act.

She'd done well to concentrate through to the point where the interval arrived, and was just considering heading to the garden to step through her lines in situ so she could work on Hermione's expressions and gestures, when a persistent voice at the back of her head won over her need to rehearse.

Rob is coming here today and I am taking him to the pub.

At first she'd been put out when Tina had confessed to

having reserved a table on her behalf, but then she'd been grateful. *I'm so used to having to do everything for myself, that I don't know how to handle it when someone does something to help without asking.*

An image of her father came to mind. She'd been a little girl of nine, sat across the kitchen table. She'd woken up with a stomach ache and feeling sick, but as she'd had no temperature her father had insisted she went to school. 'When you're older, there'll be no chance to skip work because you feel a bit off colour. Hard life lessons. Yes, Harriet?'

Harriet remembered how she'd gone to school, walked into her classroom and promptly been sick everywhere. They'd sent her straight home again. Her father had been furious.

Shaking the memory away, Harriet allowed herself to picture her and Rob at the table for two in the corner of the Stag and Hound instead. The fire to their left, roaring away in the grate, they'd talk about the play and their hopes and dreams for the future. Harriet could almost taste the mulled wine she intended to drink.

Opening her eyes, she gave herself a stern talking-to as the sounds of activity in the house around her flittered through her thoughts. 'You've got hours before Rob arrives and there are probably jobs I can help with.' Getting up she laid down her script, brushed down her jeans, and headed to the kitchen.

'Hi, Mabel, can I help?'

'Morning, Harriet.' Mabel pointed to the clipboard. 'You could cross off "make lasagne" and pass me the oven gloves.'

That done, Harriet scanned the list. 'I'll go and sort the loo rolls, shall I? Make sure there are spares in each bathroom?'

Mabel pushed the lasagne into the Aga. 'That would be very helpful. They're kept in the laundry. Do you know where that is?'

'Not yet.'

'If you head to the back door and then stand as if you've just come inside then, rather than turning left to come along the corridor to this kitchen, take the white door in front of you.'

'Into the corridor that takes you to Thea's office?'

'That's it. Just beyond the office is a narrower corridor that runs to the old laundry room and storerooms.' Mabel adjusted her apron. 'The light switch is to the right, behind the door. You have to reach around on yourself a bit to find it.'

Ten minutes later, grateful that Mabel had told her where to switch the light on, Harriet surveyed the laundry. Ignoring the two washing machines and tumble dryers, she had no trouble imagining the room as it must have once been. The long sink beneath the window, too high to see out of, with a wooden draining board and row upon row of hooks for utensils and clothes, sat above drawers and cupboards that housed the manor's linen, towels and cleaning supplies, just as she pictured it would have done in the nineteenth century. Harriet was already feeling sorry for the maids who'd have spent their time in this place, lit only by candles or gas lamps, washing and scrubbing until their unprotected hands were raw.

I have to add this to the tour I'll give Rob.

Grabbing a wicker basket from a stack by the door, she faced the dresser, which was crammed with piles of tea towels, kitchen roll and toilet rolls. Harriet scooped up a dozen of the latter and, holding a hand over a couple of rolls that were rather precariously lodged on the top of her haul, she set off, planning which route she'd take to show the house to Rob when he arrived in six hours' time.

* * *

'Let me introduce Philippa, a most excellent sonographer.' Arjun sat on a stool to the side of his colleague.

'I'm very pleased to meet you.' The sonographer held out a hand in greeting. 'Thank you for letting Arjun sit in.'

'Not at all.' Helen apprehensively eyed the equipment that lined the walls of the room.

'Don't worry.' Philippa pulled out a long sheet of blue paper and laid it across an examination bed. 'It all looks far scarier than it is. You only need to concern yourself with this.' She patted a computer monitor that sat next to an examina-tion bed.

Arjun gestured to the bed. 'If you'd like to get on, just relax your head against the raised pillow. You'll be able to see the monitor from there.'

Tom found his voice. 'You mean we'll be able to see our baby today?'

'You will.' Philippa smiled. 'Doctor Sanders has asked me to help establish how far along you are.'

'That's why I'm here?' Helen was puzzled. 'I thought it was because... well, because I'm old.'

'You are far from that.'

'But...'

'While you are an older first-time mother, I can see from your medical records that you are fit and healthy and, while I see here that your mother suffered from early menopause and cancer, you are clear of such evils.'

Tom patted the bed. 'Come on, love, hop on.'

Helen slipped off her shoes. 'I suppose I just assumed my age was why I was here. I'm pretty sure I'm only eight weeks.'

'We'll soon find out.' Philippa smiled. 'A few legal formalities first. Can you confirm your full name for me please?'

'Helen Sarah Rogers.'

'Date of birth?'

'Fifteenth of April, 1979.'

'First line of your address?'

'Fifteen Prince Road.'

'That's Tiverton, yes?'

'Yes. I work in Bath though, so...'

'No need to explain, it's all here.' Philippa pointed to her open file. 'I have to ask these things though. Can't be giving the wrong patient the wrong advice and all that. If you could roll down your skirt's waistband and lift your top a little for me?'

The sonographer pressed the screen before them, which flickered into life. 'Arjun, if you'd do the honours.'

The student selected a bottle from a row of similar-looking containers. 'Fear not, the gel is nice and warm. Not like the old days when we used to freeze expectant mothers at the drop of a hat.'

Helen, who'd been expecting the gel to be icy, sighed with relief. 'It's a silly thing to worry about, but I was getting tense ready to repel the cold!'

The sonographer laughed. 'Everyone does.'

Helen retook Tom's hand. She was sure he could hear what she was thinking. *I'm too scared to look, but I want to look.*

'Okay then.' Philippa wiped a sterile cloth over a thick probe that was attached to the computer before trailing it firmly through the gel over Helen's stomach. 'That feel alright?'

'Weird, but yes.' Helen shifted uncomfortably. 'But if I don't pee soon, I may not be responsible for my actions.'

Arjun smiled. 'You wouldn't be the first. But don't worry. That door over in the corner leads to a bathroom. The second we're done you can make a dash for it.'

'Thanks.' Helen, trying not to be distracted by the increasingly dull ache in her bladder now the sonographer was pressing on her stomach, watched as the monitor's screen changed and a large grey and black square came to life.

Tom's gasp was louder than Helen's as a tiny moving shape came into soft focus. 'Is that...?'

'Yes, Mr Harris. That is your child.' Philippa pressed a few buttons on the screen, zooming the picture into sharper focus. 'I never get tired of saying that.'

Helen craned her neck forward as Tom brought his head next to hers. 'I can't believe this.' She felt choked, and knew there were tears in her eyes.

'It's amazing. I wasn't... Sue didn't let me go with her to see Dylan before he was born.'

'Here.' Philippa took a pencil and gave it to Arjun. 'Perhaps you could show Miss Rogers and Mr Harris where everything is while I work out some measurements?'

'Please—' Tom smiled '—call us Helen and Tom.'

'Okay then, Helen and Tom.' Arjun moved around the bed. 'Let's meet your baby.'

Helen forgot how badly she needed the bathroom as, with Tom's breath brushing her cheek, they watched as their baby's arms and legs were pointed out with the tip of the pencil. Then, Arjun traced a circle around the tiny beating heart and told them that everything looked as it ought to.

Helen looked from the screen to her stomach and back again. 'It doesn't seem possible that we're looking at a human being that's inside me.'

'Weird sensation isn't it?' Philippa pressed a few more keys on her computer, before adding, 'A human being that is already twelve weeks into its life.'

'Twelve?' Helen gasped. 'Are you sure?'

'Possibly even thirteen.' Philippa turned to Arjun. 'Could you get some tissue so Helen can clean up? I'm sure that bathroom visit is pressing now.'

Taking the tissue and wiping up the gel, Helen barely noticed Tom help her sit up and walk with her to the small toilet cubicle. It was only when she returned to the examination room, considerably more comfortable, that she asked, 'How can I be that far along? I've had no morning sickness. I haven't even gone off coffee. I'm fine, just...'

'Excessively emotional,' Tom added kindly as he saw Helen welling up. 'That's what made us think that the menopause had come early.'

'That's completely understandable.' Philippa jotted some notes into the file. 'If you've had no sickness then you are incredibly lucky.'

'It's okay though, is it?' Helen was anxious again. 'I mean, I don't actually *want* to be sick or anything, but if that's what is supposed to happen, then...'

'There is no "supposed to happen" in pregnancy. Every single person is different. And, as you've just seen, your child is doing well.'

'Twelve weeks.' Tom started calculating. 'So we are looking at a new arrival in June.'

'I'd give the approximate due date at 10th June, as I suspect Helen is nearer thirteen weeks than twelve.'

'Early summer.' Helen smiled. 'I like that.'

'Me too.' Tom kissed her forehead.

Arjun looked up from where he'd been tapping on a computer keyboard. 'Would you like some photographs to show friends and family, or would you like me to email you a link to the photos? Or both?'

* * *

Helen sat in the Courtyard Café near Bath Abbey with the printout of the scan photo in her hand. She traced the tip of a fingernail around the tiny body. It was more like a kidney bean with tiny protrusions than a miniature human being.

Tom pushed a slice of carrot cake towards her. 'Eat up. You're eating for two, remember!'

Helen laughed. 'I'm not sure that means eating so much fat.'

'Nonsense. There's veg in there. This cake is one of your five a day.' Tom took the photo from her fingers and replaced it with a cake fork. 'I know you only pretended to eat breakfast, so eat now.'

'I was too nervous to eat earlier.'

'Me too.' Tom took a mouthful of his own cake. 'And we only thought we were having the pregnancy confirmed today. I wasn't expecting a trip out to the hospital.'

Helen yawned. 'Nor me.'

'Are you sure you should be going in to work today?'

'I have to.' Helen sighed. 'I'd better make an appointment to see the curator too.'

'That still sounds odd. To me, you'll always be the curator there.'

Helen smiled. 'Nonetheless, they need to be told I'm

expecting, so maternity cover can be sorted.' She fiddled with her cake fork. 'I feel bad about that. I've only just got them to readjust things so that I can change my job and work from home.'

'They'll be fine.'

'Yeah.' Helen took a tentative mouthful of cake.

'We weren't going to tell the others until you were twelve weeks, but you're already past that. What do you want to do?'

Helen knocked a stray crumb from her lips. 'I have a confession.'

'Go on.'

'Thea knows. She guessed.' Helen hastily added, 'She is sworn to secrecy though.'

'If Thea guessed, then I'd put money on Mabel having suspicions too.' Tom grinned. 'I have a confession too. I spoke to Bert about you possibly having the menopause.'

'Bert?'

'He was lovely. Told me it was probably you having way too much on and adjusting to a lack of friends around you all day.'

'He's the sweetest man in the world.'

'Ouch!' Tom stuck his tongue out playfully.

'Okay, the second-sweetest man.' Helen looked up at Tom. 'He and Mabel will be delighted won't they?'

'They will be over the moon. They're already like grand-parents to Dylan.'

'Let's not tell them yet. I mean, I do want to tell them, but with Sue arriving tomorrow, and the nativity in a few days, and then Harriet's play...'

Tom reached a hand across the table. 'I know. It's all a bit much. We'll wait until Sue and Nathan have gone home. It'll be a nice early Christmas surprise for Dylan. Help cheer him up once his mum's gone again.'

'Thanks, Tom. I might be being unfair, but I can't help thinking Sue would have something unhelpful to say about me having a baby at my age.'

TWENTY-THREE
MONDAY DECEMBER 13TH

The house smelt of beeswax. Everything that could have been polished shone, and every carpet and rug had been hoovered. The beds were made up, towels were placed at the end of each bed and the bathrooms gleamed.

Harriet had never worked so hard in her life and was surprised to find she'd loved helping to turn the house into a home for her acting friends. Glad she'd arrived first, and so had bagged the only single guest room, she was mentally allocating bedrooms to her colleagues, when Tina arrived, a bag over her shoulder and her ever-present notepad to hand.

'I was wondering if you had an idea as to who should sleep where?' Tina produced a heap of printed out and laminated name labels from her bag. 'I thought it would save a lot of hassle if we stuck people's names on the doors now; that way there'll be no "who's sleeping where" arguments.'

'Good thinking.' Harriet stood at the far end of the corridor nearest the main hub of the bedrooms. 'Matt and Ali should have a double, as they are the only couple.'

'Sorted. They can have the master bedroom.'

Harriet took the labels with Matt and Ali's names on, and, seeing they were already dotted with sticky tack, stuck them both to the main bedroom door. 'Does everyone get on? I mean, are there some members of the cast that I shouldn't have sharing a room in case of ego clashes?'

'Not now Jason isn't part of the group.' Helen looked out of the window as her cheeks began to pink. 'Although, maybe Rob should have a double. After all, he's the star after Matt.'

Tina passed Harriet Rob's name label and pointed to the next nearest double room. She didn't say what she was thinking. *And if he's in a double room, then he can't share with anyone – which may or may not be handy.* Instead she said, 'What time does Rob expect to get here?'

'About five.' Harriet checked her watch. 'Oh God, that's only two hours away! I haven't even decided what to wear.'

Suddenly reminded of her nineteen-year-old self, Tina waved towards a window. 'It's cold out there, and although Moira keeps the pub toasty, you will be best wearing layers.'

Harriet looked outside again. The light was already beginning to fade. 'I hoped to show Rob the walled garden when he got here.'

'You can. Just wrap up first and take a couple of torches from the cupboard by the back door.'

'Thanks.'

Tina stuck two name tags on the twin bedroom door that was next along the corridor. 'Look, I know you want to dress up for Rob, it's natural, but maybe take a bit of advice from someone who got rather too hung up on her appearance back in the day. If Rob is the right guy, it won't matter what you wear, but it will matter if you wear something light and sexy and go and get hypothermia!'

'But he's so out of my league and...'

'I doubt he is any such thing. But either way, if you get a cold and can't stop coughing or sneezing, then you won't get to be Hermione and play opposite him.'

'I suppose so.' Harriet grimaced.

'Your career is important to you, and from what you've said about Rob, so is his to him. You're only nineteen. I know you'll get sick of people saying that, but we change so much between the ages of eighteen and twenty-two. I'm not saying we stop changing after that, but that's when we find out who we are.'

'You think it's pointless me liking Rob, then?'

'Not at all. Loads of people meet their partner for life at uni. What I mean is, don't let how you feel blind everything else. If Rob is the one, he'll be the one whether you wear a little black dress and heels or seven thermal layers and walking boots.' Tina patted Harriet's shoulder. 'And as you'd look drop-dead gorgeous in anything, it matters even less.'

* * *

Helen's ears were ringing with lines from "Away in a Manger" as she unlocked the front door and called out to Tom, announcing their return from the nativity rehearsal.

'Hey, Dad.' Dylan pulled off his shoes and threw them into the corner of the hall. 'Mrs Harley loved my costume.'

'That's great.' Tom reached out to take Helen's coat as she kicked off her trainers.

'Can I watch some telly, Dad?'

'Wash your hands first.' As Dylan dashed into the bathroom at breakneck speed, Tom asked Helen, 'You okay?'

'Tired.'

'Hardly surprising – it's been a hell of a day.'

'Just a bit.' Helen's head turned towards the kitchen and she inhaled deeply. 'You've made dinner?'

'Casserole.'

'I love casserole!'

Tom laughed. 'That was my motivation for cooking it.'

Saying with feeling 'Thank you,' Helen headed to the kitchen. 'If I don't sit down soon, I'm going to fall asleep right here.'

'Coffee?'

'Just water I think. I know I'm lucky not to have gone off it, but I don't want this wee one to start life with a major caffeine addiction. It'll be up all night for a start!'

'They will be anyway.' Tom opened the oven and a comforting waft of beef, vegetables and pearl barley filled the room. 'Dylan was a nightmare. Never slept well until he was three. I swear he was afraid of missing something while his eyes were closed.'

Helen yawned. 'Shame we can't stockpile sleep in advance.'

Stirring the casserole, Tom asked, 'How was the rehearsal?'

'Great. The kids look so sweet in their costumes. But I'm not sure I want to hear "Silent Night" or "Away in a Manger" ever again.'

'I can well imagine.' Tom gathered three plates from the cupboard. 'How about the adults? I know from Dylan that the kids all love you, but are you okay with the grown-ups?'

'You mean, am I fitting in better?'

'More, do you *feel* you're fitting in better, I suppose.'

'Now I'm going to be a proper parent you mean?'

Tom shook his head. 'No, love, you were always a proper

parent. I meant, now you're in a position where you have to talk to them.'

'It's still only the teaching staff and me, but yes. I think so.' Helen sipped her water. 'I tried to picture telling Carol Walters about our baby, but I couldn't quite hear myself saying the words.' She tapped her stomach. 'These trousers are already too tight. It's going to be obvious soon.'

'I think the talking-to-people problem will solve itself.'

'How do you mean?'

'You just said it yourself. Soon you'll have a gorgeous baby bump. People will talk about that. They'll start the conversation.'

'You think so?'

'I do.'

'A bit like when someone has a new puppy, and folk feel they have to talk to the owner and stroke the puppy?'

Tom laughed. 'Sort of, but without the stroking hopefully.'

Helen got up to lay the table. 'Any word from Sue?'

Tom passed her some tablemats. 'I got a brief email asking for details of their room booking at the pub, but that was it.'

'You don't know what time they arrive in England?'

'No idea. They could already be here.'

Helen paused in the act of placing forks on the table. 'Surely they wouldn't come to England and not visit their children straight away?'

'Who knows?' Tom sighed. 'I'm being unfair. Sue loves Dylan. She's just got a new life. Lots of adjustments I'm sure.'

'And Nathan? Harriet seemed hurt by the manner of his coming to visit, rather than being excited to be seeing her father.'

'I only met him once, when he collected Sue to go to the

airport. I can't say I took to him. Maybe he was just nervous and trying too hard to impress me.'

Helen added cutlery to the table. 'Is it awful of me to wish they weren't coming?'

'Because of the nativity rehearsals?'

'Because I'm like an animated sack of spuds compared to Sue at the best of times, and I'm emotional enough as it is, without my hormones ganging up with my brain and telling me I'm fat.'

Tom looked up from the oven. 'Don't be daft. You know damn well you are gorgeous, not to mention being a much nicer person than Sue will ever be.'

'Thanks, love.' Helen gave him a brave smile. 'Just bear with me if I have wobbles. I may have got away without morning sickness so far, but the emotional avalanche is more than compensating for that!'

TWENTY-FOUR
MONDAY DECEMBER 13TH

Harriet didn't know if Tina had snuck out and switched the fairy lights on in the greenhouse on purpose, or if they came on every evening via a timer, but the rainbow effect against the reflection of the glass was magical.

Keen to show Rob their stage before the last of the fading daylight died away, she'd invited him to the walled garden the moment he'd stepped from his car. If he'd been surprised by her instant arrival as he'd driven into the car park, he hadn't shown it. Nor had he objected to being dragged out into the cold evening before seeing inside the house.

Beyond a polite enquiry about his journey, neither of them had spoken as they walked around the side of the house and across the lawns. Harriet realised, with some surprise, that the silence between them hadn't felt awkward. She'd enjoyed quietly strolling beside Rob's tall slim frame as he took in the evening view of the woodland beyond the garden, and peered, almost furtively, through the windows of the house.

Now, as they stood to the side of the chicken coop, the

greenhouse before them, Harriet found herself fighting the urge to slip her palm into his.

'I can see why you've fallen in love with this place.' Rob tore his eyes from the recently restored greenhouse. 'There's so much history here. You can practically hear it pouring from the walls.'

'You wait until it's light. I'll be able to show you where the Roman Fortlet is.'

'A fortlet? Seriously?' Rob's dark brow furrowed despite his smile. 'Romans on Exmoor?'

'I'm not winding you up. Promise.' Harriet gestured towards the far side of the main garden. 'If we have time tomorrow before the others arrive, maybe Thea or Shaun will show it to you.'

Rob's dark eyes shone. 'Are you telling me we have come to an archaeological site?'

'Yes.' Harriet nodded. 'You into history then?'

'You could say that.' Rob walked closer to the greenhouse. 'It was a toss-up between studying drama or history when I applied for uni. Well, more likely heritage studies to be honest.'

'Really?' Harriet experienced a totally irrational stab of jealousy towards Mill Grange itself. *How can I compete with this house?*

'Absolutely. You know my dad's family is Jamaican?'

Harriet smiled. 'Your parents brought your grandparents to the show you did in June. They were lovely. Told us tales of Jamaican summers during the interval.'

'I never knew that.' Rob looked down at Harriet. 'I'm sorry, I had forgotten you'd met my family.'

'Why would you be sorry about that?' Harriet suppressed

a sigh. 'They were there to support you. That's hardly something to be sorry about.'

'I suppose not.' Rob looked faintly embarrassed as they reached the greenhouse. 'This is lovely. Restored?'

'I'm not sure.' Harriet shuffled her feet. They were beginning to get cold in spite of being snuggled in two pairs of socks.

Rob twisted around so he was looking beyond the chicken coop to the side of the manor. 'This is a perfect spot for the play, Harriet. Thank you.'

Glad it was getting dark so Rob couldn't see her red cheeks, Harriet said, 'I just wanted to help Matt. He's so kind letting me have a stab at being Hermione.'

'He's hardly doing that.' Rob began to pace out the length of the imaginary stage. 'You auditioned and got the job on merit. He is a lovely guy, but no way would Matt give you a role you weren't good enough for.'

'Oh. Thanks.' Harriet's reply came out as a squeak.

Rob strode out a few more paces, before adding, 'I'm guessing I'd stand here – ish, and you over there for our parts at the start of Act One.'

'Yes. Maybe.' She waved a hand at the house. 'I did a rough plan of where we all might stand at the start in case it helps.'

Rob gave her a quick but piercing look, which could have been approval or might have been him questioning why she'd waste time doing that. Staring up at the chickens, Harriet asked, 'Why didn't you take the role of Polixenes when Matt offered it? You're more than good enough.'

Rob kept his attention fixed on the garden, and working out where the actors would all stand. 'I already know the Leontes role.'

'You know Polixenes' too.'

'True.' Rob gave her a flash of his dazzling smile. 'I have a few distractions going on and learning a different part as well as I'd like to at such short notice didn't feel realistic.'

Harriet was about to ask what distractions he had, but thought better of it. 'Would you like to see the house?'

'I'd love to.' Rob's smile widened.

Harriet stared at her feet as she hastily added, 'There's a table booked for us at the pub at seven. I hope that's okay?'

'Perfect.' Rob glanced at her briefly then turned to walk towards the house. 'Tell me about this place. When was it built?'

'I don't know. Sorry.' Harriet cursed her lack of knowledge. 'It's Victorian, but beyond that...'

'And a stunning example if the outside is anything to go by.'

Harriet asked, 'You are interested in the Victorians then?'

'Their architecture really. Their actions – well, some of the higher class's actions, don't exactly sit well with me for obvious reasons, but I'm not so blinkered as to deny the period had its good points. Its architecture was one of them.'

Even though Rob had spoken kindly, Harriet felt as if she'd been told off for her lack of knowledge. She changed the subject as they approached the house. 'Would you like a coffee or something? Then I'll show you your room and, if you want I can give you a tour. Although maybe one of the others should do that.'

'I'd love a tour.'

A wave of disappointment washed over Harriet as she heard herself saying, 'I'll see if Shaun or Thea are about. They give good guided tours. And they know what they're talking about.'

* * *

Thea mouthed "sorry" for the third time, as Shaun and Rob dived deeper into conversation. Harriet gave her a smile which, she hoped, said it didn't matter, and tried not to mind as she looked across the pub at the table she had imagined sitting at that evening.

Harriet blamed herself. She hadn't told Rob the table she'd booked was just for them. It wasn't unreasonable that he'd assumed it was for a group of Mill Grange folk, so when she had introduced him to Shaun, and they had instantly hit it off, it wasn't a surprise to hear Rob ask if he and Thea would be joining them at the Stag and Hound.

Cradling her glass of lager, watching the fire dance in the hearth, Harriet listened to Shaun tell Rob about how he'd come to Mill Grange and the history of the house. By the time Rob had asked Thea about the Roman remains in the garden, they had eaten their steak and chips.

When Rob and Shaun got into a discussion about a sunken slave ship that Shaun had voiced a television documentary for three years ago, Harriet got to her feet. 'If you guys will forgive me, I'm rather tired. With my father and the cast coming tomorrow, I ought to try and get some sleep. I think I'll head back.'

A flash of something crossed Rob's face. Harriet hoped it was regret, but she doubted it. 'Could you two show Rob the way back?'

Thea hooked her coat off the back of her chair. 'I'll come with you. I've got a long day tomorrow too.' Thea gave Shaun a stern look. 'You'll bring Rob back, won't you?'

'No problem.'

'And don't bore the poor lad too much with tales of site shenanigans.'

Shaun's eyebrows rose. 'But Rob asked me, so...'

'I did.' Rob sucked his bottom lip. 'Sorry if I've gone on a bit. It's just so fascinating.'

'Not at all.' Harriet brushed the point away. 'I really am tired. I'll see you both in the morning.'

* * *

Shaun climbed into bed. 'That Rob's a nice bloke.'

'For an intelligent man, Shaun, you really are a berk!'

'What?'

Tutting, Thea levered herself up from her pillows, so she was resting on an elbow. 'As soon as you get onto archaeology talk you are blind to everything else. You simply do not see the signs. But why I'd think you'd start noticing signs when you never see the obvious, I don't know...'

'Signs?' Shaun was puzzled. 'What are you talking about? That was a lovely evening – wasn't it?'

'Tell me, Shaun, what was it that Harriet said over dinner?'

'Harriet? I'm not sure.'

'That is because the poor girl hardly said a word. Neither did I for that matter. Couldn't get a word in.'

'What are you talking about?' Shaun's forehead creased as he looked up at Thea. 'Rob asked you all sorts of things about the fortlet.'

'And I answered him, and then tried to steer the subject to the play or something that could include Harriet.'

'But Rob...' Shaun raked a hand through his hair. 'Oh.'

'And the penny drops.' Thea laid her head on his shoulder.

'But if she wanted to talk to him alone, why did she invite us along?'

'She didn't. The original table booked was for two. Tina and I sorted it with Moira.'

'You did?'

'Harriet has a serious crush on the boy. But she's too shy to do anything about it, and from what she told us about him, he likes her but is too shy to do anything about it either, so...'

Shaun grinned. 'You thought you'd meddle! Talk about doing a Mabel!'

'Doing a Mabel?' Thea poked him in the ribs. 'Hardly – we were just helping out. Or trying to, and then you go and accept his invite.'

'You should have told me then shouldn't you.'

'I didn't know Rob was a *Landscape Treasures* fan and a history nut.'

'I'm not sure Harriet did either.' Thea groaned. 'Thank goodness we bailed out of your conversation before you started telling Rob about your potential local dig site.'

'My... Oh yes. Well, that's all very hush-hush for now.' Shaun stroked Thea's hair. 'Perhaps you and Tina should just let them get to know each other without trying to matchmake.'

'That's what we're trying to do!' Thea groaned. 'Give them space to talk without the rest of the cast around.'

'Why didn't you make up an excuse for us not to go?'

Thea sighed. 'Because Rob's a guest, and well, he looked so excited to be able to talk to you.'

'We did talk about the play after you'd gone. I was giving him some pointers that I picked up when I played the role.'

'You were?' Thea couldn't help but chuckle. 'Shaun, you played a different role to him, once, in an amateur production years ago. Rob's a professional. If anyone was giving anyone tips, it should have been the other way around.'

'He seemed keen to listen.'

'Oh course he was. You're his TV hero – God help him.' Thea exhaled slowly. 'Harriet was very quiet on the way home. I hope she's okay.'

'She'll be fine.' Shaun ran a finger down Thea's thigh. 'Anyway, she'll have all her friends here tomorrow. They'll be so busy rehearsing she won't have a moment to dwell on it.'

'I suppose not.' Gathering her courage, Thea took a deep breath. 'Shaun, you know how Sam and Tina got married and Tom and Helen moved into their own place and...'

'Uh-huh...' Shaun's other hand joined his first on an exploration of his partner's legs.

Determined to finish what she was saying, Thea tried to ignore his delicate touch. 'Well, I've been thinking it would be nice, you know, to move on a bit, to take a step towards...'

Shaun cut off her sentence and disappeared under the bedcovers, muttering, 'Whatever you say, love.'

TWENTY-FIVE

TUESDAY DECEMBER 14TH

Rob hovered in the doorway to the kitchen observing Harriet as she sat at the table eating a biscuit. Not sure if he should go in or not, after a moment's hesitation, he gave a light cough. 'Did you sleep alright?'

'Oh, hello. Yes thanks,' Harriet lied. 'You? Bed comfy?'

'Very. I was out like a light.'

'That's good.' Harriet ran a finger around the rim of her coffee mug. 'Shaun helped you find your room okay?'

'Yes.'

'I know I'd already pointed it out where it was, but this house can be a bit of a maze. I walked the wrong way down the corridor on my first night and couldn't find my room. Most embarrassing.' Wondering why she'd said that, knowing it wasn't quite true, and that she'd simply walked past her bedroom door and then swung straight around again, Harriet asked, 'Are you coming into the kitchen, or did you have other plans for breakfast?'

'Other plans? With Shaun you mean? No.' Rob headed to

the kettle. 'I'm sorry if I got a bit carried away talking to him last night. I've been a fan for so long and... Anyway, sorry.'

'It's okay. He's a nice guy.'

'He is. So is Thea. A nice girl I mean – woman – oh, you know!' Rob hid his face as he poured himself some tea. 'I ought to apologise to her too.'

'Don't worry about it. I get the impression Thea is used to coming second to *Landscape Treasures*.'

'Even so.' Rob gestured to the teapot. 'You want one?'

'I'm fine thanks.' Harriet tapped her mug of coffee and vowed to put the previous evening behind them. 'I wasn't expecting to see you up so early.'

'Thought it would be good to do a quick rehearsal before the others get here.' Rob gestured to the window that gave a view of the frosted garden beyond. 'Would you like to come?'

'To the walled garden?'

'Yeah. It looked good yesterday, but I'd like to see it in proper daylight.'

'That would be great.' Harriet took a small sip of coffee. 'I've finished mending the costumes by the way. You should try yours on.'

'Thanks.' Rob looked towards the window. 'I wondered if, later, you'd like to...'

'Morning.' Mabel bustled in, her arms full of shopping bags, 'Oh... hello.'

Harriet, cursing her luck, and trying not to be annoyed that whatever Rob had been about to ask her had been interrupted, got up to help the old lady unload her groceries. 'Mabel, this is Rob. Rob, meet Mabel. She's responsible for the amazing food you'll be eating while you're here.'

Rob got to his feet and reached out a hand. 'A pleasure to meet you.'

'And you, young man.' Mabel looked disapprovingly at the solo mug of tea sat before him. 'No breakfast?'

'I don't generally bother.'

'Nonsense!' Mabel brushed her palms together. 'You have a very busy day ahead and it's freezing out there. I'll get the frying pan on.'

'Really, there's no need.'

'Vegetarian, yes?'

'Yes.'

'Egg on toast it is then.' Mabel spun round and flashed a knowing look in Harriet's direction. 'For two?'

'Well I...'

'Excellent. I'll cook them up, but then I'll have to leave you to your own devices. I promised Bert I'd take him shopping.'

Harriet, certain Mabel was lying about the shopping, realised her knowing smile was in danger of giving her feelings away.

'I meant to ask you, Harriet—' Mabel took two eggs from the basket on the dresser '—did the buttons you picked to close the gap on the tunic work?'

'They did, thanks, Mabel.'

'You fixed the gap with buttons?' Rob picked up his mug. 'I'd probably just have sewed the material back together.'

'It would have torn again.' Mabel spoke with authority as she moved around the kitchen. 'You have broad shoulders. The material needed a way to have more give to it.'

Finding herself distracted by talk of Rob's shoulders, Harriet got to her feet. 'I'll fetch the tunic now.'

By the time she'd negotiated all the stairs and had returned with the costume in hand, Mabel was serving up their fried eggs on toast. 'That looks and smells amazing. Thank you.'

'My pleasure. Now then—' the old lady waved a hand towards the costume '—don't get that covered in egg. I'll see you later.'

Rob murmured a goodbye as he ran his fingers over the buttons newly attached to his tunic. 'Are these military buttons?'

'Mabel thought so.' Harriet crunched her way through a piece of toast.

'Can't you just imagine all the things these buttons have seen – good and bad?'

'I can. I love buttons, they just speak to you don't they?'

'They really do.' Rob looked closely at the three buttons on his tunic's shoulder. 'I wonder if Shaun would know where they came from?'

Harriet suppressed a sigh. 'Unlikely. Bit too modern for him. But if you're really interested, then both Sam and Tom were in the forces. They might know.'

'Do you think they'd mind me asking them?'

'I am sure they wouldn't.' Harriet stared at her breakfast, wondering if she was going to have to compete with a set of buttons as well as Mill Grange for Rob's attention.

* * *

Harriet shivered. Rob's idea to make their rehearsal into a dress rehearsal was a good one, but that didn't stop it being only four degrees outside, and without her thermals or the pregnancy suit, which was travelling down later with Ali and Matt, the silk material did nothing to keep the cold weather out, even with her coat slipped over her shoulders.

Rob, who thankfully didn't need further adjustments to his tunic, had directed them both through Act One, before he abruptly burst out laughing.

'I don't think I've ever read my lines so quickly in my life.'

Harriet held the coat closer over her dress. 'Funny how the cold makes a person talk faster.'

Rob fastened his jacket. 'I hate to say this, as you look amazing in that dress, but I think you should do your coat up.'

As she pulled her zip up to her neck, Harriet asked, 'How are we ever going to act out here? I mean, the temperature will be lower in the evening.'

'Matt was making sure the patio heaters would be delivered here instead of to Lacock as I left yesterday. Otherwise, nervous energy will keep us warm!'

'I hope so.' Harriet rubbed her arms as she looked up at the sky. 'I hope it doesn't snow. Perhaps we should go inside and finish up the scene there.'

'Good idea.' Rob checked his watch. 'I reckon we have about an hour before we're invaded.'

A sense of resentment hit Harriet as she walked up to the house. She had waited for this moment since she was ten years old, her first professional performance, but now she'd have given anything for the play to be delayed for twenty-four hours, with no one else around, so she could have enough time with Rob.

Harriet was about to be brave and ask him what it was he'd been about to say in the kitchen before Mabel had insisted they had breakfast, when she saw Thea and Shaun in the distance. They had their arms full of boxes.

'On the other hand, perhaps we should abandon the idea of rehearsing until the others get here and help out with getting things ready?'

Rob glanced briefly in her direction. 'Perhaps we should.'

A childish sense of disappointment descended on Harriet. She forced herself to shrug it off and be positive. 'We should change. It wouldn't be good if the others arrived and found us doing chores in our costumes.'

'I doubt they'd mind, but it would be a bit of a pain if we got them dirty.'

'Or lost a button and broke a zip.' Talking fast so she didn't have the chance to change her mind, Harriet muttered, 'I was going to buy you a drink to say thank you for rescuing my dignity on stage. Somehow, I never quite got the chance.'

Rob stopped walking and reached out a hand to her, only to drop it self-consciously a fraction of a second before his fingers met hers. Staring up at the house instead, he said, 'I was going to ask you. To go for a drink, I mean.'

'You were?'

'Just to say thanks for fixing the tunic, nothing umm...' Rob gnawed his bottom lip as he hastily added, 'You know.'

'Right.' Harriet scuffed her boots against the frost-tipped grass. 'A mutual thank you drink.'

'Absolutely.' Rob watched his feet as his boots resumed their crunching across the crisp lawn. 'Maybe there'll be time after the play is over?'

'Maybe. Until then, let's go and see what needs doing inside.'

'And put jeans on.' Rob's expression relaxed. 'It's freezing.'

'Possibly two pairs each!'

* * *

'Built in 1856, Mill Grange was the home of Lord and Lady Upwich.'

'But now it's used as a retreat?' Matt held his hands up to the fire as Ali wandered around the drawing room, admiring the eclectic collection of paintings that hung at intervals on the walls.

'That's right.' Thea found herself slipping into tour guide mode without even thinking about it. 'We've not been open that long, but Sam and Tina have already done wonders, and there are more plans on the way.'

'From what I've seen so far, I can see the house is every bit as beautiful as Harriet said it was.' Ali sat on the sofa next to her fellow cast members, all of whom were tucking into generous slices of lemon cake. 'And that is one hell of a Christmas tree.'

Tina picked up her mug of coffee. 'I'm glad you think so. Sam and Shaun decorated it with the expert help of Dylan – that's Harriet's stepbrother.'

Harriet, her own cake long since consumed, checked her watch. Her father hadn't mentioned what time he'd be arriving in Upwich. While it had been easy to push his impending presence to the back of her mind while she was with Rob, now her cast mates were here, the imminence of the play's first night and his arrival hit her.

Wanting to keep her mind occupied, she got to her feet. 'Would you like me to show everyone to their rooms, Tina?'

'That would be fabulous, thank you, Harriet.' Tina smiled. 'Rob, I don't suppose you could help? Maybe you could do the back of the house and the spare attic rooms, while Harriet does the front of the house?'

As they got to their feet, Harriet caught Tina's eye. *Had there been a glimmer of mischief there? Was she, like Mabel earlier in the day, conspiring to make sure she and Rob did as much together as possible?*

Dismissing the thought – knowing that Tina was probably simply glad of the help – Harriet got up as Ali announced, 'I don't know about this lot, but I can't wait to see my room.'

Rob smiled. 'I'll bring the cake munchers up when they're finished.'

'Thanks.' Keeping her voice down, as they wandered along the red and black tiled corridor to the main staircase, Harriet said, 'Before you ask me, Ali, no, Rob hasn't invited me out. I did ask him – and he said yes – but made it very clear it would be a thank you drink between friends.'

Ali opened her mouth to reply, but Harriet was already shaking her head. 'Let's concentrate on the play shall we. Anything else is clearly just wishful thinking on my behalf.'

TWENTY-SIX

TUESDAY DECEMBER 14TH

Tom realised he shouldn't have been surprised, and yet he felt a wave of sadness for Dylan and Harriet.

It was pure fluke he'd spotted them. If Sam hadn't decided that it would be wise to have some additional teabags, milk and sugar on top of the supplies already ordered and asked him to pop to the supermarket, then Tom would not have been passing through Upwich at all.

Hand in hand, Nathan and Sue were wandering up the high street.

Ducking into the pub garden, Tom checked his phone to see if he'd missed a message from Sue saying she'd arrived. There was nothing.

After weaving through the pub garden, his hands full of shopping bags, Tom headed inside to see Moira.

The landlady was behind the bar, which, for once, was relatively quiet.

'Hi, Tom. How are you?'

'Good thanks.' He cleared his throat. 'I just wondered if

Dylan's mum had checked in yet? He's so excited about seeing her.'

'I bet he is.' Moira beamed. 'They got here about eleven.'

'Thanks, Moira.'

Back in the street there was no sign of them.

Eleven this morning! He checked his watch. It was two-thirty in the afternoon. *Why didn't Sue let me know?*

Even as he had the thought, another overtook him and, hooking a carrier bag up his arm, he pulled out his mobile.

'Sorry to disturb you, love.'

'I've been expecting you to call. Sue arrived?' Helen kept typing as she listened to Tom.

'She has, but I only know because I saw her and Nathan walking through the village. Moira tells me they arrived this morning.'

'Oh.' Helen didn't know what else to say.

'Quite.' Tom negotiated a group of walkers as he kept moving. 'It's not looking like they're going to try and see Dylan today. He'll be gutted. I thought I should warn you before school pick-up.'

'Thanks for the heads-up. I'll have extra cuddles on standby.'

* * *

Stood in the back of the large van, Shaun took hold of one side of a giant patio heater, while Sam took the other. With Tom guiding them along, ready to help steady the tall slim object should it wobble in transit, the three men moved gingerly across the lawn.

'Stop.' Tom signalled their arrival at the gate of the walled garden just as Matt and two cast members he'd introduced as

Neil and Dave arrived, puffing and panting, with a second heater. 'Best put them down a minute.'

Shaun straightened his back. 'I never dreamt these would be so heavy.'

Matt grinned. 'It's so they don't blow over. It's bad enough having to deal with the health and safety implications of the cables and generator to keep the worst of the cold off us and the stage lit. But if these weren't stable... Well, you can imagine the...'

'Health and safety forms.' Sam, Shaun and Tom spoke as one, making Matt laugh.

'Similar issues here then?'

Sam rolled his eyes. 'Like you wouldn't believe.'

Tom opened the gate. 'We'll have to go through one at a time, as the entrance is rather narrow.'

Matt stepped forward. 'Actually, would you mind if I had a quick look at the garden first. I know I've seen pictures, and Rob and Harriet have done a great job in working out the dimensions of stage area, but...'

Sam gestured for them to step through the gate. 'I'm so sorry. I should have shown you the garden straight away.'

Matt brushed the issue away. 'We had to get these heaters off the van, so the driver could crack on with his rounds. Made sense to bring them this far.'

Tom nodded to the heaters. 'I'll stay here and keep an eye on these while you guys look round.'

'They should be okay on their own to be honest. As I said, the whole point is that they're so heavy, they won't fall over.' Matt smiled. 'Although your help would be appreciated when we move them again.'

'In that case, I'll nip to the shed and get the stuff to clean out the chickens. That way I'll be on hand for when you need me. Got to have Gertrude looking her best while you rehearse.'

'Gertrude?' Matt looked at Dave and Neil, who both shrugged.

Sam laughed. 'Let me introduce you to your rehearsal audience.'

* * *

Harriet watched as Rob and Matt took up their positions on the stage. Although the scenery hadn't yet been put in place, the heaters made a massive difference to the feel of the space. Not only was the heat they delivered surprisingly strong, they also emitted an orange glow which, combined with the silver frost that clung stubbornly to the greenhouse behind them, gave the air an almost summer-like haze.

She had deliberately left her mobile in the house. Her father was in the village, and had been since eleven o'clock according to Tom, and yet he hadn't called her or come to say hello. If she had her phone with her, she knew she'd be checking it every few minutes for a message from him when she should be concentrating on the rehearsal. The first performance was only four days away.

Three and a half days away.

* * *

Helen sucked the lemon sherbet sweet she'd popped into her mouth as she walked through the park towards Dylan's school. She couldn't remember the last time she'd bought a packet of sweets for herself, but today the purchase had felt vital.

Either I'm missing my regular helpings of Tina's lemon cake, or the emotional outpourings are being complemented by a sugar craving.

Remembering the number of sugar cubes she'd mainlined at Sybil's, Helen vowed to cut back on how much sugar she had in her coffee as she strode through the school gates. Three steps later she stopped dead.

Sue and Nathan were stood outside Dylan's classroom in animated discussion with Carol Walters.

Not sure if she should join them or not, Helen checked her mobile to see if Tom had sent a message saying that there'd been a change of plan concerning the collection of his son. There was nothing. She was about to call Tom, when the teaching assistant spotted her.

'Miss Rogers, excellent timing.' Carol gave her a smile that clearly held a warning in it.

'Sue.' Helen forced herself to nod at Nathan. 'Tom didn't say you'd arranged to meet Dylan and me here.'

Sue's chin jutted out in a manner she'd often heard Tom describe as something that happened when his ex was in danger of not getting her own way. Not wanting to have a scene in the playground, Helen kept talking.

'How was the flight?'

Nathan answered, 'Long and dull.'

'I can imagine.' Helen sucked her sweet hard, aware it was making her speech slur slightly. 'Dylan will be pleased to see you. Would you like to come back to the house with us for a cuppa?'

'Not particularly. I'd like to see my son, but apparently—' Sue scowled at Carol '—I can't pick him up because I didn't ring ahead. I'm his mother for God's sake!'

Conscious of the eyes of the other waiting parents, Carol

said, 'Shall we go inside and talk this over? I'm sure Dylan wouldn't like to see you arguing.'

'I'm not arguing.' Sue spoke very slowly. 'I'm telling you I have come to collect my son and take him out for dinner.'

'As I said,' Helen looked from Sue to Nathan and back again, 'Tom didn't tell me that was happening.'

'I tried to call him, but got no answer.'

'He doesn't always have a signal at Mill Grange.' Helen mentally gritted her teeth as she turned to Miss Walters. 'Thank you. I think some privacy to sort this out would be an excellent idea. I don't want Dylan upset.'

'My son's happiness is not down to you, it's...'

'Enough.' Carol spoke using a tone Helen had heard her use during nativity rehearsals when the children got too boisterous. 'If you'd all come this way please.'

Moments later, they were in the reception.

'Now then—' Carol sounded increasingly businesslike '—what you need to remember, Miss Ward, is that the school has a legal responsibility to Dylan. I am not saying you are not entitled to see Dylan. Far from it. He is very excited about seeing you. He's been telling his friends how you'd be jumping off the plane and dashing straight to see him.'

Helen glanced at Sue, and was pleased to see she looked embarrassed. No one spoke, so Carol added, 'Although you'd be very welcome to take Dylan if we'd had permission from his legal guardian, we can't just let him go with you – especially as it's clear that Miss Rogers was not expecting you.'

'But that's ridiculous; you know I'm his mum! I came here every day for months.'

Nathan, giving off an air of a man who was bored with the situation, broke his silence. 'Sue, they are not saying you aren't the boy's mother; they are complying with the law. A legal situation you agreed to before we left. The answer is obvious. Either Miss Rogers here—' he peered at Helen over his glasses as if she was an unavoidable problem '—or the school, call Tom and ask for his permission to take his son from the school grounds.'

Helen pressed a button on her phone. 'I'll call him. I am sure Tom will be fine with you taking Dylan out for dinner because your son has been so excited about seeing you.'

Not waiting to hear Sue respond, Helen dipped her head to Carol. 'Could someone tell Dylan there's been a delay and we'll be with him soon? I'd hate him to come out of the classroom and find no one waiting for him.'

'Of course.' Carol immediately headed to the reception desk to ask for a message to be taken to Mrs Harley's room. No one mentioned that it should have been Sue who had thought of that.

Five minutes after going outside to talk to Tom in private, Helen was back.

'Tom is okay with you being the one to collect Dylan from school today. He is less than amused with how you've gone about it.'

'Right then, let's go and...' Sue looked smug as she readied herself to leave the reception area.

'However!' Helen added. 'Tom insists that Dylan is not told of the manner of your behaviour here today and that, if asked, we agree to say that you collecting him was a surprise that we knew about all along.'

'So you can get credit for it!' Sue scowled like a truculent teenager. 'I don't...'

Helen had had enough. 'What is the matter with you?! Not so I get credit – like that would matter – but so Dylan does not know that you caused a scene as soon as you arrived.'

'How dare...'

'And, if you agree to that, we *won't* tell him that you didn't come straight to see him. Or go to visit Harriet for that matter.' Helen fixed her gaze on Nathan. 'Even though you've been in Upwich since eleven this morning, and so, presumably, have been in England since yesterday, if not before.'

Nathan frowned at Sue. 'You didn't tell them about the work meeting in Bristol?'

'I forgot.'

'You've been in Bristol?' Helen looked at the couple before her in disbelief. 'Only an hour away?'

'I had a meeting.' Nathan wiggled his mobile phone at Helen as if offering to show her his schedule in case she wanted proof.

'And you, Sue, sleeping off jet lag or shopping?'

'Jet lag.' Sue sighed. 'This really is the earliest we could have got here.'

'Right.' Helen felt the remains of her sweet fizz down her throat. 'Let's go and see Dylan, shall we?'

'I've never spoken to anyone like that in my life!' Helen was still surprised at herself. 'Honestly, Thea, I could have strangled Sue.'

Thea tied a scarf around her neck. 'I'd have been pretty livid myself.'

'Normally I'd have just *thought* all the things I said, but today... I don't know, they came out of my mouth before I had the chance to stop them.'

'Maybe your maternal instincts have kicked in harder now you're expecting.'

'Sssh...' Helen looked around Mill Grange's hallway. 'You aren't supposed to know.'

'Sorry!' Thea whispered. 'How are you anyway?'

'Okay thanks.' Helen pulled the packet of lemon sherbets from her pocket and offered one to Thea. 'Serious sugar craving though.'

'Oh, I love these! I haven't had one in years.' Heading out into the garden with Helen on her heels Thea sucked on her sweet. 'Does Harriet know her dad's here?'

'I'm not sure. I got the impression that Nathan hadn't been in touch with her when I saw him at school. Tom might have told her.'

Thea shook her head. 'I don't understand that couple. If my kids were usually thousands of miles away... Still, we're all different aren't we?'

'You can say that again.' Helen tapped her belly, as if to assure her child that she'd always be there for him or her.

'How long is Dylan going to be with Sue?'

'I asked them to have him back at Mill Grange by seven. By the time we get home, it'll still be late for a school night, but I didn't think I could be too stingy with the time.'

Thea nodded. 'Well it's good to see you back over here anyway, whatever the reason.'

'Thanks.' Helen smiled. 'My concentration was shattered work wise, so I thought I'd head over and have dinner with Tom. We'll grab fish and chips or something. I'll leave my car here, and we can drive home with Dylan together.'

'Good plan, but I'm sure you could ask Tina if you could stay for dinner. Mabel's in the kitchen now.'

'I might do that – but suggest we all have fish and chips and leave the guests to Mabel's culinary prowess.'

Thea laughed. 'Just the thing to accompany lemon sherbets!'

Helen paused as they reached the gate to the walled garden. 'I think I'll check with Tina that it really is okay for me to work here sometimes.'

'I'd love it if you did.'

'Me too. As I'll have to collect my car tomorrow, I thought I'd start then. I have Roman Baths work to get on with, and the final bits and bobs of the book marketing to sort if time allows.'

'I'm so looking forward to reading your book!' Thea grinned. 'It's pre-ordered on my Kindle.'

'But you know everything that's in it already!'

'So? As soon as the paperback comes out, I'll want a signed copy.'

'Daft woman.' Helen smiled. 'Thanks though. Makes sense to be able to nip over and look at the excavation while I finish up the PR bit. If I'm lucky, all I'll need to do on the day is to be around to answer any social media questions that crop up about the fortlet.' Helen patted her stomach again. 'I should make the most of being able to visit you all before this little soul makes their presence felt.'

'Surely you'll come over even more then, so we can help out and make sure mini-Tom or Helen is correctly tutored in the ways of scone eating?'

Helen chuckled. 'Obviously, that is very important.'

'And I'll want lots of baby cuddles.' Thea pushed open the gate.

Lowering her voice, Helen said, 'Shaun said anything else about you two starting a family?'

'Only that he's appreciating practising, if you see what I mean.'

'Who doesn't? But there's practising and then there's coming off the Pill and practising.'

'Something I could never do without his agreement.'

'Of course not, but...' Helen took her friend's arm as they walked towards the rehearsal in action before them '...if it is what you both want, then don't leave it too long before you bring the subject up again. Trust me, being an older mum comes with a side order of extra worry.'

'I won't.' Thea looked across at her partner. He was stood with Sam and Bert, watching the actors working on the delivery of their parts. 'Shaun's so content with life. I suppose I'm afraid of messing that up.'

'You're happy together though aren't you?'

'Very much so, but every time I try and talk about us, he changes the subject or has to dash off somewhere.'

'Perhaps he needs a nudge. You know, to stop him getting *too* comfortable?'

Thea whispered out of the side of her mouth, 'You're about to say I should propose to him again, aren't you?'

'Yep.' Helen's nod was emphatic.

'Well right now, I'd be proposing to the wrong person because, if I'm not much mistaken, he isn't himself.'

'I'm sorry?'

'He's being Polixenes. Look – he's even mouthing the lines silently to himself in time with Matt.'

'Surely he can't remember every word from when he was a student?'

Thea smiled. 'Actually, don't tell anyone, but he's been reading the script on the quiet. He doesn't realise I know.'

'Seriously?'

'Yup.' Thea took a step forward. 'Come on, let's go and see how the *real* actors are getting on.'

* * *

Huddled under several jumpers, an ancient overcoat and a tartan travel rug, Bert had to battle the urge to applaud as Harriet finished her first major scene.

He glanced up at Sam, and muttered, 'She's darn good isn't she?'

'Very good.' Sam rubbed his gloved hands together. 'I'm so glad we agreed to do this.'

'Me too, my boy.'

As the actors went into a discussion mid-stage, Bert spotted Thea and Helen and raised a hand in greeting. 'Get under here – these heater things are fantastic.'

'So they are.' Thea raised her hands up to the heat source. 'Blimey, I reckon you could fry an egg under here!'

'Very probably.' Bert chuckled, his eyes returning to the stage space before them. 'They're about to do some more.'

Thea reached Shaun, wrapping an arm around his waist. She whispered into his ear, 'Hello, Polixenes.'

Shaun frowned. 'What do you mean?'

'You've been mouthing the words along with Matt.'

'Oh, hell, have I?' Shaun grimaced. 'I hadn't realised.'

'Must be the years of practice with *Landscape Treasures*. You mouth your lines when you rehearse for them.'

'I suppose I do.'

'Don't worry. I don't think anyone else noticed.' Thea smiled. 'You're loving this aren't you?'

'I am. Takes me back to my wild youth I suppose.'

'Wild?'

'Okay, more occasionally eventful than wild.'

* * *

Matt clapped his hands to get the cast's attention. 'Okay, folks, that's enough for tonight. Great work all round.'

As everyone gathered around, he spoke to each performer in turn, pointing out improvements that could be made in movement, diction or line delivery.

Harriet's shoulders tensed as her turn for advice came. She wasn't sure why she was nervous. Matt was never unkind, and whatever he said was always helpful, but she could never shake the feeling she was being admonished for not being perfect in the first place.

'Harriet. A bit more angst in the courtroom scene, a touch more despair in your expression and you're there. Just imagine you'll never eat Tina's lemon cake again – that'll be putting despair on my face when we come to leave.'

'Mine too.' Harriet sagged with relief. 'Thanks, Matt.'

As the director moved on to Nigel, Harriet found herself face to face with Rob.

'You were great.'

'So were you. It was a good rehearsal.' Feeling her cheeks flush, Harriet looked away. 'Our practice audience seem to have enjoyed it anyway.'

'So they do.' Rob followed the direction of Harriet's gaze. 'Who's the chap in the chair?'

'That's Bert Hastings. I'll introduce you.'

'Mabel's husband?'

'The very same.'

* * *

'Harriet, lass.' Bert beamed. 'Whatever that Matt chap said to you at the end, take no notice, you're already brilliant.'

'See, I said you were good.' Rob held out a hand. 'Mr Hastings? I'm pleased to meet you.'

'Oh, Bert, please. And likewise. An excellent performance from you too. How you remember all those lines I'll never know! I have trouble remembering to get milk when I've gone to the shop specifically *for* milk.'

'Practice, that's all.' Rob slipped off the jacket he'd put over his shoulders. 'These heaters never cease to amaze me. It's tropical under here compared to the stage.'

'I'm as snug as a bug in a rug.' Bert patted the rug over his knees to prove his point.

'You having dinner with us, Bert?' Harriet gestured towards the house. 'Mabel's lasagne smelt delicious when I went into the kitchen earlier.'

'I don't doubt it.' Bert tapped the side of his nose. 'She cooks it very slowly in that Aga thing. It'll be the best lasagne you have ever tasted.'

Harriet held out a hand. 'Can we escort you to the kitchen then?'

'You certainly can.' Pushing off his travel rug, Bert held a hand each to Harriet and Rob, allowing them to lever him to his feet before grabbing his walking stick. 'Best foot forward, lass.' Bert concentrated on his footing as he asked Rob, 'Have you always wanted to act?'

'As long as I can remember.'

'Same as Harriet here then. And now young Dylan is treading the boards.'

Rob looked at Harriet. 'Your stepbrother?'

'He's in the school nativity. He's so excited, bless him.'

Bert added, 'The innkeeper no less. Mabel's made a great job of his costume.'

'As Harriet did with mine.' Rob patted the shoulder of his tunic. 'It had a rip in it that I was just going to sew together. Buttons make it look so much better. And them being military gives it a bit of a regal touch, don't you think?'

Bert glanced at Rob's shoulder. 'Very nice job, Harriet. They certainly...' The old man's footing faltered.

'Bert!' Harriet dived forward, catching a hand under the old man's elbow. 'You okay?'

'What? Yes, sorry. Caught my foot on the grass there.' Bert gestured to the ground. 'Stupid walking stick.'

Harriet's eyes met Rob's, who reflected concern back at her.

'Can we help, Bert?' Rob asked. 'Feel free to hold on to my arm again.'

'That's very kind, young man.' Bert stared at his feet. 'But you need your dinner. Perhaps you could fetch Sam for me, Harriet. He'll get me home.'

Harriet frowned. 'You not coming for some lasagne now then?'

'Not hungry lass. Thanks though. I'll wait by the chickens. Gertrude and I haven't chattered for ages.'

TWENTY-EIGHT

WEDNESDAY DECEMBER 15TH

Dylan hadn't stopped talking since he'd got up. The smart-watch Sue and Nathan had given him was strapped to his wrist.

Tom shared a tired look with Helen, before he sat next to his son. 'Dylan, what did we say to you last night about that watch?'

The six-year-old's head dropped and he mumbled, 'That I couldn't wear it to school.'

'Someone might steal it or you could lose it. You know you aren't allowed to wear jewellery, and watches are a bit like that. If you got it caught on something during PE, then you could hurt yourself or break it.'

Dylan wailed, 'But I want to show my friends.'

'I'm sure you do, but Mrs Harley would take it off you.'

Abruptly jumping to his feet, Dylan yelled as he ran from the room. 'You two are so mean! Mummy would let me!'

Tom made to get up, but Helen put out her hand to stop him. 'Give him two minutes first.'

'This is so like Sue.'

Not wanting to comment, Helen cleared the breakfast dishes from the table. 'Perhaps Dylan could invite some friends around after school if he wants to show it to them?'

'Can you really face a group of children here after school when you're trying to work?'

'It's what parents across the world have been doing for years.'

'I suppose...' Tom paused. 'Hang on, isn't it the final after-school rehearsal for Dylan today?'

'Oh hell. Yes it is. I forgot.' Helen closed her eyes. 'I don't think I can face that *and* having his friends over afterwards. They are always high as kites when they're done. And the book's out tomorrow – not to mention it'll be nativity day.'

'I know love, I know.' Tom picked up Dylan's lunchbox and slipped it into his school bag. 'Are you ready for a morning working at Mill Grange?'

Helen gestured to the laptop bag and pile of files in a carrier bag by the door. 'I was looking forward to being back in my office in the corner of the storeroom.'

'But now?'

'In all honesty, I just want to burst into tears and go back to bed.'

'Bloody Sue!' Tom cursed under his breath. 'She knows full well he is too young for a smartwatch.'

'I'm sure she just wanted to treat him.'

'Show off that she can afford treats like that now, more like.'

A heavy sigh escaped Helen's lips. 'Maybe, but that doesn't solve the problem of the little boy breaking his heart because we won't let him show his friends the gift he had from the mum he misses.'

Raking both his hands through his hair, Tom groaned as he headed for the stairs. 'I'll try and explain.'

'Good luck.'

* * *

Dylan was curled up on top of his pillow, clasping Harold the dinosaur as if his life depended on it. His face was streaked with tears.

'Cuddle?'

Crawling over to where his dad had sat, Dylan's eyes stayed on his wrist, where his new watch sat proudly, the time reflecting back at him with bold confidence.

'Do you understand why we said you can't wear the watch?'

Dylan clamped his lips together.

Tom stroked his son's hair. 'It's worth a lot of money. If it went missing, I couldn't afford to replace it. And worse, you'd have lost something precious – not because it's expensive, but because it was from Mum.'

'Suppose.'

'You know, your mum came all this way so she could see you in the nativity. She wouldn't want to see you sad.'

'But won't she be sad if she sees that I'm not wearing her present?'

'Is that why you were so keen to wear it today?'

'Yes.' Dylan wiped the back of his hand over his eyes. 'And I wanted to show my friends.'

'I doubt Mum meant for it to be worn at school. It's too special. As to your friends, why don't you ask a couple of them, to ask their parents, if they can come over for tea some-time in the Christmas holiday?'

'Can I really, Dad?' Dylan immediately bounced off the bed and undid his watch strap. 'Have friends here?'

'Yes. Of course.'

'Mum would never let me do that.'

'Really?'

'Helen wouldn't mind would she?'

'It was her idea.'

Dylan took off his watch and laid it on his desk. 'It's nearly time to go, Dad.'

'Come on then.' Relief flooded Tom as he got to his feet. 'Two friends. Once they've got the okay from their parents, we'll sort a date. Agreed?'

'Agreed.'

* * *

Bert ran a hand through the assortment of socks in the second drawer of his bedside cabinet. They weren't there. Nor were they in the drawer above or below.

He sat back on the bed and closed his eyes.

'I should have taken better care of them. I'm sorry, my friend.'

* * *

Harriet woke with a jolt. Her night had been full of dreams where she'd lost her voice, forgotten her lines, or both.

Taking a sip of the water from her bedside cabinet, Harriet gave herself a shake. 'They were just anxiety dreams. Perfectly normal as this is my first professional role.' She took a steadying breath. 'After that, all I have to do is to give another forty-nine professional performances and I can apply for an Equity card.'

It felt impossible.

Harriet thought back to when she'd first seen the advertisement for auditions for The Outdoor Players. She almost hadn't bothered looking at it properly – the idea of working in the open air, at the mercy of the British weather not being terribly appealing – but then she'd seen the magic words. "The Outdoor Players is an Actors' Equity Association theatre."

This meant any performance she did there counted towards her earning a licence to be an actor. Or "a proper actor" as her father would say.

Pulling a jumper over her pyjamas, Harriet headed to the bedroom window.

The garden twinkled in the early morning half light. The sky was a cloudless duck-egg blue, and the bare trees in the woods beyond looked as if someone had been busy spraying them with silver dust.

'It's a wonder anyone ever leaves here.' Harriet cuddled her arms around her chest. 'It's as if Titania will slide out silkily from between the trees at any moment, her fairy folk dancing around her.'

As she watched, Sam came into view, his arms around a sack of chicken feed. Moments later, Shaun and Thea were striding across the garden, each carrying a brush and a spade. Harriet was just wondering what they were up to, when she saw Rob running up behind them, a dustpan and brush in his hands and a grin on his face.

Without stopping to think, Harriet grabbed some clothes from her rucksack and raced to the bathroom. After dressing at high speed she brushed her teeth, and then, without stopping to wash, tugged on her coat and boots before hurtling down the old servants' staircase and out into the cold fresh air.

It was only once she was outside that Harriet stopped moving.

What are you doing? You weren't invited to do whatever they're doing.

She shrank back against the wall of the manor house, looking about furtively, hoping no one had seen her.

Only yesterday you'd decided to let this crush go. Now you're running downstairs before you've even had a shower!

Straightening her shoulders, Harriet headed back inside.

You are a grown woman. Stop behaving like a love-struck sixteen-year-old.

Creeping up the backstairs, listening to the sounds of breakfast being served and consumed in the kitchen, she gave herself a pep talk.

'You have a play to do, an Equity card to start working towards and your father to deal with. The very last thing you need is to be distracted by someone who only sees you as a friend. Get over it, get washed, get dressed properly and go and do your job.'

* * *

Thea helped Shaun roll back the tarpaulin that had been covering the Roman Fortlet for the past month. She glanced at Rob, noting his enthusiastic expression as Shaun chatted to him about their theories concerning the formation of the fortlet. The evening before, she'd had a conversation with a slightly tipsy Ali, who'd told her that Harriet had given up on the idea of Rob ever asking her out and had decided it was just a crush she'd get over.

Hearing footsteps behind her, Thea turned. Sure it would be Harriet, she was surprised to see Tom crossing the garden.

'Morning, Tom.' Thea smiled. 'Helen here?'

'Helping Mabel and Tina in the kitchen with the guests' breakfasts.'

Thea immediately passed her spade and brush to Tom. 'She shouldn't be doing that! Her book's out tomorrow. If she doesn't get on she'll be all of a flap tomorrow. I'll go if you don't mind taking over here.'

'Thanks, Thea.' Tom twisted slightly so Shaun and Rob couldn't hear him. 'Helen told me, you know. Can you – well, could you at least try – to stop her doing too much?'

'I'll give it a go. But you know Helen, she might be here to do her own job, but the chances of her not wanting to join in with the rest of us are slim.'

'Quite.'

'You okay, Tom?'

'Let's just say life will be calmer once Sue has gone home again.'

* * *

Mabel kicked her shoes off and placed her coat on the hook by the front door of her cottage. 'Bert, I've got sausage rolls from Sybil's for lunch.'

'That's nice.'

Expecting to see her husband sat on the sofa in the living room, she was surprised to see his favourite seat empty. 'Bert?'

'In the bedroom.'

'What on earth...?' Mabel looked at the bed. It was covered in a mass of clothing, which had been haphazardly emptied out of every drawer in the room. The whole place had a freshly burgled feel.

'Have you seen the buttons I kept in my sock drawer?'

'Buttons?' She stared around her in horror. 'You've ransacked our bedroom for buttons?'

Bert looked at his hands, his fingers pulling at each other. 'Yes, love. I have.'

Picking up on his solemn tone, Mabel checked her temper and perched next to him on the edge of the bed. 'What buttons?'

'I hadn't thought about them in years. Then I saw young Rob yesterday. His tunic had three buttons on the shoulder. They were just like the ones I used to wear – well, like thousands of us used to wear.'

Mabel nodded. 'I told Harriet they probably came from a military infantry uniform.'

'They were.' Bert laid a hand upon his wife's. 'Where did Harriet get the buttons from?'

'The sewing box at Mill Grange.'

'And how did they get in that box?'

'I suppose someone put them there.' Mabel's patience slipped. 'Bert, I have lots to do, and now we need to tidy this lot up. Honestly, what were you thinking?'

'I was thinking that my wife probably went through the drawers at some point, when she was having a clean-out, found three buttons and put them in the button box at Mill Grange. That they might be the buttons that I haven't been able to find here.'

Mabel opened her mouth to protest, but all that came out of her mouth was a puff of air.

'Did you, love?'

'Well, I... It was ages ago. I'd forgotten. I had that clear-out to find clothes for a jumble sale. Long before Thea came to Mill Grange.'

'And you found the buttons?'

'Yes.' The old lady looked troubled. 'I must have slipped them into my apron pocket, found them when I was restoring the house and dropped them into the old box.'

'Makes sense.' Bert patted his wife's hand as he stood up. 'That's that then.'

'Bert?'

'The buttons weren't mine. They were entrusted to me. I was supposed to give them to someone else when I got home, but I couldn't.'

Mabel tugged Bert's hand, pulling him back down. 'What are you talking about? And more to the point, why haven't you told me about this before?'

TWENTY-NINE

WEDNESDAY DECEMBER 15TH

Mabel hung up the phone and headed back to Bert.

'That was Sam. He was worried about you.'

'Hope you told him I'm as fit as a flea.'

'Something like that.' Mabel sighed. 'I'm sorry, love. I had no idea. Why didn't you tell me about the buttons?' She tucked the last pair of socks back into Bert's drawer. 'We talked so much about the war and what it did to you. We coped with everything together and...'

Seeing the flash of hurt on his wife's face, Bert took her hands in his. 'It wasn't that I didn't tell you. You know about everything that happened to me in Korea. I just didn't mention the buttons. They were...' Bert paused, trying to make sense of his thoughts. 'I suppose I originally kept them so I wouldn't forget how lucky I was to be alive, even though at first, I couldn't go inside or live normally or...'

'And now, all this time later, when you live as normal a life as anyone who has visited hell before their time?'

'Now, I wish I'd told you I wanted to keep them.'

* * *

'Are you sure you aren't needed in the walled garden?' Helen passed Rob the end of the tape measure as she walked backwards, double-checking the length of the fortlet's longest wall. They could hear the sound of recited Shakespearean prose drifting across the clear crisp air.

'Not until this afternoon. Matt's concentrating on the after-interval scenes set in Bohemia this morning. I'm not in those.'

'Is Harriet?'

'Not in the Bohemia bit, no. She's upstairs going through her part.'

'How's she getting on? Tom told me this is a big deal for Harriet, first step on the road to her Equity card and all that.'

'She's fabulous. Far better than she thinks she is.'

'Maybe you should tell her that.'

Rob flicked his eyes in Helen's direction, before refocusing on the wall he was crouched next to. 'Well, I...'

'She told us you were the best actor out of the entire cast here. That you were the one who'd be sure to go far.'

'Harriet said that?'

'She did.' Helen noted Rob's wistful expression as she jotted down measurements she didn't need to take. 'Thanks for this. It's so much easier to use a tape measure with a helper.'

'I'm in my element to be honest. When Harriet said she'd found us a house on Exmoor to perform from, I was sceptical. But this is heaven.'

'Shaun said you loved your history.'

'I really do.' Rob ran a slim finger over the stonework. 'I can't believe I'm getting to help on a dig, albeit only a tiny bit.'

'Maybe you should take Harriet out to say thank you?'

Rob's head snapped up. 'Do you think I... Oh, I see, yes, I suppose I ought to ask Matt about it. Perhaps we should arrange a group thank you.'

Helen bit her lips. *Thea's right, the boy will never ask her out without help.*

'That would be a lovely thing to do.' She nodded to the tape, indicating he could let go. 'Do you like scones?'

Surprised by the new direction of conversation, Rob said, 'Yes, well, apart from fruit ones, not keen on sultanas. Is Mabel planning on baking some?'

'Gosh no, Sybil would kill her.'

'Who's Sybil?' Rob's face creased in confusion.

Helen laughed. 'Forgive me. I forgot you have no idea who I'm talking about. Sybil owns the teashop in the village. Everyone local gets their scones from Sybil.'

'I see.'

'Thea and Tina have been meaning to take Harriet there ever since she arrived.'

'Oh I see!' Rob wound up the tape measure and passed it to Helen. 'And you think I should suggest to Matt that that's where we go to say thanks.'

Helen took a deep breath, 'No, Rob, I think it's where you should take Harriet right now so you can talk to each other away from the history of Mill Grange and the lure of the greasepaint.'

* * *

'You didn't!?'

'I did. I don't know what came over me. It's so clear he

likes her. His eyes sparkle every time Harriet's name is mentioned.'

'She's the same.' Tina continued to stack garden forks in the corner of the storeroom. 'Thea and I have been trying to manoeuvre things so they were alone in the same space. Full-frontal attack didn't occur to us.'

'Perhaps I shouldn't have interfered—' Helen pushed her fringe from her eyes '—but all I could think about was how long it took me to find Tom.'

'So, you gave them a push.'

'Exactly.' Helen slipped her tape measure into a drawer.

'How come you got talking to Rob anyway?'

'He was helping Thea and Shaun unroll the fortlet's tarpaulin earlier so that I could take a few photos for promoting the book.' Helen blushed. 'I pretended I needed to take some measurements, Rob volunteered to help – which I guessed he would.'

'And you waved your magic wand.' Tina laughed. 'Mabel will be so proud!'

'Only if it works. Your last attempt sounded as if it was going to work right until the last minute, and then didn't quite go to plan. All I did was plant the idea in his head. It doesn't mean Rob will do anything about it.'

'True.' Tina brushed her hands down her jeans. 'That's the stock checked ready for next session. Coffee?'

Helen pointed at her desk. 'I'd love to, but I've already used up lots of work time playing Cupid. I'd better be a good girl. I'll see you later, by which time, hopefully, I'll have got all I need to do before tomorrow's launch done!'

'What are you doing to celebrate that?'

'Nothing. Well, maybe a takeaway at home.'

'What?' Tina frowned. 'But it's a big deal, surely we should...'

Helen held up her hand. 'Thanks, but tomorrow is Dylan's day. I'll do the full celebration thing when the paperback comes out in the summer. All I want to do tomorrow is feel a sense of relief that it's out there! Then I can be ready for nativity action stations.'

* * *

As Tina waved a temporary goodbye, Helen's mobile burst into life. Frowning at the unrecognised number, assuming it was work-related, she answered, 'Helen Rogers, Roman Bath events, how can I help you?'

Her mouth went dry as she listened. Eventually she found herself saying, 'What time would that be...? Nine-thirty, yes... I'll be there. Thank you.'

The silence after she'd hung up the phone felt as if it could go on forever.

* * *

Harriet repeated the words in her head. After the fourth time she began to wonder if they were a figment of her overactive imagination.

Would you like to grab a scone at the tea rooms? Helen says we can't leave Upwich without trying one.

'It's *not* a date. It's just a friend asking me to go to a café. It's nothing more than that.' Changing her top for the third time, Harriet realised if she didn't leave soon, she'd be late. Opting for her favourite, slightly low-cut – but not too much

– black jumper, she ran a brush through her hair and headed out of the house.

It isn't a date, because if it was, Rob would have met me here and we'd go together.

Rolling her eyes at herself, Harriet slowed down. If she kept going at that speed, she'd be a sweaty mess before she got there.

This isn't the nineteenth century; blokes don't have to walk you to a date anymore.

Shaking her head at herself, Harriet's insides knotted. *Stop overthinking! This is just coffee and conversation. Anyway, I decided I wasn't going to date Rob...*

* * *

Rob was sat at the far side of the tea room. Harriet could see he was gnawing on his bottom lip.

He's nervous.

Oddly flattered by the fact, she wiped her palms down her jeans. 'Hi.'

Rob instantly stood up, and then, as if not sure why he'd done so, sat down again. 'I have to say, Helen was right, we do need to try these scones. Look.' He tilted his head to the nearest table, where a pile of steaming hot cherry scones sat, their scent as beguiling as their appearance.

'Wow!' Harriet's mouth watered. 'I love cherry scones. Mind you—' she sat down and eagerly read the menu '—Thea said life was too short to go without the cheese ones.'

'Shall we have one of each, each?'

'Perfect.' Amazed at the ice-breaking ability of scone flavour discussions, Harriet asked, 'Coffee, tea or something else?'

'Tea for me.' Rob traced a finger down the menu. 'But that choice brings with it another big decision.'

'It does?'

'Have you seen the list of tea flavours available?' He tapped the back page of the menu. 'I could be here all day!'

'Good Lord.' Harriet scanned the twenty options on offer. 'Think I might opt out of such a difficult decision and have a latte.'

'Very wise.' Rob closed his eyes and put his finger on the menu, before opening them again. 'I'm having ginger and honey tea apparently.'

Harriet couldn't help but laugh. 'A very scientific method of selection.'

'The close your eyes and point technique has been working for me for years.'

'I'll have to tell Dylan about that. He spends ages trying to make his mind up in here, although he always has the same thing in the end.'

'Which is?'

'Orange juice and a cheese scone.'

'Sensible lad.' Rob laid down his menu. 'I'm glad Helen suggested this.'

'Me too.' Harriet put her menu next to Rob's, immediately missing its presence as a face-screen, and felt the danger of an awkward silence ahead.

Speak. Say anything!

She was relieved when a waitress arrived at their side to take their order. As soon as she was gone, Rob asked, 'Was Bert okay last night? Stumbling seemed to shake his confidence.'

'Sam said he was fine. He was quite ill earlier in the year. Pneumonia. He sometimes needs a bit of peace and quiet. Apparently, it's left him less steady on his legs than he was.'

'Poor guy.'

'Dylan adores him. Bert's like a grandad to him, and Mabel's like a grandma for that matter.'

'Lucky kid.' Rob smiled. 'My grandparents are amazing. They helped bring me up.'

Harriet was glad when the waitress picked that moment to deliver their order, saving her having to tell him she'd lost both sets of her grandparents before she was born.

Taking in a mutual inhalation of sconey aroma, they burst out laughing.

'I think we can agree that they smell amazing.' Harriet eagerly reached for the bowl of butter.

Rob picked up his knife and deftly sliced a cheese scone in half. A puff of hot air rose from their centre. 'I can already feel a return visit coming on.'

'Too right.' Harriet took a far less dainty mouthful than she'd normally contemplate, immediately mumbling, 'Oh boy, that's good.'

Rob's eyes glinted in a way that made Harriet both self-conscious and hopeful. Knowing there was a very real chance of them spending their whole morning off discussing scones, Harriet asked, 'What was it that made you pick acting over a history degree? You clearly adore archaeology.'

Rob chewed a little slower. 'I meant to apologise properly for that.'

'For what?' Harriet twirled a strand of hair between her fingers as she looked at him.

'For talking to Shaun so much when we went to the pub. I sort of hoped it'd just be you and me, but...'

'But Shaun is your hero.' Harriet wrapped her hands

around her latte glass. 'It's okay. Thanks though, you know, for saying that it would have been nice if it was just us.'

Harriet's face went pink as Rob's eyes met hers.

'I've almost asked you to come for a drink before. Somehow something always happens and...' Rob broke off, his eyes moving at speed from Harriet's smiling face to a space just above her right shoulder.

'You okay, Rob?'

A hand came to Harriet's shoulder from behind, making her jump and twist her head round at speed.

'Hello, Harriet.'

'Dad!'

Her father raised his eyebrows. 'Surely it isn't that much of a surprise to see us.' He waved a hand towards the door where Sue was waiting. 'We were waiting for a table to become free when I spotted you.'

'Oh.' Harriet didn't know what else to say as she looked from her father to Rob and then back again.

'I'm assuming you don't mind us joining you. It's a table for four after all and we *have* come all this way to see you. No one seems in a hurry to move out of here, although most people have *clearly* finished their food.'

Harriet winced as several customers stared at her father, who wasn't troubling to keep his voice down.

'Actually, Dad, we were...'

Nathan took no notice as he called across the café, 'We can sit here, Sue.'

Sitting down, Nathan stared at his daughter expectantly. 'Aren't you going to introduce me?'

'Sorry.' Harriet flashed Rob an apologetic look. 'Dad, this is Rob. Rob, this is my father, Nathan Bradshaw. And this—'

she nodded to Sue as she joined them '—is Dylan's mum, and Dad's fiancée, Sue.'

Rob stretched out his hand. 'I'm pleased to meet you, sir, Sue.'

'Sir?' Sue's eyebrows rose. 'He must be after you, Harriet.'

Harriet wasn't brave enough to look at Rob to see his reaction to the careless remark, but guessed he'd be gnawing his lip. Scrunching her napkin in her fingers, she mumbled, 'I heard you arrived early yesterday. You took Dylan to the pub for dinner.'

The words: 'But you didn't take me, invite me, or even tell me you were here,' remained unspoken.

As the tension around the table thickened, Rob pointed to his teapot. 'Would you like some tea? It's ginger and honey, but there's plenty if...'

'God good no.' Sue pulled a face.

Harriet drew in a sharp breath. 'Thank you for offering though, Rob.'

He gave her a sympathetic dip of his head as Nathan fixed his grey eyes on the actor. 'Would you mind giving me some time with my daughter?'

THIRTY

THURSDAY DECEMBER 16TH

'What time is it now?'

Helen checked her watch. It was only two minutes since Tom had last asked the same question.

'Nine twenty-one.' She peered around, frantically trying to spot a parking space. 'Why don't you drop me off and park?'

'You are *not* going in there on your own.' Tom took a steadying breath. 'I didn't mean to snap. I'm nervous. Sorry.'

'Me too. And believe me, I don't want to go on my own, but the appointment is in eight minutes.'

Slowing the car, Tom pulled into the drop-off point by the maternity outpatients department. 'I hate it when you're right.'

'I know.' Helen squeezed his thigh. 'Park and come and find me. They're probably running late anyway.'

'But if they aren't, then...'

'I will tell the receptionist I'd like you to join me when you arrive. But first I must try and ring my publisher. They're expecting a lot from me today, and I can't deliver.'

'But surely you can do some work from your phone while we're waiting?' Tom sounded increasingly flustered as Helen got out of the car.

'You can't always use mobiles inside the hospital.'

'Bugger.'

'Quite.'

* * *

Harriet passed Ali her apron.

'You calmed down yet?'

'No.' Picking up her pregnancy suit, Harriet brushed off some fluff that had stuck to the bump. 'I doubt Rob will ever talk to me again.'

'It was hardly your fault.'

'They were so rude. Rob offered to share his tea. From the way they reacted, you'd have thought he was proposing they shared it from the same cup.' Harriet sighed. 'I didn't stick up for him or myself.'

'From how you tell it, Rob scuttled off pretty damn smartish. Did you have a chance to defend him?'

'Not really, although I still could have done once he'd gone. I'm ashamed to say I didn't.'

'Presumably your father had moved the conversation on by then?'

Harriet's voice was small. 'I don't blame Rob one bit for dashing out.' Smoothing the silk dress over the table, making sure the zip was holding, she remembered how Rob had admired her in it. 'You wait until you meet my father. You won't want to stay around him either.'

'He can't be that bad.' Ali's tone was soothing.

Harriet picked at the sleeve of her jumper. 'I found out

why I wasn't invited to the pub with Dylan. Apparently, Sue wanted her son to feel special. The pub trip was a treat because she'd missed him so much.'

'Oh.'

'Yeah. And I understand that, but it would have been nice to have been told I was missed too.' Harriet pulled a face. 'I honestly don't think Dad has any idea how hurtful he can be. He's just unable to see beyond himself. Always been the same.'

'Lack of empathy?'

'More like, none whatsoever.' Harriet rubbed away the tears that threatened to coat her eyes.

'Oh, hon.' Ali put her arm around her friend's shoulders.

'Dad told me how wonderful their new life was and Sue rattled on about the wedding and how much they are looking forward to their first Christmas on the beach.'

'They're sticking to the idea of Christmas without their children then?'

'Yep.'

'Ouch.'

Harriet sniffed. 'After listening for a well-mannered amount of time, during which no questions about my life were asked, I said I was needed at the rehearsals, and left.'

'I think you're marvellous for staying that long. I think I'd have said something very short and to the point and stormed out.'

'If I'd done that it would have been added to the very long list of things I'm ungrateful for.'

'I'm sorry?'

'I'm ungrateful that Dad's paying for my education, even when I'm not doing a "proper subject". I'm ungrateful for being looked after by him alone after Mum was gone, rather than packing me off to a boarding school, and so the list goes on.'

'I honestly don't know what to say.'

'No need to say anything. Thanks for letting me vent.'

'If you need to vent more, just shout.' Ali took Hermione's costume from Harriet and hung it with the rest. 'Let's go and see how the boys are getting on in the garden.'

'Good idea. I prefer the land of make-believe. It's much nicer there.'

* * *

'Did you manage to get through to your publisher?' Tom flopped onto a chair, catching his breath after running from the car park.

'Yes.'

'How did they take it?'

'Stoically. They were slightly appeased by the fact I'd pre-scheduled so many Facebook and Twitter posts promoting today's launch.' Helen threw up her hands. 'All the work that's gone into today and now I can't even share the news.'

'Well, you can't, but the others can.'

'What do you mean?'

'I've got Thea on share social media duty.'

Helen's face lit up. 'Really?'

'Really. She was more than happy to help when I told her why.'

Helen's stomach muscles unclenched a fraction. 'I should have asked her. I didn't even think! I should have...'

'You have a hell of a lot on your mind. At least the Baths

agreed to you having an official day off and, on top of that, we've made Sue's day.'

'How?'

'She was thrilled when I asked her to be at school at closing time to make sure Dylan gets his costume on in case you're late.'

'Where did you say we were going?' Helen glanced at the clock on the wall; the hands were moving extremely slowly.

'Christmas shopping.' Tom held Helen's hand. 'A bit lame, but it was all I could think of.'

'I got the impression Sue wasn't too chuffed that Mabel had made Dylan's costume.'

Tom agreed, 'I've no idea why; she can't sew to save her life.'

'We have something in common then!' Helen laid a hand on her stomach. 'I was so relieved when Mabel stepped in.'

'That's the only thing you have in common. Thank God!'

Helen closed her eyes. 'I wish this wasn't happening today.'

Tom swallowed. 'I didn't know about this sort of thing.'

'Nor me.' Helen looked at the leaflet that lay on the table before them. It had been given to them by the receptionist as they'd arrived. 'Obviously, I knew that such tests happened, and that they were for older mums but...'

'Elderly primigravida sounds so damn rude. The connotations...'

'Tom.' Helen took a sip from her water. 'I'm scared.'

'Me too, and I'm sorry it's happened on book and nativity day, but best we find out, yes?'

'Yes, but I just can't help wishing we didn't have to. Why couldn't they have done this scan with the last one? We wouldn't have known to be worried and it would all be over already.'

'I know.' Tom got up. 'I'd better get you some more water to drink.'

Helen groaned. 'I wish they'd hurry up.'

* * *

Standing by the chicken coop, Harriet sought out Rob, but as soon as he saw her, she pulled her gaze away. *What will I say to him?*

He was helping Shaun move a scene backdrop across the garden while Matt and the cast involved in the final scenes huddled under one of the heaters.

Harriet rested her elbows on the top of the fence that ran around the coop. 'I'm not sure which one of you is Gertrude, but Tina told me you were the one to bring my troubles to.'

She didn't have time to ask their opinion, however, before she heard footsteps coming up behind her.

'Are you alright?' Rob's expression was creased with concern. 'I'm so cross with myself for not staying yesterday Then I couldn't find you later.'

'You had no choice, once my father had spoken, well—' Harriet stuttered in surprise. 'I got excused from rehearsals and had an early night.'

Rob gripped the top of the fence. Harriet was touched to see his knuckles clenching in anger on her behalf. 'I don't like how your father treats you, and I don't like that I abandoned you. It was our first... We were...'

Harriet found her smile returning. 'Our first?'

Rob focused on the nearest chicken. 'Date.' He risked

looking at her out of the corner of his eye. 'It was a date, wasn't it?'

'I hoped it was, but... I wasn't sure if it was a friend thing or a date thing.'

Rob sucked in his bottom lip. 'I'm not very good at all that. I go all clumsy and shy and...' Letting go of the fence he faced Harriet. 'Would you like to come out for a drink tonight? A proper one, at the pub?'

'I'd love to.' Harriet grinned, but then it faded. 'I'm sorry about my father. I should never have let him dismiss you like that.'

'Could you have stopped him?'

'Well, no.'

'Then don't worry about it.' Rob looked back at the chickens. 'Seven o'clock in the Stag and Hound, or would you rather go somewhere where your father won't show up?'

'He and Sue are eating in Tiverton after the nativity, so we'll be safe enough.'

'Is it a date then?'

'It is.'

'Good.' Suddenly self-conscious, Rob gestured towards the cast. 'Come on. Work time.'

* * *

Helen paced the room. She'd long since given up on holding her bladder, been to the bathroom, and was now refilling herself with water while she waited for Tom to get back from updating their car park ticket.

The receptionist had already been out to apologise three times for the delay. There had been an emergency, and all hands were needed elsewhere.

What if that happens to me? What if I go into labour and become an emergency?

The hands of the clock on the wall ticked around to half past eleven. Her stomach growled with hunger. *Come on! Dylan's nativity is this afternoon!*

Everyone else in the waiting room had already been seen, emergency or no emergency.

I'll stay until twelve-thirty then I'm leaving. I am not missing Dylan's big moment.

THIRTY-ONE

THURSDAY DECEMBER 16TH

Arjun apologised for the delay for the tenth time as he led Helen and Tom into the same scanning room they'd visited only days before as the clock's hands reached twelve o'clock.

Tom, tight-lipped with nerves, mumbled, 'It's okay. But we don't have much time. My son's nativity play is at four and it's a two-hour drive.'

'We'll be as quick as we can, I promise.'

Helen fidgeted with the strap of her bag. 'Can you tell us what's going to happen?'

'Didn't they explain during the phone call?'

'They did, but... I heard the phrase "geriatric mother" and after that, well... I got a bit scared. It didn't really go in.'

The student midwife sympathised. 'I'm not at all surprised. I'm so sorry. That phrase is hardly ever used these days, and with good reason. It's so offensive.'

'Could you explain things?' Tom took Helen's coat as they crossed the room. 'Maybe without making Helen sound ninety.'

Arjun patted the examination bed, indicating that Helen

should climb on. 'All pregnant women over forty are offered a nuchal translucency scan as part of their antenatal care. It's a routine procedure, which needs to be done between ten weeks and thirteen weeks. Normally we combine it with your twelve-week scan, but as you came last time to simply confirm how advanced your pregnancy was, and it was believed you were only eight weeks gone, we hadn't scheduled enough time for that. We've rushed you in today, as you're already at the thirteen-week mark.'

The student midwife looked uncomfortable. 'Plus, I owe you an apology. I should have given you the leaflets with all the information on this last time, and I forgot. I'm terribly sorry.'

'It's okay.' Helen immediately felt sorry for Arjun. 'I hope you didn't get too much of a hard time for that.'

'A bit of one – but I deserved it.' He pulled a tray closer. 'If you are okay, I'll take your blood now. Dr Evan will be with us shortly to do the scan.'

'A doctor, not a midwife or sonographer?' Fear stirred in Helen's gut.

'Dr Evan is a specialist in such scans.'

'Blood test *and* a scan?' Tom asked.

'The nuchal check is a two-part process. The blood test looks at the levels of two hormones within Helen that are important to watch in pregnancy-associated plasma. Protein– A and free beta–hCG.'

'Never heard of them.' Tom frowned.

'No reason why you would have.' Arjun tried to sound encouraging. 'By monitoring these levels we can discover if there is a risk of chromosomal abnormalities.'

Helen gulped. 'Go on then, do the blood test while you tell us about what'll happen during the scan.'

Arjun numbed a patch of skin inside of Helen's arm below the elbow. 'That's it, just breathe naturally. Here we go.'

Helen closed her eyes as the needle slipped into her arm with a sharp prick and she listened to Arjun. His words sounded frightening and unreal.

'During the scan, Dr Evan will measure the amount of fluid at the base of your baby's neck.'

Tom kept his eyes on Helen's face so he didn't have to see the needle in her arm. 'Will we be able to see our baby like last time?'

'You will. The scan is just the same.' Arjun withdrew the needle. 'There you go. All done.'

'Thanks.' Helen hardly dare ask her next question. 'What happens if there's too much fluid?'

'All babies have fluid at the base of the neck, but babies with Down's syndrome have an increased amount.' Arjun wrote Helen's name on the vial as he added, 'Dr Evan will also check to see whether a nasal bone is visible on the scan.'

'Why?'

'Because foetuses with Down's syndrome often don't have a visible nasal bone at this stage of development, whereas babies without Down's usually do.'

'And if the fluid is okay and the nasal bone is there, then everything will be okay?' The presence of Helen's full bladder began to be echoed by the thud of a tension headache.

'We can never be one hundred per cent sure, but the chances are good if the tests are negative.'

'Right.' Helen felt distant, as if nothing in the room was connected to her as Arjun excused himself to fetch the doctor.

The second they were alone, Tom leant forward and kissed her forehead. 'It's going to be fine.'

'I should have asked more questions on the phone.' Helen looked up, her face pale. 'I should have known. I *did* know. Everyone knows there's a chance of Down's if you have a baby after forty, but I didn't...'

'Hang on, love.' Tom teased a ringlet of hair away from her eyes. 'Your reaction is totally natural. No one wants to think their child could have problems to overcome. It'll be alright.'

'But we can't *know* that.' Helen groaned. 'This is unreal. I'm longing to see our baby again, but I'm not sure I can bear to look at the screen.'

'I know what you mean. Yet—' Tom's heart constricted as he heard two sets of footsteps approaching the room '—we will look, because it's our child.'

'A child we'll love whatever? Whether it has Down's or anything else?'

'One hundred per cent.'

* * *

Mabel and Bert waved Sam goodbye as he dropped them off outside West Exe Primary School.

'It isn't like Tom or Helen to be late for anything.' Mabel scanned the queue of parents getting ready to see the nativity. 'I'm not sure I believe they were held up shopping.'

'Either way, lass, Sam has got us here, and Tom will take us home again.'

'Umm.' Mabel pointed to the school building. 'I suppose we ought to look for Sue.'

'Less of the sour face.' Bert linked his arm through his wife's. 'Whether we like her or not, she's Dylan's mum.'

'Some mum!' Mabel grunted. 'I hope Dylan's alright.'

'He'll be in his element.'

'But he was expecting Helen to be with him.' Mabel searched the throng of parents as they headed towards the door. 'I can't see any sign of any of them.'

'We have our tickets – perhaps we should go in?' Bert lifted his stick in the direction of the open door. 'I suspect Nathan and Sue are already inside.'

'Not Nathan. There's only four tickets, remember.' Mabel's lips pursed a second time as she thought about Nathan. 'Poor Harriet. She's such a nice girl. Sybil was telling me that her father and Sue launched themselves on her while she was with that nice Rob.'

Bert said nothing on the matter as he patted his wife's arm. 'Let's go inside; it's getting cold.'

* * *

'Dylan.' Helen wove her way through the children. They were all either in hyper drive or the grip of silent nerves. 'I'm so sorry I'm late.'

Holding on to Helen, Dylan looked anxious. 'Is everyone else here? Dad and Mabel and Bert?'

Crossing her fingers, hoping she was telling the truth, Helen said, 'They are. Now then, let's have a look at you.' She held the little boy out at arm's length. 'You are without doubt, the most impressive innkeeper of all time.'

Dylan giggled before his face became more serious. 'Mum was here. She sort of helped then she had to go and take a seat.'

'I'm glad you weren't on your own.'

As he ran a hand through his hair in a way that reminded her of Tom, Dylan whispered, 'I will remember my lines won't I?'

'Of course you will. And if you have a forgetful moment, look for Bert, he'll be saying them along with you.'

Helen caught Miss Walters' eye. 'I need to help your friends now, but I'll be watching. Good luck, Dylan, and most of all, have fun!'

* * *

There was hardly a dry eye in the house as the last notes of "Silent Night" echoed around the school hall. From her position at the side of the stage, her arms full of goodie bags, Helen sniffed, wishing she had a hand free to fish out a tissue and blow her nose. Dylan, his round face shiny under the lights, his smile expansive, looked happier than she'd ever seen him.

He's so like Bert – even though that's impossible. Helen glanced down at her belly. *Please be okay in there. Please.*

As Mrs Harley walked into the middle of the stage, encouraging the parents and guests to give the children one more, well-earned round of applause, Helen's eyes found Tom's. He was looking right at her, his expression full of love.

I'm so lucky. Whatever happens, we'll be okay.

'Helen?'

Helen was suddenly aware of a hand on her shoulder.

'You okay? You're awfully pale,' Carol whispered. Her arms similarly laden with goodie bags, she tilted her head to one side to indicate they should step back from the stage.

'Tired. I'm so sorry I was late.'

Carol smiled. 'Does Dylan know yet?'

'Know?'

Carol dipped her head towards Helen's stomach. 'Obviously, I'll keep my lips sealed if not.'

Helen's eyebrows rose. 'No one but my best friend and Tom know. How did…?'

'Primary school working. Lots of our mums become mums again while their offspring are here. We get to recognise the signs.'

Not sure what to say, Helen heard a fresh crescendo of applause cross the stage.

'Brace yourself. They'll be back here any second.'

Seconds later, Helen was handing each performer a bag of treats, as twenty happy children fidgeted, skipped or meandered offstage.

* * *

'A triumph!' Bert engulfed Dylan in a bear hug as he bowled up to the group of adults waiting for him outside the hall.

'I remembered all my words.'

'You absolutely did.' Bert beamed. 'Wasn't he brilliant, Mabel?'

'You'll be giving Harriet a run for her money.'

Tom picked his son up. 'It was wonderful. Did you enjoy it?'

'Yeah!' Dylan held up his bag of goodies. 'We got these. Sweets, crayons, notebook and I got a ruler with knights and dragons on it.'

'A perfect ruler then. Is Helen nearly done in there?'

'Yeah.' Dylan looked round. 'Where's Mum?'

'She's nipped to the loo.' Tom put Dylan down. 'Ah, there she is.'

Sue was threading her way towards them, looking like a fish out of water. Dylan dashed towards her.

'Did you like it, Mum? Did you?'

'You were very good.' Sue wiped her hands down her skirt. 'Unlike those toilets. How on earth is anyone supposed to sit on those seats?'

Tom shot her a stern look. 'They're for children, Sue.'

'Ummm.' Sue avoided Mabel's disapproving gaze as she bent to Dylan. 'I have to go now, but I'll see you at Harriet's play on Saturday, okay?'

'Okay, Mum.' Dylan held on to her waist until Sue had to peel him away.

Holding out her hand to the little boy, Mabel said, 'Come on, let's get some chips.'

Dylan looked back at Sue. 'You could come, Mum. And Nathan too. Couldn't they, Dad?'

'Certainly they could.'

'Ah, oh well, umm... Nathan's booked us a table at the Indian.'

Tom's eyes narrowed. 'Just for the *two* of you?'

He didn't need to say, *And what about your son?* The look of guilt on Sue's face told him all he needed to know.

'You'd best be off then.'

As his mum dashed away, Dylan clutched his reward bag to his chest and whispered to Mabel, 'I think Helen must have picked the ruler I got especially for me.'

Harriet sipped mulled wine as she stared into the fire. The pub heaved with life. She could hear Moira and her staff chatting with their customers as they greeted a steady stream of people ordering food and drink.

Rob had texted her to warn her he'd be a few minutes late. He'd been held up talking to Matt about a few last-minute scene direction changes, and told her she should go inside and keep warm.

Spiced liquid slipped down Harriet's throat, soothing her insides and making her smile widen. *I'll be tipsy before he arrives if I drink this too fast.*

Sitting back on the cushion-padded settle by the fire, Harriet ran through her lines in her head.

* * *

Tom pulled the car into the drive of Bert and Mabel's cottage to the sound of Bert and Dylan snoring.

Mabel chuckled. 'Will you look at the pair of them?'

Helen laughed as a yawn escaped her. 'Whatever they have is catching.'

'I'm a bit tired myself.' Mabel undid her seatbelt.

'It was the fish and chips that did it.' Helen stifled another yawn. 'They were lovely. The ultimate comfort food.'

Tom helped Mabel out of the car.

'Thanks for the lift home.'

Tom smiled. 'I'm sorry we couldn't collect you as originally planned.'

Mabel looked straight at him. 'I'm sure you had a *very* good reason.'

Tom half expected her to wink, and saw in that moment that Mabel suspected she knew why they'd been late. Rather than saying anything to confirm her suspicions, he pointed to Bert. 'Seems a shame to wake him.'

Mabel grinned. 'We could throw a few blankets over him. He'd be fine until tomorrow.'

'He'd be a bit nonplussed if he woke up on Mill Grange's drive though.'

'You staying over at the manor?'

'Sam invited us once he knew we'd be driving you back. Dylan's on holiday now until January, so no school in the morning.' Tom gently shook Bert's shoulder. 'Come on, mate.'

A few grunts later and Bert came round. 'Oh... oh sorry.'

'No worries. You're home,' Helen said softly, before putting a finger to her lips to indicate a sleeping Dylan.

Bert whispered, 'Say goodnight to him for us if he wakes up.'

'Will do.' Helen got out, stretching her cramped muscles as she moved around to sit in the front of the car with Tom.

Moments later, as they were heading up the drive to Mill

Grange, Helen whispered, 'Carol Walters guessed about the baby.'

Tom pulled his Fiesta into its usual parking spot and switched off the engine. 'Just as well school is closed for Christmas. There won't be anyone for her to tell, although I don't suppose she would anyway. Are you alright?'

'Exhausted. The nativity was wonderful though.'

'It was fabulous.' Tom swivelled in his seat to look at Dylan; his head lolling to one side, he snuffled like a hedgehog.

'Maybe we'll have another one to go to in five years.' Helen smoothed a hand over her stomach. 'Tom, the scan was clear, no extra fluid on the neck, so why can't I stop worrying that something's wrong?'

'Because you're in love with your baby. It's natural. Whatever age you are, that worry is part of the process.' He rested a hand on her thigh. 'If Carol knows, then the others will work it out soon too.'

'Not long until Harriet's play is over.' Helen undid her safety belt. 'We'll stick to the plan and make it official after that, yes?'

Tom patted Helen's stomach. 'I think we'll have to. I'm not sure the baggy jumpers are going to hide that gorgeous mini bump for much longer.'

* * *

Thea, Tina, Sam and Shaun were sat in the kitchen when Helen joined them. The sound of chatter and laughter from the cast members in the drawing and living rooms occasionally drifted along the corridor.

'How was it?' Thea waved a mug in her friend's direction. 'Hot chocolate?'

'Please.' Helen sat down, kicking off her shoes in relief. 'Excellent. Dylan was wonderful. They all were.'

'Where is our little innkeeper?' Sam asked.

'Worn to a frazzle. He slept most of the way home. Tom's carrying him straight up.' Helen took a biscuit from a tin on the table. 'Thanks for letting us stay.'

'Pleasure. Anyway—' Tina passed her a drink '—Dylan has had his moment – now it's your turn. Have a look at this.'

Tina passed Sam's tablet across the table. It was open on the cover page of a book – her book.

'Wow! I haven't had a chance to see this yet.' Helen pressed the screen and found herself flicking through the e-pages of her own book. 'You bought one?'

'We all bought one!' Sam laughed. 'And when the paperback comes out we'll put in a bulk order to sell here at Mill Grange. Plus, there will be an open day in the summer with, if you're okay with the idea, a book signing and, very probably a bonfire party afterwards.'

Helen traced a finger over the photos of the fortlet on the page before her. Each one was annotated with her own words. 'Thank you. I don't know what else to say.'

Sam picked up his phone and waved his own copy of *Upwich: A Roman Fortlet* under Helen's nose. 'You did this for us. We are the ones who should be thanking you.'

Battling a yawn, Helen clicked through a few more pages. 'It's weird seeing it like this. It's not like a proper book.'

Thea shook her head. 'It's very like a proper book. Identical in fact, but I know what you mean. The photographs and plans will look much better in hardcopy.'

'I've been so worried about this, so nervous about having

everything ready for today, but when it came to it, with the nativity and everything, I forgot all about it.' Helen looked at Thea. 'Tom said you'd offered to do the social media bit. Was it okay?'

'It was.' Thea looked a bit embarrassed. 'I rather enjoyed pretending to be you! There were lots of questions about the site. I have linked everything to the Mill Grange website, so hopefully we'll get some interest when the site opens to the public.'

'That's brilliant. Thank you.'

Thea reached into her handbag. 'A little well-done present.'

Helen laughed. 'A box of sugar cubes!'

'Our trips to Sybil's reminded me how much of a sweet tooth you've got.' Thea smiled.

Helen, who desperately wanted to tell Thea about the real reason the book had flown from her mind, held the sugar cube box to her chest. 'I'm ever so grateful.'

'I wouldn't be that grateful.' Tina leant forward, a mischievous expression on her face. 'Our kindness comes at a price.'

'Go on?'

'We wondered if you'd like to stay at Mill Grange until after the play. Full board and lodging in return for help getting everything ready.'

Helen laughed. 'No need to bribe us with board and lodging – we sort of assumed our services might be required.' She raised her mug to her lips. 'I'll need to work during the day tomorrow, but everything I need is either here or in the car. But after five o'clock I can be all yours.'

A shriek of laughter from the drawing room made them

all turn as Tom pushed open the kitchen door. 'Whatever the cast are up to in there, they're having fun.'

'It's nice to hear them relaxing. I'd be a nervous wreck if I was about to perform in front of loads of people.' Helen held her mug against her chest.

'They're used to bigger audiences than can fit in the walled garden.' Shaun tapped a teaspoon against the table as he thought. 'I performed in the same play to more people, and that was just an amateur thing.'

Thea rolled her eyes. 'For someone who claims to have had a terrible time in that play, you don't half go on about it.'

Shaun tousled his fringe. 'I've hardly mentioned it, I...'

'Come off it, mate.' Sam grinned.

Shaun hid behind a gulp of tea. 'Maybe I've mentioned it a bit.'

'A bit?' Thea chuckled. 'I'm beginning to think you'd like to swap *Landscape Treasures* for the stage.'

'Never!' Shaun laughed as he saw the knowing expressions on his friends' faces. 'Okay, I might have got a bit over-interested. I will admit to being curious about how Matt will tackle being Polixenes.'

'Well, you don't have long to wait to find out now.'

* * *

Harriet finished her drink and checked her phone.

There was nothing. No texts. No missed calls. No emails.

Should I send him a text?

Glancing covertly around the pub, wondering how many of the customers were trying to work out if she'd been stood up, Harriet shifted uncomfortably against the wooden settle.

He said he'd be late, but an hour?

Harriet's glass had been empty for at least forty minutes, but she hadn't wanted to risk getting up for another in case she lost her seat by the fire.

Ten more minutes. Then I'm leaving.

Picking up her empty mug, Harriet pretended to drink from it, hoping the act made her look less like she was waiting for someone.

What will I say to the others? Ali is bound to want to know how the date went. Then there's Helen and Thea and... A low moan escaped from between her gritted teeth. *Why did he ask me for a drink if he never intended to turn up?*

Suddenly not sure why she was bothering to give Rob another ten minutes, she got up, hooked her bag onto her shoulder, grabbed her coat and scarf, and dashed outside, making sure she didn't catch anybody's eye.

As the evening chill hit her, Harriet tucked herself in against the wall of the pub and zipped up her coat. Angry humiliation battled in her head with a nagging voice that shouted, *This isn't like Rob. If he didn't intend to be here, he'd say.*

'So where is he then?'

A trickle of unease tripped down Harriet's spine.

Looking around, relieved that the main street through Upwich was empty, while simultaneously willing Rob to appear, Harriet took a deep breath and called his number.

The mobile only rang three times before it was picked up.

'Hello. This is Rob Peterson's phone. Who is calling please?'

There was something about the tone of the female voice that made all the hairs on the back of Harriet's neck stand up.

'Um, I'm Harriet. Who are you?'

'My name is Sara. I'm a paramedic attached to the Musgrove Hospital in Taunton, and I...'

'Hospital?' Harriet's hands started to shake. 'What's happened? Is he okay?'

With practised calm, Sara said, 'He'll be fine. Can I ask, are you family?'

'Family? Um, no. I'm his... I've been waiting for him. We were on a date.'

'His girlfriend then, right. So, I'm sure you can understand I can't tell you much as you are not next of kin but...'

She broke off for a second. Harriet could hear muffled conversation in the background. Every second that passed felt like forever as the words "next of kin" made her slump backwards against the pub wall.

'Harriet, is that you?'

'Rob!'

'I'm so sorry.' He winced as if in pain. 'If I hadn't stayed to help Matt then...'

'Where are you?' Harriet gripped her mobile harder, pushing it closer to her ear.

'In an ambulance on the way to hospital.' Rob's voice sounded strangled. 'I think my ankle is broken.'

'Oh thank God.'

'What?'

'Sorry, I just meant that when the paramedic said "next of kin" I was imagining far worse.'

'I was running you see. I knew I was late, but then this deer came out and...' Rob's voice faded for a second before it came back to clarity. '...Can you hear me?'

'Just. Did you say a *deer*?'

'Yes, look, I'll explain later. I have to go – we've arrived. Can you tell Matt I'm sorry?'

'Oh my God, the play!'

'Yes.'

Harriet had the impression Rob was trying not to cry. 'Don't worry about a thing. Just get that ankle seen to. Phone me as soon as you can. Promise?'

'Promise.'

Harriet could picture him biting his bottom lip as he muttered, 'I'm sorry I missed our date. We'll do it again, if you want to.'

'We *will* do it again, and then we'll...' Harriet stopped talking and stared at her phone. The line had gone dead.

THIRTY-THREE

THURSDAY DECEMBER 16TH

Although she didn't recognise the car as it drove from the road into the car park behind the Stag and Hound, Harriet did recognise the man in the passenger seat. Before she'd allowed herself to consider what his answer would be, Harriet ran after the vehicle.

'Dad.'

'Harriet?' Nathan brushed his suit down as he stepped out of the hired Jaguar. 'What are you doing here?'

'It's Rob, Dad, he's had an accident. I need to get to the Musgrove.'

'What?'

'The hospital. It's Rob, Dad. The man I was with at the tea rooms. He's had an accident. I need to get to him. Will you take me?'

Joining her fiancée, Sue frowned. 'Was that man your boyfriend then?'

'Yes!' Hoping that was the case, Harriet could see her father's expression hardening just as it always did when he considered she was asking something unreasonable of him.

'I'm sure the hospital would rather you weren't hanging around while they sort out whatever he's done.'

Harriet's words came out as a strained squeak. 'He's in hospital with no car to bring him home and no clothes or anything.'

'I can't. I've had a drink. I doubt they'll keep him in anyway.' Nathan shrugged. 'I'm sure he'll be fine.'

As she stared at her father in disbelief, something inside Harriet snapped. 'He'll be fine. That's it? That's all I get?'

'Now look here, Harriet, we came all this way...'

'No!' Harriet heard herself shout at her father. She felt as if she was watching herself from above as she flung her words at her startled parent's face. 'I can take you arriving in England and not telling me you've got here safely, even though you must have known I'd want to know. I coped when you took Dylan out for a meal and didn't invite me. I can take that you went out for a meal tonight, and again, didn't think I might like to come. And I have *long* since got used to you never asking how *I* am or having any sort of conversation with me that doesn't involve you telling me about *your* life or about how I *ought* to live mine.

'But now, for the first time since I was a child, I have asked for your help so I can be there for someone I care about, and you brush it off. Why did I even bother to ask? Tough love, you call it. Teaching me to survive with your hard life lessons – well, guess what, Dad? I learnt! And most of all, I learnt that tough love leads to *no* love!'

Leaving stunned silence behind her, her head a tumult of emotions, Harriet marched from the car park. The sound of footsteps behind her made Harriet move faster. She was about to break into a jog, not wanting to face her father's rage, when an unexpected voice called out to her.

'I'll drive you.' Sue shouted. 'I'll take you to see Rob.'

* * *

Apart from firing off a text to Ali, telling her what had happened, Harriet sat in silence, staring out of the window. She wanted to ask Sue why she was helping her and, more to the point, what had been said to persuade her dad for him to part with the car keys, but she wasn't sure she wanted to know the answers.

Rob won't be able to play Leontes. Ali had sounded devastated when Harriet had gabbled off her news, although she hadn't said anything except that she'd tell Matt and sent best wishes to Rob. *We've got no understudy. The play will have to be cancelled after all.*

Steering out of the country lanes and onto the link road that would take them to the motorway and then Taunton, Sue finally spoke. 'He'll be okay. They're good at the Musgrove.'

'You know it?'

'Dylan hurt himself not long after we moved here. I was so scared.' Sue kept her eyes fixed on the road. 'He was being an aeroplane and was convinced he could fly down the stairs. His first lesson in the power of gravity.'

'Tom never said.'

'He doesn't know.'

'Oh.' Harriet had known Sue ever since she'd first met her father, happily babysitting Dylan while they dated. They'd never been what Harriet considered friends, but they'd always been friendly. Since Sue had graduated from her father's girlfriend to his future wife, Harriet hadn't known what to say to her.

'He does love you, your father I mean.'

Harriet looked out of the window. The fields that ran off to the left of the motorway were shrouded in a foggy gloom that matched her mood. 'And yet all the evidence points to the contrary.'

'I'm sorry.'

Harriet was surprised by the sincerity of Sue's tone. 'Thanks, but he's treated me like an inconvenience ever since Mum...' She sighed. 'I was foolish to think he'd help me now. I hardly saw him when we lived in the same house. He locked himself away in his study night after night. Why would I think thousands of miles would make a difference?'

The silence lasted longer this time. Harriet felt an overwhelming sense of relief as they swung into the hospital's car park and found the Accident and Emergency department.

'Thank you, Sue.'

'That's okay.' She manoeuvred the Jaguar into a space that hadn't been designed for such a large vehicle.

'Is it?'

'Of course.'

'What about Dad? Is he going to give you hell for helping me?'

Sue, her hands still on the steering wheel, turned to face Harriet properly. 'Whatever you think, we did want to see you. He misses you as much as I miss Dylan. He's just appalling at showing it.'

'To put it mildly.' Harriet nodded towards the hospital. 'I don't know how long I'll be.'

Sue pointed to a pile of magazines on the back seat of the car. 'I'll be fine. If they are keeping him in, let me know, okay?'

'Thanks, Sue.'

* * *

'A deer?'

'That's what Harriet said.' Ali wasn't sure what to say. Matt had gone pale. She knew he was madly trying to work out how to save the show, without being so heartless as to say that was his prime concern.

Tina looked at Sam. He'd also gone pale, and she knew why. So far the battle with his PTSD had remained unspoken amongst their guests. None of the visitors had had any reason to notice he suffered if he spent too long indoors – but if Rob couldn't climb stairs... Tina concentrated on staying positive as she asked, 'Will Harriet call when she knows the full situation?'

'I'm sure she will.' Ali reached a hand out to her partner.

'Either way ' Matt sighed ' thanks to Jason, we have no understudy.'

Tina closed her eyes. 'You mean...'

'No Rob, no play.' Matt felt helpless. 'Let's hope it's just a sprain. A limping Leontes we could work with, but one on crutches, especially outside on grass in winter, is not going to happen.'

'But surely...' Ali shook her head. 'No. I was going to say the audience would understand, and they probably would, but standing around on cold ground, rather than keeping his leg rested, won't do Rob any good.'

'And if he acted and, as a result, the break didn't heal properly, we'd feel awful.' Matt groaned.

'If Rob can't play the role, then, we'll need to start undoing all we've done. Give back the ticket money and so on.' Tina tried not to think about how much they'd spent on food and drink.

'I'm so sorry.' Matt shook his head.

'It's not your fault.' Sam sat up straighter. 'Are you insured for this sort of thing?'

'To an extent. Don't worry, your costs will be paid.'

Sam brushed that away. 'I didn't mean that; I meant, your cast will expect to be paid.'

'You're very kind, but your expenses will be covered first.' Matt smiled. 'Maybe you'd consider having us back another time.'

'We'd be delighted.' Tina hugged her arms around her knees. 'I know some of your cast were hoping this would earn them Equity points. I don't suppose there's another play you could put on instead? One with one less actor in it?'

'Wrong scenery and, to be honest, I wouldn't be too thrilled if I had paid to see *The Winter's Tale* and turned up to find I'd be watching *Waiting for Godot*.' Matt got up. 'I'll go and tell the others we're having a meeting at nine tomorrow morning.'

'Will you tell them about Rob?' Ali asked.

'Tomorrow. Let's wait until we've heard from Harriet.'

As Matt left the kitchen, Sam spoke the words that had been on Tina's mind. 'Rob will need the downstairs room.'

'I know.'

Ali frowned. 'But that's your room.'

'We'll swap with Rob.' Sam said the words quickly before he could change his mind.

Tina glanced at him as she said, 'Ali, would you mind seeing if Thea and Shaun are in the living room? I think we should let them know what's going on.'

The second Ali had gone, Tina muttered to Sam, 'Are you sure?'

'No, but what else can we do? Even if Rob has only

bruised or sprained his ankle, stairs will be painful. It's that or he sleeps on the sofa, which won't do him any good. And I don't fancy sleeping on the sofa in front of all these people. Nor do I relish explaining why I'm putting a tent up in the garden in the middle of December.'

'But...'

'No.' Sam shook his head. 'Thanks to Dylan, I've been upstairs before, and it's not like I have to go up to the attics. It's just a little way along the corridor and there's the big window and...'

Tina leant forward and interrupted him with a kiss. 'You're an amazing man, Sam Philips.'

'Not that amazing.' Sam gulped and hoped the pain that had shot across his temples wouldn't linger. 'Let's not do a room swap until we've heard whether he's coming back here tonight or not.'

THIRTY-FOUR

FRIDAY DECEMBER 17TH

Harriet sat on the bench in the walled garden with Matt and Ali. The early morning sunshine melting the frost beneath their toes, she filled her friends in on Rob's condition.

'The damage is minor. A hairline fracture rather than a major break, so no operation is required. He has a plastic boot over his foot rather than a cast. But it will take six weeks or so to heal, and he has to keep it rested most of the time.' Fidgeting with her scarf, Harriet added, 'Rob's so cross with himself. I've tried to make him see it wasn't his fault, but...'

'It's not Rob's fault, just bloody bad luck. But the fact of the matter is we can't go ahead. If this had happened a week ago, then maybe Neil or Dave could have rehearsed enough to swap to being Leontes, but neither of them know the part well enough, and the opening night is tomorrow. *Was* tomorrow.' Matt got up and began to pace. 'We owe it to our audience to let them know before midday that it's off so that those travelling from Wiltshire or Bristol don't set out.'

Ali put an arm around Harriet. 'You look wiped out.

You've been up all night – why don't you head to bed for a while? We can do the bad news bit.'

'Thanks, but I feel responsible. I ought to at least be here to take the flak.'

'This isn't your fault.'

'If Rob hadn't been coming to see me at the pub, then he wouldn't have been running along the road in the dark in the first place.'

Matt disagreed. 'And if he hadn't stayed late to help me with the scenery, then he wouldn't have been running in the first place. The blame game isn't going to help.'

Disappointment welled around Harriet. 'Will you go for a postponement, or is that it? I mean, will we get to do the play another time?' She stared at her booted feet. 'I feel awful even asking that.'

'It's a fair question.' Matt brushed his hands down his jeans as he saw a few of their fellow actors enter the garden. 'Sam has offered us Easter week here if we want it.'

'That's very kind.'

'He's a good man.' Matt turned to face the group of actors walking across the walled garden. 'Right then, you two, ready for this?'

The guilt at the play being cancelled suddenly mixed with the anxiety concerning her relationship with her father, sent nerves circling through Harriet and tensed her tired muscles. All night, sat next to Rob in the hospital, she had privately replayed her car park outburst. Sue might claim that her father loved his daughter, but she wasn't convinced.

So, why do I feel so damn responsible for the fact that the show they've come to see isn't going to happen?

'Would you think me a coward if I changed my mind and went to see how Rob is?'

Matt laid a reassuring hand on her shoulder. 'Harriet, this really isn't his fault or yours. Tell Rob that we aren't cross and he'll definitely be offered roles with us in the future. And so will you.'

* * *

The bonfire crackled in the brazier as Sam threw in an armful of branches and brambles that had been cut back from Bert's garden. 'We're almost clear of these now. One more fire and your garden will be all neat, tidy and ready for spring.'

Bert held his palms over the flames, which swayed in the light breeze. 'I'd best save the last lot for Dylan to burn, or he'll be disappointed.'

'He's at the house, so I expect you'll have a visitor before long.'

Bert nodded, but his customary good humour was missing. 'You didn't come over this morning to help with the bonfire though, did you, Sam.'

'Not entirely.'

Bert pulled his flat cap down further over his forehead. 'Mabel phoned and told me about the play being off. How invested were you?'

'Financially things will even out. Matt has his head screwed on. The company is insured and we've invited them back. The food will be baked or cooked and frozen ready for the retreaters in the spring.'

'Good.' Bert looked satisfied. 'I knew you'd all be sensible about it. How is Rob this morning?'

'Poor chap. Harriet says the pain isn't the issue so much as disappointment about not getting to act and guilty that the show is cancelled, although I'm sure he's suffering.'

'The ankle is definitely broken?'

'Yes.' Sam threw a stray twig into the brazier. 'Talk about a freak accident. He was late for his date with Harriet, so was running full pelt along the road between the house and Upwich. A deer ran out from the fields to the right and bowled straight into him. He remembers the stench of fur and fear from the animal, but little else.'

'He was lucky he wasn't killed!'

'He was. Hit his head, but no damage done on that front thank goodness,' Sam agreed. 'He's also lucky that a driver came past and found him so quickly after he'd been hurt. You can go hours without seeing traffic along there.'

'Is he in plaster?'

'Foot brace. Solid plastic. And he's got crutches of course. Harriet and Sue got him back to the house at nine this morning.'

'Sue?' Bert turned in surprise. 'Mabel didn't mention that.'

'She doesn't know yet; at least, she didn't when I left. Once Rob was safely tucked up on one of the sofas when they got back this morning, Sue went up to Dylan. I wouldn't be at all surprised if she wasn't fast asleep on the lad's bed after a night in the hospital car park.'

'Tom and Helen okay with her being there?'

'If they aren't, they're hiding it well.'

Bert gave his friend a searching look. 'And the real reason you're here is because?'

Sam laughed. 'Sometimes I think you're more intuitive than Mabel.'

'So I've been told.' Bert patted the arm of the chair next to him. 'Talk to me.'

'Rob can't do stairs.'

'Ah.' Bert understood in an instant. 'Which means, if he stays while he recovers, you and Tina have to give up your room for him.'

'Yes.'

'And although you've been upstairs once, you are having serious heebie-jeebies about doing so again, let alone sleeping up there.'

'Yes.'

'Tell me—' Bert moved away from the fire and wandered towards the cottage '—when a guest in a wheelchair comes to Mill Grange, what do you do?'

'Use the tent.'

'Which works until the winter comes.'

'We aren't normally open in the winter, so it's not a problem.' Sam groaned. 'I'm just not ready to sleep upstairs, Bert. I want to. I know, logically, that the house is solid but...'

'I understand. What does Tina say?'

'That if I need to sleep in the tent, she'll come with me.'

'Which is just what I'd expect her to say. Meanwhile, you will have told her it is too cold, and she should sleep indoors.'

'Same conversation we have every time something happens to stir the demon.' Sam took off his coat and followed Bert into the living room. 'But I'm sick of it. I'm sick of having the same conversation with my wife. I thought I'd moved on and started to get better, but now I'm having internal panics on a loop because some poor sod's broken his ankle.'

Bert lowered himself into an armchair. 'I like young Rob. We only met briefly, but I took to the lad right away.'

'He's a nice guy.'

'Did you see the buttons on his tunic?'

Sam opened his mouth and closed it again. 'Buttons?'

'Three of them on his shoulder. Harriet got them out of the sewing box at Mill Grange.'

'No, I can't say I noticed them.' Sam tilted his head to one side, thrown by the change in their conversation's direction. 'You okay?'

'I'm always okay, young man.' Bert closed his eyes and rested back in his chair. 'Oh, and, Sam, the solution to your night-time problem is obvious.'

'It is?'

'Rob can stay here.'

* * *

Helen looked up from her desk as she heard a familiar footfall approaching the converted stable block. 'I thought you'd pop in.'

Tom gestured to the mobile phone lying next to Helen's laptop. 'Any word?'

'It's a bit soon yet. Arjun said it would be this afternoon at the earliest, but more likely Monday before we got the results.'

'I was wishful thinking.' Tom perched on the edge of her desk.

'How's Dylan?'

'Happily giving his mum a tour of the house.'

'Sue must be shattered.' Helen pushed a stray coil of hair from her eyes. 'I can't believe she stayed at the Musgrove with Harriet like that.'

'Nor me, but I'm glad she did.'

'Weird that it was Sue that took Harriet to the hospital and not her dad.'

'Umm.' Tom headed to the shelves of archaeological tools

that lined the walls opposite Helen's desk and began to restack a set of trowels that didn't need restacking. 'If Sue and Nathan have fallen out then...'

Helen got to her feet. 'You think that might have happened?'

'She's still here, rather than heading back to the pub. Sue has a pattern in relationships. I grant you they've never included talk of marriage before, but they usually last about this long, ending when she won't change her life to fit in with someone else's.'

'You're worried she'll come back and take Dylan with her?' A lump formed in Helen's throat.

'It crossed my mind.'

Helen exhaled slowly. 'If that happens, there won't be a thing we can do.'

'I'm not having her disrupt Dylan's life with a move away from Tiverton. Not after all she's put him through already. Not now he is settled at school with friends of his own.'

Helen placed a hand on her stomach. 'For now, can we stick to worrying about a problem we know exists? Sue and Nathan may be perfectly alright. Nathan might not have gone to hospital because he'd drunk too much to drive.'

'Sorry. I was panicking without reason. It's so obvious. Why didn't I think of the drink-drive thing?'

'Because I'm brilliant and you're daft?' Helen blew Tom a kiss. 'Now go away and let me catch up on yesterday's book launch stuff before my concentration totally deserts me.'

* * *

Harriet rescued the red crayon as it landed on the floor, catching it in mid-roll towards the Christmas tree.

'I think we need to teach Rob how to control his colouring in.'

Dylan giggled as he took the errant crayon back and gave it to Rob. 'You've gone out of the lines.'

Rob peered at the colouring book open on the lap-tray before him. The castle he'd been helping Dylan fill in now had a flag with a less than perfect red cross running through it. 'How did I manage that?'

'Mrs Harley would say you need to go slower.'

Rob laughed. 'Is that your teacher?'

'Yeah.' Selecting a grey crayon from his pencil case, Dylan addressed the castle's battlements. 'She's nice.'

'I'm sorry if I've ruined your picture.' Rob laid down his pencil crayon and flexed each leg in turn as he half sat, half lay on the drawing room sofa.

'It's okay. I can fix it.'

As Dylan concentrated on his picture, Harriet asked, 'Shall I go and fetch some tea?'

'Please.' Rob winced, his leg giving an involuntary shudder.

'Are you in pain?' Harriet immediately regretted the question. 'Sorry, that was a stupid thing to say. Maybe we should leave you to sleep?'

Rob rested his head back against the pillows Mabel had put behind him. 'I'm not sure I'll be able to sleep until I've faced the others.'

'They will understand. It's not like you broke your ankle on purpose.'

'Even so.' Rob sucked in his bottom lip. 'And it's not just the cast is it. Tina and Sam put themselves out for us and now...'

Seeing that it was only Dylan's presence that was keeping

Rob from going to pieces, Harriet mumbled, 'I'm just as much to blame. If you hadn't been coming to see me then, well, you know.'

Rob reached out a hand and took hers. 'Do you think we'll ever get a proper date?'

'You still want to date me?' Harriet stared at their connected palms in wonder. 'First Dad was rude to you and now this. I've not exactly been good for you so far.'

Rob didn't have time to answer, for Dylan had looked up from his work. 'Don't be silly, Harriet. You're a lovely girl and Rob is very lucky to have you.'

'I couldn't agree more.' Rob laughed, instantly regretting it as the involuntary movement it caused jarred his leg. 'What made you say that, Dylan?'

'It's what Mum said.' He selected a green pencil to colour the grass that surrounded the base of his castle. 'She really likes Harriet.'

The sight of Nathan walking up the drive to Mill Grange, his face like thunder, did nothing to calm Tom's anxiety.

Suspecting Harriet would be feeling bad enough about the play being cancelled, without having to face a speech from her father about how disappointed in her he was, Tom called across the drive. 'You looking for Sue?'

'Oh, Tom.' Nathan dipped his head in acknowledgement. 'Yes. Where can I find her?'

'She was with Dylan, in his bedroom, when I last saw her.'

'He has a room here as well as at home?'

'In the attic. We stay as often as we can.' Tom swung an arm around to encompass the view. 'It's good for him to be able to spend time in the countryside.'

'If you say so.' Nathan pointed to the main door. 'Am I allowed in that way, or would you prefer me to find the tradesman's entrance?'

Tom opened the double doors. 'Take the staircase to your right once you're inside, then walk along to the end of the corridor and go up the narrow set of stairs you'll see to your left. Dylan's room is the third door along the corridor.'

'Thank you.'

'And, Nathan—' Tom balled his fists in his pockets '—the house is currently full of guests. If you intend to have a blazing row, I'd ask you to save it until you are well away from Mill Grange.'

'How dare you tell me how I should behave?'

'I would not be so foolish.' Tom battled to keep his tone neutral. 'I merely ask you to respect those around you. Now, if you'll excuse me, I'm going to see how your daughter is. You remember Harriet? She's in the house too if you're bothered about her at all.'

Marching to the kitchen before Nathan had the chance to either reply or punch him, Tom was cross with himself. He should never have said that about Harriet, but there was something about Nathan that made him so angry. *He has an amazing daughter. If I had one then...*

Slowing his pace, Tom caught his breath. *I might have a daughter or another son. It doesn't matter which, but please, let them be alright.*

* * *

Harriet looked up from where she and Dylan were showing Rob how it was possible to colour within the lines without making a mistake.

'Dad!'

'About bloody time!' Nathan snapped. 'I've been walking around this rabbit warren for ages searching for you.'

Harriet's cheeks burnt crimson as she whispered, 'Please don't swear in front of Dylan, Dad.'

'Oh for God's sake, Harriet, he'll hear worse in the school playground.'

'Maybe, but that doesn't make it alright.' Not sure where her boldness was coming from, but desperately hoping it would last, Harriet felt Rob's silent encouragement radiating into her back. 'Why were you looking for me?'

'He wasn't.' Tom put his head around the door. 'Sorry, Harriet, he came looking for Sue.'

'Of course. Silly me.' Biting the insides of her cheeks, Harriet asked Dylan, 'Do you know where your mum went?'

'Out for a walk.'

'Dylan.' Tom crouched next to his son. 'Did Mum say where she planned to walk to?'

'No. She couldn't sleep, so I said that when Helen was tired and couldn't sleep she got fresh air. Mum thought that was a good idea.'

Tom's eyebrows rose in surprise as Harriet explained, 'Sue dropped Dylan off with me about half an hour ago. I assumed she was heading back to the pub.'

Without another word, Nathan spun on the heels of his expensive brogues and left the room.

Breaking the silence, Dylan scrambled off his chair. 'Can we go and see the actors now, Harriet? I want to see if your play is as good as mine was.'

Tom reached out a hand to his son. 'There's been a bit of a hiccup, Dylan. Now Rob's ankle has been hurt, there isn't anyone to play his part.'

Dylan thought for a moment. 'Are there lots of words?'

'Lots and lots.' Rob sighed. 'I'm sorry if I've disappointed you, Dylan.'

'That's okay.' Dylan let go of Harriet and went back to his

picture. 'If there hadn't been many words, I'd have done it for you, then everyone would be happy again.'

Tears pricked in Harriet's eyes as she looked from Rob to Dylan. *Everyone except my father.*

Rob shifted on the sofa. 'That's very kind of you, Dylan. I'm sure you'll make a fabulous Leontes when you're older, if you decide acting is what you want to do.'

'I might be an... arky-ologist. Or a palentolo... thingy.'

Tom smiled, 'Palaeontologist.'

'That's it.'

'You could do both.' Rob's smile turned into a yawn.

'We should leave you to sleep, Rob.' Tom turned to Harriet. 'What with your dad and everything, I forgot why I was here. Matt is asking to see you.'

* * *

Back on the bench nearest to the chicken coop, Matt and Ali told Harriet that the cast's response to what had happened had been as expected. A mix of frustration and disappointment.

'No one blames you, Harriet.' Ali gave her friend a reassuring nod.

'That's nice, but it doesn't make me feel any better.' Harriet's gaze moved from the giant patio heaters to the scene cut-outs, to the pile of chairs, neatly hidden beneath tarpaulins, that Tom and Sam had helped carry into the garden ready for the audience.

'I'm going to take Sam up on his offer of rescheduling to Easter.' Matt watched the hens wander around their pen. 'I know Jason's parents would probably have us back, assuming the flood damage is sorted, but I'm not keen on working with that particular actor again.'

'Aren't you booked in elsewhere at Easter?' Harriet followed Matt's gaze in time to see Gertrude flap Betty away from Tony Stark.

'Next show isn't until we go to Hampstead Heath in London in July.' Matt got wearily to his feet. 'For now, I need to call the patio heater suppliers to arrange collection and change our people carrier booking from next week to today.'

'Today?' Harriet looked up so quickly she made herself dizzy.

'The cast are mostly students; they can't afford to pay to stay here without reason. I can't pay them for work they haven't done.'

'Can't pay them?'

'It's in the contract. If we don't act, we don't get paid.' Ali patted Harriet's arm. 'I'm sorry, but we're a shoestring company. It's how it is.'

Harriet's moment of freedom from guilt evaporated. 'I'll go and tell Rob.'

'I suppose he'll have to stay here though.' Ali frowned. 'He came in his own car didn't he? And he won't be driving again anytime soon.'

'I'd forgotten about that.' Harriet remembered the late-night romantic notions that had accompanied her most nights since she'd first suggested coming to Mill Grange, of her and Rob driving off to explore Exmoor between performances, walking and talking together in the winter sunshine. They seemed so ridiculous now. 'Will there be room for him in the people carrier with his bound ankle and crutches? He could come back for the car later.'

'I'll book one with a disabled space in case.'

* * *

Thea ran from her scullery office to the kitchen.

'You alright, Thea?' Mabel looked up from her baking, surprised at the speed of her friend's arrival.

'Have you seen Shaun?'

'He said something about having to pop out.'

'Again!' Thea's brow furrowed.

'I presumed he was Christmas shopping.'

'Possible I suppose, but I thought he had all his Christmas presents. It's not like we have loads of people to buy for.' Thea was dubious.

Mabel picked up on her friend's uncertain tone. 'Maybe it was something for the house, or presents that Sam needs collecting?'

'You could be right. Sorry, Mabel, it's just that, every time I look for Shaun he's slipped off without saying anything. Have you seen Sam or Tina then?'

'Sam's helping Bert with the garden at home and Tina is in her office doing the accounts.'

'Thanks.' Thea didn't hesitate. Leaving a curious Mabel behind her, she ran up the stairs to the attic. Without pausing to knock, she dived straight in. 'I've had an idea. You got five minutes, Tina?'

'Literally.' Tina pointed at her computer screen. 'Then I'm going to help Mabel get drinks for the cast. They'll be craving strong coffee, along with decent cake, to help take the edge off the bad news.'

'What if there was a way the play could happen though?'

'What way?' Tina's fingers paused over the keyboard.

'It's so obvious.' Thea slapped a palm against the desk.

'He's more or less told us on repeat how much he loved playing the role.'

'Shaun?'

'Yes!' Thea pulled her mobile out of her pocket and pressed in her partner's number. 'You didn't send him to get anything from the shops did you?'

'No. Sam could have, I suppose.' Tina was struggling to keep up. 'Hang on, Thea, Shaun didn't play Leontes at uni. He played that Poli... whatever, bloke.'

'I know, but what if...' Thea broke off as the phone connected. 'Shaun, where the hell are you?'

* * *

Shaun pulled into Mill Grange's driveway seconds after Sam and Bert had arrived at the house.

'Hi, Bert.' Shaun opened the car door for his friend. 'Have you two been summoned too?'

'Summoned?' Sam retrieved Bert's walking stick from the back seat. 'We're here to see how Rob's doing.'

'I was Christmas shopping, but Thea called. She made it sound urgent.' Shaun waggled his mobile at them.

Sam checked his own phone and swore. 'I've got a missed call from Tina.'

'We'd better find our womenfolk.' Bert pulled his mobile from his pocket. 'Uh-oh, I've got one from Mabel I missed too. Brace yourselves for an earbashing lads.'

Shaun laughed. 'What makes you think we're in trouble?'

'Experience.'

THIRTY-SIX

FRIDAY DECEMBER 17TH

Shaun stood at the kitchen window, wishing he could see into the walled garden from there. He shook his head as he turned back to Tina, Thea, Sam, Bert and Mabel. They were all sat around the table looking straight at him.

'It's a mad idea.'

'I know it is.' Thea watched her boyfriend. 'But it's the only one we've got. Think about it. If Matt agrees, then the show will go on!'

'I think this theatrical lark has got to you.' Shaun's laugh came out as strangled hysteria. 'The play is tomorrow!' He checked his watch. 'It's almost eleven-thirty, which means the first night goes up in thirty-one and a half hours! And I'll need to eat and sleep at some point.'

'All the more reason to try and save the show.' Tina added, 'Think how disappointed our audience will be to have it cancelled now, at the last minute. We've all invested so much in this, and I don't just mean money.' Twirling her pigtails through her fingers, Tina said, 'If it works out, then maybe The Outdoor Players will come back every winter.

Think of how much good that would do us in terms of publicity as well as finance.'

'We could start saving to get the old mill building converted at last.' Sam nodded. 'I know this is coming across like peer pressure, mate, and I know it's a lot to ask, but the fact is, you're famous – whether you like that fact or not. If people knew you were performing, the last few tickets would be snapped up.'

'But I haven't acted for over twenty years. Can you imagine the outcome if I messed it up? The press would have a field day *and* I'd let Matt and co. down. They'd look like an amateur set-up because of me!'

'Or the press would shower praise on you for stepping in at the last moment to save the day.' Thea saw the conflict on Shaun's face. 'I'm sorry, love, I should have asked you privately first. But it's the eleventh hour and every time I think about Harriet not getting her first professional performance and Mill Grange not delivering something it has promised, I feel awful.'

Shaun raked a hand through his hair. 'Finances aside, what do you really think, Sam?'

'I think it's a harebrained scheme.'

'Sam!' Tina turned to her husband.

'But, to coin a phrase: "It's a million-to-one chance, but it might just work."'

Shaun's forehead creased in thought. 'Wasn't that Terry Pratchett?'

Sam nodded. 'Yeah, the *Guards* series. Brilliant, although other authors have...'

Thea coughed loudly. 'Can we leave the literary appreciation until later?'

'Bert, you were right. We were in for an earbashing.' Sam

winked at the old man as he went on, 'The thing is, Shaun, you're a natural performer, and even if you need the prompt to help you every now and then, you are good at learning lines.'

'Often with only a moment's notice,' Thea chipped in. 'I've seen you do it.'

Shaun stared at his friends. He wasn't sure why he was arguing. They knew he'd say yes, and so did he. A little part of his brain was already working out how to deliver the lines, while wondering if they had a costume big enough to fit him when a new thought nudged itself centre stage.

'Hang on. You're all missing a vital point here. I can't replace Rob because he *wasn't* Polixenes. That's the only role I know. Sort of know.'

Mabel grinned. 'That's okay, Matt can be Leontes and you can be Polixenes.'

'What?'

'When I was helping Harriet sort Rob's outfit, we got talking. Rob was offered the role of Leontes when that nasty-sounding Jason walked out. Rob declined, so Matt, who knows *both* roles inside out, took that part. He could just as easily have been Leontes.'

'Oh.' Shaun fixed his gaze on Thea. 'So we suggest that Matt swaps his role and I take on Polixenes. Is that what you're saying?'

'Complicated I know, but...' Thea clasped his hand. 'For Harriet? For Mill Grange?'

'Okay. But *only* if Matt agrees. If he says no, then that's that. Agreed?'

'Agreed.' Thea and Tina replied together.

'Well one of you lot can suggest it. I'm certainly not going to put myself forward.'

'I'll do it.' Sam got up as he heard a group of people coming in through the back door.

Mabel got to her feet. 'Time for operation coffee and cake then, Tina.'

'I'd better go over my lines – just in case Matt agrees.' Shaun felt his insides clench with nervous excitement.

'Thanks for this, love.' Thea gave him a gentle kiss. 'You'll be amazing.'

'Matt could say no.'

Thea whispered in his ear, 'You'll be disappointed if he does, won't you?'

'Maybe.'

* * *

Heading into the living room, Bert wove his way through the men and women who formed The Outdoor Players. They were seated, their faces downcast. No one said much.

As he reached the double doors that divided the living room from the drawing room, Bert paused. He could see Rob sat alone on the sofa nearest the Christmas tree. His expression was as solemn. Bert wondered if any of his friends had been in to see him; he guessed not.

'If you want to rest, say so and I'll push off.'

'Resting doesn't seem possible just now.' Rob motioned towards his colleagues on the other side of the connecting door. 'I can almost taste their disappointment.'

'They'll get over it.'

Rob readjusted his leg as it lay out before him. 'Even as a kid I never broke a bone. I can't say I'm enjoying the experience.'

Bert sat on the armchair nearest to Rob and propped his

walking stick next to him. 'Broke an arm once. It's not all it's cracked up to be.'

Rob found himself chuckling at the pun. 'I bet you weren't treated like a bowling ball by a frightened deer.'

'Nope, I fell through the ceiling of a house during the Korean War.'

'Oh.' Rob's laughter stopped. 'Sorry.'

'Not at all.' Bert gestured to the adjoining room, ignoring the slight patina of sweat that had dotted across his shoulders. 'Your friends will come round.'

'I hope you're right, but just now that would take a miracle.'

'Didn't anyone tell you? Mill Grange is a place of miracles.'

'Do you know something I don't?'

'Loads of things I suspect.' The old man smiled.

Rob smiled back. 'Do you know if Harriet's okay? Matt sent for her after the others came in.'

'I haven't seen her, but I suspect she feels as disappointed as you do.'

Slamming a hand down on top of his nearest crutch handle, Rob groaned. 'I'm useless. I haven't even had the chance to get the hang of these yet. By the time I've hobbled to see her, she could have walked back to Bristol.'

Understanding Rob's frustration, Bert said, 'Give yourself time. Your body is in shock and you're exhausted. Anyway, I didn't come to see you to tell you the obvious. I came to ask if you'd like to come back with me this evening. Or now, if you want to hit the sack.'

'Go with you?'

'Mabel and I have a spare room in our bungalow. You'd be very welcome to have the use of it for a few days while the worst of the pain dies away. If you stayed at Mill Grange you'd have to sleep on the sofa, which isn't the best idea while you're in recovery.'

'But we'll be going home, won't we?'

'Eventually, but you drove here, young man. You won't be driving anywhere for a while.'

* * *

Matt had serious reservations. It was clear Shaun did too now that he'd had time to think. Ali, however, had no qualms.

'It's a brilliant idea.' She danced around the chicken pen in a manner designed to make Gertrude dizzy.

'Ali, will you please keep still.' Matt held out a hand and guided her to his side. 'You're like a jumping cracker.'

'The play has been granted a reprieve. Again!' Ali spoke practically. 'As I see it, we have two choices: we cancel or we go ahead with a last-minute cast change and an explanation to the audience prior to each performance.'

Shaun was getting up to let them discuss things in private when Matt asked, 'Are you sure you're up for this? I mean, it's a big role and there's hardly any time to prepare.'

Shaun licked his lips. 'I'll be honest, I have no idea how well it'll go. I am prepared to try, but *only* if it's what you and *all* of your cast want. If there's any unease about the idea, then you must cancel.'

'Are you kidding me?' Ali gestured towards the house. 'Not one of those people in there will want to let this chance go by. You wait until they hear they'll be acting alongside a television celebrity.'

'I'm an archaeologist, not an actor.'

Ali slipped her hand into Matt's. 'How about you? It isn't

just a matter of how well Shaun can play Polixenes. Are you cool with switching to being Leontes?'

'I've played the role several times, and I've been reading all the lines with everyone for this performance. I can't promise it'll be perfect, but I could give as close to perfect as I can.'

Shaun peered into the chicken run. 'Only one soul left to ask about the wisdom of this enterprise then.'

Matt frowned. 'Rob?'

'Rob will be fine with it because he'll want Harriet to have her chance to start earning her Equity card. I meant Gertrude.' Shaun waved a hand at the chicken who was staring right at them. 'If she says it'll be okay, then it will be.'

Harriet's mouth dropped open, but no words crossed her lips. She looked at Rob. He was also speechless.

Shaun hovered anxiously. 'Does your silence mean you think this is a terrible idea and you're both trying to think of polite ways of saying so?'

Bert shuffled towards Shaun, one hand outstretched to shake the archaeologist by the hand. 'Well done, my boy.'

Shaun gave Bert a shrewd stare. 'You knew this would happen as soon as Thea suggested it, didn't you.'

'Let's just say, I'd have been surprised if it hadn't.'

Rob cleared his throat. 'Is this what you meant by a miracle, Bert?'

'Might have been.' The old man wiggled his eyebrows playfully. 'Now then, Rob, if you could get young Harriet here to gather up all your bits from your bedroom, Sam is happy to drive you to my place later. For now, I'll leave you three to talk acting tactics and I'll go to see what Mabel is up to. I imagine now that the mood has lifted and everyone is staying, she'll appreciate help buttering the bread for a mountain of bacon sandwiches.'

'Now you're talking my language, Bert.' Shaun smiled. 'It's going to take some of Mabel's finest butties to get me through this.'

* * *

Helen picked up her mobile and then put it down again. There were two calls she needed to make, and she couldn't face either of them.

Surely the blood tests results are back by now.

Clicking her computer's mouse over her inbox list, Helen forced her attention back to the *Children of Roman Britain* exhibition she was supposed to be organising.

And that's the other call I need to make.

Since realising she'd be on maternity leave when the exhibition was due to take place, Helen had lost heart in the idea.

I have to call the museum. I have to tell them I'm pregnant.

A treacherous voice at the back of her head, cruelly whispered, *But what if you're not by then. What if...* The word "amniocentesis" ricocheted around her head.

We might not need one. If the bloods are clear then Dr Evan said that the chances were slim, although there was still a risk.

Helen sighed. 'Stop putting things off!'

Picking up her phone, she pressed the screen. Seconds later the line to the new curator of the Roman Baths was ringing.

* * *

'I've never seen anything like it!' Mabel retied her apron as she hurried towards the fridge. 'And there I was thinking that former military folk ate fast. These theatre types are like vultures!'

Thea laughed. 'Nervous energy food in Shaun's case and much-needed fuel in everyone else's.'

'We'll have none left for the rest of the week at this rate.' Mabel served a frying pan's worth of perfectly crisped bacon onto a hotplate, ready for Tina to fold into the bread that Bert had pre-buttered.

'I'll get some more – don't worry.' Thea jotted the job onto her list.

'Shaun's in his element.' Mabel stepped back from the hob, as oil in the pan spat at her.

'He'll claim otherwise, but he does love his moment in the limelight.' Thea had to agree. 'He's a different person in front of the camera. More confident and assertive.'

'You okay, lass?'

'What? Oh yes.' Thea parcelled the last batch of butties into tin foil. 'Just thinking out loud. I'll take these out to the vultures.'

* * *

Helen's hands shook. Automatically she placed them on her stomach. With each day she could feel a more definite bump. It was only small, but it was there.

Her boss had taken the news well. More than that, they'd been thrilled for her, telling Helen that the job was hers for the keeping after maternity leave. The only thing they had asked her to do was make sure the *Children of Roman Britain* exhibition was good to go, and hand over to her temporary replacement, before she went on leave.

The relief at having got the call over with had been quickly overshadowed when, seconds after she'd hung up, her mobile phone screen had lit up with the arrival of another call.

She knew she should go and find Tom, but she was too exhausted to move. Instead, she picked the phone up for a third time.

* * *

'Tom. They called. Everything is going to be okay.'

Three minutes later, Helen heard the sound of boots running in her direction before she was engulfed in the biggest hug of her life. A hug that was abruptly curtailed as Tom registered how tightly he was clasping her. 'Oh God, sorry.'

Helen laughed. 'Are you apologising to me or your child?'

'Both. Is that it now, or do we need to do anything else? Any more extra checks we need to do?'

'That's up to us.' Helen sat back down. 'Dr Evan said that, with me being over forty then an amniocentesis is an option. She also told me that there is a non-invasive screening test that can be done—covers a host of chromosomal abnormalities—but it's not available on the NHS in this region so...'

'So, we'd have to go private?'

'Yes.' Helen nodded, 'But as the scan and bloods were clear, then the need is lessened. Obviously, we can't rule out any problems, but...'

'But there is a risk in having the test that is on offer. We could lose our...' Tom found he couldn't finish the sentence.

'It's a slim possibility, but yes.' Helen fiddled with her pen. 'What do you think?'

'I think we'll love our child whoever they are.'

Helen stood back up and looked into her partner's eyes. 'I don't want the amniocentesis. I know some would think us irresponsible, but if we lost our child because of it...'

'I know,' Tom hastily agreed. 'If there had been even a hint of worry from the scan or bloods, I'd say differently.'

'Me too, but I'm assured there are no indicators.' Helen's words trailed off, before she added, 'A Down's syndrome child would be a hell of a responsibility, but we could do it. We *would* do it.'

'Of course we would.' Tom kissed her forehead. 'I love you.'

'You too.' Helen snuggled into his shoulder. 'I'm scared stiff and yet massively excited all at once.'

'There's a lot of that going on today.'

Helen looked up at him. 'You too?'

'Very much so, but in this case I meant Shaun.' Tom tilted his head towards the door. 'You should see him out there.'

'What are you talking about?'

'No one told you yet?' Tom grinned. 'Although, it's fresh news so...'

'Told me what?'

'Shaun is going to act in the play so it doesn't have to be cancelled!' Tom tangled a red coil of Helen's hair through his fingers. 'Talk about in at the deep end.'

Helen patted her belly. 'There's a lot of that going on too.'

* * *

Tina couldn't keep up with the phone calls to the manor. All she'd done about announcing the cast change since lunch was call Sybil and Moira at the café and pub to ask them to swap Rob's name to Shaun's on the poster advertising the show. Now, an hour later, the village jungle drums had beaten sufficiently for the locals who hadn't yet bought tickets for the performance, to snap them up.

Knowing there was scope to add at least another ten seats to the proposed audience space, Tina hadn't had time to get up and track down Matt or Ali to ask if she should sell extra tickets, when the phone rang again.

'Mill Grange, Tina Philips speaking.'

As soon as the caller announced themselves as being a researcher from the BBC *Spotlight* news programme, Tina left her desk and talked as she walked, heading towards the walled garden at top speed.

* * *

'Sam.' Shaun gestured to his friend as he took a break between scenes to talk to him. 'Can I ask a favour?'

'Sure. What is it?'

'I had an appointment in... Hang on, that's Tina.' Shaun saw Sam's wife racing towards them, a phone to her ear.

'What's the favour?'

Shaun whispered, 'I'll tell you later.'

A little out of breath, Tina arrived at their side, holding the phone out to Shaun. 'BBC News, the local one. They want to talk to you about the play.'

'What?' Shaun held his hand over the mobile. 'Who told them?'

'Well don't look at me – I haven't had a minute.' Tina

gestured towards the garden. 'But the word is out. I've sold every ticket we had left in the last hour. Where's Matt? I need to ask him about adding more seating.'

'More?' The contents of Shaun's stomach did a barrel roll.

Sam gestured to the phone. 'Better take that call, mate. If they want to come here to film an interview with you, the answer is yes.'

* * *

Ali and Harriet rummaged through the costume bag.

'I can't see anything big enough for Shaun in here.' Ali dropped a tunic that had briefly caused a flicker of hope, but on closer examination, it was clear it wasn't long enough. 'How tall is he again?'

'Six-four.' Harriet began to fold up the pile of rejected clothing. 'We're going to have to call in the big guns.'

'I'm sorry?'

'Mabel. She'll know what to do.'

'I'm not sure she'd like being compared to an artillery piece.' Ali picked out a belt and sword from the spare supplies. 'At least these will work whatever size he is.'

'I'll see if Mabel's free.' Harriet put down an extremely creased shirt.

'Won't she be busy with food for the hordes?'

'She will, but as you and I are never going to get jobs as seamstresses, then I don't see what option we have.' Harriet got up. 'I'll offer to take over in the kitchen.'

'Can you cook?' Ali asked as they headed along the corridor.

'I was thinking more of offering to peel any veg that might be needed for dinner.'

'Won't you be needed for rehearsals soon?' Ali checked her watch. 'It's just gone two.'

'Matt said he'd call me when I was wanted. Shaun is doing a full walk-through of just his part first.'

'In that case, I'll help in the kitchen too.' Ali leant against the doorframe. 'And while we're peeling spuds, you can tell me if Rob has got his act together and kissed you yet.'

THIRTY-EIGHT

FRIDAY DECEMBER 17TH

The birds overhead sang as if it was the start of spring rather than mid-winter as Helen wandered through the woods at the foot of the garden. The sun, low in the sky, was doing its best to illuminate the land.

Her planning notebook to hand, Helen headed towards her favourite bench. Hidden among the trees, it had been positioned years ago, to overlook the river that meandered off into the distance at the point where Mill Grange's land met the moor.

She'd taken the route many times since first coming to Mill Grange, but this was the first time Helen had found someone else sitting on the bench when she got there.

Sue?

Helen hesitated. Tom's ex hadn't noticed her. Staring out across the moor beyond the thinning trees, Sue's face was lined with care. Helen realised it was the first time she'd seen Sue without make-up on. Torn between her natural instinct to help and a desire to creep quietly away, Helen's decision was taken from her by the abrupt ring of her phone.

Swinging round, Sue looked startled as Helen answered the call.

'Tom?... Yes, no problem. About half an hour...? Okay, see you later. Bye, love.'

Slipping the mobile into her coat pocket, Helen apologised. 'I didn't mean to make you jump. Hardly anyone ever comes here.'

'You were after some peace, away from all the acting chaos.'

Helen lifted her notebook. 'I thought I'd get a few ideas jotted down for an event I'm running in Bath.' She looked out across the view. 'This place always gives me inspiration. I hadn't realised you knew about it.'

'I didn't.' Sue shrugged. 'I was walking and stumbled across it.'

Knowing she couldn't leave without asking what was wrong, Helen sat on the bench next to Sue.

'I imagine I'm the last person you'd want to talk to, but if you do need to offload, well, I'm here.' There was a short silence, before Helen groaned. 'God, that sounded so, so... trite. Patronising, even. I was just...'

'Being nice.' Sue kept her gaze on the river in the valley below. 'I know. Everyone here is so *nice*.'

'You say that like it's a bad thing.'

'It can be a bit hard to take sometimes.'

'Oh.' Helen fought the urge to apologise.

As the awkward seconds lengthened into minutes, Helen shivered under the shade of the naked trees that sat behind the bench. She got back to her feet. 'I should go. Tom's expecting me.'

Helen had taken two paces when Sue, her tone unusually

subdued, asked, 'Is Dylan alright? I mean, has he been okay since I left?'

'He misses you, if that's what you're asking, but yes, he's been alright.'

Sue played with her perfectly manicured fingernails. 'Thank you for looking after him for me. I know Tom does, but you... It couldn't have been what you planned. A new man with a full-time son in tow.'

Offended on Dylan's behalf, at the implication that he was some sort of inconvenience, Helen bit her tongue. 'He's a pleasure to have around.'

'Hard work though.' Sue's eyes met Helen's. There was a pleading to them that Helen hadn't expected to see. '*Please* tell me you find it hard work sometimes too – it can't just be me can it?' Now she'd started talking, Sue's words sped up. 'I love Dylan to bits, but there was never time for me. I had no energy for anything. I lost myself, turned into someone I didn't like, but then I met Nathan and he liked me. He gave me a way out. Freedom from the daily routine and I grabbed it. It's just...' Sue's gaze fell back to the hands folded in her lap. 'I hadn't banked on the guilt. Then I saw Nathan with Harriet. Am I like that?'

Helen didn't know if she was supposed to reply or not. She sensed there was more that Sue had been about to say, but had thought better of it.

Eventually, unable to stand the silence that even the bird-song couldn't fill, Helen said, 'You aren't Nathan, and although you sometimes have a funny way of showing it, neither Tom nor I have ever thought that you don't love Dylan.'

Sue gave a weak smile. 'But you think I'm a neglectful mother sometimes.'

'Neglectful, no. A little self-centred perhaps.'

Sue laughed. 'Is that better than being outright selfish or not?'

'Better, definitely.' Helen sat back down. 'Perhaps you could talk to him a bit more on Zoom, send him postcards, that sort of thing? So that he knows you're thinking of him.'

Sue muttered, 'I mean to, but it's hard. I miss him. Sometimes not talking to him, missing out on seeing his happy face, is easier than actually seeing it.'

'I understand that, but Dylan doesn't.' Helen sighed, aware that she might have been doing Sue a disservice. 'It isn't my place to say anything, but please don't compare your parenting of Dylan with Nathan's of Harriet.'

'Because he clearly does not care about his daughter, whereas I love my son to pieces.' Spoken as a statement and not a question. Sue exhaled a slow frost-tinted breath. 'Harriet is a good kid. When she asked Nathan for a lift to the hospital, he'd had a drink so couldn't drive anyway, but rather than being sympathetic he reacted as if she'd asked to take all the money from his bank account.'

Nausea swam in Helen's stomach. *Was Tom right? Was Sue going to leave Nathan and come back?* Not sure what to say, she muttered, 'Rob was very grateful to you for driving Harriet to the Musgrove.'

Sue held her fingernails up before her, as if checking for blemishes. 'It crossed my mind that Nathan was unwilling to help because he didn't like the idea of Harriet dating a black man, but although he's a self-centred bastard, he isn't a racist.'

'Then, the only question you have to ask yourself is, do you love Nathan despite his less attractive traits?'

'You make it sound simple.'

'Nothing worthwhile is simple.' Helen checked her watch. 'I'm sorry, Sue, I have to go.'

'Because Tom called.' Sue flexed her long slim fingers out before her. 'You came here to work; if I hadn't been here to disturb your plans, and you'd started work, would you have answered his summons?'

'It was a request, not a summons. The play is tomorrow and they need help.'

Sue shook her head. 'And that's the difference between you and me. I'd have stayed to finish what I needed to do first.'

'I'm not going to apologise for that just so you feel better.'

Sue's eyebrows rose. 'Good for you.'

'Are you coming up to the house? I'm sure Dylan would like to see you.'

'I told him I'd see him tomorrow night.'

'That doesn't mean you can't surprise him with extra mum time.'

Sue stood up. 'Maybe I'll pop by again later; now I think I'd better face Nathan. We have a few things to sort out.'

* * *

Shaun stalked across the stage. His script was in his hand, but remained unopened. Approaching Matt, he flew into his lines as if his life depended on it.

Two minutes later, his speech as Polixenes defending Hermione, pleading their innocence of an affair delivered, Shaun collapsed onto a chair at the side of the stage and took a long draught of water.

'That was fabulous.' Thea passed him a bar of chocolate. 'I knew you'd be good, but that was awesome.'

'Hardly.' Shaun blew out an anxious breath.

'If you weren't good, Matt would be here talking you through how to improve, but look, he's over with Neil and Dave setting up for their scene.'

Shaun shook his head. 'It was so long ago, and yet the words are just coming back.'

'Maybe because last time you delivered them was tainted for you, part of you has been waiting for the chance to prove that you can act the role well?'

'Or it could be that I tend not to forget lines once I've learnt them. I could recite pretty much every word I've ever delivered on *Landscape Treasures* should anyone wish me to.'

Thea laughed. 'I think I'll pass thanks.'

'What if... what if I'm no good when it comes to it?'

Thea glanced at Shaun in surprise. 'You'll be fab. All you need is a costume, and you'll be the King of Bohemia through and through.'

'Thanks, but I was like that last time. I knew every word, every position, every gesture, and still I got slated.' Shaun took her hands in his. 'Thea, I'm really nervous.'

'But you never get nervous.' Thea was amazed. 'You stand in front of television cameras all day.'

'You can stop cameras rolling and start again if it goes wrong. Theatre's a very different proposition. There's no retakes. You cock it up and everyone remembers and everyone is let down.'

'You won't let anyone down.' Thea gave Shaun a cuddle. 'Pretend the cameras are there. Tell yourself it's the same as when you're filming. You rarely need to do retakes.'

'Rarely isn't the same as never.'

Thea wasn't used to seeing Shaun unsure of himself.

'Everyone knows you're stepping in to save the show. No one is expecting you to be perfect.'

'But I want to be. I want Matt to be able to trust me not let his troupe down.'

'I can't promise you won't slip up here and there, but hardly anyone in the audience will know the words to *The Winter's Tale*. As long as you keep going, a minor mistake here and there will go unnoticed. All that matters is that the play happens. You're doing this for Mill Grange as well as for Harriet's Equity card and The Outdoor Players.'

'Yeah.'

'And let's face it, Shaun, you're doing this because you need to prove to yourself that you can. Am I right?'

He kissed her softly. 'Aren't you always?'

'Finally, the penny drops.' Thea laughed. 'Seriously though, love, I feel bad about backing you into this, but it's for a good cause.'

'It really is.' Shaun tugged Thea gently to one side. 'I keep meaning to say, I'm sorry about the new dig check taking so long. Every time I think we're sorted I need to check something else and...' Shaun's mouth closed mid explanation as he caught a movement out of the corner of his eye. 'Oh God.'

'What is it?' Thea followed the direction of his gaze. 'Hell, I'd forgotten about them!'

'Wish me luck.' Shaun got up to greet the television news crew that Mabel was excitedly ushering into the walled garden.

'Just now you were longing for the comfort of television cameras.'

'And if they were here to talk about archaeology, then I'd be running in their direction.'

'You really are nervous, aren't you?'

'Now the penny drops.' Shaun kissed her forehead. 'Once more unto the breach, dear friends...'

* * *

Helen found Tom in the kitchen. He was making up two giant flasks: one of tea and one of coffee.

'You got a thirst on you?'

'They're for the television folk as well as the audience.'

'What audience?' Helen passed a pile of teaspoons across the table for Tom to place on a tray.

'The cast not currently rehearsing are watching, as are Dylan, Thea and Sybil.'

'Sybil?'

'Yeah.' He pointed to three large plastic tubs near the larder. 'She popped in for two minutes to deliver the food for tomorrow's interval refreshments an hour ago. She's not gone yet.'

'Are they watching the rehearsal or the TV crew filming Shaun?'

'Both probably.' Tom tilted his head towards a lemon sponge waiting to be cut into slices. 'Sorry I had to disturb your work, love. Would you mind sorting out the cake for me?'

Helen selected a knife from a stand by the Aga. 'I was already pre-disturbed.'

'How do you mean?'

'Sue.'

'Sue?' Tom's hand rested on the kettle handle as he paused in the act of filling the first thermos. 'She came to your office?'

'No, I went for a walk to try and think through everything

I need for the exhibition that lands smack in the middle of my maternity leave. She was on the bench in the woods.' The knife sliced through the sponge. 'I think you're right. I'm not sure she'll go back to Australia with Nathan.'

'Shit.'

'Exactly.' Helen laid down the knife. 'I know we should want her around for Dylan's sake but...'

'But life is easier when she isn't here.' Tom continued to fill the flasks. 'Did she say why?'

'Nathan's treatment of Harriet.'

'Really?' Tom lowered the kettle to the table. 'At least that's a good reason.'

'To be honest, Tom, although I'd be stretching the truth if I said I found myself liking Sue, I found myself respecting her a bit more. She was very honest. She feels as guilty as hell about leaving Dylan.'

'Sue actually said that?' Tom sealed the lid to the tea flask. 'I'm impressed.'

'She left me to go and talk to Nathan.' Helen gathered a pile of plates from the cupboard by the door. 'Um, Tom?'

'Uh-huh.'

'Sue said something that made me think. She said that, when she was looking after Dylan full-time she lost herself. She became someone she didn't like. What if...?'

'If you're about to ask me if you'll turn out like that, then stop.' Tom dropped a hefty spoonful of coffee powder into an empty flask. 'You're nothing like Sue. And don't forget, Sue was on her own. You aren't. I can't say I like much of how she brought Dylan up early on, but I have to credit her with turning her life around once he went to school. Raising him alone – even though that was her choice – can't have been easy.'

Helen nodded. 'Thanks, Tom. It's all so scary.'

'Exciting scary.'

'Very exciting scary.' Sliding the cake slices onto the waiting plates Helen gave her partner a meaningful look. 'Tom, if you don't put at least five more spoonfuls of coffee powder into that flask then you'll be delivering possibly the most disgusting beverage of all time to some very thirsty people.'

Tom laughed. 'Still not lost your taste for caffeine then?'

'Heaven forbid.'

THIRTY-NINE

FRIDAY DECEMBER 17TH

'A vastly different experience for you, Shaun, compared with giving us the ins and outs of a Roman villa or Saxon farm.'

The young woman from the local television news beamed at Shaun as she held out her microphone.

'Very much so. This, I have to admit...' Shaun twisted so that he could gesture an arm out across the walled garden, to where The Outdoor Players were waiting to continue their rehearsal '...is far more daunting for someone used to hiding behind the safety of a television camera.'

'I understand you will be playing Polixenes, one of the lead roles in Shakespeare's *The Winter's Tale*.'

'Indeed. Sadly, due to circumstances beyond his control, one of the original actors, a fabulous young talent called Rob Peterson, is now unable to perform, and so, yesterday, I was invited to step in. Years ago, I played the role of Polixenes at university. I will be apologising in advance to the audience for any mistakes I might make!'

The presenter laughed dutifully, managing not to make her humour sound forced as the camera panned across the garden. 'Mill Grange, a Victorian house now used as a retreat to help recovering military personnel learn new skills on leaving the forces, is a fantastic venue. You performed the opening ceremony for the manor when the new owner purchased it from the Exmoor Heritage Trust – is that right?'

'I did. It was an honour to cut the ribbon, an act that has led me to have an ongoing association with this amazing place, and the good people of Upwich and Exmoor.'

'And finally, are there any tickets left for the three performances of *The Winter's Tale*, here at Mill Grange tomorrow, Thursday and Friday evening?'

'The owners of Mill Grange, Sam and Tina Philips, have released ten extra tickets for each night. These will be available on the door, on a first-come, first-served basis. So if anyone would like to see the brilliant Outdoor Players, and find out if I can remember my lines after just twenty-four hours to rehearse, then do come along.'

'Shaun Coulson, thank you very much.'

Keeping his smile firmly in place until the red light on top of the camera went off, Shaun let out a gust of air. 'Okay for you?'

'I think so.' Tucking a lock of chestnut hair behind her ear, the presenter opened her laptop ready to run through the film. 'I'll check the sound quality, but it felt good. You agree?'

'Absolutely.' Shaun watched as he appeared on the small screen. 'While you're checking it over, can I tempt you to a sandwich, a slice of Tina's most excellent lemon cake, or both?'

* * *

Mabel pounced the second Shaun had delivered lunch to the news team. 'Can you come inside a moment, please?'

'Well I...' Shaun glanced over his shoulder. He could see Matt looking in his direction, clearly expecting him to return to the set. 'I think I'm needed over there.'

'I'm sure you are, but if we don't get you a costume sorted, then you'll be performing in that garden-stained shirt and jeans. Not exactly kingly regalia.'

'You're right.' Shaun raked a hand through his hair. 'Thanks for helping with this, Mabel.'

'I'm not sure if I have helped yet. I've adapted a plain T-shirt of yours that Thea found for me and sewn it into the tunic Rob was going to wear.'

'How on earth did you manage that?' Shaun regarded the formidable old lady. 'You never cease to amaze me.'

'I'd hold off being amazed until we've seen if it fits.'

'When you said you'd adapted a T-shirt into a tunic I wasn't sure what to expect.'

Shaun held up the pale blue and navy garment. It was hard to tell that it had been two different items of clothing only a few hours ago. The shiny military buttons Harriet had sewn in place on the original tunic no longer functioned as an opening, but added decoration to one shoulder. Pulled over the head, the enlarged tunic had a hidden opening, for ease of dressing, that Mabel had disguised with a flap of fabric Velcroed in place.

'How did you manage to do this so fast?' Shaun flexed his arms as he threw the cloak Rob had passed to him earlier that day around his shoulders, hiding all evidence that the neck of the tunic had a T-shirt neckline.

'Where there's a will... Anyway, it isn't finished. I wanted you to try it on before I over sew the stitching.' Mabel walked around Shaun, her sharp eyes examining how the garment sat. Every now and then she tugged at the material to make sure it wouldn't split on the seam as he moved around the stage. 'I think we may be lucky. This looks good. Comfortable?'

'Comfortable would be a lie, but it fits and I can move in it.' Shaun went to remove the cloak again. 'Better take it off. Wouldn't be good to get it dirty so late in the day.'

Mabel reached out to stop him. 'Normally I'd agree, but don't you think you should do at least one run-through with it on, so you get used to wearing it while you're out there?'

Shaun smiled. 'As ever, Mabel, you are absolutely right.'

Mabel's eyes hovered over the outfit. 'If you think those buttons are coming loose, you will say? I'd hate one to get lost.'

'Uh, yeah sure.' Shaun's hand automatically went to the buttons. 'They feel fast to me, Mabel.'

'Right. Good.' Wishing there'd been time to switch the buttons for others, so they could be returned to Bert, Mabel tilted her head in the direction of the drawing room. 'I think it's time Rob had a go with his crutches and came to help. He'll be feeling bad enough as it is, but if Matt doesn't give him a function, albeit behind the scenes, he'll be even more miserable.'

Swishing his cloak in true Elizabethan style, Shaun bowed at Mabel. 'You are a genius.'

The old lady giggled. 'Why thank you kind, sir. But why am I a genius?'

'Because—' Shaun lowered his voice '—I'm scared stiff about forgetting what I'm supposed to say. Ali has enough to do being prompt to everyone else when she isn't on stage herself. When she is on stage, now Matt is in the show, we have no professional prompt, so we'll just have to hope no one goes wrong.'

'I don't follow.'

'Rob could be my personal prompt. He knows the role inside out.' Some of Shaun's anxiety eased from his shoulders. 'If I knew he was listening out for me the whole time, I'm less likely to mess up.'

'The psychological advantage of having someone in your corner you mean.'

'Exactly.'

* * *

'My prisoner? Or my guest? by your dread. Verily...' Harriet reached her hands towards Shaun. 'One of them you shall be.'

'Your guest, then, madam. To be your prisoner should import offending; which is for me less easy to commit, than you to punish.' Still dressed as Polixenes, Shaun shook his head at Harriet's Hermione.

From his seat under the patio heater, Bert chuckled quietly to Rob. 'Shakespeare really did use "verily" then? I thought that was made up.'

Rob kept his eyes on Shaun as he whispered, 'He really did.'

Clutching his mug of tea in his gloved hands, Bert watched as his friend moved around the stage with Harriet. A moment later, as Shaun's character, in a moment of frustrated tension, pushed his cloak away from one shoulder, Bert caught a glimpse of the buttons he'd seen Rob wear a few days before. The old man's breath caught in his throat, sending a coughing fit flying from his lips.

'Bert?' Rob made to fetch his companion some water,

before realising he couldn't use his crutches and carry water at the same time.

Rob's curse was curtailed as he saw Dylan dashing to his friend, with Thea behind him; a glass of water in hand.

'That silly new-moaner playing up, Bert?'

'Just swallowed the wrong way.' Bert patted Dylan's arm. 'Nothing to worry about.'

'Good, cos you won't want to miss the play.'

'True.' Bert whispered, 'We've got to see if Harriet is as good an actor as you are haven't we.'

'She's a proper actor. I was just pretending.'

Rob laughed. 'Dylan, acting is all pretending. I hear you are very good at it.'

'Oh. Ta.'

As Dylan watched Harriet moving around the stage area, Bert looked back at Shaun. Or more truthfully, he watched the buttons on the tunic as his memory took him to a time and place he'd tried hard to forget.

* * *

Pausing in the act of unfolding chairs for tomorrow's audience, a sense of unease shot through Sam as he heard Bert coughing. His palms prickled and the thump of a headache began to nag his skull. *This is ridiculous – I'm outside. Keep calm. Breathe slowly and...*

Sam's thoughts faltered as he saw Bert flex his hands. He looked at his own palms. He was flexing them in exactly the same way as the old man.

Wiping away the patina of sweat on his forehead and ignoring the thud behind his eyes, Sam put down the chair he'd been about to wipe clean.

What do I do?

In all the time Bert had been helping him battle his claustrophobia Sam had never seen any sign of the old man's private war with the same enemy. He knew about it of course, how Bert had developed similar PTSD after the Korean War. There had been no help for him like there had been for Sam. Bert had survived and coped because of one reason only. He had Mabel.

And I have Tina.

Sam looked round for his wife, before remembering she'd gone inside with Mabel. Returning his gaze to Bert, he saw that Thea had moved away, taking Dylan with her.

Go and see if he's okay.

Sam shoved his sweating hands into his coat pockets. Cross with himself for not dashing to his friend's side in the first place, he took some solace from the fact that, if he'd immediately run to Bert, it would have drawn attention to his coughing, which he wouldn't have liked. Sam observed Bert as he got closer. The old man's eyes were fixed on Shaun, but he was looking through him, as if he was watching something that wasn't there.

Sam frowned, until he saw Shaun move, the winter sun catching on the fastenings of his tunic, throwing out a glint of light.

The buttons.

'Fancy heading inside?' Sam crouched next to Bert's chair. 'If you see the whole play now, then you'll know how it ends before tomorrow night.'

'What?' Bert looked up, suddenly realising that Sam was there. 'Oh yes, of course.'

Lifting out a hand, Sam helped his friend rise to his feet and muttered, 'You alright?'

'Not on top form, my boy, but I'd rather keep that under wraps.'

'Understood.' Sam passed Bert his walking stick. 'How about we head back to your place rather than go inside? It's busy here and about to get busier. Now the light's going I can't imagine they'll rehearse outside for much longer. We'll have no privacy.'

Bert nodded, his eyes shining with the gratitude he wanted to express, but no words would form.

FORTY

FRIDAY DECEMBER 17TH

As he went through the motions of making tea, Sam racked his brain for a way to open the conversation. Getting nowhere, he concluded that he should treat Bert in the same manner that he'd treated him.

I'll dive straight in.

Placing the mug of tea in front of his friend, Sam said, 'I had a panic attack outside today. That hasn't happened since long before I came to Mill Grange. I know what triggered it and I'm concerned, not for me, but for you, Bert.'

'Oh.'

'When we spoke yesterday, you told me about the buttons on Rob's tunic. The ones Harriet had sewn onto his costume without realising that they were the only remains of a uniform from your time in the war.'

'Yes.'

'And today I saw your face when you saw those same buttons on Shaun's costume.'

'I hadn't expected them to be there. I thought Rob's

costume would be too small for Shaun. I'd told myself I wouldn't see them today.' Bert picked up his mug, the slight tremor to his hands forcing him to concentrate on not slopping his tea.

'I've never seen you like this before.' Sam added, 'A claustrophobia attack?'

'More the memory of one. An echo of the battle fought for so long.' Bert sighed into his mug. 'It's been a while.'

'Does Mabel know?'

'She knows.' Bert took a sip of tea. 'She is also busy wishing that she hadn't taken the buttons and put them in the sewing box at Mill Grange after finding them in a clear-up ages back. Bless her, she didn't know I'd hidden them from myself in my sock drawer. She thought she was helping by putting them in a place where they'd find use. She knew they weren't off my uniform. My buttons are in her jewellery box.'

'Bert, I am not going to push it if you don't want to tell me, but if our roles were reversed you'd encourage me to talk.' Sam paused, before adding, 'Do you want to tell me about the owner of the buttons?'

Placing the mug back on to the coffee table with slow deliberation, Bert took a deep breath.

'I was part of the 1st Commonwealth Division in Korea.'

As his friend lapsed into silence, Sam waited patiently for Bert to start talking again.

'His name was Jacko. Corporal Jacko Jackson. His family arrived in the UK from Kingston, Jamaica, in late 1949. He never told me the circumstances of that arrival, but I know he joined up straight away, keen to represent the country that had taken in his family. We fought alongside each other. Jacko was a good soldier. Never took a life he didn't have to take and saved more people than most.'

The pause went on far longer this time before Bert went on.

'He never made it home. I was with him when he slipped away. He was so proud to wear the uniform, he asked me to cut the buttons from his jacket and bring them home to his family.'

'And you did what he asked.'

'I tried to.' Bert rubbed at his eyes. 'Several buttons got lost along the way, but those three made it to England with me. As soon as I was back, even before I returned to Mabel, I made enquiries about Jacko's family, but it was too late. While we'd been away, his parents had been killed in a traffic accident in London.'

Sam saw the sorrow in his friend's eyes. 'Any brothers or sisters? Grandparents?'

'It had just been the three of them. Jacko and his parents.'

'I'm so sorry, Bert.'

'Seeing the buttons again after all this time, it made me think of him. I couldn't save him and then I failed to carry out the only thing he ever asked of me.'

Sam's insides tightened. 'Wars are full of comrades we can't save. It's not your fault you couldn't, nor that you were unable to give the buttons to his family.'

'Logically I know that, but...' Bert stared into his drink. 'He was shot on patrol. I was supposed to be with him, but I'd gone for a pee. I heard the bang of the gun. I heard him fall. I just froze.'

Sam's headache doubled as he watched his friend; anguish at his failure marked his face. 'You know that if you had been stood next to Jacko, you'd be dead too. You know that is a *fact*.'

'I do.' Bert lifted his face so his eyes met Sam's. 'Just as you know that knowledge makes not a blind bit of difference to how I – or any soldier – feels in that situation.'

'True.'

'It was after that the claustrophobia began. Tightly packed trees. I was in a copse when he died. There weren't many trees around, but these seemed to move, enclosing me. Preventing me from running to his side and...' Bert stopped, his breathing laboured. 'Then there was another incident later, inside a barracks... the walls were blown inwards – shell fire – we couldn't get out. Not for ages. That, on top of Jacko...'

As his friend's words faded into silence Sam moved to the sofa and sat next to him. 'You taught me how to cope with those feelings. *You* helped me move from living a daily nightmare, to living a life with only episodes of immobility and regret.'

'Thank you, Sam.'

'Jacko. He sounds like a nice man.'

'He was the best.' A happier memory nudged some of Bert's pallor away. 'Always smiling this great big grin. I didn't know many coloured folk back then. I once told him his smile was more impressive because of his dark skin. The second the words had left my lips I could have kicked myself and began to apologise. I hadn't meant anything, but...'

'I understand.'

'So did he. In fact he laughed his head off. Said it was the gentlest comment on his complexion he'd ever heard.' Bert shook his head. 'Gentle. That's a good word for him. He was truly gentle.'

* * *

Matt stuck his thumb up at Rob, signalling a job well done, before he turned to Shaun.

'What can I say? Only three requests for help from the prompt. That's quite something.'

Shaun pulled a face. 'Thank you, but it isn't good enough.'

Harriet wrapped her coat around her costume as they called the rehearsal over for the day. 'Are you kidding, Shaun? Most of us need more than that on our first run-through without a script, even when we've been practising our lines for weeks.'

'She's right.' Ali came up behind Harriet, untying her apron as she approached. 'And let's face it, people are dead keen on seeing you perform. Tina has sold every ticket and Sam has already dug out extra chairs for folk who arrive hoping for on the door tickets after the news piece goes out tonight.'

Flexing his numb fingers, Shaun sighed. 'That's my point. If I mess up more than once, then it'll be all over the village. Five minutes later the local press will know. I don't care two hoots about what they think about me – I'm just an archaeologist stepping in at the last minute. But I do *not* want to ruin your reputation. I've seen the write-up you guys get after each performance. You're good. You have a good reputation. What if I damage that?'

* * *

Helen switched off the light to her storeroom office and locked the door. She smiled as she saw Tom walking in her direction.

'I was about to come and tell you that everyone is finishing up for the day.' He slipped a hand in hers as they walked towards the kitchen door.

'My stomach rumbling became impossible to ignore.' Helen looked across the garden to see Harriet, Rob and Shaun come through the walled garden's gate.

Helen stopped suddenly. 'Do you think I'll look like that soon?'

'I'm sorry?'

'Harriet. At least, Harriet's costume.'

'I see, well yes, you will.' Tom smiled. 'Weird seeing her pregnant, even if it's only pretend.'

Helen started to walk faster. 'Come on, I'm starving.'

'Dinner will be an hour or so yet, love.'

Helen laughed. 'Believe me, I shall eat every scrap when the time comes. For now, I have a hot date with the biscuit tin.'

'A cookie and coffee starter. I may join you. Just to show solidarity you understand.'

'Naturally.' Helen briefly patted her stomach. 'We appreciate your selfless show of support.'

'It's a sacrifice I'm prepared to make. I'll even...'

The sound of feet moving quickly over the gravel path behind them caused Tom and Helen to spin round.

Sue, mascara streaked down her face, her eyes blotched with tears, was running towards them, her heels making her wobble with each step.

* * *

Having checked with Thea that they could use it, Tom left Helen to find some food, ushered Sue into the scullery office and closed the door behind them.

'What's going on, Sue?'

Crossing her arms in front of her chest, looking as if she was going to launch into an angry tirade, Sue's expression abruptly crumpled.

Unsure if he was supposed to comfort her or not, Tom stayed by the door. He'd only seen Sue cry once before, and that was when she told him she was leaving Dylan to live abroad.

Pulling a soggy tissue from her skirt pocket, Sue blew her nose and gave a rattling breath. 'Sorry. I bet you were about to have dinner.'

'An apology?' Tom's eyebrows rose. 'Wow.'

'Please, Tom.' Sue lifted her gaze to meet his. 'Don't.'

Moving to Thea's desk chair, Tom sat down. 'Come on then, tell me what's going on.'

'It's not really…'

'If you are about to say it's not really any of my business, the fact that we have had a son together makes me beg to differ.' Tom folded his arms. 'I'm assuming this is about Nathan?'

'Uh-huh.'

'So then?'

Taking the chair opposite Tom, Sue perched on its edge. 'You've heard the dismissive way he talks to Harriet.'

'I have. I don't like it.'

'Nor do I.'

Tom raked a hand across his closely shaved head. 'But you knew how he treated her before you went away.'

'It was different then.'

'How?'

'We were...' Sue blew out a heavy sigh. 'I've been so naïve.'

Wishing he'd collected a mug of coffee before he'd started talking to Sue, Tom said, 'Because you were in love and everything looked exciting. New life, new country, new man.'

'Yes.' Sue's voice was small. 'I was consumed by the need to escape my life.'

'To the extent that you no longer had to be a mum.'

Tom's words had been delivered softly, but nonetheless they cut into Sue. 'Don't ever think that I don't love Dylan.'

'I've never said you didn't. But I don't think you like being a parent very much.' Tom rested his elbows on the desk. 'It's hard work. And, let's face it, you did so much of it alone for so long.'

'I did.'

'You didn't have to.' Tom knew he was effectively saying "I told you so", but couldn't seem to stop himself. 'I would have been there for him whenever you needed me.'

'I know.' Sue clasped her arms tighter around herself. 'I made mistakes. There's no need to rub it in.'

'I'm sorry.' Tom got up and held his arms open. 'You really need a cuddle don't you.'

'Yes, but... Helen?'

'Helen will understand.'

'She will, won't she.' Sue allowed herself to be engulfed in Tom's familiar, and yet somehow alien, embrace. 'She's a good person.'

'And so are you.'

'I'm not. As Helen told me, I'm a self-centred person.' Sue felt herself relax as Tom stroked her hair.

'A fact that you accept and, when you stop and think, fight against.'

'Unlike Nathan.'

Tom looked into Sue's eyes. 'Which brings us back to the point. Why are you here talking to me and not sat in a posh restaurant with him?'

'Because I've left him. At least. I think I have.'

The mood around Mill Grange's giant dining room table was jubilant. A stark contrast from the post-breakfast gloom that several hours earlier had coated the manor like Victorian smog.

Listening to the excited chatter, her cast mates marvelling at how many problems the coming performance had overcome, Harriet discreetly shuffled her chair closer to Rob's. Battling the urge to lay a hand on his leg, she couldn't shift the idea that something else was going to go wrong. That, at any minute, their hard work would be for nothing after all.

Rob flashed her a brief but dazzling smile, before switching his attention to Matt. He was doing what Harriet knew she should be doing – listening to The Outdoor Players' manager, producer and director, giving his final guidance points for tomorrow's performance. Her eyes, however, found themselves continually drawn to a single figure at the end of the table.

Sat playing with her food rather than eating it, Sue looked like a fish out of water.

Why isn't she with Dad? Have they broken up?

Harriet shifted her gaze to Helen and Tom, one sat either side of their unexpected guest, both trying and failing to engage her in conversation.

Is Sue being here my fault? If I hadn't asked for a lift to the hospital then...

'You okay?'

Harriet turned to see Rob looking at her in concern.

'Matt asked you a question. Did you hear it?'

Harriet muttered an excuse for not paying attention. 'Sorry. I was going through my part in my head.'

Matt stabbed a piece of chicken onto the prongs of his fork. 'Don't worry. I was just asking everyone if they were comfortable with the run of their offstage tasks during the performance.'

'Yes, sorry. I'm good. I'll be on hand during the second half to help with scene changes until I'm needed on stage at the very end.'

'Fabulous.' Matt pushed his food into his mouth. Chewing, he added, 'That's everything sorted then.'

'As long as it doesn't snow,' Sam chipped in, his eyes straying to the window.

Matt stopped chewing. 'You don't think it will – do you?'

'Always possible.' Sam immediately regretted mentioning snow as he saw the cast exchange worried glances.

'Take no notice of him.' Tina nudged Sam in the ribs. 'He's just gone all Bear Grylls on you. If it does snow, then we'll dig out the stage, provide extra blankets for the audience, and shove up a load of marquees. No problem.'

'Really?' Ali sagged with relief.

'Absolutely.' Sam nodded. 'Snow, we can deal with.'

'But people might not be able to get to the manor if snow blocks the road.' Harriet's sense of foreboding returned.

Tina rounded on Sam. 'Why did you have to mention snow? Now everyone is panicking!'

'Sorry!' Sam sighed. 'I just have a feeling it might snow soon, that's all.' He turned to Matt and Ali. 'But really, even if there was an avalanche, the villagers from Upwich would get here. Trust me.'

'That's true.' Shaun nodded. 'No way would anyone local want to miss out. They'd come via sled wearing snowshoes.'

Matt laughed. 'Okay then, if you guys are sure. Then we are as ready as we can be.'

Ali's eyebrows rose. 'What's this, Matt? Aren't we having your usual "Don't go out and get plastered between now and the end of the run" speech?'

Matt swallowed his mouthful. 'Not that many opportunities to go out and get bladdered here, but Ali's right. I should ask you all, very nicely, to refrain from getting plastered in the name of calming last-minute stage fright. It's no fun, and terribly unprofessional, to give any performance with the remnants of a hangover.'

Shaun laughed. 'There speaks a man whose cast is largely comprised of students and recent graduates.'

'Don't you make fun.' Thea pinched a chip off his plate. 'Or I'll tell everyone how much practice your drinking arm got when you were a graduate TV presenter doing the conference circuit.'

Rob grinned. 'I hadn't realised you two knew each other at uni.'

'We didn't.' Shaun rolled his eyes as Thea stole another of his chips. 'We met at a conference about Roman Britain. Then we met again here several years later. It must have been fate.' He tapped the back of Thea's hand as it crept in for another chip. 'Although I do think fate could have found me someone who didn't steal food off my plate!'

Thea stuck her tongue out and took another chip. 'I only steal chips. I've finished mine.'

'Eat your chicken then.'

'I am.'

'You two are worse than Dylan.' The words from the other end of the table, muttered without malice, were so quiet, that Thea almost missed them.

'He is a good example for us, Sue,' Thea answered without thinking. 'A boy to be proud of.'

'I *am* proud of him!'

'Oh I...' Taken back by the snapping tone, Thea's fingers prickled with anxiety. 'I didn't mean to imply you weren't. I was just...'

'We know what you meant, Thea.' Tom nodded. 'He's a great lad. We're proud of him, aren't we, Sue?'

'Yes,' Sue mumbled, aware that the entire Outdoor Players cast were suddenly tucking into the remainder of their meal in silence. 'Sorry, Thea. I'll um, I think I'll go and see how he is. Excuse me.'

Harriet saw Tom and Helen exchange looks, silently asking each other if one of them should go after her.

'Why don't you go?' Rob whispered as he placed a hand on Harriet's leg. 'I don't think you'll be able to relax until you find out what's going on with Sue and your father.'

Harriet realised she had unconsciously placed her hand over his, and the presence of his hand under hers gave Harriet strength. 'You're right.'

Rob smiled. 'Tell me how it went afterwards.'

'You want to know?'

Rob leant forward. 'If it wasn't so damn awkward to move, I'd come up to your room and ask you in person, but as I can't do that, you'll have to come down to find me.' He paused. 'Will you – come and be with me before I go to Bert's?'

Placing a hand over Rob's again, Harriet held it there for a second, breathing out her answer. 'Yes.'

Getting up before Tom could beat her to it, Harriet excused herself from the table, and headed in the direction of Dylan's bedroom in search of her almost stepmum.

* * *

As soon as she left the friendly camaraderie of the dining room Harriet wondered what she was doing. If she was the one who'd caused a rift between her father and Sue, surely she was the last person Sue would want to see.

If you don't try and help, you'll feel terrible.

Harriet walked up the stairs to the attic and old servants' quarters where Dylan ought to be asleep. As she climbed she realised what it would mean for Tom and Helen if Sue and her father really had split up.

Okay, so I can feel worse than I do already.

Harriet was wondering how she was going to concentrate on acting the next day, her guilt swelling so much that even the promise of time alone with Rob later wasn't making her feel better, when she heard a faint sound.

She stood and listened.

There it was again. A slight shuffle, as if something was moving around the corner ahead of her.

This place is not haunted. Someone would have said.

Harriet went cold as she stood still, her hand gripping the

thin wooden handrail. Making herself focus on what might
happen when she saw Rob later, rather than the presence of
spirits, Harriet moved forward again.

*He put his hand on your leg. You put your hand over his
hand – he didn't pull away.*

Her mind a conflict of tumbling thoughts and contradic-
tory emotions, Harriet took the sharp right-hand turn halfway
up the narrow staircase, and came to a full stop.

Sue looked up with a start. 'Harriet!'

Taking a step backwards and crouching down so that she
didn't tower over Sue, Harriet mumbled, 'I came to see if you
were alright.'

Sue nodded. 'Dylan's asleep.'

'He's had a busy day.' Harriet felt awkward as she
mumbled, 'And so have we. I don't know about you, but I
haven't had any kip since we spent all night at the hospital.'

'I slept in the car while you were in with Rob.'

'Right.' Talking about sleep made Harriet feel tired. 'I
think my lack of sleep is catching up on me.'

'Do you need me to move so you can head to bed?' Sue
shifted to the side of the slim walkway.

'I'm on the floor below. Anyway, I told you, I came to see
if you were alright.'

Sue gave an overly dramatic sigh. 'You mean, have I split
up with your dad, and if so, what does that mean for you?'

Harriet felt her patience waver. 'No, Sue, I came to see
how *you* were. You were very kind to me and Rob last night.
Why is it so hard for you to believe I'd like to make sure
you're okay?'

Sue muttered. 'Sorry.'

'Do you want to talk about it?'

'I'm not very good at that.' Sue grimaced. 'Too long alone

or, if I'm honest, too long with the wrong sort of men. I've got out of the habit of sharing.'

Not sure she wanted the answer, Harriet asked the question anyway. 'And is my dad the wrong sort of man?'

Meeting Harriet's eyes, Sue shrugged. 'I hoped not. I don't know. He's so...'

Harriet sat down. 'He is, isn't he.'

'You don't know what I was going to say.'

'True, but I'd guess it would go hand in hand with him being stubborn, a bit controlling, and used to having things his own way.'

Sue said nothing as she nodded.

'Dad was on his own for a long time after Mum... went.' Harriet was amazed to find herself defending her father. 'It was just him and me, a six-year-old girl. He was out of his depth and coped by setting rigid rules, not just for me, but for himself.'

'He's had girlfriends since then though, he told me.'

'He did, but they were one-date wonders for the most part.' Harriet realised for the first time that she'd never questioned her father's lack of long-term relationships before.

'Nathan didn't want you to get used to a new woman in his life, only to have her ripped away from you again if the relationship didn't work. He told me that too.'

Harriet's mouth dropped open. 'He stayed alone because of me?'

'You didn't realise?'

'No.'

Sue chewed a fingernail for a moment, before saying, 'Your dad wasn't impressed with me for taking you to the hospital.'

'I worked that out.'

'But do you know why?'

'Because he doesn't like anyone doing something he doesn't want them to do.'

'No, Harriet, it was because he truly believed that it would be better for you, and for Rob, if you let him manage at the hospital alone.'

'How on earth could that have been better?'

Sue sighed. 'That's what I said. Your father responded by saying it would be a mistake for Rob to become dependent on anyone, and a bigger mistake for you to do the same at your age.'

'Dependent? Being there for a friend isn't being dependent, it's being kind.' Harriet closed her eyes. 'Dad's never got the hang of kindness.'

'You'd be surprised.'

'I would actually.' Harriet groaned. 'Look, Sue, are you and Dad together?'

Standing up, Sue brushed down her short skirt and picked specks of dust off her tights. 'I don't know. I told him I would give him time to think.'

'Think about what?'

Sue ruffled a hand through her perfect bob as Harriet got to her feet. 'I reminded him there is a massive difference between putting yourself first and acting as if you aren't interested in your child's life. And told him his way – his "hard life lessons" being the best policy – isn't good. I know it comes from him being hurt, and him not wanting you to ever feel pain like he did, but it's created a barrier between you.'

Harriet couldn't believe it. She found herself stuttering her words out. 'You really said that to Dad?'

'Yes.' Sue examined the nail she'd been chewing. 'His response was brief, as was my resulting ultimatum.'

'Ultimatum?'

'Either he accepts that you are a woman in her own right who doesn't need Daddy's overly stern protective hand anymore, or I leave him.'

'Sue!'

'I know.' The anguish Sue was doing her best to hide became visible for the first time. 'He acts like he does from a place of self-preservation, but even so.'

'Self-preservation?'

'You look like your mother.' Sue stared at her palms. 'Every time he looks at you he sees her.'

'Mum?' Harriet sank back down, perched on a stair, her hand steadying herself on the rail. 'But he never said.'

'Your father hasn't said much to anyone for years, not about what's important.' Sue flicked a hair from her eyes. 'And if he doesn't start now then he'll be going back to Oz on his own.'

Harriet's head spun. 'So, now what?'

'Now, I go back to the pub and see if I'm packing my suitcase and bringing it back here or not.'

'Back here?'

'Tom and Helen said I could share with Dylan until I'd sorted myself out.'

'Oh.'

'They are much nicer people than I am. Dylan is lucky to have them.' Sue paused. '*I'm* lucky Dylan has them.'

'I...' Harriet wanted to say something, to ask a million questions, but she found her words had run out.

'Don't worry. Thea will tell Harriet.' Shaun guided Rob into the passenger seat of his car, passing him his crutches, before shutting the door.

'I promised we'd talk after she'd seen Sue.'

'I know, mate. I'm sorry to whisk you away, but if you don't get to Bert and Mabel's cottage soon they'll have fallen asleep on the sofa.'

Rob looked up at the side of Mill Grange. Its granite walls projected both shadows and the moonlight. 'I appreciate them putting me up and you for driving me over to them.'

'No problem.' Shaun saw the anxiety on the younger man's face. 'Harriet will be fine. There's good phone signal at Bert's – you can call her.'

Rob tried to flex his toes and immediately regretted it as a band of pain ran up from his ankle. 'She might be too tired to talk. Neither of us slept last night.'

'All the more reason for getting you to Bert's.' Shaun switched on the engine and drew the car from its parking space. 'Matt won't thank you for being too tired to be my prompt. Something I am really grateful for by the way.'

'My pleasure. Not everyone can say their claim to fame is to be Shaun Coulson's prompt.'

Shaun laughed. 'I am confident you'll have far better claims to fame soon.'

'Depends how the ankle heals.' Rob looked down at his booted foot. 'There are limited roles out there for actors with a limp.'

'I'm sure it'll be fine.' Shaun glanced at his passenger. 'Just make sure you rest it and, when the time comes, do all the exercises they give you to get it back to full strength.'

'The exercises won't bother me. The resting bit is already proving a challenge.'

'Especially as you'd like to be taking Harriet out and about in your car, rather than sitting with your leg up on the sofa.'

Rob almost denied it, but then changed his mind. 'Something like that.'

'Thea informs me that Harriet likes you beyond friendship.'

'She does?'

Shaun wasn't sure if he should have said anything. 'I assumed you knew.'

'Hoped, yes. Suspected, maybe. Knew – nope. I mean, each time we try to have a date something happens.'

'And now, tonight, you said you'd chat to her, and you aren't going to be there.'

'Yep.'

'Sorry, mate.'

'It's okay. I understand why, and so will Harriet. But all

these obstacles do make me wonder if she and I are meant to be.'

* * *

Thea opened a bottle of Pinot at speed, while Tina grabbed three glasses and poured a jug of water.

Less than ten seconds later, having operated like a well-oiled machine activated in time of crisis, they had sat Harriet down at the kitchen table, pushed a half-full wine glass into her hand, and turned the Aga up, so that it pumped a comforting heat out across the room.

'I'm not supposed to drink until after the play's over.' Harriet, her eyes heavy from lack of sleep, focused on the pale liquid in her glass.

Thea disagreed. 'You are not supposed to get drunk. Big difference.'

Harriet gave a massive yawn, prompting Tina to ask, 'Are you sure you don't just want to go to bed?'

'I do, but I'd never sleep. There's too much in my head, and...'

'And?' Tina picked up her glass.

'What if I am too preoccupied to remember what I'm supposed to do?' Harriet shuddered, 'I have this image in my head of standing in front of all those people, and nothing coming out of my mouth. Hermione may as well be mute!'

Thea disagreed once more. 'I've been watching you out there. You're word-perfect. Shaun reckons you're the real deal acting wise.'

'Oh.' Harriet gulped. 'That's kind of him, but...'

'I think you'd better tell us – if you want to – what Sue said.' Thea gave her a coaxing smile.

'It isn't Sue that's the problem. It's my dad, or rather me. Apparently, I was the problem all along, but he hadn't told me.' She took a small sip of wine.

'Go on,' Tina coaxed.

'He never had girlfriends as I was growing up. Actually, he did. There was an occasional one-night stand here and there over the years. Maybe two or three times a year I'd find an unfamiliar female face sat across me at the kitchen table for breakfast.'

'Not surprising. Your father is a handsome man.' Thea spoke practically. 'He must have cared for you a great deal for there not to have been more women.'

'So I've just discovered.' Harriet swirled the remaining liquid around her glass. 'Thinking back, once I got to about ten, there was no one at all.'

'Because you were old enough to understand why a woman might stay the night?' Tina asked.

'I suppose so.'

'And this is why Sue was here?' Thea played the stem of her glass through her fingers. 'To tell you that, despite appearances, your father cares for you?'

'No... Sue's walked out on Dad.'

Thea gave a sharp gasp. 'She's left Nathan?'

'Unless he starts treating me better, yes.'

'Oh God.' Thea glanced at Tina as she said, 'Sorry, it's just...'

'I know. Helen, Tom and Dylan. I get it.' Harriet took another mouthful of alcohol before repeating everything Sue had told her while they were sat on the attic stairs. 'How am I supposed to concentrate on the play, when I'll be looking out to see if it's just Sue in the audience, or just Dad, or both of them together? Sue said she'd come back here to sleep if they split up – but she hasn't come back yet. So maybe... oh I don't know.'

'And that's what you were going to talk over with Rob?' Tina asked.

'Yeah.' Harriet gave another almighty yawn. 'And that's the other thing. I've been so *stupid*. I started to dare to think that perhaps...' Her shoulders sagged in defeat. 'We *almost* talk. We *almost* go on a date. It's always *almost*. Life keeps getting in our way. It's as if we aren't meant to be. And let's face it, he could have anyone he wants, so why would...'

'Stop right there.' Tina raised a hand. 'We went through this before he broke his ankle. Rob likes you. You like him. Rob's a good bloke, but if you're thinking he is too good for you, then I shall withdraw the Pinot!'

'Thanks, Tina.'

'You can't control what your dad and Sue decide to do, Harriet. Nor are you responsible for the decisions your father made while he was bringing you up.'

'Tina's right,' Thea agreed. 'Whatever cockeyed way your dad did it, he did a damn good job of raising an intelligent and talented young woman.'

'Well I...' Harriet's cheeks bloomed.

Tina nodded. 'And as to Rob, remember what I said when you arrived here. If he is the right man for you, it will happen. Sounds simplistic, and I can't promise life won't keep throwing boulders at you, but if he is the one, then it will happen.'

Thea looked up at the clock on the kitchen wall. 'It's almost nine-thirty. That's late for someone who has been up all night and has to act their socks off tomorrow. Why don't you head to bed?'

Harriet rose to her feet. 'Sue does love Dad. I can see it in her face when she talks about him. Perhaps it'll be okay.'

'Perhaps it will.' Thea gave Harriet a hug. 'Either way, what's really important is that she has taken a stand on your behalf.'

* * *

Shaun climbed into bed next to Thea, wrapping an arm around her. 'You have a good evening?'

'More interesting than good.' Thea rolled around to face him. 'Sue might have left Nathan and Harriet has decided it's all her fault.'

'Why would it by her fault?'

'It isn't, but I can see how she has jumped to that conclusion.' Thea reached up for a kiss. 'It doesn't help that she is coping with the pressure of her first professional performance at the same time.'

'That, I can understand.' Shaun pushed a strand of Thea's straggly brown hair away from her face.

'And the situation with Rob hasn't helped either. She's close to giving up on them happening.'

'So is he.' Shaun cupped Thea's face in his hands. 'Rob's got to thinking that they aren't meant to be.'

Thea sat up. 'I must text Tina – we need to make sure they get breakfast together, undisturbed, in the morning, and then...'

Shaun placed a palm on Thea's shoulder. 'No you don't.'

'But they're meant to be together.' Thea sighed. 'Rob has told you he likes Harriet, right?'

'Yes.'

'And Harriet has told me, Tina and Ali that she likes Rob.

You only have to see them together to know they feel comfortable around each other.'

'I'm not disagreeing with you, love, but you can't make things happen for other people.'

'And if our friends had taken that attitude with us, where would we be?' Thea focused her gaze on his. 'You know as well as I do that our mutual stubbornness would have dug us into the sort of hole we couldn't get out of, archaeologists or not.'

'I know, but with the play just around the corner, surely it's best to hold off the matchmaking. What if you go all *Blind Date* in the morning and it goes wrong? The last thing Matt needs on top of everything else is a Hermione and Leontes who are too embarrassed to look at each other.'

'I suppose you're right.' Thea rested her head on Shaun's shoulder. 'But, what with Nathan being such an arse, Harriet might be glad of someone to hug before and after the show.'

Shaun sat up. 'You aren't going to let this go are you?'

'I can't help feeling it's our fault they aren't a couple already.'

'Our fault?'

'We ruined their first date in the pub.'

Shaun rolled his eyes. 'You mean *my* fault for not being able to read everyone's mind and guessing it was a date.'

'Pretty much.' Thea poked him playfully in the ribs. 'But either way, if we could just nudge them in the right direction.'

'I still think it would be a mistake to push it.'

'I'm not suggesting we push it, I'm suggesting we steer things a bit.'

Shaun's eyes narrowed. 'Define steer.'

'Make sure they are in the same room together with no

one else around. Perhaps there are errands that they could run together?'

'The man's on crutches!'

'Ummm.'

Shaun lay back again, pulling Thea down on top of him. 'You've had an idea haven't you?'

'I have insurance forms everyone needs to sign.'

'How romantic.' Shaun frowned.

'And Mabel needs a bit of shopping from Bampton. I wonder if Rob and Harriet would mind fetching it?'

'But...'

Thea put a finger to his lips. 'I promise I won't ask them to do anything that doesn't need doing. I just intend to ask them to do those things together.'

Harriet was surprised she'd slept. When she'd rested her head on her pillow the previous evening, her mind had see-sawed between confusion over her father's motives for pretty much everything he did, and nerves for the performance that was only hours away. Exhaustion had won the day, however, and the sun had been streaming through the chink in the curtains when she came round a little after eight o'clock.

Now, having checked there was no snow and breathing a sigh of relief, she smothered her body in two jumpers, tights, jeans and her coat and boots, and headed into the walled garden. Having taken the precaution of collecting some slices of apple to offer as a bribe, Harriet went to see the chickens.

'Everyone who lives here tells me this is the place to come for advice.'

Gertrude looked up at the newcomer, her questioning gaze softening as the apple pieces were dropped into the coop.

'The thing is, I'm acting here tonight.' Harriet looked

towards the greenhouse. 'And I'm scared I'm going to let Matt and Ali down. Let myself down.'

Two more hens joined Gertrude, making short work of the apple.

'What if I can't concentrate? My mind'll be on whether or not my father will come to see the performance. If he's there, but not with Sue, I'll be worried about Dylan. And if he doesn't show up at all, I'll feel even more wretched than I do now. I don't think Sue came back to the manor last night, but that might not mean anything.'

Gertrude stared at her human companion with such a knowing look that Harriet couldn't help but laugh. 'You're quite right, that isn't the only issue. There's Rob too, but at least I've made a decision on that front.' She sighed. 'I think you could say that my time at Mill Grange, although it's been spent with lovely people at a great venue, hasn't turned out as I'd hoped.'

Cocking her head to one side, Gertrude clucked in enquiry.

'I had silly romantic notions that I'm going to put it down to wishful thinking.' Harriet watched as the rooster emerged from the henhouse, a smug expression on his face. 'Rob is such a nice guy. I'm lucky to have him as a friend.'

Not sure if she'd imagined the positive incline of the head from Tony Stark or not, Harriet felt her phone vibrate in her pocket.

'It's a text from Thea. She needs me up at the house. An insurance form to sign in her office.' Harriet stepped away from the coop, 'Thanks, Gertrude. Duty calls.'

* * *

'Hey,' Rob raised a hand in greeting as Harriet walked into the scullery office.

'Oh, hi.' Harriet smiled. 'I was expecting Thea.'

'She had to dash off to help Mabel with something.' Rob pointed to the laptop. 'There's an insurance form to sign. Public liability, in case one of us hurts themselves during the show.'

'Sure.' Harriet sat down at the desk and pulled the laptop closer. 'You signed yours?'

'Yes.' Rob raised the leg he had stretched out in front of him and flexed his knee before lowering his booted foot again. 'Seems a bit like shutting the stable door after the deer has bolted, but there you go.'

Quickly signing, Harriet asked, 'How is it today?'

'Let's just say I'm extremely grateful to the inventor of ibuprofen, in all its forms.' Rob rubbed his ankle. 'Fancy helping me out – if you aren't expected at rehearsals?'

'Sure.'

'Shaun has asked me to pop into Bampton for him and Mabel. Apparently there's a bus, but as I have a car, I wondered...' He gestured to his ankle. 'Can you drive?'

'Well, yes, but I'm not insured to drive your car.' Harriet's heart began to beat faster as she double-checked she'd understood what Rob was saying to her. 'You'd trust me with your car?'

'You're my friend; you're sensible.'

'I quite like driving actually.' Harriet wasn't sure why she felt shy. 'I've been saving up for a car – along with everything else I'm saving for.'

Rob leant forward and opened up a tab on the laptop screen. 'Please don't think I made an assumption – but I made an assumption.'

Harriet laughed. 'Another insurance form?'

'Yeah. So you can drive my car as much as you need to for the next week.' Rob chewed his bottom lip as he regarded Harriet. 'But only if you want to. I could get the bus or...'

'Rob.' Harriet stemmed his flow as she read the form before her. 'I'd be delighted to drive you. Thank you.'

'You're doing me the favour, I should be thanking you.'

'I meant, thank you for trusting me with your car.' Harriet pressed send and the screen announced that the request was being processed. 'And strictly speaking, we're doing Shaun a favour. What does he want you to go to Bampton for anyway?'

* * *

Helen threw cold water over her eyes. She hadn't meant to oversleep, but as she stared into the bathroom mirror, she knew she'd needed every second of it. Stretching her arms up over her head, she tried to ease some of the muscles that had balled themselves into tight knots overnight.

As full consciousness claimed her, the two questions that had replayed themselves over in her head every few minutes, for the last two days, began their relentless cycle. *Should I have agreed to the amniocentesis?*

Helen spoke sternly to herself, as she did every time the thought revolved to the front of her mind. 'It isn't worth the risk of losing our child in the process, especially as there's no way we'd abort our baby either way. They will be who they are, and we'll love them whatever.'

The moment she had reasoned through her argument the second worry leapt to the forefront of her mind.

Will Sue stay, and if she does, will she take Dylan away?

For what felt like the thousandth time, Helen told herself that whatever happened with Sue and Nathan, Dylan would be fine, and that was all that mattered. As long as Dylan was loved and looked after, it didn't matter which parent he lived with.

'Except it does matter, because losing him now would break my heart – and Tom would...' Helen gulped down a rush of emotion and picked up her toothbrush. 'This is something you can do nothing about. Just wait and see. In the meantime, look after Tom, look after your baby and look after Dylan.'

* * *

From the other side of the garden, Tom saw his son drag the branch of a fallen tree towards Sam. Judging by the puffed expression and his red cheeks, it was taking all his strength to manoeuvre it. A moment later, Sam was taking the branch with a look of approval. Tom knew his friend would be congratulating Dylan on finding such a great addition to the bonfire they intended to light after the final performance of *The Winter's Tale* in two days' time.

'Are you standing here worrying about the same things I'm worrying about?' Helen arrived at Tom's side and passed him a mug of tea.

'Doesn't matter how many times I tell myself to stop fretting, my mind won't let it go.'

'Same.' Helen slipped a hand into Tom's as she followed the line of his gaze. 'Dylan looks happy.'

'It's going to be a bonfire to rival any we've ever had at Mill Grange.' Tom nodded. 'I believe Mabel has got in some extra-large spuds to jacket for the occasion.'

'Nothing like bonfire-cooked jacket potatoes.' Helen watched Dylan pass Sam an armful of dead leaves to throw into the heart of the twigs and branches. 'He's going to be filthy.'

'And have another story to tell his school friends when they come over to see his watch.' Tom found himself choked. 'I don't... I don't want to lose him.'

Helen sounded more certain than she felt. 'Sue made the decision to leave Dylan in England for his own good, and it was a hard choice to make. If she does stay this time Dylan will still be with us part-time. You won't lose him.'

'You're right. I know you are. But...'

Helen finished off his fear for him. 'What if Sue stays in the UK, but gets a job miles away?' She sighed. 'I can't answer that. I'm doing all I can not to think about the possibility.'

'A good line to take.'

'What time is their flight back to Australia tomorrow?'

'Late afternoon.' Tom stared up at the house.

'So if Nathan wants to watch Harriet in the play, it really is today or not at all.'

'Yes.' Tom threaded a hand around Helen's waist. 'Come on, let's go and help get the place prepped for tonight. There is an epic list of things to do on the kitchen table. I swear each time I look at it, Mabel, Tina or Thea have added more to it.'

* * *

Harriet had decided not to tell Rob that she hadn't driven for almost a year, just in case he had second thoughts about allowing her near his car. As she pulled into a parking space along the side of Bampton's main street, she was relieved that she'd neither stalled the engine or crashed the gears.

'So, where are we picking up this shopping for Shaun?'

'The antique shop.' Rob adjusted his footing on the crutches and winced.

'Do you want to wait in the car?' Harriet glanced at Rob's booted foot. 'I should have come without you. The doctor said you should take a few days before you moved much.'

Rob shook his head. 'Shaun has been very kind to me. I'd like to do this for him.'

Harriet hooked her bag onto her shoulder. 'Come on then, hop-along. Let's go and find this shop. Do you know what you're collecting?'

'A necklace.' Rob winced. 'Rats, I wasn't supposed to tell you in case you told Thea.'

'I'd never do that.' Harriet was hurt for a moment, but then she reasoned, Shaun didn't know her. 'But I can understand him not wanting to risk ruining the surprise.'

'At least it's something small.' Rob took a couple of awkward steps along the narrow pavement before finding his stride. 'I had visions of being asked to transport a chest of drawers or something when he said antique shop.'

Harriet laughed. 'Or a grand piano strapped to the roof of the car.'

'We'd look like something out of a sitcom, with me on crutches and you trying to rope a musical instrument to the roof of my little car!'

'So, where is this antique shop then?'

'Top corner of the street apparently.' Rob tore his gaze from his feet, and looked ahead. 'Actually, Shaun warned me it was a tiny shop. Why don't I go in while you fetch the bits Mabel asked for from that shop over there.'

Using his crutch to indicate a mini supermarket on the

other side of the road, Rob added, 'It looks busy. I'm not sure I'd do well being jostled among the shopping baskets.'

Harriet agreed. 'I don't think we should be too long either. I know we have all morning until we're needed to check props and costumes, but I feel bad not helping at the house – even though we are helping.'

'I know exactly what you mean.' Rob smiled. 'Shame though, that café over there looks nice.'

Harriet saw a small coffee shop, with a neat bay window and a beguiling collection of cakes on display. 'It does rather.'

'Once the play is over, I'd like to take you there – or rather, ask you nicely to drive us there so I can buy you lunch.'

'I'd like that.'

'And now you're covered to drive my car, maybe we could do two trips? One tomorrow, and one on Monday. Get some exercise before we have to prepare for the performances. Explore Exmoor a tiny bit.'

Harriet smiled. 'I'd like that, but—' she gestured to his ankle '—won't it be a bit tricky?'

'Not if we find some short, flat walks.'

'Alright. You're on.' Harriet hugged the shopping bag to her chest.

'Excellent.' Rob grinned. 'Do you think that touristy-looking shop over there might sell maps of the local area?'

FORTY-FOUR

SATURDAY DECEMBER 18TH

'What on earth?'

Mabel heard a crash, as if something large and hollow had fallen over, hitting the gravel outside the back door. Holding her clipboard to her chest like a shield, she hurried to the drive in time to see Sam and Tom manhandling a large green plastic box.

'Are you two alright?'

'This Portaloo fought back.' Sam helped Tom right the mobile lavatory. 'It literally fell off the back of a lorry.'

Mabel's eyebrows rose. 'What lorry?'

Tom wiped his hands down his jeans. 'It's taken the other loos around to the side of the house.' He pointed to the offending toilet. 'This one didn't want to join in the fun.'

Sam noted Mabel's disapproval. 'It looks as if the securing rope snapped. The driver was lucky it didn't give way while he was on the road.'

'Is it damaged?' The old lady eyed the contraption with the suspicion of someone who knew they'd rather wet themselves than use a Portaloo.

'A dent at the back corner.' Tom gestured to the far side of the cubicle. 'I think we'll leave looking inside to the driver when he has the other ones set up.'

'Wise.' Mabel referred to her clipboard. 'The toilet rolls are in the laundry. Thea's allocated three per toilet per play. Two to be put in position, and a third to be added after the interval.'

'Right you are, Mabel.' Tom aimed for the back door. 'I'll get them now.'

As Tom headed off, Mabel hurried to Sam's side. 'I didn't have the chance to thank you for helping Bert yesterday.'

'Least I could do. Bert's something of an anchor for me.' Sam dropped his tone to a hushed whisper. 'Seeing him having a semi-panic attack – it brought home just how far I've come since he began to help me. It's easy to forget that Bert's never really beaten it himself. It's just...'

'Something he deals with.' Mabel finished the sentence with a sombre dip of her head. 'And he does deal with it. As you do.'

Understanding the closed expression on Mabel's face, knowing there was no point in going over old ground, Sam asked, 'How is he today?'

'Appears to be happy as a lark. He's Dylan-sitting until Sue comes to collect him for lunch at Sybil's.'

'Dylan'll like that.'

'Time with his mum and scones.' Mabel approved. 'I hope Sue appreciates what a good lad she has there. Old-fashioned values in a six-year-old don't come along often and are easily ruined.'

'Tom's worried Sue will take him away.' Sam frowned. 'He hasn't said anything but... well, with Sue turning up at the manor last night and the atmosphere between Harriet and Nathan, it doesn't take a rocket scientist.'

'Bert would be devastated if... so would I come to that. But Sue *is* the boy's mother.' Mabel's head rose as she heard the faint sound of boots crossing gravel, the sound shaking her out of a rare moment's inaction. She patted Sam's shoulder as a harassed-looking man appeared from around the corner of the manor. 'Your luckless loo provider, I presume.'

* * *

Tina poked her head around the door of the scullery office.

'It didn't work.'

'Sorry?' Thea looked up from her laptop. 'What didn't?'

'Yours and Shaun's plan to throw Harriet and Rob together to sign forms and go shopping for Mabel so they could be alone to talk, realise they were madly in love, and live happily ever after.'

'Rats.'

'Beyond obviously having a nice time together, they are not – unless they are deliberately hiding it from everyone – a couple.'

'How do you know?'

'I was watching for them to come back. They looked happy and relaxed, but there wasn't a hand-hold or an exchanged knowing look in sight.'

Thea closed the lid of her computer. 'That's it, I give up! You need a hand getting lunch?'

'That would be great, thanks. I've sent Mabel home for a rest before this evening.'

'I'll just clear this and then...'

Tina's eyebrows rose as she saw a smile crossing her friend's face. 'What is it? What are you up to?'

'How about one last-ditch attempt?'

'But Thea, you *can't* engineer someone else's happiness.'

'No, you can't.' Thea sighed. 'Sorry, I think it must be exposure to this theatrical lark making me think in fairy tales.'

As the friends left the office and passed the back door, they saw Harriet and Rob in the driveway. They were stood by Rob's car with a map unfolded on the bonnet.

'Looks like they're planning a few trips now Harriet's insured to drive his car.' Tina smiled. 'Your meddling may not be needed after all.'

'Maybe not.' Thea smiled. 'Or maybe... Can you manage without me for five minutes? I want a quick word with Shaun.'

* * *

The scent of fresh baking hit Harriet as she pulled off her boots by the back door. She could hear some of her actor friends tucking into their lunch and her stomach rumbled. It was a shame that she and Rob couldn't have had lunch in Bampton; they'd had such a nice time together.

Hanging her coat on a hook by the door, Harriet glanced back through the window to Rob's car. They'd found several walks on Exmoor that were both short enough and flat enough to attempt with crutches, and had eventually, after much indecision, picked two. It felt good to have something to look forward to beyond the play's opening night – something she could enjoy once her father had left to go back to Australia – with or without Sue.

Feeling her worries about her father encroach on her

mood, Harriet took Shaun's keys from her pocket. He'd asked her to drop them into Thea's office on the way to lunch; apparently they kept jangling in his trouser pocket and the sound was driving his co-stars mad.

Hungry, Harriet dashed along the tiled corridor towards the old scullery. As she reached the open door, Harriet went to knock as she stepped inside, and stopped dead.

The papers that had been piled up in haphazard heaps on Thea's desk earlier were gone. In their place was a tablecloth laden with a pot of coffee, a plate of freshly cooked muffins, a rack of toast, pots of butter and marmalade, a jug of orange juice, two glasses and – sat with his leg supported by a stool – Rob.

'I hope this is alright. I know it's more like breakfast, but I didn't want to put anyone to more trouble than necessary.'

Harriet stood in the doorway staring at the picnic in disbelief. 'When did you, I mean... how did you...?'

'Shaun and Thea.' Rob was chewing his bottom lip in a manner that made Harriet want to hug him. 'I would like to claim it was my idea, but that would be wrong, although...' he risked a look at Harriet '...as soon as Shaun suggested it I was all for it.'

'Why didn't you say anything this morning? We've been planning walks and trips for lunch after the play. As friends.'

'Because we *are* friends.'

An embarrassed flush covered Harriet's face. *I've jumped to the wrong conclusion.* 'Well yes, of course we are.' She swallowed. 'So is this another thank you then? For coming to the hospital and driving to Bampton?'

'Yes.' Rob's voice wavered as he saw Harriet's uncertainty; privately cursing that he couldn't rush across the room to reassure her with a hug. 'But not just that. I keep trying to tell you that I'd like you to be more than my friend, but life kept getting in the way, so I told myself to let it go. I felt something was telling us we weren't meant to be.'

A small spark of hope ignited inside Harriet's chest. 'Me too. I told Thea as much.'

'And I told Shaun.' Rob gestured to the lunch picnic. 'Apparently they are fed up with us not quite admitting how we feel to each other, so they've helped.'

Conscious that she'd been gripping the doorframe, Harriet stepped inside the office. The click, as the door closed behind her, led to a silence that was filled with a tension she didn't want to break.

After a moment, Rob said, 'If this was a movie, I'd dash over to you, hold you in my arms and kiss you.' He gestured to his leg. 'As it is, I'm stuck here, but I can offer you toast.'

'Or the movie could play out differently.' Harriet stepped forward. 'How about a version of the film where the girl crosses the room, pulls the chair next to the boy very much closer to his side and...' Harriet pushed a chair next to Rob '... kisses him. Would that work do you think?'

Harriet's pulse accelerated as Rob's eyes met hers, his neck tilted in her direction.

'I think that would work. Tell me though—' he placed a hand on her cheek, tracing the contours of her face with a single finger '—how do you feel about cold toast? Because that's the penalty for a kiss before we eat.'

Harriet put her hands in his. 'I can live with the sacrifice if you can.'

* * *

Shaun glanced towards the kitchen door and then back at Thea, before picking up his sandwich.

'They'll be fine.' Thea grinned. 'Meddling always wins in the end.'

Shaun laughed. 'You've definitely worked with Mabel too long.'

Tina shook her head with a grin. 'Says the man who asked Rob outright if he wanted to set up a lunch date with Harriet.'

'Only so Thea would drop the subject and I could concentrate on being Polixenes.'

Thea nudged her partner in the ribs. 'Talking of which, shouldn't you be outside having one last run-through?'

Glancing at the kitchen clock, Shaun got to his feet. '"It's a far, far better thing that I do now..."'

'That's Dickens not Shakespeare!' Thea headed to the dishwasher, ready to swap a heap of clean cups and plates for dirty ones.

'Fitting though.' Shaun winked. 'And for goodness' sake, no listening at the office keyhole in your impatience to see if Rob and Harriet have got it together, or if they've decided to stay just good friends! We have done our bit – it's up to them now.'

* * *

'Cold toast could grow on me.' Rob brushed a crumb from Harriet's shoulder.

'It has a certain something to recommend it.' Harriet reached for a second slice, before burying herself back into place. 'I can't believe this.'

'Nor me.' Rob abandoned a crust to his plate. 'I wish I'd

thought of this myself, but even if I had, I'd never have had the nerve to ask for all this. Especially not today.'

'Thea and Shaun are so lovely. Everyone at Mill Grange is.'

'Bert told me it was a place of miracles.'

Harriet twisted around in surprise so she could see his face. 'I was told that too.' She smiled. 'I don't usually believe in miracles, although right now I'm wondering if Bert was right.'

'Bert *was* right.' Rob took the triangle of toast from her hand and kissed her buttery lips with slow deliberation. 'At the risk of killing the mood, you couldn't pass me a coffee so I can take some painkillers, could you? I can't quite reach the pot to refill my cup from here.'

'Seeing as you asked so nicely.' Harriet got up. 'I'm glad we weren't needed this morning. I've had ever such a lovely day, and what with my dad and everything, I really didn't think I would. Plus, I think if I ran through my lines again I'd start to forget them rather than remember them.'

Rob sighed. 'I hate that I'm not going to be up there with you.'

'I'm sorry.' Harriet suddenly felt awful. 'If it hadn't been for...'

Rob shook his head. 'Ask yourself, would I have been running if I hadn't been keen to get to you?'

Colour infused Harriet's cheeks. 'I hadn't thought of that.'

'There you go then.' Rob reached out his hand to hers and held it tightly. 'So, where are we going to walk and hobble in the morning?'

FORTY-FIVE

SATURDAY DECEMBER 18TH

Thea brushed non-existent dust off Shaun's shoulder before taking a tissue and polishing the buttons on his tunic.

'It's hard to think how much history these have seen.'

'Not to mention how much sorrow.' Shaun took a deep breath. 'I felt awful when Sam told me where they'd come from.'

Thea touched each button lightly before hiding them beneath the cloak. 'I'm surprised Bert didn't want you to take them off the costume.'

'I did offer to swap them for some other buttons from the box when I dropped Rob at the cottage last night, but he said to leave them until after the play was over. That if they held even a vestige of the goodness of the man who once wore them, then they would bring me luck.'

'I can just hear Bert saying that.' Thea stepped back to examine Shaun. 'You look every inch a Shakespearian hero.'

'I'm every inch a nervous wreck.'

'It doesn't show.'

'Nonetheless.' Shaun checked the time on his wristwatch before taking it off. 'Half an hour till lift-off.'

'You know you'll be fabulous.' Nervous on Shaun's behalf, Thea said, 'Rob will be there if you need him. Everyone will be cheering you on.'

'Including the local radio station.'

'Local radio?' Thea headed to the window of their bedroom to look across the garden. 'I knew the *Mid Devon and Somerset Gazette* were here, but not the radio.'

'I don't think they are officially, but that guy there—' Shaun pointed to a man stood back from the steady trickle of people milling around the garden '—the one in the cloth cap and brown leather jacket.'

'I see him.'

'BBC Radio Somerset.' Shaun gulped as the nerves in his gut threatened to escape in the form of an almighty burp. 'He's interviewed me before.'

'Maybe he just likes outdoor theatre. He doesn't have to be working to be here.'

'True, but that doesn't mean he won't notice if I cock up. Would make a good talking point on his programme wouldn't it? "Celebrities who overreach themselves". I can hear it now!'

'Not becoming paranoid at all then?'

Shaun exhaled a gust of pent-up adrenalin. 'A bit, maybe.'

'You are going to be fantastic.' Thea kissed his cheek. 'Come and find me in the interval for a drink yes?'

'Definitely.'

'Now, off you go. The others will be waiting. You don't want to be late and come across all prima donna.'

'God forbid.'

'Love you,' Thea called as he reached the door of their

room, but there was no reply as Shaun's boots clattered along the corridor.

* * *

Having poured its contents into a large metal, thick-bottomed jug, which was stood on a portable hob, Mabel placed a third, empty mulled wine bottle in a box under the table. Stood with Tina, beneath a marquee Sam and Tom had placed in the main garden, she passed a recyclable cup of the deliciously aromatic drink to the latest customer in a seemingly endless queue. 'Can we get more bottles from the kitchen? I've only got two left here.'

'I'll dash up there as soon as I can.' Tina poured milk into a cup of tea, while directing a customer to a box of sugar sachets sat at the far end of the table. 'I can't believe how fast the drinks are selling.'

'We could do with some more help.' Mabel tucked an errant hair behind her ear. 'Where are Tom and Sam?'

'Tom's on the drive, doing ticket duty until Thea has helped Shaun dress. Sam is making sure everyone gets to their seats once they reach the stage area.'

'And Helen?'

'With Bert and Dylan in the walled garden.' Tina paused to take an order for two black coffees and a hot chocolate. 'Sue hasn't arrived yet.'

Mabel pursed her lips. 'Any sign of Harriet's father?'

'Not that I've noticed.' Tina counted out some change and moved on to an order for an orange squash while Mabel emptied the fourth mulled wine bottle into the warming jug. 'Thank goodness I ordered extra from Moira!'

'Indeed, but it's no good to us in the house rather than here.'

Tina threw Mabel a concerned look. It wasn't like the old lady to sound flustered. 'I'll get it as soon as the demand for tea and coffee dies down.'

'Bert said Sue was on time to take Dylan to Sybil's for lunch.' Mabel slopped some milk, mopping it up distractedly. 'And that she dropped him back at the cottage on time as well. That, in itself, is an improvement on the Sue of the past. Before she went to Australia, promised deadlines were things for other people.'

Understanding what was making Mabel edgy, Tina passed a couple of cup lids to a customer before whispering, 'Whatever her faults, Sue loves her son too much to uproot him again.'

'I hope so.' Mabel sighed. 'Either way, I hope Sue hurries up if she's coming, because we need Helen's help, and right now we don't even have time to text her an SOS so she can leave Dylan with Bert!'

A pointed cough made both Tina and Mabel look up from stacking up a new row of biodegradable cups ready to be filled.

'What's all this I hear about errant toilets?'

'Sybil!' Tina chuckled. 'This village's gossip network never ceases to amaze me! One of the cubicles dropped off the lorry, that's all. Apart from looking a bit battered, it works fine. I wouldn't like to be in the driver's shoes when he gets them back to the depot though.'

'So, what can I do to help?' Without waiting for a reply, Sybil shimmied her way around the table and helped herself to a healthy dose of hand sanitiser. 'Teas and coffees or money-taking?'

'Has anyone ever told you, you're a saint?' Mabel's shoulders visibly relaxed.

'Once or twice, darling, once or twice.'

* * *

Sam counted the tickets he'd collected. Every single person expected had arrived, bar one.

Looking out across the main garden, he could see Mabel and Tina clearing the stack of used cups into bags for recycling. Their queue gone, Sybil had left them to it and taken her seat in the audience.

He could see Tina say something to Mabel, before she jogged over to join him.

'Is Nathan here?'

'Not to my knowledge.' Sam stared towards the driveway, willing Harriet's father to turn up.

'Damn.' Tina pulled on her pigtails as they walked to the walled garden. Peeping inside, she could see several rows of people, swathed in thick coats, hats and bundled under travel blankets.

Sam gestured back towards the refreshment tent. 'You fetch Mabel, and go in. Tom and I will clear up and prep the tent for the interval. Then I'll send him in to join you and I will catch the play tomorrow.'

'You sure?'

'Yes.' Sam nodded. 'I'll keep an eye out. If Nathan does make a last-minute appearance, I'll sneak him in.'

* * *

Stood beneath a patio heater at the side of the stage, hidden behind a cardboard cut-out of the Sicilian court, Ali wrapped Harriet in a giant hug.

'Boy it's weird cuddling you when you're pregnant.'

Harriet gave a nervous smile. 'Not as weird as wearing the outfit.'

'You okay?'

'Ask me after the show.' Harriet brushed out the creases Ali had put into her dress. 'How about you? Ready?'

'As I'll ever be.' Ali picked up her apron and tied it around her waist. 'I should go and join Matt.'

'Good luck.' Harriet exhaled slowly.

'Don't look so worried – you'll be fine.'

'But what if...'

Ali smiled. 'If you weren't nervous, then I'd be worried. Anyway, you know the role inside out.'

'Yeah.' A thin layer of sweat was gathering at the back of Harriet's neck. 'It's just that...'

'Your father?'

'Uh-huh.'

'I can't promise you he'll be here, but I do know it's his loss if he misses your first professional show. In the meantime, think of the positives.' Ali gave her friend another hug. 'For a start a little bird tells me, you and Rob headed out on a jaunt this morning. Have you been holding out on me, young lady?'

'Shaun asked us to pick up his Christmas gift for Thea. As he's doing us such a big favour, then we could hardly say no.'

'True. But Rob didn't need to go with you, and let's not forget, he let you drive his car.'

'I'm beginning to think you've got me bugged! How did you know that?'

'I overheard.' Ali smirked. 'That's a heck of an act of trust.'

'Well, I suppose...' Harriet felt self-conscious.

'Has he kissed you yet?'

Harriet didn't need to answer. The smile that involuntarily took over her face said it all.

'Yes!' Ali jumped into the air. 'Well stop moping then!' She checked her watch before taking it off and slipping it into her apron pocket. 'I must go. I'll give Rob your love shall I?'

'Don't you bloody dare.' Harriet poked her tongue out.

'Break a leg!'

Harriet gave her friend a friendly shove. 'I think a broken ankle has caused enough trouble, don't you.'

FORTY-SIX

SATURDAY DECEMBER 18TH

Harriet's neck muscles ached with the effort of not looking at the audience. She could hear them though. There was no chatter or, God forbid, heckling, but the background rustle from an assembled group of people – all listening, breathing and reacting to the action on the stage – rang in her ears. Normally the sound of a rapt audience gave her a rush of pleasure. A surge of adrenalin hit like no other. Today it just reinforced the fact that it was there, and she daren't look at it.

During the first scene, a confused pheasant had crash-landed near the chickens, sending a cacophony of concerned clucks from the sleepy hens, but otherwise all was quiet. The sound she'd been straining her ears for hadn't come. No one had got to their feet to allow a latecomer to shift along a row of the chairs Sam and Tom had laid out. And, although there had been an occasional intermittent cough cutting through the air, there had been no pointed, targeted, cough – the sound her father made when the world wasn't paying him enough attention. *If he was here, I'd know.*

While delivering her lines as Hermione, engrossed in her role, Harriet had been fine. But now, stood at the edge of the stage, hidden from the audience by a makeshift curtain, hung behind two large fake Sicilian hedges, she could feel a strong urge to look; to find out for sure if her father was in the audience after all. Before the confrontation with her father, Harriet had looked forward to the quieter part her character played in the second half of the play. It was a time she'd earmarked for sipping a hot drink to ease her voice back to top condition, before returning to the stage for the final few acts. Now she dreaded it. Another hour of waiting, while trying not to peer out over the blanket-swathed crowd.

This is ridiculous. It won't make any difference if he is there or not. Knowing she was lying to herself, Harriet focused on the stage. She could see Shaun and Matt. They were delivering a heated argument as the drama grew towards the mid-show climax.

What if Dad's gone back to the airport already?

Staring across the stage, Harriet could just see Rob. He was sat on a chair, his leg up; his eyes fixed on Shaun. Every now and then he turned a page of the script, keeping up with Polixenes' speeches as they were projected into the audience.

Letting the sound of Shaun's voice wash over her, Harriet closed her eyes and allowed herself to remember the sensation of Rob's hand in hers. Just minutes before the curtain had opened, he'd hobbled across the stage, drawn her aside and kissed her with a tenderness that promised so much – not to mention announced their relationship to all those around them. He'd whispered into her ear, telling her that, whether or not her father came, he was there for her. *'I hope I'll always be there for you.'*

Harriet opened her eyes in time to see Shaun hastening to the side of the stage, as if running from the land of Sicilia. Suddenly, the audience erupted into peals of glove-muted applause and the curtain was drawn across the stage. The cast members who'd been waiting quietly on either side of the wings dashed forward, moving the few pieces of stage furniture to the side.

As Matt used silent hand signals to direct the placement of the next set, Ali rushed towards Harriet.

'You were fantastic!' Keeping her voice low so it didn't carry to any members of the audience who had decided not to leave their seats, Ali added, 'And yet, you look like you've seen a ghost.'

'More, not seen one. I haven't dared peep to see if Dad is out there. Sue is, but...' Harriet's words disappeared into a rush of exhaled air.

Ali waved a hand towards the curtain. 'Would you like me to look?'

'You don't know who you are looking for.'

'True. But I know what Sue looks like, and if there is a man I don't recognise with her, then it has to be your father.'

Harriet crossed her arms over her chest. 'It's okay. I'll have to go out there in a minute anyway. I'm dying for a hot drink and a pee!'

'I'll come with you.' Rob's soft voice reached them before he did as he negotiated his crutches over the grass. 'If you don't mind waiting for me to lumber my way along.'

'Ali!' Harriet blushed, but her friend was already jogging towards Matt.

Rob smiled at Ali's hasty retreat. 'Shaun was brilliant. I only had to prompt one line, and even then, he remembered it as soon as I said the first word. I don't think anyone even noticed.'

'I certainly didn't. I'm sorry it isn't you on stage though.'

'Me too, believe me.' Rob glared at his booted foot. 'I'm getting seriously itchy feet on both levels.'

'Is the boot hot to wear?'

'Very.' Rob shuffled his leg. 'One foot is cold, despite a thermal sock, and one is experiencing the sort of humid, itchy heat you get in a sun-drenched greenhouse.'

'Maybe you should ask Mabel for a kebab stick from the kitchen. You could ease it in and have a scratch.'

Rob laughed. 'Funnily enough, the doctor told me to avoid all scratching devices. I got the impression far too many people use things that break off mid-scratch and end up back in casualty with foreign objects lodged in the boots. I'll take it off and have a good itch once we're inside.'

'I hadn't realised it came off. That's something I suppose.' Harriet flexed her toes. 'My feet are freezing.'

'And you wanted the loo and a drink. Do you fancy that hobble? I need to move. My circulation's fried.'

'I do, but...' Harriet faced the closed curtain.

Rob shuffled both crutches into one hand so he could take her palm. 'All your friends are out there. They will want to congratulate you on your fabulous performance. After all, you are halfway through getting the first tick on the road to having a valid Equity card. It's a big deal.'

'But...' Harriet sighed. 'Look, I know it's stupid, but if my father is there, I won't have been good enough.'

'Is that the problem – not that he won't be here, but that if he is he'll undermine your confidence?'

Harriet shrugged. 'Maybe.'

'I'll be with you.' Rob bit his bottom lip. 'I know that's no compensation for family, but...'

'It's more than compensation.' Rocking up onto her toes, Harriet stole a quick kiss. 'And the irony is, I don't even know why I crave his presence so much. It's not as if he's ever been a loving father.'

'Sue told you, it isn't that he doesn't love you, it's just that you...'

'I remind him of my mum,' Harriet mumbled. 'That's not my fault.'

'I know, but we are dealing with complex emotions of loss. When did fault, or fairness come to that, ever come into play, with those?' Tucking an arm around her shoulder, Rob kissed the top of her head. 'God, you smell good.'

Harriet giggled as some of her tension faded. 'Shea butter and almond shampoo.'

'I approve.'

'I'm very glad to hear it, although, if you hadn't approved...'

'It would have been my hard luck because you aren't changing your shampoo.'

'Precisely.'

'Glad to hear it.' Rob laughed, before he dropped his voice. 'Perhaps it's just as well my ankle is broken, or I'd have to jump on you right now, which would be unseemly in such a public sylvan setting, not to mention rather presumptuous on my part.'

Holding his hand a little tighter, Harriet experienced a rush of heat that had nothing to do with her thermals. 'While I am in agreement re the unsuitable setting, you have my permission to be presumptuous.

'Now, father or no father, I need to find a loo!'

'Don't you want to change out of the pregnancy suit first?'

'Not as much as I want to visit the bathroom! Believe me it's a devil to take off.'

'Come on then.' Rob looked around as they began to walk. 'After that, I must talk to Shaun.'

'To chat about the script for the second half?'

'Something like that.'

FORTY-SEVEN

SATURDAY DECEMBER 18TH

Shaun had managed to make it into the main garden and halfway to the refreshment tent before the journalist from the local press came to his side; Dictaphone optimistically to hand.

Greeting him politely, Shaun looked ahead to where Thea was holding out two mugs of coffee expectantly. *So much for five minutes with my girlfriend.*

'Quite a departure for you Mr Coulson.'

'Please, call me Shaun.' He hooked his cloak up over his arm. 'And yes it is. This isn't something I've done since university...'

* * *

Thea saw Shaun's apologetic glance and returned to the refreshment tent with his drink.

'Shaun's been ambushed by the press. Can I do anything?'

Tina motioned towards the last full scone tub. 'Could you

open that for me? We've almost sold out of Sybil's finest creations already.'

'No problem.' Arranging the mix of cheese and plain scones onto a platter, Thea inhaled the aroma. 'They may not be fresh out of the oven, but they still smell of the promise of delicious calories.'

Tina laughed as she took payment for a cup of tea. 'Shaun was brilliant.'

Thea passed some butter sachets across the table. 'I'm wondering how long it'll be before I lose my partner to the stage rather than an archaeological dig.'

Mabel, moving from the tea urn to the jug of mulled wine, patted Thea's shoulder as she passed. 'You make that sound as if that would be a bad thing.'

'I doubt it's a thing at all, but as I've hardly seen him, apart from at bedtime, since he got back from Northumbria, how would I know? Whenever he's around I'm working, and whenever I go to look for him, he's off somewhere or he's rehearsing.'

Tina and Mabel shared a troubled glance, before Tina said, 'You two are okay though, aren't you?'

'We are. There's been no rows or anything, but...' Thea sighed. 'Ignore me. I was looking forward to having an interval chat that's all. You'd think I'd be used to the celebrity thing getting in the way by now, wouldn't you. Of course he had to rehearse all the time – and it's paid off. As you said Tina, he's really good. I'm sure we'll get to spend some proper time together once the play is over.'

* * *

Having taken Rob's last-minute advice, and skirted around the audience, not looking for anyone until she'd tested the Portaloos, Harriet was saved facing the moment of truth. Dylan was hurtling through the kitchen door towards her.

'You were fabulous!' Throwing his arms around Harriet's legs, Dylan peered up at her. 'I can't wait to tell my friends that you're going to be a famous actor.'

Harriet picked him up. 'I don't think I'll ever be famous, but I'm glad you liked it.'

'You were great.' Helen, arriving at Dylan's side, agreed, her eyes lingering on Harriet's fake bump, hoping that her moment's disquiet didn't show. 'Doesn't look easy holding him while wearing that outfit.'

'It's not too bad actually.' Harriet looked at Dylan. 'You're sort of lodged on top, aren't you, mate?'

'Yeah.' He prodded the squashy fabric.

Helen gave an involuntary wince. 'You wouldn't do that if it was a real baby bump, now would you, Dylan?'

'Course not.' He wriggled back to the floor and reclaimed his orange juice. 'You gonna be on stage again in a minute?'

'I'm dead, remember?'

Dylan looked troubled. 'Mum said that makes no difference in Shakespeare. That dead people often come back to life all the time.' He leant forward and whispered in Harriet's ear, 'Is it okay that I don't understand what the play is about?'

'It's very okay. Don't worry. Lots of people find Shakespeare tricky.' Harriet hugged him tight, before asking Helen, 'Sue still here?'

Waving a hand towards the car park, Helen spoke gently, 'She's gone to talk to your dad.'

Harriet's body flashed hot and cold. 'He came?'

'Sam said he arrived about ten minutes late. Stood by the

chickens for the entire first half. Didn't take his eyes off the stage the whole time you were on it, apparently.'

'Oh.' Harriet wasn't sure if she was relieved or not. She looked at Dylan, who was waving at an approaching Bert.

'Why don't you see if Bert needs help with his walking stick?' As he scooted off, she took her chance. 'How was Sue, Helen? Did she know my father was here before the interval?'

'She got a text as the curtain went up. All she told me was that Nathan was here, but didn't want to interrupt things.'

'Was she okay?'

'She didn't burst into tears, but nor did she smile.'

Harriet's throat felt drier than ever. 'So you don't yet know if...'

Pre-empting Harriet's question, her eyes on the little boy moving back towards them, his hand in Bert's, Helen shook her head. 'No, not yet.'

Harriet sighed. 'If I hadn't upset Dad then...'

Tom appeared holding a cup of orange juice and a coffee. 'Here. Thea sent over a drink; she guessed you'd be parched.'

'Wonderful. Thank you.' Harriet gulped back a mouthful of liquid. 'I hope she's saving a few bottles of mulled wine for later.'

'You'll be lucky, lass.' Bert joined the group. 'Mabel says it's selling even faster than Sybil's scones. Maybe you and your young man can go to the pub for some after the show.'

Helen smiled. 'It's official then is it, you and Rob?'

'Well...' Harriet stuttered.

'It's obvious, lass. You only have to look at each other and we can see how you both feel.' Bert appeared extremely satisfied with the situation. 'Where is Rob anyway?'

'Bathroom by the kitchen.' Harriet lifted her glass in the

direction of the house. 'There's no way he could do Portaloo steps with crutches.'

Bert held a hand out for Dylan. 'Well then, young man, how about you help me to get through all these people so I can use the bathroom too?' He patted his pocket. 'There might just be a mini packet of chocolate biscuits in here as a reward.'

As soon as Dylan was out of earshot, Helen spoke to Tom. 'I was just telling Harriet that Sue and Nathan are talking in the car park.'

'Talking—' Harriet felt sick '—or splitting up?'

Tom attempted to be practical. 'Look, I know our lives would be different if they broke up and Sue stayed, but this is none of our business. As much as Sue can be a pain in the arse, I wouldn't want her to be unhappy.'

Harriet passed Helen her cup. 'I'm going to go and see if they are okay.'

'Are you sure that's a good idea?'

'No. I think it's a terrible idea, but if I don't then there is no way on earth I'll be able to concentrate during the second half. Anyway, I want to know if Dylan is going to be my step-brother or not.'

* * *

Harriet had no idea what she was going to say when she got to them. Her mind raced as she heard the crunch of gravel beneath her feet. She hadn't realised how much noise her boots made as she walked along the path between Mill Grange's garden and the small car park, until now.

Tom's right. Dad and Sue's life is none of our business.

Harriet's heart thumped in her chest.

But it is sort of my business, a little bit. He's my dad.

Reaching the corner of the house, Harriet sidled around it, feeling like an inappropriately attired spy. There was no one there.

Aware of the press of time, she hesitated.

What would I have said anyway?

Harriet had just decided to go back when the sound of two raised voices, in urgent discussion, floated through the air. There was no doubt who was speaking, even though she couldn't make out their actual words. They were coming from a spot just beyond the row of parked cars.

As quietly as she could, Harriet crept forward.

'...so, is that it then?'

Harriet swallowed as she heard Sue speak. *Is what it then?*

'I think so.' Nathan sounded tired.

With the conversation she'd had with Sue flashing through her mind, backlit by an image of Helen and Tom's worried but accepting expressions, Harriet moved forward.

'Hello, Dad. Tom told me you'd made it.'

'Harriet?' Nathan shuffled a foot against the gravel. 'Do you think you could give us a minute? We're having a private conversation?'

Folding her arms over her fake bump, Harriet stood her ground. 'A private conversation or a teenage-style row?'

Nathan opened his mouth to speak, but Harriet raised her hand. 'Before you ask "how dare I?" I would remind you that what you do – what you *and* Sue do – has consequences for other people. It's time to stop acting like you live in a bubble, Dad! This isn't just about you!'

Sue, her eyes looking heavy from lack of sleep, patted Harriet's shoulder. 'You were excellent up there.'

Harriet's hackles lowered. 'Oh, thanks, Sue.'

Nathan took a step towards his daughter. 'She's right. You were good. I wasn't expecting much, but...'

'And that's the problem right there isn't it.' Tom strode out of the shadows. 'Rob sent me to fetch you, Harriet. There are only a few minutes until you're needed back behind the scenes.'

Harriet nodded her thanks. Her head was a whirl. Her father had complimented her – in a back-handed sort of way.

'My relationship with my daughter is not your concern!' Nathan growled at Tom.

'It isn't.' Tom's gaze fell on Sue. 'But your relationship with my son is. So, are you both coming back to see the second half – together – like adults who know how to set a good example to Dylan, or not?'

Sue's face flushed, but she held her tongue as Tom added, 'Personally, I don't care if you stay together or not. But Dylan will care, so if you could sort yourselves out one way or another, we would all be very grateful.'

Tom gave Harriet a rueful smile. 'Let's go. Rob's waiting to walk you up to the stage.'

Gathering her skirts, so they didn't drag on the ground as she hurried back to the walled garden, Harriet faced her father. 'I know I'm a disappointment to you. I don't mean to be, but I do love you anyway.' Waving a hand towards Sue, Harriet suddenly felt exhausted. 'And so does she.'

FORTY-EIGHT

SATURDAY DECEMBER 18TH

Shaun's interview with the local press had developed into a myriad of interviews with various papers and a chat with the radio presenter he'd spotted earlier about setting up an interview time. Having agreed to the latter, but only if Matt was part of that interview, Shaun reached the refreshment tent as a bell rang out, loud and clear, across the garden. With a groan, he saw Dave walking around with a hand-held bell, the signal that the audience had ten minutes to take their seats, and that the actors were needed backstage.

Thea held out a cup of coffee. 'Here, you can drink it as you head back.'

'Thanks.' Shaun looked around. 'You'll be in to see the finale won't you?'

'I expect so, Shaun, I...'

Continuing to scan the crowd around them, Shaun interrupted, 'You haven't seen Rob have you?'

'No, I haven't. You were...'

'Better go.' Shaun spun round, his feet taking him away

from Thea, towards the walled garden so quickly that he didn't hear her parting words.

'You were good by the way.'

* * *

Matt and Ali were waiting for Shaun. Both had changed their costumes ready for the second half.

'I saw you being interviewed. I didn't like to interfere.'

'Next time, definitely interfere, Matt. We have a radio thing to do by the way. On Monday. BBC Radio Somerset.' Shaun looked anxiously around the cramped space. 'Where's Rob?'

'BBC Radio?' Matt's mouth dropped open. 'Really? Do we need to go somewhere, will they call us here or...'

'What? Oh, yeah. Ummm, they'll call us here, via Skype. I said I'd only do it if you were there. The Outdoor Players is your baby, not mine.' Shaun adjusted the cloak across his shoulders as he looked around the small space. 'Shouldn't Rob be here by now?'

Ali peered across the stage. 'He should, and so should Harriet, but don't worry. Neither of you are on for a bit, so you won't need a prompt.'

'Prompt?' Shaun shook his head. 'Oh yes, of course. Well, I hope I won't. It's good to know Rob's there though – just in case.'

Ali peeped out through the side of the curtain. 'The audience is back.'

'But no Hermione or Rob?' Matt looked worried.

'They'll be here.' Ali scanned the audience. 'Neither of them would ever let us down.'

* * *

Helen was back in the audience, but unlike everyone else, her eyes were not on the stage. Twisted in her seat, her line of vision was fixed to a spot beyond the chicken coop, towards the gate into the walled garden.

'You alright, lass?' Bert, sat beside Helen, pulled his cap over his head and tucked a thick travel rug over his legs.

Keeping her voice down, so Dylan wouldn't hear, she said, 'Tom should be here by now, and Harriet and Rob aren't back yet.'

'A fact that is connected with Sue's absence?'

'Uh-huh.'

'Would you like me to go and look for them?' Bert was already reaching for his walking stick.

Helen put a hand on his arm. 'Thanks, but I don't think either of us joining them would speed things up.'

Bert followed Helen's line of sight just as the young couple dashed through the gate, before separating, each moving as quickly as possible along the opposite outside edges of the garden, heading for their positions behind stage.

'Thank goodness. And there's Tom, and...' Helen exhaled shakily '...Sue and Nathan.'

'They look sheepish if I'm any judge.' Bert settled back in his seat. 'If Mabel wasn't sorting out the refreshment stand, she'd be able to tell us what had happened by just looking at them! But as it is, we'll have to wait until after the show before we find out what's going on.'

Standing to let Sue and Nathan shuffle past her, Bert and Dylan, Helen reached a hand out to Tom, as he sat on the aisle chair next to her just as the music struck up and the curtains opened. He answered her unspoken enquiry with a motion of his shoulders.

Helen bit back a sigh. *Is Sue still with Nathan, or not?*

It was going to be a long second half.

* * *

At the very back of the waiting area, on the left-hand side of the stage, Harriet took three slow deep breaths. Then, lifting a bottle of water from a crate that someone had left on a table, she unscrewed its cap with a quiet click and had a much-needed drink.

On the stage she could faintly hear the shepherds of Bohemia discovering Hermione's sixteen-year-old daughter, Perdita.

An abandoned daughter who is, eventually, reunited with her father. She gulped down several mouthfuls of water. *Are you trying to tell me something, Mr Shakespeare?*

As she sat, the sound of her pulse thumping in her ears drowning out the action on stage, Harriet wasn't sure how things had been left. She stuffed her cold hands into the folds of her outfit and listed the events of the interval through her mind to try and make sense of things.

Sue had said her performance was good. And her father had agreed, qualifying the statement with the fact he hadn't been expecting much. *God forbid he should give me a whole-hearted compliment.*

Tom had accused them of behaving like kids and then she'd told her dad she loved him.

Why did I do that? He'll see it as blackmail.

Harriet shifted a little on the hard plastic seat as she recalled the shocked expression on her father's face when she apologised for being a disappointment to him. *Perhaps, if I hadn't had to rush off, he'd have said something.*

As she'd raced back to the stage, part of her had wondered if that was the last time she'd see her father; if he'd leave then and there. But a peep out into the audience had quickly taken that fear away.

He is out there. With Sue.

Harriet took another drink from her bottle and gave herself a shake. *Enough of the guilt. I've said my piece. It's up to him now.*

Getting up from her seat, she moved to the costume rack at the back of the waiting area. She was about to change out of her outfit, losing the baby bump, when she caught sight of Rob on the opposite side of the stage. He was with Shaun. They were huddled together, a little distanced from the action.

What are they up to?

* * *

Tina, Thea and Mabel stacked the last of the unused cups onto a tray, emptied the dribble of tea left in the urn onto the grass, and put the lid on the plastic tub of sugar sachets.

'I feel like I've been run over by a herd of hungry elephants.' Tina stretched her arms above her head.

Mabel chuckled. 'No stamina, you young people.'

'We're going to have to order in more supplies. Mind you, even if we had three times as many of Sybil's scones on offer, we'd still sell out.'

'Can't blame people for having good taste.' Mabel knocked a pile of used napkins and empty sugar packets into a bin liner. 'I'm looking forward to being able to sit and watch the entire show tomorrow, mind.'

'Me too.' Tina glanced towards the walled garden. They could just hear the actors as they worked. 'I fully expect the hens to be clucking out the lines by the final performance, they'll have heard the play so often.'

Mabel chuckled. 'Accompanied by Tony Stark's crowing?'

'It goes without saying.' Tina folded the tablecloth from the trestle table. 'Can't you imagine it, Thea?'

'What?' Looking up from where she'd been collecting a few dropped cups, Thea said, 'Sorry, I was miles away. What did you say?'

'Just something silly about the chickens. You okay?'

'Of course.'

Mabel's shrewd eyes narrowed as she said, 'Shaun's loving his moment on stage. I hope he calms down a bit after tonight's debut is over.'

Tina glanced at Thea. 'He's been rather consumed with this hasn't he?'

'Just a bit.' Thea dropped the rubbish into a sack.

Mabel lifted the cash box and gave it a satisfied shake. 'Shaun's obsession with his role aside, this play lark has been a good move for Mill Grange.'

'Now that was a heavy-sounding jangle. We'd better get that inside.' Tina picked up the laden tray. 'If we're lucky, we'll be able to join the others for the final curtain so we can add to the applause.'

'You guys go on over. I don't think I'll bother today.' Thea took the money box from Mabel.

'But it's Shaun's first show?' Tina rested the tray back on the table. 'Surely, you...'

'There's two more.' Thea took the tray from Tina and put the money box on it. 'Go on. I'll see you later.' Then, before they could stop her, she walked up the sloping lawn towards the house.

* * *

Harriet concentrated on being statue-still – literally.

As Matt, Shaun, Ali, Ian and Sara, in their roles as Leontes, Polixenes, Paulina, Camillo and Perdita, walked around her, as the statue of Hermione, she stared out across the audience, unblinking.

Wishing that Shakespeare hadn't written quite so much script for her fellow actors, requiring her to be static for so long, Harriet forced her gaze to rest on the chicken coop.

Out of the corner of her eye she could see her father. He was looking right at her. *I bet he's waiting to see if I move so he can remind me that statues don't do that.* The thought was knocked out of her head when she noticed that her father was holding Sue's hand.

Harriet was so surprised by this open act of affection that she almost forgot to react when Ali, as Paulina, announced, 'Dear life redeems you. You perceive she stirs...'

Moving slowly, flexing Hermione's stone stiff limbs, Harriet stepped towards Shaun and embraced him. Catching Rob's encouraging smile from the wings, Harriet faced the audience. Delivering her final speech with her hands clasped together over her chest, her eyes fixed upon her father. 'You gods, look down, and from your sacred vials pour your graces upon my daughter's head! Tell me, mine own. Where hast thou been preserved? Where lived? How found thy father's court? For thou shalt hear that I, knowing by Paulina that the oracle gave hope thou wast in being, have preserved myself to see the issue.'

Then, in what felt like only a few more seconds, the final words were exchanged and the audience was on its feet, clapping as the cast took a final bow.

Suddenly it was all over. Matt was thanking everyone for coming on such a cold night; making everyone laugh by thanking the sky directly for the lack of snow, despite Sam's fears. Then, with a very Shakespearean bow, he publicly thanked Shaun for stepping in at the last minute.

Calls of approval came from the crowd as Shaun humbly accepted the thanks before, to Harriet's surprise, he invited Rob onto the stage.

Rob, however, had clearly been expecting the call. He was already making his way out of the wings and onto the stage, to a generous round of sympathetic applause, his crutches under his arms.

'As much as I have loved every second of playing Polixenes, I heartily wish Rob here hadn't had to sustain injury for me to do so. However...' Shaun paused dramatically '...it does allow me to do something I've wanted to do for a very long time.'

Harriet exchanged a confused look with Ali as she saw Rob take something from his pocket and pass it to Shaun.

'I think Matt would agree that there are so many people who work at this wonderful house to thank. First of all, there's Thea.'

Tina froze. *But she isn't here.*

She was about to tell Sam, embarrassed on Shaun's behalf as he was about to thank his partner, when Shaun called out, 'Thea Thomas, would you join me on the stage please?'

'She isn't here.' Tina nudged Sam. 'What do we do?'

Seeing his wife's worried expression, Sam shook his head. 'Yes she is. At the back. Look.'

Tina turned to see Thea standing by the chickens. Relieved that her friend had had a change of heart, she watched as Thea headed towards them. When she reached Sam, Thea muttered, 'What's he playing at? I don't want to go up there. It should be you and Tina he thanks on stage, not me.'

'I'm sure we'll be next.' Sam gave her a gentle shove. 'Go on.'

Reaching out his hand, pulling a reluctant Thea into the limelight, Shaun wasted no time. Swishing his cloak over his shoulder, he got down on one knee, a velvet ring box held out before him. A hush rippled backwards from the front row of the audience, as everyone realised what was about to happen.

'Thea Thomas, will you marry me?'

FORTY-NINE

SATURDAY DECEMBER 18TH

As Tom and Sam ushered the final members of the audience towards the drive and the cast headed to the manor, Thea sat on a chair near the makeshift stage, holding her ring finger out before her.

'Is this what you've been popping out for every five minutes since you got back from Northumbria?'

'It is.'

'So there was no local site for *Landscape Treasures* then?'

'A little white lie.'

Thea sighed. 'I almost didn't come to see the end of the show. One minute you've been so loving, then the next so distant. Not listening to me or seeing me, so...'

'I'm sorry, love. I was trying so hard to keep this a secret.' Shaun kissed the top of her head. 'What made you decide to watch in the end?'

'I love you, you idiot.'

'I like that answer.' Shaun smiled as Thea admired the ring. 'I saw what I thought was the perfect ring in Berwick, but the only day I had free the shop was closed. Then, when I emailed them to ask about the ring, I got an automated message saying they were away for two weeks, which was...'

'After you'd left.'

'Right.'

'So...' Thea felt awkward '...so while I've been thinking you didn't want to move us along...'

'I've been searching for a ring and trying to find the perfect proposal moment.'

Thea kissed his cheek. 'I'm sorry if I've been pushing you a bit, I just...'

'I know. I want the house, the family – all of it too, but...' Shaun looked sheepish '...I got rather carried away with the adventure of the ring hunt.'

Thea laughed. 'Like a true archaeologist.'

'Indiana Jones has nothing on me, kid!' Shaun's smile faded as he went on. 'Honestly, I knew you were ready for the next step, but I wanted to do it properly, and then the play meant I needed to rehearse all the time and there wasn't a free slot when I could pop out. I didn't want to let Matt down – but that meant I had no time to collect the ring when I finally found it, so Rob went to the jeweller's for me.'

'Is that why you wanted to talk to Rob in the interval and not me?'

'He was keeping the ring safe for me.' Shaun held her closer. 'I didn't mean to blank you. I just ran out of time after the interviews and, well, I couldn't propose in front of everyone without a ring, could I?'

'Probably not.' Thea rested her head on Shaun's shoulder as she held her hand out between them.

'I knew what sort of ring I wanted, but to get the exact one.' He shook his head. 'I've been all over the country since spring, and all over the south-west over the past fortnight. But there it was, in Bampton all along.'

Thea's mouth dropped open. 'You've been intending to propose since the spring!'

'Since the second Tina and Sam were married.'

Amazed by her boyfriend for the second time that day, Thea found herself stuttering, 'How come Rob had to collect the ring for you? Why couldn't you just bring it back when you bought it?'

'I wanted it professionally cleaned. Don't get me wrong, it wasn't covered in mud or anything archaeological, but it's a nineteenth-century ring. It had a patina on it that I wanted lifting.' Perched on the final chair in a deserted row of seating next to Thea, Shaun was suddenly anxious. 'Is it okay? If it isn't, I'll change it.'

'Of course it's okay. It's perfect. I love it. I love you.'

Thea stared in wonder at the three perfectly cut stones. Two opals and an almost midnight blue sapphire were set in a simple gold band. She held it up to the light provided by the heaters and gasped. 'Shaun, look.'

The two opals had appeared milky in colour at first, almost as if they were pearls, but now, as Thea moved her hand towards the light, they burst into shimmers of colour; showing shades of pink, green and blue depending on how she tilted her finger. 'Wow!'

Shaun took hold of her hand and kissed it. 'The jeweller showed me. He said it was a miracle ring, that once you noticed its hidden rainbow, you'd always love it. Apparently, every time you look at it in the light the colours will be fractionally different. He went on about diffraction and the prism effect after that, but I'll be honest, I zoned out. I was too busy planning how to propose.'

'A proposal in full Shakespearean style.' Thea laughed.

'It took me so long to have the courage to do it at all, that when I did, I wanted you to be in no doubt I meant it. Having an audience seemed the best way.'

'Why courage?' Thea kissed his lips softly. 'You can't have imagined I'd say no.'

'I was afraid you might. I've not always been the easiest man to live with.'

'True, but I'm not the easiest woman sometimes, so, as Mr Shakespeare would say, "we are a pair well met".' Thea ran a fingertip over the stones. 'It is the most amazing ring I've ever seen.'

'And you are the most amazing woman I've ever met.' Shaun lowered his voice, his eyes fixed on Thea. 'As soon as the jeweller used the phrase "miracle ring" I was sold. After all, Bert always says...'

Thea joined Shaun, and they both quoted their friend, 'Mill Grange is a place of miracles.'

* * *

Deep in thought as he returned to the walled garden, Sam folded up the last few chairs as his friends collected up a few stray takeout cups and checked the chickens. 'I don't know about you lot, but I think an early celebration bonfire is called for, albeit without my famous jacket spuds.'

'Fabulous idea.' Tina clapped her hands. 'What do you think, Thea, Shaun – an impromptu engagement party?'

Thea rested her head on her fiancé's shoulder. 'I'd love to. Shaun?'

'Providing I can change out of this costume first. We should invite Matt, Ali and the others.'

'Everyone is welcome.' Sam grinned. 'I'm sure Dylan won't mind helping me put a second bonfire together for the last night's celebration.'

* * *

As Shaun and Sam unfolded a tarpaulin, Tina asked Mabel, 'How much mulled wine do we have left?'

'Six bottles.' The old lady tugged her woolly hat further down over her ears. 'We were saving them for tomorrow's interval sales, but if we drink it all tonight, then the world won't end.'

Bert chuckled. 'Spoken with true pragmatism, my girl.'

'Shush with your cheek.' Mabel's eyes twinkled as she brushed her hands down her apron. 'If this was a fairy tale, now that the prince has asked his princess to be his wife – at last...'

Shaun cut in with a low bow. 'I'm no prince. I'm the King of Bohemia I'll have you know. And my good lady is...'

'An archaeologist!' Thea laughed. 'A princess, I am not.'

'As I was saying,' Mabel continued, 'in the fairy-tale version of events, Sue and Nathan would stay together in this country so Dylan could live with Tom and Helen, but be able to see his mum whenever he liked. Rob and Harriet would have an uninterrupted date and all The Outdoor Players' members needing Equity cards would magically have earned them already.'

Bert laughed. 'You've always loved a fairy-tale ending, lass, but before we start working out how to pull off a new round of miracles, someone had better tell Helen and Tom about our bonfire plan. They were off to tuck Dylan into bed. He'd be gutted if we had a bonfire party without him.'

* * *

The contents of the six bottles of mulled wine, warmed with additional sticks of cinnamon, had been distributed, just making it around the Mill Grange team and the cast before it ran out.

Thea sipped from her mug, relishing the smooth liquid soothing her throat as she sat before the bonfire. The vivid orange and yellow lick of the flames consumed the wood and leaves with comforting crackles as her gaze moved from the fire to the Victorian engagement ring on her finger, and on to the house, to her right.

She could hear Matt congratulating his actors on their performance, before reminding them that they shouldn't overdo the drink, as they had two shows to go. Bert was telling an exhausted-looking Dylan a story about William Shakespeare and a dragon, which the old man was clearly inventing on the spot, while Harriet and Rob were huddled close to each other on the opposite side of the fire. Thea smiled to herself as she saw Rob's hand in Harriet's. They had slightly self-conscious expressions on their faces.

Next to her, Thea could hear Shaun in full *Landscape Treasures* anecdote mode with Ali and Dave, while Tom and Helen sat quietly together, a little to the side, watching the flames sway in the light breeze. Next to them, sat Sue and Nathan. Every now and then, Thea saw Harriet shift to steal a glance in her father's direction.

Matt frowned. 'Did you hear me, Harriet?'

'What, oh, I'm so sorry. I was just thinking.'

'I was suggesting that you audition for our summer play on Hampstead Heath. The role of Titania in *A Midsummer Night's Dream*.'

'But that's the main female role!'

'Why so surprised?' Matt asked. 'You have the main female role in *The Winter's Tale.*'

'Well, yes but...' Harriet wasn't sure how to diplomatically continue '...there's a difference between giving a lead role in the depths of Exmoor, and giving one in London. I'm not belittling this, but Hampstead Heath! That's a big deal. I'm not sure I'm good enough.'

'You are more than good enough.'

The voice that came in reassurance did not belong to Matt or Rob.

'Dad?'

'I mean it. You were outstanding.' Nathan dipped his head towards Matt. 'Wasn't she?'

'Harriet is always good, but yes, today's performance was excellent.' Matt, sensing they should leave Harriet alone with her father, turned to Rob. 'I wonder if you have a minute to come and chat about auditioning as well. I need an Oberon and a Puck – you'd be welcome to try for either.'

* * *

'I meant it. You really are an excellent actress.'

Harriet stood with her dad, staring at the sheet of blue tarpaulin that covered the excavation. 'Thank you.'

Nathan shuffled his feet, his expensive brogues looking out of place on the uneven ground. 'Sue has been good for me.'

Surprised by the statement, Harriet said nothing, hoping her father would continue.

'She's made me see that, although I believed I was doing

the best for you when you were growing up, that wasn't always the case.'

Harriet watched her father out of the corner of her eye as she said, 'I like Sue. She can be a bit prickly sometimes, but she was always good to me when I used to babysit Dylan and then, when she drove me to the hospital...'

'That should have been me.' Regret laced Nathan's words. 'But somehow...'

'You couldn't break the habit of a lifetime. I should fend for myself. Sort out my own problems. That way, no one will let me down. No one will hurt me.'

'Yes.' Nathan risked facing his daughter. 'And well... hospitals... Even now, I...' He cleared his throat before going on, '...I find them difficult. With your mother, it was so unexpected. So quick. She was at home, then in hospital and then she was gone.'

Harriet found herself biting her bottom lip, reminding herself of Rob as her father, his glasses slipping down his nose, appeared to age before her eyes. They'd rarely talked of her mother since her death. It had been easier for both of them to pretend she had just nipped out, or had gone away for a while.

'Sue asked me about your mum not long after we met. And I, for the first time in years, found myself able to answer the questions.'

'I miss Mum.' Harriet spoke the words softly, an out-loud admission she rarely allowed herself to make.

'Me too.' He shrugged. 'Perhaps if the cancer had been spotted earlier, perhaps if...'

'No, Dad. Don't.' Harriet reached out and held his hand. 'I've asked those questions a million times, but it's no good. If the doctors had found it earlier, yes, we'd have had Mum longer, but then she'd have spent months, if not years, in pain. The way it was – three weeks... it meant she didn't suffer as much as she could have.'

'That's what Sue said.'

'And she's right.'

Nathan regarded his daughter as if he was seeing her properly for the first time in years. 'How I raised you, hard life lessons. I thought it was for the best. We were always just us. But I knew I couldn't be there for you forever, so...' His words dissolved into thin air.

'So you made sure I knew how to survive alone from the start.'

'Yes.'

'Not everyone goes through life alone, Dad.' Harriet gulped against the lump that had formed in her throat. 'Mum wouldn't want you to.'

'I know.'

'Don't push Sue away.' Harriet met her father's eyes. 'As you said, she is good for you. Not everyone you love is going to go away.'

Tom couldn't stand not knowing any longer. He could feel the tension radiating off Helen, and feared for what it might be doing for their baby. *Probably nothing, you fool... but...* He shuffled across to sit on the blanket laid out next to Sue. 'I know it's none of my business, but I have to ask, are you and Nathan okay?'

Sue's gaze landed on Dylan. He was curled up, fast asleep on Bert's lap, his little chest rising up and down. The old man was stroking his hair.

'They are like grandparents to him.'

'Yes.' A lump formed in Tom's throat. 'That's one of the reasons I need to know.'

'If I'll be staying and demanding my son back?'

'Please don't make this into a row.' Tom shook his head. 'You wouldn't have to demand anything. If you stayed, then we'd share custody. I'd miss him always being there, but you and I have coped with such a situation before and we would again. So would Dylan.'

Sue uncurled her legs. 'You don't need to worry, although it means a lot to me that you'd do that, if I stayed.'

'You're Dylan's mum.'

'I am.' Sue watched as her son rolled over in his sleep, narrowly avoiding falling off Bert's knees. 'Which doesn't make leaving him behind easy, but I know he's safe and loved.'

'You're with Nathan then?'

'For now.' She paused as they saw Nathan and Harriet come back into view, arms around each other. 'But if he makes his daughter feel worthless, or as if she has to cope with everything in life alone again, that situation will change.'

Tom leant forward and kissed her cheek. 'I always knew you were a nice person.'

Sue snorted out a laugh. 'Let's just say that I'm a work in progress.'

* * *

Thea looked around at her friends, and noticed that both Sam and Mabel were absent. Before she could start to wonder where they had gone, Shaun took hold of her hand and glanced towards the house as Sam and Mabel arrived back, holding trays of champagne-filled glasses.

'This is very kind of you, Sam, but there's no need to do a speech or anything.'

'There is every need.'

Before Shaun could protest, Tina tapped the side of her glass, breaking through everyone's chatter and Sam began to speak.

'Ladies and gentlemen, as you know, Thea and Shaun became engaged this evening. I would like you to raise your glasses to wish them every success and happiness for the future.'

As cries of "congratulations" resounded across the garden, Shaun got to his feet and lifted his own glass to toast Thea, before addressing their friends.

'A special thanks to Matt, Ali and their amazing company, The Outdoor Players, for trusting me with a role I was barely equipped to perform – which gave me the chance to propose to Thea in style.'

With a nudge from Ali, Matt rose to his feet. 'It is us who should be thanking you. If you hadn't stepped into the breach, then there would have been no show.' Matt then turned to Sam and Tina. 'And to you both, for allowing us to come to Mill Grange at the last minute.'

'It has been our pleasure.' Sam raised his glass.

'Which means there is only one person to thank left. And that's Harriet.'

'Me?' Harriet blushed as Rob concurred.

'Absolutely. Without Harriet, we'd have had no venue. Mill Grange is the perfect sylvan setting for outdoor theatre.'

'It is,' Matt agreed.

'You are welcome anytime.' Sam retook his seat on the travel-rug-covered ground.

'This time next year?' Ali piped up from behind Matt.

'Deal!' Tina clapped.

'Brilliant.' Matt listened to the murmurings of approval rippling through his cast before he held up his hands. 'And now I must put my director hat back on and ask all you actor types to go to bed. There are two more performances before we can really let our hair down.'

* * *

With the exception of Harriet and Shaun, the cast of *The Winter's Tale* disappeared into the manor as Nathan and Sue stood up.

'Harriet, we should be going too.' Nathan took Sue's hand as they rose. 'Our flight back is tomorrow.'

'Right.' Harriet found she meant it when she said, 'I'm glad you came.'

'So am I.' Letting go of Sue's hand so she could go and speak to Tom, Nathan added, 'We would like to take you and Dylan to breakfast at the pub tomorrow, if you'd like to join us before we go? I'd love to hear all about life at uni, if you'd like to tell me?'

'I'd love to.' Harriet gave him a hug. 'Thanks, Dad.'

* * *

Bert waited until the cast had drifted away before he called Shaun to his side. 'I'm not sure how to ask, I just wondered if...'

Shaun placed a hand on his friend's shoulder. 'Wondered if, when the play's over, I'd cut the buttons off the tunic and give them back to you?'

'Yes.'

'Don't worry, Bert, I'll make sure you get them back.'

* * *

Helen nudged Tom's side. 'I know there are still two performances to go but...' She paused, before whispering in Tom's ear.

He smiled. 'Are you sure?'

'I'm sure.'

Taking Tom's hand, Helen stepped forward, and called to all their friends. 'Before we go inside, now it's just the Mill Grange team here, we have something to tell you.'

'Umm.' Harriet put up her hand as if interrupting a teacher. 'Should Rob and I go? We're not really part of...'

'Harriet, you are very much part of the family, so, if you are happy to risk Matt's wrath and stay for a couple more minutes, I'd like you to stay.'

Helen glanced at Tom, their expressions suddenly joyous as she said, 'The thing is...'

'I knew it!' The words burst out of Mabel's mouth before she could stop herself.

'They haven't said anything yet!' Bert rolled his eyes.

Helen laughed. 'I was sure you'd guessed, Mabel.'

Tina's frown morphed into an expression of delight. 'And now I've guessed!'

Tom laughed. 'No such thing as a secret here.'

'Well I haven't a clue what's going on.' Sam glanced at Shaun, who looked equally clueless.

Helen patted her belly. 'We're going to have a baby. In June.'

Through the calls of congratulations, a shuffling on Bert's lap turned into Dylan sitting bolt upright. 'Baby? Really? Dad? Am I going to be a brother?'

'You are.' Tom reached out his arms so he could either comfort or congratulate his son. So far, the expression on Dylan's face suggested his reaction could go either way. 'Is that okay?'

Helen tensed. Every sound around her disappeared. She couldn't hear the flicker of the fire or the congratulations of her friends, just the beat of her heart as she waited for Dylan to respond.

Looking from Bert to Mabel, as if to check his impending brotherhood was alright with them, the little boy punched the air. 'Yes!'

Helen almost burst into tears as Dylan ran forward and embraced her, then abruptly broke away again.

'Is it okay to hug you? I don't want to hurt them.'

'Your hugs are always welcome. You're going to be a fabulous brother.'

'And Bert and Mabel will be their sort-of-grandparents, won't they. Just like they're mine?' The earnest tone of Dylan's voice laid a hush across Mill Grange's garden.

Taking his son's hand in one palm and Helen's in the other, Tom led them to where the elderly couple sat.

'Helen and I couldn't manage without you two.' Tom glanced at Helen who blinked in encouragement. 'Would you mind, perhaps – if you wanted to – consider being proper, official, grandparents to our baby and Dylan?'

The elderly couple's mutual reply of "yes" were lost as Dylan whooped around the bonfire in a victory dance, before plonking himself between Bert and Mabel, a very important question on his lips.

'So, Nan and Grandad or Gran and Grandad or Grampa and Nana?'

'Whichever, Dylan, whichever you like.' Mabel fought tears as she held a hand out to Harriet. 'You're Dylan's step-sister, or soon will be.'

'Well, yes.' Harriet guessed what Mabel was about to say, and had a horrible feeling she was going to cry.

'If you wanted, but not if you don't, because you are a grown woman now and everything, but...'

Harriet didn't wait for the words to be spoken before

throwing her arms around the old woman. 'I'd love it, thank you.'

'Isn't this wonderful, Bert?' Mabel reached a hand to her husband, but the old man didn't hear her. He was too busy hugging his newly adopted grandson as if his life depended on it.

FIFTY-ONE

TUESDAY DECEMBER 21ST

Harriet waved until the second people carrier was out of sight. 'I can't believe it's over.'

Thea played her new ring around her finger as a fluttering of snowflakes flew around them in the wind. 'Three performances gone in three days, a splash of mulled wine, Shakespeare and cheese scones.'

'I think it's going to take longer than that to get the lines I relearnt out of my head again.' Shaun massaged his forehead. 'I'll be dreaming Polixenes' speeches for months.'

Rob laughed. 'That happens to me after a play run. Takes a while to remember who I am for a bit.'

'Thank goodness it didn't start snowing until this morning.' Thea held up her palms to the heavy grey sky. 'An audience huddled up against the snow is one thing, but being dug out of a snowdrift is something else entirely!'

Shaun laughed. 'We'd have had to get the trowels out at the end to excavate people out of their seats.'

'Talking of excavating—' Thea looked up at her fiancé '—

has the world of archaeology lost you to the lure of the greasepaint?'

Tina turned towards Thea. The question had been spoken with humour, but she knew her friend had been making a serious enquiry.

Shaun pointed along the garden path behind them that led to the fortlet. 'And miss moments of discovery like we had here? Not on your life.'

* * *

'Are you sure we shouldn't be helping the others?' Harriet relaxed back in her chair, tucked in a cosy corner of Sybil's Tea Rooms.

Rob raised his coffee cup. 'I was given permission to spirit you away.'

'You were?'

'I believe Mabel's exact words were: "Get yourself out with that girl before you lose her to someone else."'

'Mabel said that?' Harriet's eyebrows rose in surprise. 'That sounds more like a Bert thing to say.'

'He must be a good influence on her.'

Harriet cut open a piping hot cheese scone. 'I'm sorry my dad ruined our last visit here.'

'It doesn't matter.' Rob smiled. 'All that matters is that you two finally talked.'

'According to a text I got this morning, they've got over their jet lag and are preparing for their beach Christmas.'

'I'm sorry he didn't stay for Christmas.'

Harriet smiled to show she didn't mind. 'He might be texting me now and again, something that in the past only happened when he wanted something, but he is still the same person he always was. He wanted Christmas on the beach, so that's what will happen.'

Rob reached a hand across the table and took Harriet's palm in his. 'It was so good of Sam and Tina to invite us for Christmas.'

Looking at their entwined fingers, Harriet said, 'I can't remember the last time I looked forward to Christmas.'

'I'm glad I broke my ankle.'

'You are?'

'Yeah. If I hadn't, Shaun would not have played Polixenes, so may have put off proposing to Thea for longer, and I would have been able to drive home. As I can't, I get to have Christmas with my clever, funny and beautiful girlfriend.'

Blushing, Harriet asked, 'Your parents weren't too upset not to have you home for Christmas were they?'

'My brothers and grandparents will be there. Although—' he took a bite of scone before the butter completely melted '— they have issued an order to meet you as soon as I can drive again.'

Harriet shuffled nervously. 'I hope they like me.'

'My grandparents already like you. They remembered you as the smiling girl from last summer.' Rob let go of Harriet's hand so he could grab a napkin and mop up the butter threatening to dribble down his chin.

Harriet hid her nerves behind a sip of coffee. 'They remembered me?'

'They did. And now you have grandparents too.'

Harriet smiled, still filled with the sheer joy of being included. 'I'd hate to think that Bert and Mabel felt they have to ask me just because I'm going to be Dylan's step-sister.'

'Mabel strikes me as someone who does not say things she doesn't mean.'

'That's what Tina and Thea said.'

Rob put out his hand. 'I've a confession.'

'Go on.'

'You remember when Matt asked me if I'd like to play Polixenes?'

'You said it was because you didn't have time to relearn the part and because you'd been...'

'A little distracted.' Rob nodded. 'Distracted by wondering how to ask you out. You're so out of my league and... well...'

'You are joking?' Harriet couldn't believe it. 'But that's what I said to Tina, Thea and Ali – that you were out of my league and I should forget it. Anyway, we were becoming friends and I didn't want to mess that up.'

Rob held her hand a little tighter. 'I hoped you liked me, but I told myself you were nice to everyone so that I shouldn't get my hopes up.'

'That's what I did! And then, when we did try to see each other, and life kept getting in the way, I tried to convince myself it wasn't meant to be... but...' Harriet smiled into his dark brown eyes '...perhaps it was after all.'

'It was.' Rob freed one hand. 'I was going to save this until Christmas Day, but the chance of having any time alone then will be slim. Here.'

Harriet's heart beat faster as Rob passed her a small rectangular parcel done up in festive wrapping paper. She ran a single fingertip along the top. 'Can I really open it now?'

Rob laughed. 'That's why I have it here.'

Making sure her fingers were free of butter and crumbs, Harriet reverently turned the package over and undid the sticky tape. With a glance up at Rob, who was anxiously chewing his bottom lip, she removed the paper. Confronted by a slim, green-velvet-covered box, Harriet found that her hands were trembling as she eased the lid open.

The words 'Oh, Rob,' morphed into a hushed gasp as she lifted the necklace from its cushioned bed.

'You like it?' He sounded as nervous as he looked.

'I love it.' Harriet held the silver chain out before her so she could examine the tree-shaped pendant. Caught in a perfect circle of silver, the branches of the oak tree stretched out to each side. As she peered closer, Harriet saw that, at the base of the miniature trunk, a Harlequin mask had been etched into the metal. 'It's perfect!'

'Really?'

'Really.' Harriet put it around her neck, the clasp catching first time beneath her chestnut hair. 'What better pendant for an outdoor actor?'

'Hopefully it will always remind you of Mill Grange.'

'It will.' Harriet held the pendant between her fingertips. 'Thank you.'

'I spotted it when I collected Thea's engagement ring.'

'No wonder you were so long!' Harriet took his hands back in hers. 'I thought it was your crutches slowing you down.'

'You truly like it?'

'Truly.' Harriet squeezed his hands. 'And you. I like you really rather a lot.'

* * *

Silence enveloped the manor. There was always a split second of adjustment to the atmosphere of the place between groups of guests – a moment when Mill Grange held its breath and allowed the dust to settle. A second when the house gave the distinct impression it was savouring having no one but its owners inside it.

Today the emptiness seemed bigger, the pause slightly longer. With the exception of Rob and Harriet, The Outdoor Players had gone. The Portaloos had been collected, the beds had been stripped and Thea and Shaun had gone for a walk, while Mabel, Bert, Tom, Helen and Dylan had returned to their respective homes.

Stepping through the front door, Tina let out a contented sigh.

'So, there's going to be another wedding at Mill Grange.' Sam came in behind her. 'I'm glad Thea and Shaun want to tie the knot here. It'll be the talk of the village.'

'And a baby. Helen was saying it would be lovely to have a bonfire party and a naming ceremony here.' Tina shook the snow from her coat and hung it on the stand by the door. 'I wonder what flavour it'll be?'

'Strawberry or blueberry you mean?' Sam laughed.

'Or maybe a mixed flavour   could be a them rather than a him or her.'

'Can't see Tom or Helen minding as long as they have a healthy wee one.' Sam tilted his head to one side as he looked at his wife. 'You're ready aren't you, to try for a child?'

'Yes.' Tina stepped into his arms. 'But only if you are. I know you've been upstairs once, but...'

'You haven't wanted to rush me.'

Tina smiled her agreement.

'A fact for which I am extremely grateful, but you aren't rushing me. I'm ready too. I'd love to start a new generation at Mill Grange.'

Sam faced the wooden staircase. 'I've made it up there

once to help get the decorations down with Dylan, so I know logically, that I can do it again.'

'If you can face trying with me, I'm willing whenever the time is right.' Tina twirled a pigtail around her finger.

'Now.' Sam took her hand and focused his gaze on the second step.

'You're sure? Now?'

'*Now*. Providing you reward me afterwards.'

'Like I did last time?' Tina held Sam's hand tighter. She could feel it trembling. A light perspiration had started to form across his palms, but he was obviously determined to ignore it.

'Exactly like last time!' Sam kissed her nose. 'With an incentive like that, even if it takes me three hours to reach the attic, I know it'll be more than worth it!'

EPILOGUE
SATURDAY 18TH JUNE

Helen got out of the car and stretched. The summer sunshine reflected off her face. She knew her freckles would be darkening in its presence.

She stifled a yawn as Dylan jumped from the car, Harold the dinosaur under one arm and Daisy the diplodocus under the other.

'Come on, Dad, I can see them waiting!'

Seeing that his son was bouncing from one foot to the other in excitement, Tom nodded towards the giant marquee on the lawn. 'Go on, we'll catch you up. But remember, not a word.'

Pulling a hand over his mouth in a "my lips are sealed" motion, Dylan rushed ahead.

Helen hooked her backpack over her shoulder. 'That's Rob's car isn't it?'

'I think so. Harriet said they'd try to make it.' Tom leant to undo the baby seat strapped securely into the back of the Fiesta. 'They are staying with Mabel and Bert so that Sam and Tina don't have to remake up any bedrooms before the new guest intake on Monday.'

'It can't be long until they go on their glamping honeymoon.' Helen watched as Tom lifted their baby from its chair.

'Two weeks' time.' Tom looked at their child. 'And you, young 'un, were supposed to stay asleep when I lifted you up!'

'Fat chance!' Helen laughed. 'And miss a second of what's going on? As if!'

'You okay carrying the bag if I hold on to this one?'

'Yep.' Helen looked ahead to their friends. 'You ready?'

'I have no idea how we've managed to keep the name a secret for a whole week. It'll be a relief to share!'

* * *

Sat in a circle of deckchairs under the marquee, which was keeping the glare of the mid-morning sun off them, Mabel and Bert were making a fuss of Dylan as Tom and Helen arrived.

'Look at this! It's my being a big brother present from Gran and Grandad.'

'Is it now?' Tom thanked Bert and Mabel as he watched Dylan kneel on the array of travel rugs covering the grass, and begin to study the construction instructions for a gigantic Lego castle set.

Tina got to her feet, her arms held out. 'Do I get a cuddle with this wee one before you put us out of our misery and tell us what your child is called?'

Tom passed his youngest son over, smiling as Tina rested him in her arms, lodging him above her tiny baby bump.

Thea got up to embrace Helen. 'You knackered?'

'Just a bit.' Sitting on the nearest chair, Helen kicked off her shoes and gestured to the collection of house particulars on the chair Thea had vacated. 'How's the house hunting going?'

Shaun selected a leaflet from the top of the pile. 'We've *finally* found something we both like. We put in an offer on this one this morning.'

Helen took the house details. 'Bampton. Three bedrooms, ohhh... an acre of garden. Nice.'

Thea laughed. 'Shaun is already dreaming of buying a ride-on lawnmower.'

'Let's hope you don't find an archaeological excavation in the garden!' Tom took a seat next to Helen.

'And if you do,' Helen added, 'do not ask me to write a book about it!'

'You all ready for the paperback book launch next month?' Sam smiled. 'I'm still happy to hold a book event here if you think you'll have the energy.'

'Thanks, Sam.' Helen looked towards her two children. 'Providing babysitters are on hand, then I'd love to.'

'You bet.' Tina and Thea spoke in unison, making Helen laugh.

'Writing a book about your fortlet was the hardest thing I've ever done.'

Tina kissed the baby's cheek and passed him to a patiently waiting Mabel. 'You sure about that?'

'Okay, the second hardest thing I've ever done.'

'Worth every push.' Mabel nuzzled the top of the baby's head.

Tom raised his eyes to the sky. 'And every minute of the twelve-hour labour! Pest.'

Helen took a sip of coffee. 'Can't believe it was only a week ago!'

'And I can't believe you haven't told us his name yet!' Bert held a finger out to his grandson, who immediately latched a tiny hand around it.

'Well, I have the champagne here.' Sam gestured to a table to the side of the marquee. 'Would you like to put us out of our misery?'

'Oh please do!' Harriet smiled. 'I can't wait to tell Ali. I have orders to text her as soon as we know.'

* * *

Standing as one, the friends raised a toast as, from the middle of the circle, Dylan – his brother snug in cushions on his lap – announced in his proudest voice, 'Please raise your glasses to my baby brother: Albert Thomas Harris.'

'Albert?' Bert breathed the name as Mabel looked at her husband.

'We call him Albie, don't we, Mum.'

'Mill Grange.' Mabel looked at the two little boys sat on the ground before her, her hand finding Bert's as they muttered, 'Place of miracles.'

The best thing that you can do to support an author or a book you love is to write a review. If you enjoyed WINTER FIRES AT MILL GRANGE and would like to support the author, please leave a review.

ACKNOWLEDGMENTS

When I first created the characters that live in and around Mill Grange, I never dreamt I'd be lucky enough to pen four novels about them. Writing the adventures of Thea, Tina, Shaun, Sam, Tom and Helen – not forgetting Mabel and Bert – has been a total delight. I'm going to miss them very much.

I'd like to thank a few people who've helped me along the Mill Grange journey.

First, the team at Aria (Head of Zeus), especially Martina, Hannah, Lizz and Rhea, who have been so supportive and passionate about the series, from beginning to end. Also, to my agent, Kiran; many thanks for your support, guidance and encouragement.

To my family and friends, who are always there for me, despite my obsessive need to write on a daily basis.

Finally – to Northmoor itself. The Mill Grange series would never have come to life if it hadn't been for Northmoor House – a manor in Exmoor where I, and my colleague, Alison Knight, take many of our Imagine students on a writing retreat every year. A place of beauty and wonder, it remains the inspiration behind everything that happens within Mill Grange.

ABOUT THE AUTHOR

JENNY KANE is the bestselling author of many romantic fiction series. These include the Mill Grange series, Abi's Cornwall series, and the Another Cup series. She has had bestsellers in the Amazon Romance, Contemporary Fiction and Women's Fiction charts. If you enjoy Jenny's writing, then why not follow her author page, for updates on all of her new releases!

Hello from Aria

We hope you enjoyed this book! If you did, let us know, we'd love to hear from you.

We are Aria, a dynamic fiction imprint from award-winning publishers Head of Zeus. At heart, we're committed to publishing fantastic commercial fiction – from romance to sagas to historical fiction. Visit us online and discover a community of like minded fiction fans

You can find us at:

www.ariafiction.com

🐦 @ariafiction

f @Aria_Fiction

📷 @ariafiction